Dedication

I want to dedicate this book to my family,
because they were so supportive,
even after I killed them in the first chapter.

=-}

Introduction:

Thank you for picking up my book.
I sincerely hope you enjoy it.

Moogie Covenant
By Morgan Routh

Published by Routh Enterprise
Phoenix Arizona, USA
MorganRouth.com

Cover design by Lilie Routh

First Edition Paperback: 2012
Printed in the United States Of America

Summary: Frozen in a child's body, young Moogie must face eternal life as she has come to know it. Violent, trying, and cumbersome as she makes decisions of the shades of evil she is, whether it is murder, identity, or her struggling obsessions. Moogie is not pronounced like a cow moo, it sounds like: muh-gee.

ISBN: 978-0-9887155-0-9

RRT 130501   Cover 1

This page is left intentionally blank.

1
In the Classroom

2010

Is the clock trying to be slow? Tic, tic, tic, I watched the second hand slowly inch closer to the twelve. Come on! I squirmed in my seat as my impatience craved for it to go faster. Just ten more seconds until spring break. Ten, nine, eight, seven... I counted down until that poorly recorded dinging sound projected through the out-of-date intercom system. Finally, I was beginning to believe it would never come.

I slung my backpack over my shoulder and slipped out the door. In the hall children raced to escape, including me; nobody wants to be at school more than they have too.

In the midst of the chaos, slamming lockers, squeaking tennis shoes, and the rumble of hundreds of conversations, I watched my peers manage to dodge out of each other's way to the sunshine.

I rode the crowd to the double doors where the bus pick up is just outside. I took one last glance behind me at the halls. In the corner of my eye I noticed somebody fall over, their possessions scattered everywhere, and she fell victim to the stampede of feet trudging passed her.

Nobody bothered to help, and she hesitantly picked up her shoe printed notebooks before disappearing into the crowd. I was helpless to fight against the rowdy kids to reach her, so I turned to soak up the heat, barely giving it a second thought. Good-bye seventh grade homework for a week!

I boarded the bus and tried to dodge the flying objects and ignore the industrial smell. At the back of the bus I plopped down on the tough, gray fabric seat my best friend Angel always saved for me.

Angel glanced up from her phone's screen and smiled. I greeted her with the usual enthusiasm and she closed the flip phone.

Angel and I have been best friends ever since I can remember. She's my only friend, and it seems the other people at school just don't see me.

Usually I'm the girl everyone forgets about unless they are staring at me directly in the face. She, unlike everyone in my life, sincerely wants to spend time with me, and I'm as happy as somebody with thousands of friends.

Angel has frizzy, poofy, dark, deep red hair that contrasts her round and soft face. She's squishy and very big, but not exactly overweight, and awkwardly too tall. She looms over everyone, including me, and has bulky, uncomfortable braces.

Angel had been made fun of for her looks, and her name Angelica, because it sounds a little strange. In fifth grade I renamed her Angel, and she was overjoyed to be called the better substitute.

I remembered the conversation we had, she crossed her arms and said, "You know if you get to rename me, I should give you a better name too!" And in our little fifth grade minds it made complete sense, from that day on forever I will always be Moogie, and she will always be Angel.

The bus rumbled to life, adding smoke to the dusty smell. I dug around for the last few pieces of gum in my backpack and shared it with Angel while we talked. The kids on the bus yelled and chatted, still throwing various objects and trying to yank the windows down.

A pencil ended up in my hair; I pulled it and stuck it in my backpack. Finders keepers right?

"Did you hear about the party at Justin's house?" Angel chatted. I racked my brain to think of it; nothing came up, I shrugged, "No, when is it?"

"Next weekend, are you going to go?"

"No, I'm going on a family camping trip all spring break." Her sky blue eyes turned slightly dismayed, "Oh."

I looked out the window, nothing exciting there, just a lot of desert landscaped lawns and one-story houses, although, nearly every house I can see has an infestation of desert daisies.

Around the same time every year they spring up. No other plants exist like the daisies, appearing out of nowhere, blanketing yards as far as the eye can see, and then dying suddenly when the temperature hits the horrible summertime heat. Amazing how such a pretty flower, a marvel to life, could be known as a weed, and do so much damage when they finish their life span.

My street sign appeared and I prepared to leave. Angel's house is one more stop. The bus came to a sudden jerk and threw everybody forward. I scrambled to shove everything back in my bag before getting up and leaving. Three other kids rose and we left the bus. Parting down at the crossroad to home, I headed towards my cul-de-sac on the next street.

Today it was extremely bright outside, and of course, it was hot. That's everyday in Phoenix, Arizona. But today, in the distance, I could see looming storm clouds. It might rain tonight! We only get rain around five times a year; this is almost a special occasion for me.

My house is at the edge of the cul-de-sac. In the front yard there's a pull-through driveway with large river rocks bordering it. Behind that where the house's façade should display our front porch and door, a giant white wall spanned from side yard to side yard encapsulating the house into a private, fortress-like building.

Back when the wall had just been built, I painted flowers all over it so the front didn't have to look boring. The flowers are faded some, but everyday I admire them.

Going around to the back I strolled through the gate. My backyard is the opposite of the dusty Arizona streets and gravel lawns, across the yard is lush, green grass. I passed the boat parked along the fence and stepped across the porch.

Out in the middle of the yard is the new trampoline from last Christmas, and like all other houses on the block there is a large pool built in the middle. I noticed the trees planted around the area were full of fruit. It's time to pick again!

My sister and I love to make orange juice from the fruits. I made a mental note to pull out the baskets from the shed when we get home from the cabin.

To get into the house I used the key around my neck to unlock the glass paned backdoor. A gust of cool air-conditioned air blew into my face, and it felt spectacular.

In the kitchen, I prepared myself a snack. While the microwave was going I picked at a crack in the brown wall. Every wall in my house is brown, one shade or another, I always feel warm and welcome here.

The microwave beeped, I opened up the popcorn and carried it with me to my bedroom.

My Great Dane came in to see what I was eating. She sat down next to me on the floor and I fed her some popcorn. Lilie has a gray and white fur pattern with black splotches here and there. She is petite and a runt compared to other Danes, but she still weighs more than me. Her most striking features, what I love the most about her, is her intelligence. She always gets what she wants, and if she doesn't she uses patience and cunning to get it.

For example, one time I was sitting on the couch doing homework and she was trying her best to eat the shoes on my feet. I shooed her away and she waited ten minutes just watching me. At one point I fell asleep there and when I woke up she had kidnapped my left shoe and was chewing on it in the comfort of my parent's bed down the hall.

She isn't completely evil though, along with her princess-like attitude she has distinct splotches on her back shaped like a diamond, a club, a spade, and a few hearts. I've loved that dog since she was born, and I would do anything for her.

Lilie laid her head on my lap and closed her eyes, that is, after I gave her the rest of my popcorn.

We sat like this until a dog started barking outside, and she jumped to life and sprinted out of my room to return the call. I was left alone.

I started packing my suitcase early out of boredom. My little sister arrived home shortly after.

Everyday she sees me and some how she acts as if I haven't seen her in years, today was no exception.

I heard her loud shoes clomp down the hall, and then they stopped right outside my door. She threw open my bedroom door and ran in saying "Hi Moogie!" I was then trapped in a bone-crushing hug. She let me go and stared at my forehead "You have a giant zit on your face." With my personal space violated and my face insulted I jumped up and shoved her out of my room. She shoved me back and ran away to the kitchen before I could retaliate.

I went to the bathroom to gather my hair brush and tooth brush for the trip. I checked myself in the mirror and noticed I did have a gigantic red zit right in the middle of my forehead.

For around five minutes I tried popping that zit. I usually don't have zits on my pale white face, but when I do they really stick out; they don't even look like my freckles! My waist length golden blonde hair doesn't cover up any of the zits either. Maybe if I had bangs they would cover them up.

It was sixish when my parents arrived home. My sister had her suitcase packed and she was in the car twenty minutes before we were going to leave. After five minutes she returned to the living room bored from sitting in the car alone. I went back to my room and checked to see if I forgot anything, nope.

Everybody was already in the car when I got in. My sister was bouncing off the walls happy. Lilie had laid her head on my lap and I noticed something green sticking out of her mouth. I grabbed it and realized it was the limb of one of my sister's dolls. Lilie snatched it back and it disappeared in her mouth.

Mommy drove everybody down the freeway until Dad realized they needed to go to his office to pick something up. My dad and mom work as scientists doing DNA stuff for a private company. Honestly, that's all I really know.

The office is pretty far away, and in the middle of the desert. There aren't any offices near it.

When we got there I needed to use the restroom, so I entered the office with Dad. The place has a small waiting room. There was a desk in the middle and a woman in a lab coat sitting behind it. The room had plain checkered tile with cream colored wall paper. Behind the desk the room split into two halls, I went down the left while Dad went down the right.

Before I took any steps though, the lady, which I remembered her as some sort of assistant for my dad caught me and said, "Hello again! I haven't seen you in so long!" I turned to look at her. She was very plain, just like the rest of the room. A cordate face, brown eyes, and she had her brown hair tied up in a lose bun. I smiled and nodded, I didn't know what to say, I didn't even remember her name. So I smiled some more and said I needed to run to the bathroom. She said we would talk afterwards.

The restroom was pretty boring, three stalls and sinks that were a little too short. I need to find something to talk about too, or I'll look like an idiot in front of her. If only my sister could come in to save the day. Once she starts talking she doesn't stop.

I spent a while looking in the scratched up mirror trying to find any zits I hadn't popped yet.

My sister is probably dying of boredom right now; she hates it when I take my time. Maybe I should take a little longer.

I stood staring at my reflection. I'm definitely not grown up, my face is too young, and I'm short and under developed. I wish I was a little taller; some kids in my seventh grade class can already pass as twenty-year-olds. My eyes don't seem to have a specific color, sometimes greenish blue, other times bluish green, I couldn't tell what they were today, they just seemed dark.

When I finally finished, I reached for the door handle, then stopped. Sharp, screeching sounds pierced my ears from outside the door. What was that? I pressed my ear against the door. Is that high pitched singing?

I opened the door a crack; a tall man with wild black hair in ripped clothing was holding the assistant against the wall. The man with the wild black hair was saying "You left the cage open!" Or something like that, and laughed at her. The assistant was sobbing hysterically.

Where did he come from?

Behind them was a girl with lava red hair who looked around fifteen or sixteen, she was the one singing and she twirled in a smock like from the doctor's office.

"P-please don't. I-I" He shushed her lightly and put her down, he smiled fondly at her, and I let out the breath I realized I was holding.

He looked kind of scary for a moment. The redheaded girl stopped singing and snickered. And the tall man grabbed the bun of her hair and pulled it back.

The girl started singing again and the assistant screamed. The lyrics of the girl's song finally processed in my brain, "Kill! Kill! Kill! The stupid human! Kill! Kill! Kill! So we can escape! Come on Ja-Ja-Jonathan, Kill! Kill! Kill!"

I blinked, and the assistant was on the floor. The man, Jonathan had nearly ripped her throat out of her neck. Blood poured out onto the checkered tile dripped off his face.

I trembled, my head was in a daze, everything suddenly got slower. She's dead, she's dead. It didn't exactly cook in my mind. I bit my lip to hold back a scream; what if he sees me? Where's Dad? I need to get out of here.

The man named Jonathan smiled brighter at the body. The girl started skipping around the room, "Jonathan killed EVERYBODY, YAY!" Jonathan turned to the girl slightly irritated, "Twenty years with you, Marit, and you are still annoying." The girl-Marit smiled sweetly and said "But you love me. And we'll always win together." They turned to leave, and he looked down at Marit and affectionately pet her hair. His dark grin baring yellowed teeth stained my mind. "Let's go home."

I stood frozen, petrified he would return for me. He just killed her with his teeth! What if he's still outside?

My knees grew weak and I dropped to the floor. I held my breath and scooted backwards behind the trash can. I clasped my hands around my ears, I pulled my legs in and closed my eyes, focusing on the blackness.

Outside I could hear sounds, first a shrill scream, my dog barking and then her sharp yelp. Two screams now, one choked up and then silence. I held my breath and pressed my hands harder to my ears.

"Help." I whispered in my mind, I shook my head and pressed my face into my knees.

I curled up for several long moments after that, trying to quiet my breaths as much as I could, trying to make myself silent.

The moment came when I was sure they left, I gradually crawled out of my hiding place behind the trash can, and still on my hands and knees I pushed the door open with one hand. A stream of blood advanced and touched my other hand, I flinched and pulled away, but I lost my balance and my elbow splashed in the fresh blood to catch myself.

I squealed and jumped to my feet before sprinting though the waiting room in terror. My foot splashed in a pool formed near the woman's pale broken neck.

Down the hall I slipped on a mess of papers and landed hard on my knees. I shrieked and caught a sob before holding my breath again to stay silent. I frantically stumbled forward but turned my head to see the waiting room door. Nobody was there.

I scrambled into the main lab. My father's other assistant was on the floor. My mouth dropped open as I realized his head was completely turned the wrong way, and a big unnatural bluish bulge stuck out on his neck.

I noiselessly screamed in abhorrence, and dashed way with blurring tears. "Dad!" I cried. "Daddy!" I sobbed louder.

I slammed through the door of the second room of the lab, cages aligned along the walls. Two of the cage doors were thrown open and nearly broken off their hinges. I searched with my eyes around the room. The overthrown equipment and papers along with computer apparatus scattered the floor. "Dad! Dad! Where are you?" I called.

I dropped to my hands and knees again and I checked under broken tables and other things. Directly ahead of me a man lay nearly dead on the floor with a pearly white bone ripped out of his leg, blood dripping off of the end.

"Dad!" I whispered. Blood spattered onto me as he fought to breathe through his torn throat. The sight of him stunned me, "Dad." I whimpered.

The nearly detached skin that used to exist on his neck hung on loose threads that threatened to rip off as he twitched and jerked. I watched his hand move.

"Dad, they are all dead! And those bad people are gone, we need to go before they come back." I started back up; he didn't make effort to get up with me. "Come on!" He couldn't talk, he tried but just made gurgling sounds, blood trickled out of the side of his lips, and out of the hole on his neck. I sobbed his name, "Dad, the hospital, we need to go, everything is going to be alright!"

I dropped back to my knees, and his head twitched to one side. He stroked my hair with a bloody hand. My voice cracked between sobs, "Dad, Dad! We need to leave!" He twitched his head again, and then reached for the briefcase next to him.

He opened it and put together a syringe with a strange liquid. I wiped my tears away "What is that?" Dad didn't answer; he only raised the syringe and stabbed it into my leg.

The force sent a dull but powerful shock through my leg, and I did nothing to stop him as he pressed down the plunger. The thick, dark liquid stung as it disappeared into my leg, "What-" Dad's hand dropped and his chest fell.

"No!" I shook him,

"No!" I screamed.

I found myself rocking back and forth, his blood was on my hands, and I balled my small fingers into fists. Fear pushed me to scoot away from him, the syringe needle stuck out in my leg; I ripped it out and threw it across the room. My leg felt so cold now, and hot. I sucked in my breath, my sobs never lessened, and my frantic movements made my hand slip.

I dropped and smacked my elbow on the hard tile, the pain startled me, sending a shock into my funny bone, I managed to jump up but hit my shoulder on a table.

"Ow!" Around me my world started soaking in the finer details. The room looked sullied and torn, thick puddles of bloody crimson gleamed and glistened brighter near me.

My father's body looked more real. I could see every aspect of everything magnified. My clothes looked intricate, braided down to the very fabric strands.

I struggled to push myself back up, the fresh blood from my hands made light imprints on the floor. My breathing slowed down, my heart thumped slower. I felt less of a need to breathe, the adrenaline heating up my skin. The outside layer of skin grew hotter than the blood and muscle on the inside, the room I understood, was increasing in heat.

I rose and turned, smoke filled everywhere in the lab. I could almost see the individual particles floating around. A fire had broken out in the other room. Down the hall, smoke subsisted everywhere, and it was so thick! It was so hard to breathe, my leg, shocked and hurting, pushed me to run faster. The fire broadened, consuming everything. I quickened my pace, though it wasn't chasing me.

My shoe splashed through the puddle of blood again. My socks soaked, but I didn't stop, the doors were feet away.

My hand shoved the door open, and I fell to the gravel and breathed the dusty air. "This can't be happening." I mumbled dourly to myself.

I didn't know if it was the smoke or the dryness outside but my tongue was sandpaper, I felt like I had eaten mountains of salt and dust, and no water was in sight. My thoughts felt broken.

Home, I want to go home. So I started for the car at the end of the parking lot, a heap of gray and white fur laid limp in the middle of the road.

"Lilie?" I asked.

My dog didn't move.

"No!" I croaked louder. My feet couldn't carry me fast enough, "No!" I cried.

My legs had given away under me. Dusty, jagged rocks pierced my cheek as I sobbed into the ground. I banged my fists and scratched my face trying to hold on to sanity.

Her eyes stared blankly back at me, she laid still, more still than I had ever seen her. I reached out to touch her stomach, it was still warm. I shook her, "Lilie, Lilie," My hand pushed her body harder, "Lilie!"

I violently shook her, "Lilie!" The sobs returned, I heaved and gagged as I wailed over her. "No, no, no, no." I repeated my denial and turned away, and my eyes caught the building.

The building burned; I had never seen such large fire in real life before. It was so uncontrollable, so scary. The mesmerizing fire held my attention, I clutched my dead dog's head in my lap for a long while. I tore my eyes from it and looked at the car. My voice hushed.

"Mommy?"

I could see one of her arms hung from the car. "Mom!" I called, nothing stirred in the car, "Baby?" my voice higher, I called to my sister's nickname.

Silence.

I stopped; emptiness filled my stomach with realization. And my eyes caught something scratched in corner of the car, right above the bumper, MARIT.

2
The Diner

My vision spun; my innards consumed me. I turned around pulling my eyes from the car. Gingerly I lifted Lilie's head off my lap and placed it back on the ground.

I clambered up, pushing off the gravel. I need to leave, without a last glance my feet started away from the awful site. *Run, run away coward, child.* My thoughts were broken, incomprehensible mush.

The crackling of the building behind me sounded further and then away. A piece of the building crashed to the ground, was it the roof? The loud sound drove a stark jolt of fear in me.

My walk changed to a stride and then a near sprint. My legs never slowed, nor did my breath feel short.

I coughed and tears streamed down my face. And I came to an abrupt halt.

My body quivered, I stared into the nothingness ahead of me. Something was inside of me, I could feel it, almost elemental. And with a full breath of air in my lungs it heaved itself up me, and I bellowed a scream. It was beyond any other, and it bolted exactly what I felt.

I, had *hatred.*

I watched my trembling hands become still when I clenched them. The looming thunder clouds boomed and cracked with the same ferocity as my scream, answering the deep, natural call.

Water poured to spite me as I shot through the desert. My feet touched the ground lightly and silently in a dangerous, predator efficiency. I wasn't running away anymore, I was running toward something. Someone.

The dirt turned to mud, it poured and poured, matting my golden hair and soaking my bloody shoes and skin.

I will kill them.

Of nothing ever in my life have I been so sure.

I will end their lives.

The night was dark; the moon sometimes peeked through the clouds in rays of silvery light particles.

All around me for miles was just lonely desert. Not the slightest sign of humanity. I felt alone, as if the only human existing. Animals and plants scattered sparsely on the hard, wet dirt, and the moon occasionally faded. It didn't affect my vision.

When the moon showed I could see almost as if it was daytime, and when the moon disappeared it was as if somebody had put a sheet over a lamp. Not quite turning it off but still taking away most of the light.

Of all the camping trips and hikes with my family, I find that even at sunset it wasn't as bright as I see now. On top of that I still see so much more detail, the spines of the cactus, movement of the little rodents and bugs. This night is unlike any other night I've ever lived, I feel as though a microscope focused into a finer detailed world.

A coyote passed from the bushes, but didn't dare step towards me. I stopped and met eyes with it, and then the small creature cautiously sauntered back into the bush, putting space between us. Lizards scuttled on the wet rocks and I strode on.

Continuing into the night the rain stopped and started, my mind changed from misery to hunger. But the hunger wasn't like any other hunger; it had so much more depth, as if I hadn't eaten in days.

Images went through my head as I moved through the night, over and over. So detailed, I couldn't get over that fact.

My tears started and stopped at different points of the early hours, I don't remember how long I would cry or when it stopped. Sometimes for the hunger to go away, new untapped emotions of uncertainty, animosity, and sorrowfulness darted around my head. Marit and Jonathan's face were there, laughing at me, they will feel what I have felt if it kills me.

Of all the emotions, I knew I loathed the strongest.

The need called for me to make their lives miserable before I kill them. I wanted to rip them limb from limb. Claw at their screaming faces; dig my nails into their soft, untainted skin. Remembering the horrors they've done to me, I need them to have double, to scream at their faces and make them see.

I indulged in violent dreams on how I would end them, trying to fathom it, how they would pay, it didn't matter what the cost.

At midnight I reached a road, and walked alongside it. At dawn I reached a diner called Johnnie's by the Tracks, and a train screeched by pushing my long golden hair forcefully behind me.

It was so quiet, isolated. No other structure beset the far spread desert, as if the lone diner was waiting for me.

My stomach snarled, the hunger ascended to the point where every thought was diverted to putting food in my mouth.

I dug deep in my pockets and found three crumpled up dollars and fifty two cents for a burger, it will have to do.

I walked in; a thin, middle aged lady with a pencil in her unnaturally blonde hair was smoking a cigarette behind the cash register. To my right I saw a businessman at a booth drinking coffee and typing on a computer. Everything was so loud; the cook in the back bustling around, the tap, tap, tap, of the man on the laptop, the waitress's heavy breathing. I half ran across the room to put the money on the table.

"I'd like a cheese burger, with everything on it please." The waitress tired and bored, replied "You don't have enough for that, you can have a plain burger. Want it for here, or to go?" Where would I go? I replied "For here," and stepped to the booth behind the businessman.

The waitress was taking too long, my eyes darted to the clock.

I swung my legs back and forth, and tapped my thumb with the ticking of the clock. Why isn't she here?

Then something caught my eye, something on the man's neck. Was it a bug? No, my eyes watched it closer, a pulse. I could see it move, it looked so fragile under that thin film people call skin.

I swayed to the side a moment, my mouth dry and sandy, the hunger clawing down on my stomach, searching for morsels to indulge on. His back seemed closer to me, I don't exactly remember moving, but I found myself crawling on the table to get closer. Thump, thump, his smell, under that stingy cologne his oily neck made my mouth water. My jaw clamped, sucking the air through my teeth, I wanted to bite it, feel the warm meat crush under my teeth, letting the flavor gush down my throat.

It reminded me of the fruit snacks I used to own, every time I bit into one, sweet juice squished out. Sweet, only what I wanted tasted like meat.

The door from the kitchen swung open and I shot back in my seat. She didn't notice. The waitress carried a burger to my table. She muttered robotically, "Here you are," and almost dropped the plate onto the table, letting a greasy, wilted French fry fall to the table.

I snatched it up and shoved it in nearly whole. The burger didn't help; it was almost as if I shoved a tasteless, warm hunk of foam down my throat.

Disgusting. It didn't fix it! I had so much anger built up in me, everything hurt; I wanted to lash out at the waitress. She had a mean attitude and I'm still in pain! I don't want to cry anymore; I want her head! But she returned to the kitchen.

At that moment the man took out a letter and opened it. It was a small movement, but I noticed it right away. His thumb scraped the paper, I watched the thin edge sink under the top layer of his thumb. He pulled away and a droplet of red swelled outside his thumb. I could smell it from my seat; raw, warm, my head felt so foggy, my skull wanted to collapse into my brain. Everything slowed down, my emotions hushed and the noise of the diner drifted away.

He didn't see me when I sank my teeth into his neck and drew deeply. I clamped my hand over his mouth to prevent screaming. He was so weak and fragile. I nearly broke his neck when he struggled.

More, more, I closed my eyes in bliss. His struggling was feeble to my arms, it was similar to holding my seven-year-old cousin down when she thought she could wrestle me into a headlock.

Then the juice stopped coming, it thinned and stopped. I needed more, now! I pulled myself from the dry body; it fell onto the keyboard with a thud. More juice, that's all I need, just a little more.

I went into the kitchen, a smelly old guy was at the grill, and the cook didn't even have time to look at me. His flavor wasn't as good as the first, and his skin tasted like grease and dirt.

He struggled too, his head moving. But I clamped my hands down and thrust it away from me to hold the neck better. Bone snapped and he finally stayed still enough to draw more warm meat taste.

I dropped him when he finished, I spat out the hairs from his sweaty neck and picked a few from my mouth before wandering to the freezer. The waitress was unpacking something; she saw me and pleaded with me in a tired voice, "Honey, you aren't supposed to be back here. Please go back to your booth-what is on your face?" She reached her thin arm out to take my hand but I was fast. I took her arm, and easily as if she was one of my dolls, slammed her into the wall.

I threw her so hard her head cracked, and a trail of blood smeared on the wall as she slid down, but that didn't matter. I bit into her arm, and my cheeks started filling up with liquid. I released her and swallowed before taking into the wound again. She by far tasted the worst, and she smelled like smoke, but the pain subsided. I was relieved.

I sat down next to the body, and looked at it for a moment, not really comprehending what it was. My head cleared a little, but I was still pretty drowsy.

My eyes slipped closed, for a second, and I startled back open.

Did I just go to sleep? No, it felt like I just woke up though. My head sharpened, all focus was completely back now. I looked around, then down, startled at the sight.

I stopped. Is it truly here? I didn't really know what I was looking at until now. But now that I know what it is I remember everything else too. How could I forget it? It was seconds ago, but did I really forget?

My head started to hurt with all the confusion, everything felt loud in my mind, but an alarming silence only surrounded me.

I closed my eyes, maybe this is all a very realistic dream, and I just need to wake up.

I opened my eyes and looked at the body. It was so fresh, almost as if she was sleeping, maybe she was.

I imagined her getting up and scolding me for killing her, I almost smiled. What am I doing? What am I thinking? What have I done?

That thought went through my head over and over again, like a broken record but it didn't feel right. It wasn't real.

I wanted to cry again. She's dead, they're all dead! I killed them.

I couldn't be here any longer; I sprinted out of the freezer. I tripped over something big. My face hit grimy ground, I glanced up. Another body.

I instantly flinched and almost screamed. I got up to my knees and scooted back until I hit the wall. He was so lifeless, a pool formed from his neck, just like what Jonathan did.

I stared at the cook lying on the floor, his eyes staring into nothingness. There was a large foot print on his stomach. My footprint, I calmed down somewhat; I'm alone. They are harmless, defenseless.

My heart rate was slow, my head was cleared, and I shuddered. Nothing made sense.

They did nothing to me to ever deserve to die, those people have families and normal lives, and pets like Lilie. I'm just as bad as Marit and Jonathan. I couldn't control myself. Why couldn't I control myself?

Blood was dried on my face; I spit on my sleeve and wiped it off my cheeks.

What have I become? Why can't everything just go back to normal? What did Dad do to me? I want to go home and pretend this never happened. But everybody is dead. Their bodies flashed through my mind. Marit's singing echoed in my thoughts.

Anger and adrenaline spread. I slammed my feet into the cabinet, everything is all wrong!

With my own strength the cabinet snapped in half, jagged splinters scraped my leg.

It made me feel more relaxed, but the cook still laid there. The problem wasn't going to go away. I shuddered again and cried, "This doesn't make sense!" I sobbed into my sleeve. The silence didn't answer me.

I brought my knees into my chest and wrapped my arms around them.

Sometime after I cried I realized I couldn't leave the bodies where they were. Somebody was going to discover them and call the police; my DNA and fingerprints are all over the bodies! What am I going to do with them? I could call the police myself and say I just discovered them here. I could bury them, that would take a while and there is blood all over the diner. I would have to bleach the place or something.

What if I really did just walk out? I might be on the run the rest of my life. I imagined them dragging me off and shocking me in a big iron electric chair. Or giving me a lethal injection.

I don't want to die even if I deserve it. But I still don't know what to do. What did I remember from the crime fighting shows? What mistakes did they make? I couldn't conjure much from my memories.

What did go through my mind was a strange girl in my class that loved survival and crime fighting shows.

I went through a lot of different elaborate schemes, one involving me flying to Australia with the bodies disguised as mannequins. Then I came up with the simplest one yet.

Maybe I could just burn the diner down with the bodies left in it. Nothing would be left to get evidence from.

How am I going to burn it down though?

I left my curled up position and I searched the waitress's pockets, and found a little cigarette lighter. Firewood, where is firewood now? Maybe the foam in the booths? I checked the booths, but the seats were plastic. I tried lighting them anyway. Nothing. Stupid! I kicked the chair getting a sharp pain in my big toe.

I ground my teeth, everything was hurting, sobs erupted from me. "I'm going to die!" I gasped. How am I going to burn this diner down?

I finally got up and started pacing, I had never paced before to think, then I wandered around, what to do, what to do. I wandered out to the parking lot and noticed three cars.

I could drive deep into the woods and be a hermit, isn't that what the Unabomber did? He got caught in the end though; the police could still find me and arrest me. What if I needed gas? I don't know how to buy gas! I don't know how to drive.

A movie scene went through my head, the police are chasing down a serial killer and they just found out where he was. They run in just in time as the killer was pouring gasoline on the bodies. The police arrest him and the main cop turns to him and said a cheesy line I can't remember.

I remember saying it weeks after every time I played cops and robbers with kids at school. What if the serial killer got away?

I need to get the gas out of the car. How am I going to do that? Is it even the right gas? Is there special lighting gas, or does car gas not work? I went back in the diner and found a few buckets and a mop. I took the mop out and carried the buckets outside. I stared at the first car; gas from the gas station goes into the hole on the side of the car.

Then where does it go? I dropped to my knees and crawled under the car.

Underneath the car looked dirty, completely different than its shiny paint job I was just looking at.

Several tubes connected to a tub-looking thing. I was pretty sure the tub thing was the gas tank and one of the tubes led to it.

I grabbed and yanked on a tube that led to a part of the tank, it didn't budge. I yanked and yanked until I got tired.

Why couldn't anything work? I yanked one more time, nothing. I got out from under the car; I kicked the side door and yelled at it, in stupid rage I punched in the back window, the glass shattered and my hand painfully scraped the shards, little streaks of red appeared on my hands when I shook it out.

It all stung and I hated myself more. Why couldn't this go away? I returned into one of the diner booths and started crying again.

Something seemed wrong; I'm crying next to a body. Everything is wrong. I stared through the cracks of my hands at the table. Under the table I noticed something shiny in the body's pocket. A clip? I reached down and pulled it out. It was a clip-on pocket knife. The blade unfolded, projecting my reflection, and I closed it back up.

Back under the car I started cutting the tube, it easily penetrated the plastic. After the tube was cut I aimed the open tube into the bucket. A small amount of liquid drained into the bucket and stopped. Wait, shouldn't there be more? I looked into the bucket, it doesn't look like gas. I wonder what it is.

Whatever it is, it isn't enough to burn down the diner. I hadn't gotten the gas. Maybe if I just stab a giant hole in the tank.

I gripped the knife tightly and thrust it at the tank. My hand slipped up and I cut the soft stretchy skin between my thumb and finger. The knife ricocheted off the tank and tried closing back up. It ended up cutting into the back of my thumb which opened the gash further.

Blood oozed out; I gripped my hand and bit my tongue. I tasted blood in my mouth. Blood was staining my clothes now. I scooted out and ran into the diner's bathroom. My hand more than stung, it burned and I held my sobs again.

The blood from my tongue slid down my throat, I swayed in bliss at the delicious taste. What kind of psycho am I?

A rush of water from the faucet blasted into the wound. I stood frantically trying to clean the gaping cut. When the pain eased back, I tore a piece of the towel off and tied it around my hand. The smaller cuts around my hand had already scabbed and almost disappeared, it was abnormally fast.

With my new sight, the cuts showed so much more detail, and my skin had rugged little squiggle lines. The hairs on my arm were so clear and individual; the dried blood was cracked and flaky-looking.

The towel wasn't enough, blood soaked through. I tore the towel again, untied the first ripped piece and wrapped it back up. This was very difficult to maneuver with my left hand and I had to use my mouth to help tie some of it.

I washed the dried from my face and tried to fix my hair to make it not look disgusting. It was just procrastinating though, I didn't want to go back and face my problems. I just wanted to be in this small, neglected bathroom for the rest of eternity.

I filled the sink with water and drained it a few times just to watch the water swirl with the blood muddled in it. I had never seen water so clearly. After that I paced around the room again. Ideas, ideas! I need to get the stupid gas out!

If only I could suck out the gas magically. I thought about that, maybe I can, I darted out to the parking lot and picked up the pocket knife with my undamaged hand. I quickly sawed off the rest of the hanging down tube. My palm turned black with all the new soot on it.

I threw open the little door people use when they put gas into the car and I slid the tube in the dark hole.

Back when Dad had a fish tank he would siphon old fish water out and add new water to keep the fish tank from getting dirty. Now how would he get the water out? I sighed, I can't remember.

With no hesitation, I put the dirt covered tube in my mouth and sucked as hard as I could. A revolting liquid rushed into my mouth and almost down my throat. The nauseating taste made me heave and my stomach acid burned going back down. The soot tasted like the road, and I spat as much as I could to eliminate the taste of fuel from my mouth.

Gas started flowing into the bucket. The bucket filled quickly and I replaced it with another. I carried the gas inside and put it down; then started dragging the bodies all together into a pile.

I poured the gas all over the bodies and through the diner, and then returned to the parking lot to switch the buckets. I repeated this process until all the cars were drained, the dreadful taste of gas lingering in my mouth.

After the cars were drained I stood back and admired my work. The bodies were neatly lined up, and they all had sufficient amounts of gasoline on them.

I felt strange, nobody knows I am here. No one will save me. I felt like I didn't exist anymore.

I reached over to the table and picked up the dead man's laptop. The laptop had internet and I found out where I was. The diner I found was in the middle of nowhere and Phoenix was pretty far away. The laptop also had the time; which was 1:35 pm. I had spent several hours here, it felt like days.

Then I walked over to the cash register and took all of the money. I wandered to the body of the business man and took his carrying case for the laptop. After I loaded all the money, the pocket knife, the laptop, and the lighter I slung it around my shoulder and returned to the front area.

My body leaned against one of the booths as I glanced back around me. What am I going to do after this? Where am I supposed to go?

I had made a trail of gas from the bodies to outside, and I stood where I didn't think the fire would get me. I started the lighter a few times until a small flame appeared, and brought it to the puddle of gas. The flame engulfed the gas, spreading through the room quickly. Smoke immediately filled the large room. I stood watching the flames until a beeping noise sounded. What was that?

To my horror, little droplets of water started to spray down at my fire. "No!" I roared. Warm tears started rolling down my cheeks "No! This is not fair!" The sprinklers put it out; the fire I worked so hard to get was ruined! No, no, no!

My tears splashed in one of the puddles.

The bodies were charred and there was a wretched smell of burning flesh. I backed up, leaving the scene, giving up. And I returned back on the road.

Night appeared before I reached the next town, my eyes drooped. I thought I even fell asleep a few times walking. I was somewhat thirsty but I was too fatigued to care. The streetlamps gave a russet, disgusting glow, shining every few yards.

Loneliness, dread of death and gasoline tasted in my mouth, it pulled me down. I took a few more steps and it took a long time. My knees hit the ground and I didn't have the strength to get back up. Maybe I scraped my knee, I didn't really notice, only the smell. I started crawling, crawling into the near-by alley. My hand might have landed on some glass at one point of time; I don't really remember any pain. I moved behind the tall dumpster and collapsed.

I had several dreams, but only one became apparent in my memories. It wasn't a dream really, more in the nightmare category, and most of it was blurry.

Strong, bright colors filled my head; a blur of brown and checkered, red was next to the brown, no, coming out of the brown, but it was moving over the checkered. I had not the slightest idea what it was then, but I definitely knew I was scared out of my mind.

The dream shifted then, lots of red, a fire maybe? It was so bright, like a tidal wave of red...I just wanted to stare at it forever...

My eyes cracked open, the sun light showed immediately and was too bright. My eyes hurt, daylight is too much. I blinked them a few times until they adjusted. The sky was cloudless, and had returned back to its pale blue color. I examined my surroundings. Glass, dirt, and trash were scattered around the area. My head rose and my back stiffly with it as if I hadn't moved in a very long time. I brushed all the dirt off my face and tried to avoid imagining what my hair looked like.

My dream appeared in my head again and I realized what it was. Stresses of my life came back to me in a tiresome, grasping surge.

I wanted to layback down and close my eyes, but the ground looked too disgusting to lie on.

For the rest of the day I continued walking, following the laptop's map. The whole day was extremely hot. The sun still hurt my eyes enough I had to stop sometimes and close them a minute or two. Through the journey I didn't really think, I just walked. I didn't see the scenery, people, or cars but I knew they were there.

At around five o'clock I made it to my street, the houses were so familiar but new. Unseen blemishes displayed very visibly now. Even the daisies were different.

3
Hope

My house seemed to be the only thing in this twisted world to be the same. I almost didn't expect it; as if it would never be there to relieve me from my exhausted journey. Inside the back gate I stood for a moment and shuddered with sudden disappointment, and then awe.

The grass looked alive, and so GREEN, each blade danced together forming waves in a sea. The trees looked as if they had been half dying for years, and the white paint on the trunks cracked into fragile shapes. The world I've lived in, even here, was undeniably alien, and frightened me.

Bugs scurried and scuttled as unseen worlds lived in the cracks, crevices, and niches I never noticed until now, and I'd rather have never known about them.

The house froze in time. Nothing was there, no loud TV playing stupid kid's shows my sister loves, no sound of a collar jingling, not the tap tap of the keyboard at Dad's desk. It was only empty.

I stood still a very long time. No sister to appear at my door and annoy me, her cheerful face never to smile at me with all the love in the world. My parents would never sweep me into a warm, suffocating hug. The cracks in the walls weren't the same, nor did the brown paint seem welcome and warm, just depressing.

Holidays, events, memories evaporated from the house. I stood right in the middle of the emptiness. The place felt like the turtle shell I found on the beach when I was six, empty, cold, and dead.

My world is empty; I'm monstrous, and everything is so scary. What if I hurt somebody else? Nothing is here to stand in my way; I never knew what violence really was until today. I've killed, and I'm going to kill Jonathan and Marit.

My hands balled into fits as I thought about murdering them, about feeling sticky and warm red coat my hands while they lay on the floor with holes in their chests.

Warmth flooded into my cheeks, what am I thinking? Something sunk lower in my stomach, an eating desire. I ground my teeth to keep from screaming and collapsing.

What was that liquid? What has it done to me? Or is this just me on the inside? I let go of my fists.

The thumb cut by the pocket knife ached every time I flexed it. But a scab had formed and the normal skin had healed into it. I stared at it, running my finger over the ridges of the scab, fascinated with the marvel.

The rest of the night I watched the news; at about three in the morning I gave up, took another shower and went to bed.

I woke up before the sun rose and watched more TV. Jonathan and Marit didn't appear on it, nor did anything involving me or the diner.

Through the night the strange hunger occasionally poked at me, a twinge of pain in the numbness. I noticed when I calmed myself down for long periods of time I didn't breathe right. My pulse had become significantly slower, slower to the point it might have been half what my heart usually beats. And if I sat up quickly my head grew light and I would feel sleepy.

Days melted by. I mourned and longed for my parents to come comfort me, or my sister to hug me and tell me she loved me. Why did I shake her off so many times? Why didn't I enjoy her love instead of feeling embarrassed, pushing her away?

I pulled the blanket closer to me, it smelled like Lilie. Shouldn't I be doing something? Or at least feel something other than this cold, bleak nothingness, how can I escape this stupid self pity? I'm afraid to go back out there. What if I do something bad?

I hate doing nothing. I hate Jonathan and Marit. I hate dead bodies. Nobody I trust is here to ask for help or confess my problems; they're all dead. This house feels so big and cold now.

I'm fed up with the cold, and this blanket smells like a muddy puppy, where dog hair stuck to my clothes and poked my skin. After slowly prying myself off the part of the couch I hadn't moved in for twenty minutes I sulked over to the air conditioner remote to turn up the heat.

After flipping a few switches, pressing the up arrow a couple times with a little too much anger and strength, it started beeping ERROR!

I guess it doesn't want to go very high. To try to reverse the issue I pressed the down arrow some. It kept beeping ERROR! And I smacked the little white box. The box smashed to the floor, and I bent down to pick it up. The pieces of the box had broken off and glass shards split everywhere, traveling as far as the other wall. "Stupid box." I muttered to myself, and I dropped to my hands and knees to crawl over to the glass.

I picked up some larger ones but stopped and stared at all the tiny crystals sparkling on the floor, this will take forever. Creating a kind of broom, I started to scoot my arm across the floor to collect the pieces of glass into a pile. I followed the shards until they brought me right up to an old vent.

It rumbled and hissed through the cover's slits caked in dirt. The vent, I knew about a secret behind the dirt, there was something very special, something I never dared to think about in years. Under the house Dad kept a secret lab. I was never allowed in, except one time when I was six.

Hesitantly, I opened the vent and poked my head inside. The cramped and dark box was bigger in my memories. I couldn't see anything on the bottom except filters. Dad changed the air filters every two weeks, and he kept them stacked inside here.

I moved the filters out of the way to find there wasn't a door latch. I think I remember him pushing a secret button somewhere to the left. Where in the left was it? I ran my hands around the wall; it was completely smooth until I got to a knot in the wood. The knot felt indented, and I pushed it further in with my thumb. The knot disappeared into the wood adding a sound like "chink".

Got it! A piece of the floor dropped, opening up a dark hole. I reached down and felt a piece of rough, splintery wood, no wait, two. One connected to the other. A ladder! I placed my foot onto the horizontal piece and slowly descended.

The place was pitch black until I touched the floor. A motion sensor went off with a soft beep and a light came on.

The lab was slightly smaller than my room; the floor was like the concrete Dad poured outside a few years ago. His techniques didn't change; I saw rough parts, smooth parts, and uneven hills here and there. "Definitely Dad." I mumbled.

To my right, a bookcase that reached the ceiling was filled with tons of books. Some old, others newish, all of them looked thick and heavy. I didn't recognize the titles, they were all about cells, cloning, and telomeres. I don't even know what a telomere is.

Two of the upper middle shelves were dedicated to well-worn black, non-titled books. Another shelf held an equally large series of burgundy untitled books.

In the far right was a black briefcase-looking box with a glowing light on the side. It was plugged into the wall. I wonder what it is.

Tall, odd machinery stood along the walls and in the middle a large table and chair with numerous objects sat in the middle of the table. I sat in his chair and scooted around. Dad would have killed me if I ever sat in his spot, now I'm in his private lab, touching his research, and scooting around in his big, comfy chair. I pushed a little too hard and smacked against the bookshelf. It rumbled, threatening to fall over, and I quickly covered my head as the books showered down. One particularly thick burgundy book landed in my lap sending a shock into my legs. Opening the front cover the first page read in my dad's neat handwriting:

Lilie project- Book 23

Lilie? I flipped through the pages, the photos and diagrams were the only things I could understand. The words were lost on me. The book was dated before I was born, but it showed pictures of Lilie growing up.

But I watched her grow up, from when she could fit in my lap until she was taller than Dad on her hind legs. They couldn't really be the same dog, could they? I flipped back and read the pages over again, scrutinizing the fur coat against my memories. In every picture of the dogs I saw her hearts, the spade, the club and the diamond shaped splotches.

My mind spun in disbelief, and I started rereading most of the pictures and their captions one more time.

How can that be possible? I flipped through the book more, and then started an attempt on reading the other twenty-two books. The book explained what the black box was, a storage container that holds the embryos or the fertilized eggs which can be used to create cloned Lilies.

I examined the black box; Dad's book said something about the box has liquid nitrogen freezing the embryos inside a microrefrigerator unit. I glanced at the case again. A little green light glowed on the side. After checking the book I entered the codes on the key pad under the light.

The black case split in the middle and a blaring white light shown out. I counted fifteen slots; twelve slots had tubes attached to them.

It always has to be plugged in to an outlet, after a month of not being plugged in, the battery runs out and stops keeping the embryos from warming up and being destroyed.

I tried to pick one up but the moment I touched it the icy tube stung my hand. So I leaned closer to gaze at the tubes. Each tube was at filled with a clear liquid, and I couldn't see the little egg or circle I expected to see; I didn't realize they would be microscopic, but they are cells I guess.

My head grew cold, so I pulled my head out and closed the cold case, reverting back into the mysterious black metal box with the little green glowing light.

Astonishment and butterflies swelled in my stomach making me jittery. It's real, Lilie clones are real. I stared at the case for what felt like forever. How could she be so real? And yet still be the dreamlike, science fiction phenomena that she is? Why did my dad do this? I thought about the twelve embryos for a while.

Maybe I could have Lilie my whole life. I did a few math calculations: Great Danes live until about twelve years, and I have twelve embryos, so I would have... I counted on my fingers a little. Ah! A hundred and forty-four years. That's more than the oldest person alive's time span, plus, a couple extra years. I could have Lilie my whole life, and then pass her on to my kids.

The books explained, as I read on, how to create another dog and a bunch of other gobbley-gook about Dad's different tries to clone her. I never realized Dad knew or used so many big terms. Hours and hours passed, maybe days, I couldn't tell down in the lab. It was completely silent down here. I read the books once through, then twice through, constantly trying to make sense of all the confusing terms. At one point of time I left the lab in search of a dictionary, but looking up the terms in the notebook brought on an entirely new wave of confusion. I still didn't understand anything.

Even without a slight understanding of the technical part, I did understand the part about how to use an embryo to make a new Lilie. The books explained the process as simply placing the embryo into a female dog's womb while it is in heat or ready to breed and it will grow and be birthed like all of the other dogs that the mom produces herself.

I closed the final book I was thumbing through and leaned into the folds of the cushy chair. No matter what, I can't tell anybody about this.

Fuzzy memories of news reports and articles in the newspapers flooded into my mind. Years ago when somebody else tried cloning an animal, the government had a big scandal and giant lawsuits invaded every channel on TV. Lots of people were thrown in jail, restrictions and laws were passed against genetic experimentation of any kind in every way possible.

Then the warning my father had always pounded into me about this stuff appeared in my conscience, his voice wrung true and urgent in my head, "Never tell anybody, and I mean anybody about my job or the lab. The police would take me and your mother away for a very, very long time."

I stared at the freezer in bewilderment, jail time, life ruining qualities, misery, and hardship surround this case and what is held inside. So many things to process, but one idea raced above all else. It cleared the path of confusion. One idea makes all the other punishments and prices affordable, even tolerable. I'm not alone anymore, I can get Lilie back.

4
This Section Left
Intentionally Empty

Of my long life, the next six years became the worst I had ever experienced. It was a hard, dark time, and that story is to be saved for another day.

5
All Grown Up

2016

I examined myself in the mirror again, the low cut blouse dipped lower than what I usually wear, but it made the necklace dangling loosely from my neck look better. I shifted my weight around in my four inch high heels to make it less uncomfortable and more ignorable.

It was an average Friday night. I had picked up a new location buried knee deep in strange disappearance stories and possible gang activity, it looks promising. I wonder how much of it is my kind of crime and how much are the works of real gangsters.

The heavy make up aged my face a few years, it was the price to pay to look normal. The only thing that felt uncomfortable seemed to be my hair grazing and irritating my shoulders. I need to cut it again.

I took the lightrail downtown and wandered through the city, keeping my eyes open for a bright neon sign.

At finding the blue sign, I turned and waltzed right in. The guard in front carded me haphazardly; not that he would discover anything. My new identity, Tracy Herald, lived on the other side of town and the new card maker is a perfectionist. This counterfeit hasn't failed me yet.

I blended easily with the rest of the young people. After picking a seat at the grime encrusted bar I scanned the area. Nobody else sees the filth in these bars; I can't believe America's prettiest and handsomest young inhabitants flock to these disgusting and unsanitary places to perform such important mating rituals. But dirty or not, this is where my job is.

I boredly tapped my fingers on the counter and then picked at one of the spots on my beer glass. The bar's atmosphere and temperature felt pretty normal; warm, humid, loud, drunk people everywhere. Nobody was acting suspicious, although a redhead at the crowded table across the bar just glanced at me, once, twice. I locked eyes with her the second time. She didn't pull away.

Her big blue eyes drew curiosity out of me.

I didn't think I knew her, so why did she notice me? I slightly shifted in my seat uncomfortably but continued to get on with my job.

The television's feedback buzzed, irritating me as people yelled at the baseball players on the screen from the other side of the bar.

My eyes drifted everywhere except where she was. In the corner she continued unremittingly to gawk at me, and my internal red flags shot up. Something is definitely wrong. Then she leaned over and whispered something to the boy next to her.

He glanced up and then lost interest. Seconds felt like hours as they passed, I observed everyone, conversations, body language, and interaction. The commotion would have driven any normal person insane; of course, I am not normal.

They all were completely oblivious to me as I monitored them more meticulously than even the most competent scientists observing their life's work. And after spending so much time perfecting my already natural talent of discreetness, that girl, that completely careless kid has been staring at me the entire time.

I glued my eyes to the beer glass as she started to get up and head towards me.

I wonder why. My face grew hot, wait, maybe, she was one of them. That could explain the keen observing. I heard that last coven bust had some escapees, was she one of them? How would she have known what I was? I knew I was a little sloppy getting the last one, but I didn't think anyone saw, and I don't show my face in big hunts except for special occasions. No, no, I shouldn't get worked up about this; I probably just look like somebody she knows. Besides, she couldn't kill me here, way too many witnesses.

The girl was exceptionally tall, and taller with such high heels; almost seven feet, her features were sharp and slender. Not something I see everyday, I wonder if she's a model...or a turned model.

With such a long stride she only had to take a few steps, I felt too small and insignificant. But as every other person I've come across, I slipped into one of my fixed expressions, casual, half-noticing her. When the tall redhead reached me she slightly tilted her head in confusion. "Moogie?"

My face dropped and my eyes grew very wide, I looked up at her. She knew my name, how? I smiled and asked as lightly and innocently as I could, "Do I know you?" The redhead stared at me for a long minute. I broke the silence by repeating the question.

She continued to stare, but slightly nodded. The redhead finally snapped out of her trance and said quickly "I'm Angel, from seventh grade? We were, uhh, best friends. Or at least I thought I was."

It was my turn to stare dumbfounded, this couldn't be that Angel. There are millions of people in Phoenix, how can this coincidence in running into her now, while I'm hunting, be possible?

I offered her to sit down. She slid gracefully into the disgusting seat as if royalty, saying in a slightly off tone, "You look just the same as then, really similar. Where did you go?"

I started into my usual story, "Uhh, well, on our way to the family cabin, on spring break, remember? We got into a car crash, everyone died except, well, me, and I was passed around in the system. I never really stayed in a house permanently until I grew up and I've been on my own ever since." Angel mumbled some sort of consolation that sounded like "I'm sorry."

I continued with my story in more detail, "Since we were up in northern Arizona I went to families up there. I haven't seen much of Phoenix since then."

After the story was finished I concluded with a short message, adding a little to my standard lies, "I tried to block out my life after the crash, and I'm living a new life now, perfectly fine."

Angel chewed on a thought for a moment, her eyes burned into mine as she analyzed my story. I stared right back, concealing a dread of her coming out and saying "Bull Moogie. Tell me the real truth!" she knew me.

I've lied to the law; every person I've met in the past few years I've always worn a clever façade, but her, her glassy, bright blue eyes could always see into the lucid emotions absorbing me.

She released me from her everlasting stare and replied, "I tried finding you; I thought you were dead, or, or worse." She paused momentarily, recomposing herself, and she reached for my wrist. "I missed you." She started to say other things several times, but kept choking up and the conversation ended with a silence.

I glanced at her one more time in distress, trying to convey the truth of my sincerity "I'm sorry for everything Angel."

I reached for my purse, in a gesture of leaving, but she stayed locked on holding on to my wrist.

She smiled but kept a serious and final tone. "Stay, nobody should be alone on a Friday night."

I held my breath, and smiled, "Really, I should be going." She still held my wrist, not replying.

Then something inside me stopped, the noise and the fine details of the world that usually bombarded and overloaded me dissipated; rounding and morphing into just the background. Everything about her was enticing, her voice, her face, enthralling me to stay with her, and my senses faded.

The night slipped out of my grasp while I listened to her talk. I lost track of the people filling the room, and the seconds and minutes didn't linger, they sped by just like time does for normal people.

I didn't even notice a bar fight until it was halfway over. One of those iniquitous beings I spend so much time hunting could have been stalking a naive girl right next to me and I wouldn't have noticed.

Angel's determination to spend every second with me grew, our conversation rolled at a quick pace. She talked to me about her life, her career in working in the local ice rink; she seemed to be a fun teenager. Her dreams were short sighted, no ambition and no pressure for college or extra schooling. Her life was care-free. She was even out tonight with all of her friends celebrating her birthday, how more fun can her life be? My birthdays just turn out to be another tiresome day of work.

All of my focus directed to her. Her perfume, her perfect make-up, her stature, she was infallible in every way. Comparing her to me or comparing her to her old self seemed like comparing the brightness of a supernova to a glowing ember. I would have never guessed this was Angel.

I always dreamed of growing up, and blossoming into something near her. I wanted to be her. I wanted to leave my short, under developed body, oversensitive emotions, and sense, to turn into a cheerful, lighthearted adolescent like Angel.

At one point I followed her over to her friends and she introduced me. I didn't know any of them, but by that time Angel and everyone else was too drunk for me to understand the names she alleged. So I, an expert in the language of drunk people, slurred out various sounds similar to what Angel said they were, and I was accepted into their little circle.

The world ignored them and their rowdy laughter. They could do what ever they wanted, without consequence.

They were my opposites. Every single day I'm trying my best to blend in, keep my head down, and survive. And if I fail to do so, even the slightest mistake could lead to more discrimination, punishment from police and enemies, death or torture. In the same city, Angel and her friends were normal kids, never giving any attention to anybody except their phones and their other simple entertainment sources. What I would give to have a fraction of their bliss.

After a few rounds of drinks, my edge rounded and softened like a well used bar of soap, I turned off my busy thoughts and painful analysis of the group's conversations. After a few more, I almost numbed into one of them.

I just wanted to laugh and spend time with Angel and her friends. And I did. I listened with bated breath just as the others when they talked about their parents or teenager problems. I felt like one of them, my pain, my hatred lightened to where I didn't think about it.

We whooped and shoved ice cubes down each other's backs, the girls gossiped about celebrities, somebody turned the music to something we liked and we danced in the open end of the bar.

It was when I would get a moment of clarity and my conscience reminded me of my obligations, great, another wave of guilt swept over me. I need to hunt; somebody might be dying because I'm not doing my job, only indulging myself in these childish pleasures.

Even with the dread and knowing that I'm wasting precious time I stayed with Angel and her friends. An hour passed, then two, maybe I'll stay for cake and then I'll leave. Three hours, then four slipped. We danced, we talked, we laughed.

Then came gift time, her friends supplied her with boxes of jewelry, clothes, make-up; I quickly slipped a napkin with a poem in her gift pile feeling guilty I couldn't give more. When she reached the napkin, she almost wiped her mouth with it at first, and then noticed my scratchy handwriting.

Roses are red, violets are blue, I can't write poetry, but happy birthday to you.
   -Moogie

She stared at it, and then stared at me. To everybody else it was merely a napkin with pen markings. But of all the presents that night, she kept that one with her the whole time. No words to me, no thank-yous, but she smiled. It was not over radiant, or fixed, or light. A smile only understood when seen.

At around two o'clock in the morning the bar cleared out, it was closing time. I drove everybody home, being the soberest one and probably the best driver, even though I don't own a car. Soon it was just me and a sleeping Angel behind me in the car. She was lying across the seats in the back curled up, using her arms as pillows.

She was beautiful; I was mesmerized. As I watched her candid, sleeping expression something inside me fell into a quiet, pulling languish.

The car glided across the smooth and empty freeway, we were the only people in the world. My senses were still dull, almost as an average human's. I drifted through the wide, empty lanes and slowed to regular speed when I noticed the radar detector.

The lightrail sped through the middle of the freeway, glowing, and brilliant white, nearly empty of people. Suddenly the last train car disappeared as fast as the first had come.

I remember watching it being built, opening day, entering it for the first time. Now it looked as if it has always been there, shooting across town, carrying passengers of every kind.

I always liked this time of night; it's one of the only parts of the night when I can think. The rest of the time the world is rushing around and hurrying from place to place, enslaved into obeying endless agendas or plans.

I knew her address almost as if it were muscle memory; I mechanically turned the right streets and pulled into her driveway. It reminded me of the hundreds of times I rode to her house on my bike in the spring and summer.

I turned the ignition off and looked to the backseat of the car, Angel's face half-illuminated in the moonlight.

The night was better than I could have ever hoped it would be, I enjoyed it more than the relieved feelings I have when I crack a beer with slayers after a hunt, this was some new, obscure and mindlessly fun.

But it isn't me.

Ever so carefully I leaned back and slid my hand into Angel's purse, two of my fingers found the napkin with the penned poetry and I carefully plucked it out. No memory will be left.

She's drunk, her friends don't know me, nor do they remember my name. I would become a blurry memory to her, time could pass and she would think I didn't even exist tonight. It is time to go.

I silently rolled the window down and put my feet out first. Out I slid, torso and then head, she didn't stir as my high heels touched the smooth concrete of the driveway.

I disappeared, out of her sight and out of mind.

My mind crept back into the normal state; it's time to return home, and back to work.

My heels lightly tapped the sidewalk in a brisk rhythm, bouncing me out of the sleeping neighborhood. I noticed the desert daisies were already wilting away into dead weeds throughout the cracks in the sidewalk.

I turned the corner and my mind was back to full power. The slayers in Northern Arizona were hinting about another medium to full-scale job they were sniffing out, and the nightclub I hunted in last week turned up in the papers again for disappearances. I might lose the bar I discovered tonight and hunt there instead.

My blades need to be cleaned and sharpened, again, and I need more clothes, and I need to start that burn pile for all of the blood stained outfits still sitting in the bathtub. The condo still needs a little cleaning, and I need new gauze for my medical kit, oops, I should have gotten that at the drugstore I was already at today...

The crunch of a desert daisy under my heel startled me.

I lifted my right foot up to discover the healthy flower broken and smeared on the concrete. The petals seemed old and wilted now, unlike what it was moments before, and the moisture leaked and evaporated quickly.

I stepped back and hesitated for a moment, watching it. Then I looked across the long sidewalk I just passed through.

All of the daisies in the middle section of the cracks looked like the daisy I made, these flowers weren't wilted. They were crushed.

All of them were pressed down and left to die by mindless people like me. I started to the way back home again, conscious of the dying and dead flowers, and then now irritated at myself and the other passing people who were too wrapped up in themselves to realize the unnecessary loss.

I shook my head at the destroyed thing, its beauty wouldn't be realized, it wouldn't be appreciated. It was killed with lack of consideration, and will go forever without notice.

Then my feet stopped tapping forward, I looked down at the daisies, and the back at the corner I turned minutes before.

I've never felt connected to anybody except her. But it is for the best, her world and my world should never be overlapping. Angel could be tortured, killed, and thrown into oblivion because nobody cares. The idea of her body skewed and distorted, lying dead in a barrel of acid or a ditch as I have done to my victims is unbearable.

I closed my eyes, forever, never seeing her again.

What am I doing?

I shook my head and turned back to home.

Where am I going?

I glanced at the corner.

What am I crushing?

My foot stepped towards the corner.

I silently paced closer to where I came, then to the middle of the street. I stood motionless, watching the car she was still asleep in. The open and dry night let dusty winds move my fluttery hair and graze across my shoulders.

The flavescent pool from the streetlight above me projected my shadow. As I stayed, nothing else tried to move except my hair. My shadow did not age, my body did not grow any closer to a natural death, it was irrevocably still.

Bringing her into my life is wrong to existence, I am the oddity and unnaturality of life. I would crush daisies she would never see, crush her ability to live in a defined normality. It wouldn't be fair.

I took another step forward to her. My perpetual circle of life ticks away years, she doesn't have very many.

I could stay until she gets bored of me. Or I could keep my other life a secret. She could go her whole life without knowing about my job or my world.

I'm smart, if anyone could do it, they would be me. I wouldn't let anyone get to her without having to deal with me first.

I have torn people to bits, bashed brains, and carved throats. Slayers even fear me for what I am. My fingers clutched to a fist, I would like to see somebody try to defeat me.

I started back to the darkened car, faster and faster my feet carried me until I was throwing a sprint. When I was back to the driveway I silenced again, careful not to wake Angel, and slid back through the window.

The crumpled napkin in my purse found its way back into hers.

Angel's eyes gingerly fluttered open when I reached back and shook her. She yawned and shined her sparkling white teeth at me. "Where are we? Where did all of my friends go?"

I smiled, "I took them home, the bar closed and nobody was sober enough to drive so I dropped you guys off at home."

"Oh, that's so nice of you Moogie. Thank-you for taking care of me." I gazed at her half dazed, slightly lost in her voice.

Then Angel reached out and riffled through my bag, removing my cell phone and started typing something into her phone.

"What are you doing?" She quickly placed my phone back in my purse. "I copied your phone number to mine so I can call you. And return the favor sometime."

"Oh, okay." I mumbled and I half carried her out of the car and to the door. I turned to leave, and the soft, memorable voice behind me stopped me dead in my tracks, "Bye Moogie, call me." The words lingered as a weak but lasting echo in my mind.

In the blindingly white illuminating train car I tried sorting through my confused, overreacting senses. The bulky metals clunking together from the train and the music playing a little too loud in the teenager's earphones a few seats away drove my mind to headaches and irritation. I shut my eyes and plugged my ears to attempt concentration on logical plans about Angel.

My stop arrived and I slowly rose to leave the public transport. It's Angel, she isn't just a kid from my old life; she was the reason my short childhood was so fulfilling. The bugs chirped and wheezed as I headed towards my home. This is the only person that matters, the only one I care about, not as an asset but as a companion.

A loud and obnoxious crowd of giggling girls on the other side of the street laughed their way into the condo complex I was heading toward. She's Angel, I'm going to get Angel back.

6
Moving Forward

It wasn't dawn just yet when I reentered my shabby, claustrophobic condo. I reached under my skirt and pulled out the hatchet from my hand-sewn holster strapped to my leg and tossed it onto the counter. Another day gone to waste. I flopped on my sofa and hit the new messages button on the telephone.

A monotoned robot voice said "One new message" and beeped. Joey's voice came on with a slightly hurried tone "Moogie, my dad and I are on a hunt, only two of them this time and we followed them to a house. Dad just got out of surgery and isn't up to it, I need you to come out to the job with me. Call me when you get home." The phone beeped again and I sat up. Maybe tonight wasn't so bad.

Joey, a lanky boy with light coffee-colored hair and light brown eyes was one of the first slayers that I'd met. He's my age, just out of high school, and his family has been hunting for generations. Slaying is embedded deeply into his roots, and he has a kill count higher than me, with his first at the age of ten. He goes to the college near here and is the only slayer that knows anything about modern day technology. Most of the others barely know how to work a computer.

Of every slayer I've ever encountered he is the most open minded, he doesn't care that I have a form of the virus he's been trying to exterminate. When his father and every other slayer showed disapproval of helping me he still thought that I should have a chance at pursuing my career in slaying.

I prefer to hunt with him than hunt alone or with anybody else. But even as diplomatic and understanding as he is, sometimes being a born and raised slayer means clouded judgment.

I don't trust slayers and I would gladly kill any if they turned on me, but I don't mind that we are on the same side. With that I try not to immerse myself in slayer politics or the lives of the local slayers except business and occasionally hanging out with Joey. All I really want to do is hunt as much as possible before somebody finally ends me.

After returning the call I suited up into more comfortable clothes in case there's a chase; I took off my mask of make-up and applied a lighter one. Joey knows I'm going to be thirteen forever, but he doesn't need to be reminded every time I see him. I picked my hatchet back off the table and put it on a loop I had sewn onto my belt and went outside to wait for Joey.

He arrived in his family's old, banged-up truck. I jumped inside and we headed off across the freeway without speaking.

We traveled to a high-end housing area where places were two or three stories high. The ones we were stalking lived in a gorgeous two story, old, painted blue with a black frame. The lawn had a black iron metal fence surrounding the perimeter with a healthy spread of dark green grass; a hefty oak impended over the thick grass on the far left. An elegant, curvy walkway of glossy black stepping stones led to the front porch.

I glared at the magnificent structure with envy, remembering how much I detest my condo. I shuddered at the thought of going back to the barely breathable dwelling.

Joey pulled over a block away from the house we were about to raid. With his new phone he pulled up a holographic map of the block where the house was located and I stared at it. "Wow! I want a phone like that!" Joey shrugged, "The holographics didn't turn out to be as good like they said on TV. And it is not nearly as high-quality as computers; loading anything on this piece of junk is a bitch."

Joey's grumblings soon made sense. With the holographics constantly reloading every time Joey tried marking it up with a plan we decided to give up being high-tech and went back to a paper map and a pencil. I didn't know paper maps were carried in cars anymore. I guess Joey's family still lives in the Stone Age.

It was ironic, because not too long ago Joey set up chatrooms on the internet and trained all the slayers in Arizona to use it for faster and more secure communication. I don't use the chatrooms unless I'm desperate for work, though I heard it's become so popular it's going international now.

The plan was simple, Joey will go up to the front door, ring the door bell and attack whoever answers the door while I sneak around to the back and kill the other one. Joey unsheathed his weapon, a big knife, and we both left his car to follow through on our basic plan.

It worked like clockwork; they reacted predictably. Joey rang the door bell as I hopped the fence and positioned myself next to the back door. Although I couldn't see who answered the door I did hear the sound of a door chain rattling, the whoosh and screech of door hinges working and then a crunch with a sound of furniture falling over. Finally it ended with a sort of half-screaming half-gurgling.

From above my head on the second floor I heard thumping on the staircase. I poised towards the door. With a click and the door disappearing inside the house I jumped out of my hiding place and swung my hatchet as forcefully as I could into the person exiting. The hatchet didn't quite chop the woman's head off but it did go about halfway, and she dropped to her knees while her head flopped backwards.

I stepped inside the house and looked up at Joey. He was retracting his knife from a man's stomach in the foyer room, next to a broken table. With a disappointed tone he mumbled slightly frowning, "Too bad I broke that table; it looked like it was worth something." I answered him with a shrug.

After a quick look around to find that nobody else was in the house, I returned to Joey who was knee deep in cleaning supplies from his truck.

He passed me a garbage bag and we started loading the bodies into the trash and sealed them with tape. Then Joey brought in two wardrobe boxes and a hand truck and we wheeled the garbage bags away in the boxes. After the bodies were cleaned up I moved onto to scrubbing the tiles to destroy any evidence of a fight.

I toured the house, flipping the lights on as I went, enjoying the great taste in furniture. Everything had an old-fashioned air to it that gave the house a welcoming vibe. These people reminded me of spiders.

Joey took all the remaining trash bags, cleaning chemicals, and scrubbing utensils to his car and drove home to pick up his trailer so we can start splitting the house up.

Most slayers after they finish a job end up selling everything owned by the victims. Joey got himself a realtor's license and we end up flipping houses like this. It earns a decent living; usually he ends up paying all of it toward college while I just try to make ends meet. Sometimes, Joey and I keep the properties to live in. Joey has two larger houses than this, which he kept from hunts, one he lives in and the other is where he dumps all of the stuff from other houses to be cleaned and sold.

The furniture and other valuable items go on the internet, to antique dealers, or the local flea markets.

The house was just as beautiful on the inside as it was on the outside. On the first floor, I noticed some big money makers: a flat screen TV with a built-in holographic projector, antique furniture, and a video gaming set. At the back of the house the kitchen looked like it had a substantial tableware set and a strong collection of kitchen knives. The most intriguing part of the house was in the very back. A sealed door stood with a bulky padlock keeping it protected. I tried to kick it down, it wouldn't move, I tried to ram it with my shoulder, it still didn't budge.

Even though I have just a thirteen-year-old's body, I can still push a massive amount of weight around. If I can't break through this door then something really valuable is meant to be locked up in here.

When Joey returned we ended up staring at the door trying to figure out how to open it. "Got any ideas?" We tried ramming it, and that ended up with bruised shoulders, after that Joey put a crowbar to it, but the door still wouldn't open. Then Joey resorted to picking the lock; that worked! As the door peeled open, I imagined of all the exciting things that would have been in there. The first thing we saw was a dried up dead body hanging upside down on a hook with his throat slit.

Joey shook his head, "Aww, I just put the cleaning supplies away." I nodded in understanding, "Yeah, I expected it to be ancient buried treasure too."

The room looked pretty standard, it wasn't a torture dungeon like some I've seen before, but it's a good sized, efficient station, not like the converted bathtub draining stations in places like when I first took the condo.

The room had smoothly poured concrete flooring with a drain at the bottom; right below the body was a catch basin that smelled very strongly of dried blood. To the right of the catch basin a tall, bathtub-like sink and the end of the metal counter stood knives, gloves, funnels, and empty wine bottles. "Wine bottles?" I muttered, Joey shrugged, "I guess they wanted to be more sophisticated."

In the back of the room four fifty-five gallon barrels stood sealed up, I wandered over to them, "Hey Joey, can I borrow that crowbar?" He tossed it over and I flipped the top up.

I cringed as nasty chemical smells I knew a little too well filled my nose. A body in almost chunks floated around in the barrel filled with acid, I see why they have the drain now; they drop the bodies in the acid, then drain and refill the barrels until the bodies are broken up enough to wash away. All the barrels probably have people in them. I remember doing the exact same thing a few years back, except I did it in a bathtub, but I didn't add water to the mix. When I drained the acid out and refilled the bathtub the acid ended up corroding my drain.

I shut the lid back up and Joey brought in a hand truck to wheel out the barrels. When that was finished we took care of the body hanging upside down and left the rest of the room to be scavenged for later.

We continued the look around and found a refrigerator full of wine bottles in the downstairs pantry. The refrigerator was huge, bottles of all different labels and sizes filled it from head to toe. Joey reached in and opened one of the middle ones and handed it to me. "Does this smell good to you?" he asked harmlessly. I took a whiff, "That is definitely my kind of drink." I handed it back to him, "Too bad I only let myself drink pig's blood." He smelled it and cringed, "Ugh, if you won't drink it who will?" I pondered that for a second. "Hey! Maybe we can donate it to one of the local hospitals." I imagined wheeling in a cartful of these wine bottles to a hospital and just walking out.

"Eh, we'll worry about that later."

I shook my head and took the bottle of blood from him and smelled it again, mmm, even with cold blood I know one swig would get me back to my addiction, life would be killing spree central all over again. Joey gave me a skeptical look and took the bottle back.

We opened a few more cabinets, these people had a wide selection of random pantry items. I picked up a box of old macaroni and cheese, the label was from the nineties, the company had long since changed the label.

"Huh." I huffed, "Did you know macaroni could go bad?" I mumbled.

Joey picked the box up from my hand, "I thought their kind could only drink human blood and a few other types of liquids. Why would they have cereal and canned stuff like this?"

I nodded, "Yeah, they'd end up barfing anything substantial after about a half an hour. So they might be props to look normal or these guys might have had normal people over for dinner."

Joey looked up at me, "You're saying these people were so wicked they purposely fed innocent victims expired macaroni and cheese? Whew, I'm glad we got them off the streets."

I pulled one of the soups off of the shelves, chuckling at his sarcasm. They even had my favorite alphabet soup. I opened one of the cupboards and pulled out a few fine white porcelain plates and stared, everything is so nice here. I twirled one around in my fingers.

"Do you want some breakfast, Joey?" I made him some toast while he read the news on his phone. I cracked open that can of soup before we prepared to go through the rest of the house.

After breakfast I jogged upstairs and checked each room; one of the rooms was a study, a few carved shelves packed with books lined one wall and a matching ornate wooden desk stood in front of the bookcase. An intricately designed rug was placed in the middle of the wooden paneled floor, and a large buck's head was placed near one of the windows, barely out of my reach.

The light of dawn shined down onto the room through the rounded windows. It added a calm and warm atmosphere; I stepped into the middle of the pool of light and closed my eyes, taking in the feel of the room.

A silver computer sat on top of the desk. It seemed out of place in such a stately room. This will be fun to sift through; I stared at the books guessing which ones are first editions.

The master bedroom had a walk in closet, a king size bed with satin sheets, and a huge wooden vanity. The rooms down the hall felt like museum exhibits, they were filled with hobby and recreational things.

We discovered a safe in the back of one of the closets we searched. After breaking into it we found their fake papers to support their fake identities, social security, birth records, and insurance from what I see. It would definitely catch somebody's attention if somebody was opening a bank account with a driver's license saying they are three hundred years old. So after about thirty years my kind tends to become a new person and move to a new home.

I did it too, nobody would let me check into hotels or go into bars being a teenager, especially a teenager that disappeared off the face of the earth with her family during spring of 2010. So I adapted, I traded life as a nobody wandering around lost and primitive, sleeping in alleyways, for a shadow of somebody's identity, everything is fake, down to my very name. But now I sleep in hotels and live comfortably in houses of my victims.

My eyes stayed steady on the page I was examining, but my mind drifted to the slayers and Joey. They don't even know my name, they just call me Moogie.

"Looks like these are the only owners of the house, it wasn't a rental, the mortgage seems to be paid off, and escrow payments are fine." Joey thumbed through the papers more, "The cars are paid off, and I don't see any debts. It seems like they're clean to sell."

I leaned forward and started sifting through the papers again "They might have just been lone wolves too. No partner ownerships of businesses or documentation of anyone besides the two we killed. I'm kind of glad, I really don't want to have any family relations or coven friends coming to the house at four in the morning, because that has happened before." Joey smirked, "Yeah, me too, if only my relatives stopped coming to my house at four in the morning, and then forcing me to eat their casserole."

I playfully shoved him and we continued to rummage through the safe. In more papers I found passports, bank account pins, and a set of spare keys.

Joey moved on from the safe to the hat boxes and shoe boxes while I gathered the important papers to put in the keeper pile. It's the perfect house. Why should I live in a condo when I could live in this? No noisy music playing in the condo attached to mine; it has a wide space, nice furniture, and a backyard. It's perfect. "I think I'm going to keep this house and sell the condo."

He smiled, "Good, I was wondering when you were going to give up that thing. I always felt claustrophobic in there." He opened one of the shoe boxes and found a pair of high heels encrusted with diamonds. "Look at these! You can keep the house, I want these shoes." I examined the shoes, "Alright, but honestly they clash with the blood on your shirt and they look a little too small." Joey snickered, "They are not for me, I need to get my girlfriend something for her birthday next week."

I nodded, "Deal, do you want my condo to sell too? I don't need fifty houses like you." He nodded, "Sure, I'll take the condo."

By ten o'clock I was playing dress-up in all the jewelry and designer clothes I found in one of the bedrooms, Joey and I talked and guessed how much they were worth and divided them up loosely. I'll end up pawning or selling the ones I kept with all the payments and bills that come with assuming identities, electric, gas, heat, and escrow, etcetera, etcetera. That is what I do; I become these guys to own the house and the cars, just as I did with the condo, and the apartment before that.

After playing in the clothes and getting all the diamonds and big gems we brought the safe with all of the papers downstairs and put them in a pile on the kitchen table. "Do you want the deeds signed over to a new identity, or do you want to keep living as them?"

"I think I'll keep going as them. Since they owned two cars you can have one and I'll take the other." He nodded and got up to go outside, "Since you're moving in Moogie, we're going to have to fool the neighbors." He reached his truck and grabbed from the back a for-sale sign and a hammer. "Where do you want it?" I sighed at the thought of a giant hole in my grass but pointed to a spot in the corner. "You'll need to keep it up for about a month, then we'll slap a sold sign on it and you'll get to become the new neighbor."

After that Joey and I started going through the CD, record, video tape, and whatever else is used in entertainment collection. Most houses I've raided have a bunch of old souvenirs from years and years ago, immortals are the biggest hoarders on the planet. The amount of useless stuff I find is unbelievable.

The condo had a complete dancing disco music discography and a library full of bad eighties exercise training videos. But no matter how much starving, running, exercising, or weight loss programs participated in, I and all the rest like me are incapable of growing older, changing weight, or changing physical appearance. The eighties videos still baffle me today.

At the very end of the hall a closed door had a wooden title plate named playroom. It drew my attention quickly, what would be in a playroom? Or do I not want to know?

Curiosity burned as I reached for the golden door handle. The door was unlocked, but the hinges squeaked as if it hadn't been used in a long time. I stood still, my breathing slowed and almost stopped. A certain feeling set over me, the vacuum of dry, stagnant air made the room a place of forgotten. The room was fashioned with furniture under white sheets, an exceedingly thick coat of dust blanketed every inch of the room.

As I stepped, my boots imprinted the dusty wood floor, around me the walls were painted in a deteriorating jungle theme, neglected for what might have been years, peeling elephants and marred giraffes peeked through the cracked and faded trees. I meandered over to the middle and largest piece of furniture set in the room to draw the white sheet back.

Dust clouded the air, sprinkling and resettling on my hair and nose along with the rest of the room.

Under the white cover a carved wooden crib balanced on aged, vacillated pilings. The sheets were yellowed in age, old fabric toys were positioned precisely around the edge. I stared at it in wonder. Then I moved on to the smaller sheet covered figures. One by one each revealed itself to be another contributor to a small child's playroom, rocking horses, wooden soldiers and smaller toys packed away in neatly stacked in boxes, old fashioned baby clothes, untouched paints and a blank easel.

This room was an abandoned dream, what I and all others like me face. Sterility.

I swayed as my somber thoughts were suspended in that unattainable initiative. The ancient crib stabbed my heart with a thorn of universal grief; I've seen rooms like these. It's one of the many things I missed in my short and abrupt end to average humanity.

Joey's head popped inside, "Wow! Look at this room!" He stepped in and started poking around cheerfully, "Almost near perfect condition, we hit the jackpot! I know this toy dealer around here that just eats this kind of stuff up! Man, and this crib, a buddy of mine could take this thing apart and make it into a totally tricked out new one that could sell for buckets of money, and..."

His voice faded out of my mind, the loud enthusiasm never faltered with him. I smiled and tried to support him, even when I was so far away.

Noon rolled along and we started working our way to the garage. Two sleek black cars with tinted windows occupied the majority of the space in the garage. "I call the big one!"

I laughed and then huffed a sarcastic sigh, "I wanted the big one." We walked over to each car and examined them thoroughly, both had GPS systems, holographic map systems, voice and phone communication systems, and satellite radios. "This car is just too unbelievable!" Joey muttered. I sat fascinated by the attractiveness of the machine. I have a car now, this will be a lot more fun than riding next to homeless people on the city buses and lightrails. Can this day improve any more?

I got in the smaller car and gripped the steering wheel. The grip morphed to my finger placement, "I love this car! But maybe I'll get it painted in blue or silver; the black sinister bad guy look is just not my image." Joey nodded, "Yes, black evil serial killer car is not your scene, blue evil serial killer definitely suits you better."

It took me twenty minutes to peel Joey off his new car to move on with the day, we couldn't play with the cars just yet. I still have a job to do.

The garage had a workshop filled with various power tools and half finished projects. The only thing in the garage Joey didn't recognize was a giant plywood box that had a curved back standing up in the side of the garage. It looked nothing like the pretty wood furniture inside the house; it was opposite, ugly, rough, and unpainted. The middle had loosely fitted boards haphazardly shoved into the middle to hold a couple paint cans.

"What do you think it is?"

I shrugged, "I don't know, I guess it is a make-shift shelf. The way it's curved doesn't make any sense for being a shelf." I reached up and picked up one of the paint cans. The other cans lost balance and collapsed, smashing the shelves and creating a domino affect out onto the floor. It ended in an ear piercing, tinny clanging. "Yep, I didn't think it was supposed to hold shelves."

"What do we do with it?"

"Leave it there; worry about it tomorrow. Mañana is the greatest labor saving device ever." And with that I shut the garage door.

The day passed and we filled the trailer up with tons of goodies that need to be appraised, fixed, or cleaned. I could see a lot of work ahead of me, and we haven't even scratched the surface yet. We still have bank accounts, deposit boxes, and storage containers to look through, plus the drives all over Arizona to get rid of all this stuff at thrift stores, pawn shops, and flea markets. I looked forward to moving into my new home, selling the condo, and getting used to driving a car on a regular basis.

7

It's all Downhill From Here!

Three days passed, Joey and I moved and cleaned up all of the furniture I didn't want on the bottom floor. I kept the matching tableware, the living room furniture set and the TV, but got rid of the gaming system after losing to Joey four times in one of the car racing games.

My condo, which contained virtually nothing of value, was cleaned and most of the belongings I wanted to keep had been packed up and moved to the new house. We were nearly ready to sell it.

During one of our breaks after attempting to clean out the garage in my new house, we removed the giant pseudo shelf with the curved back and used it as footstool.

After digging out lawn chairs from the side yard Joey and I half napped under a giant umbrella stand we found by the pool. Second by second we were becoming sizzling bacon in the Arizona oven.

"What are we going to dig through next?" Joey mumbled sleepily. I shrugged, flipping over to dissuade the heat from burning my face, "Maybe we could go through the power tools; they seemed brand new-" My cell phone cut in with a whiny, repetitive tone.

I slowly turned over and started feeling around the end table to turn it off. Lemonade, nope, Joey's phone, nope. My hand gripped the slightly jolting square and I squinted into the glare of my screen: ANGEL.

Angel? I answered it. She invited me out to a slightly familiar sounding coffee shop, I agreed and in no time, completely forgetting about the agenda I was just planning.

"What?" Joey propped himself up on his elbow alarmed. "Did somebody die?"

"No, not this time, but I do have to leave." "What about the power tools?" He asked, his voice tipping into disappointment.

"We'll go through them later, help me move the ugly box back to the garage."

Barely twenty minutes later, Angel's car pulled up to my house and parked. The driver door flung open and Angel jumped out with an enormous grin on her face. Then, after waving at me in the yard she ran up to my house and threw the front door open. "Where's your bathroom? I really need to go!" I almost shrugged and said "I have no idea." But luckily, Joey, who was on his way out, pointed and gave her the directions. Angel stared at him slightly confused while he was exiting my house but yielded to where he pointed.

I smiled gratefully and he departed in his truck. Angel returned a few minutes later bright as ever. "Who are the people in the pictures?" She leaned back and pointed to the portraits hanging in the foyer room. I gave her a confused look, "Huh-oh! Umm that is my cousin and her husband. I'm getting their house because they're moving up to New York, and I haven't packed up and shipped their stuff yet." She bought my improv. "I didn't know you had cousins, anyway..."

In no time I was drinking a slightly bland cup of coffee with Angel and watching kids on well beaten skateboards at the local skate park endanger themselves with serious bodily injury.

We were here supporting an ex-boyfriend of a friend of Angel's that had just gotten his cast off from an accident a few months ago. Some of Angel's other posse joined us and we watched him do dangerously entertaining tricks. He would fly through the air, looking determined to impress us, and a few times he would spin or flip a certain way on a request from a spectator.

I gleefully watched him as the others did, commenting on a particular move to my new friends, and in between tricks we talked the hours away about stories of people I haven't thought about in years.

Half of the group broke off to go shopping and visit a yogurt shop that just opened up next to one of the strip malls a few miles away. Angel and I hopped in their overcrowded van to join them.

We bounced around trying to hold ourselves in because there weren't enough seat belts, laughing whenever we hit a speed bump. I crammed in between Angel and one of the twins. I watched amused as the twin tried putting on mascara while the van was moving.

She decorated the right eye fine but when the driver took a sharp turn her hand missed and a purple line of mascara crossed her forehead.

Everybody roared with laughter and ooos while she frantically tried to wipe it off. The guy driving parked and we all rushed out of the car and in a giant blob, and made our way to the strip mall and the opening yogurt shop.

The yogurt was truly atrocious. I had never tasted such a sour strawberry flavor in my life, but the rest of the kids who got my flavor loved it, and after shoving about half in my mouth I gave up on it. Instantly, one of the other piranha kids snatched it up.

The sun turned the endless blue afternoon sky into a starry gray hue while Angel and I walked along a slightly hidden garden behind the mall. Everybody else had broken off to eat breadsticks at the Italian restaurant down the street or to find fun elsewhere.

Music danced in the background, I recognized it, an old 2006 hit, and the meaning was about something ending tonight and fireworks. I could mouth almost every lyric and remember every note played in the piano line; it vibrated the air as it crooned to my magnified senses.

We strolled and talked, I found no end to the pleasure in the stories she tells. She worked with a few of her friends on shifts at an ice rink and they would have oodles of fun playing on the Zamboni and skating in the empty rink after hours.

I wanted to be in her shoes, skating on the ice rink for fun. The last time I was anywhere near an ice skating rink I was hunting somebody who was trying to decapitate me with a skate blade.

We departed from the main path into our own niche, I leaned against a towering pine, spanning across twice my width, and near my knees somebody had carved a heart and the initials MO + RC 4ever. The MO was crossed out and marred until it actually looked like K squiggle I + RC 4ever.

I observed this out loud to Angel and she snickered at it as she laid on the grass next to me. We never stopped laughing or chatting the entire time. She would go into huge, animated stories that could have been summed up in ten words or less, I loved to hear every aspect of them.

Angel's musical laugh caught me into a daze, I felt bubbly and childlike with her. It was as if I had never left and we were goofing around again, ignoring the rest of the world because they ignored us.

The sun finally allocated the moon to rule over the stars and signify to Angel that she had to leave. "My shift is coming up, let's do this again sometime." she said, dismayed of our parting I nodded in agreement. We should do this again.

I lightly sprinted home, my feet gingerly propelling from sidewalk square to sidewalk square while humming the old piano line, my mind was blissful. I leapt and bounded from handrails and benches following the streets to the bus stop, completely oblivious to the world around me, almost passing the city at nearly inhuman speeds towards home. Street lights blurred together, scenes and signs stopped mattering; I wanted to dance through the city like this forever.

I reached my beautiful sapphire colored house, partially in lassitude from my run, eager for bed, though I haven't changed the sheets in any of the beds yet. Oops, I was supposed to do that today.

I cleaned and adjusted the house, slipping back into a quiet, sharp mood, reminiscing in the childish fun.

I ignored the quiet voice that preached the regret I should have been feeling in my mind. Today for once, I, will be ordinary.

"That's the fourth time you've texted in the past five minutes!" I quickly shoved the phone back in my pocket and started folding the clothes again. "Sorry." Joey shook his head, "For the first time in the history I've ever known you, you're texting! What is the matter with you?"

I bit my lip, should I tell him what's going on? I resorted to telling him the bare minimum, "A friend of mine is in town and we were just doing some catching up, and I didn't get enough time to finish our conversation yesterday."

He raised his eyebrows at my sudden cautiousness in tone and I looked down at the clothes I was folding. Switching to a lighter tone I said "Could you go get the next box down? That top one, I've been eyeing it for a while, I bet it has the sadomasochism stuff." I grinned; he shook his head with irritation, but didn't press for more information about the subject before. He reached to the top self and brought down the box, "Ha! You're dead on! Look at this..."

The next day at about noon the door bell rang. I almost missed it with Joey's annoying rock music pounding through the house. The doorbell rang again and I stared at the book I was reading; today I was digging through the study looking for first edition copies of books that usually sell to private collectors for a lot more than a book should.

I closed the dusty, well worn cover and jumped up to head downstairs and answer the door. In the foyer I stood on my tip toes, curiously gazing through the peep hole in the door. Angel, with two giant brown boxes stood there ginning like there's no tomorrow.

I threw the door open and Angel shoved the boxes into my arms. "Surprise!" I stumbled around and dropped the boxes into the living room while Angel brought in another box and two cases. I looked at her astounded and half shouted over the music "What are you doing here?"

She laughed at my reaction, "I had some old stuff I wanted to give back to you."

I walked over to the giant stereo by the TV and hit the pause button to end the deafening music. Then I turned back to the boxes. What kind of stuff is she talking about? Joey, who was in the process of cleaning up and throwing away useless artifacts, was balancing a box of pictures on his way down the stairs. "I'm getting this out to the dumpster, I'll be back-" Angel ran up and grabbed the box from Joey shouting in a shocked voice. "Wait! That's Moogie's cousin's stuff!"

Joey, caught completely off guard jumped back defensively, but relaxed when he saw it was just Angel. "When did you get here? What do you mean cousin-"

I cut in, "Oh, Angel! That's Joey, uhh, he means the post office, we were in the process of mailing everything to New York, to my cousins, or what he calls the dumpster."

Angel calmed down and handed the box back to Joey, "Oh, sorry, uhh, Joey, I'm Angel by the way. I just came in a couple minutes ago to drop off some stuff." She smiled, and Joey stiffened and blushed.

In a shaky voice he tried to shrug back into his attitude, accepting the story. "Yeah, no problem." And turned to me saying, "I filled the truck up with enough boxes of things to mail back to your cousins and I think that's enough for today. See you later." And he quickly stepped out the door, taking one last look at Angel. Huh, Angel has that affect on everybody, waiters, people on the streets, her friends sometimes. Even the most confident ones fall into a stutter.

"Where did all of this come from?" I asked as Angel helped me open up all of the boxes. "When you guys disappeared, the house was foreclosed on and the bank people put all of your stuff into a gigantic dumpster parked in front of your house's driveway. I dug out a few things knowing they meant a lot to you. When you came back you might miss them."

She shrugged, as if it was expected of her.

I glanced at my long lost bass and violin cases now standing up against the couch.

Angel presented my stuff back to me as if she were one of those infomercial sales women. She would display the items one at a time and then give me a very wordy and funny story about how she obtained my belongings. In one, she illustrated how she wrestled the old lady across the street from me for one of my old sweat shirts. She also found one of my old pillows under a moldy, open mayonnaise jar had to run all around town to find and open laundry cleaner because both of the ones near her miraculously closed.

It still smelled like mayonnaise. At the end of each presentation I kept waiting for her to say "Buy Now with four easy payments!"

Another box had my old wardrobe of t-shirts and sweaters, my backpack overflowing with papers came out of another box. Following that she brought out a comforter I used all the time that had my name embroidered in it. They shared a space with all the songs I had half written and stuffed in an old shoe box.

I was speechless the entire time, completely overcome in gratitude. I had lived with the thought of never seeing these things again, and here they were, saved from the untold horrors of the dump. The same place I just sent Joey to drop off the same type of memorabilia.

The last box she opened had my old laptop where I had kept all my pictures and favorite short stories. Sitting next to it my junkie old mp3 player with every song from the 2009 top forty pop singles chart sat wrapped up in an old pair of ear buds. I looked up at Angel with a smile, she grinned, sheepishly mumbling. "I knew you would come back."

I tightly hugged her. She can never know what I've come back to be, a murderer, an unworldly being, somebody who had just lied blatantly to her face.

We started putting the things in their proper new homes while I gave Angel a grand tour of my half finished house. We avoided certain rooms including the playroom and the dungeon. And when the tour finished I noticed Angel dug something out of her purse. Concert tickets, "I almost forgot! I was going to a concert with my boyfriend, but he dumped me today." Her voice slightly faltered at the last part. "So do you want to go? It's tonight."

I raised my eyebrow, "You had a boyfriend?" Angel frowned "Yeah, do you want to go or not?" I nodded and smirked "What other exciting things haven't you told me?" She stopped and smiled, showing off sparkling teeth, "A lot." She over enunciated the last word, as if she was keeping a secret from me, I strode to the passenger side door at her car. "Really? Tell me about them."

The concert was ok, to get there was a long drive, and the band really sucked, but I didn't mind. I couldn't understand any of the lyrics or tunes, just noise bashing into my brains. But I might be complaining just because my overly sensitive hearing picks up the softest noises. I can hear down to the breaths of people across a room and I'm not accustomed to bass lines that are cranked up to where the music literally shakes the stadium, and is blaring directly at me.

Ear plugs are a necessity next time. Nevertheless, Angel sincerely enjoyed it, so the night went pretty well. Angel bought t-shirts from the band and we laughed and enthusiastically sang the songs on the radio while speeding home down the empty, dimly lit freeway.

It was nearly midnight when we arrived back to my house, I nearly fell onto the concrete when I opened the door to get out of the car, she giggled and I merrily stumbled back to my house.

I turned back to wave at Angel and she leaned out the window hollering, "There's a new horror movie coming out tomorrow night, and I've been waiting for months to see it. How about I pick you up tomorrow at eleven and we go to the midnight premier!" I nodded and laughed. "Sure! See you at eleven!"

From that night on for weeks I spent every night playing with Angel. I stopped hunting, I stopped fighting, and I became a teenager. A silly, irresponsible teenager.

No systematizing my life anymore, just living. And the world didn't stop. Nobody turned around and slapped me upside the head saying "Moogie, you're being childish! Stop neglecting your life and get back to your job!" My bills were paid because I'd work on cleaning and selling the memorabilia from the house with Joey, but I stopped hunting in bars and stopped looking for those predators.

I was normal. I would drive for hours all over Arizona, or make lengthy phone calls, or run down to sell this or that, easy mindless work. Joey and I constantly worked shifts all day at flee markets, bargaining with strange bearded men that wandered up to my table.

Then, when night fell, while Joey spent the rest of the night hunting like I used to, I would run off with Angel and her friends.

We'd go far and wide around the city, either goofing around with Angel's posse loitering or attending a party where the only person I knew was Angel. We rolled around town as if we owned it, instead of merely hiding in it.

Other times we would just stay at my house, where she kept her guitar, and we would dance, sing, and play all night long trying to finish all of my half written songs. Her friends would come over, making movie nights. I would even pull out my violin once in a while, if we were really drunk, and I'd play Angel little fiddle tunes or simple songs. My violin squeaked horribly, and I've forgotten where my fingers go. My education of classical music training ended as a seventh grader, but I still laughed and played.

Maybe one day I'll learn something more sophisticated than Twinkle Twinkle Little Star.

Joey would invite me to hunts, big and small, but I'd make up some excuse that I was working on something elsewhere. Or I would be across town at some nightclub and I wouldn't even bother to pick up the phone. My brain shut off when I played with Angel, when I acted normal I never wanted to turn my brain back on, ever again.

I never missed or regretted not hunting, I didn't even think about it. I stopped waking up every morning dreading if I was going to die tonight, bruises and aches from fights stopped hurting and no more appeared to replace them.

My stress, my anger, and my self loathing washed away with regular doses of play time with Angel. My normal and wound up attitude grew fainter and fainter as my conscious and newfound bliss shoved all of my worries back into a locked, forgotten part of my mind.

The only adrenaline rushes and fear stricken inside my body were the simulation games at the arcades and friends' houses that Angel dragged me to. Or when Angel got excited about a new engagement opening or a new fall line coming out, and I'd share her anticipation. I never knew life could be so easy to ignore.

One month slipped and fell into the past, then two. My life turned into a happy blur, no worries, no 'situations', no death.

One night Angel took me to one of her favorite nightclubs. Angel and I joined up with our circle of friends, about three or four of them. We had flashy, light clothing and our hair had been put up in different temporarily dyed styles of odd multicolored streaks. I fit perfectly in with them, although I went easy on the temporary dye. I was wearing one of my electric pink plaid miniskirts, a skin tight, off cut blouse with premade holes in them and accessorized in clunky, ugly jewelry that clashed with my neon colors.

Altogether I looked like chaos with a purpose, somewhat mild, but still only next to Angel's deep dark crimson vinyl corset and amplified scarlet hair. She towered over the other girls with an intimidating beauty nobody could measure too.

Angel and her court of friends followed her through the door and she elegantly led us into the crowd. Colorful lights randomly flashed everywhere, the blaring music and thumping bass line drew my mind to migraines until I had a few drinks. I disappeared into the music with the other completely self absorbed humans.

The time ran, and I had no idea how long I was there. Angel was always with me, yet I still felt distant, letting the music flow through me. We were gone together, completely leaving boring society.

Tomorrow they'll return to being stiffs, sitting and typing in their small suffocating cubicle cells. Freedom, I always felt like this when I danced, I love dancing.

I swayed and twisted to the thumping of the synthesizer music, letting go, not caring how fast and inhuman I acted. The utter escape liquefied my almost non-existent stress into an insignificant puddle; I spun around Angel as she moved stylishly and tastefully around the floor.

Every move made, every part of her was right, veneration and almost worship of her was drawn from me merely watching her dance. Even after forever I wouldn't be a tenth of her greatness, how can I live immortally knowing she, such an insignificant human with a blink of a life span coincide on the same planet as me?

The song ended and the next didn't appeal to Angel. She left the floor and went straight to the glow-in-the-dark bar in the corner of the club. I tagged along staying close to her heels. When she noticed me she advanced over to two open chairs. The young bartender glanced at us and his face lit up "Hello Angel! Long time, no see! The usual?" Angel nodded. I smiled; I've probably gone here more often than she has and he still had no recollection of my face.

I adjusted my top and shifted straighter as I noticed four other girls wearing the same thing as me. That's my job, and I do it so well.

I decided to order whatever Angel's "usual" was, and it turned out to be very fruity. Angel turned around and surveyed her subjects, subconsciously I identified everybody's basic locations and behavior, several turned their back to us when Angel turned around and I kept finding people's attention naturally drew to where we were sitting.

Or correctly, where Angel was sitting, I'm probably invisible to the world next to Angel, glowing in beauty. But my attention sharpened after seeing something over Angel's shoulder.

The girl next to Angel rose and disappeared for a moment and the guy she was with dropped a tablet into her drink. It dissolved in seconds. She returned and drank the whole glass while the guy smugly beamed at her.

I pulled my eyes away, casually.

Oh no, not here, not now.

The hatchet strapped to my leg weighed me down with sudden consciousness that I had it.

I had a few minutes until the rupees started working; the alcohol and the bliss compartmentalized in my mind as my brain switched to a working phase.

I tried to subdue it with an attempt to engage in a conversation with Angel.

The girl was now slowly losing the confident stature she carried before the drink. Slipping into a daze, she will die tonight.

I looked down at my drink, pretending not to see them. Nobody would know, and it's a greater risk for Angel to find out about me then for some girl to get drained. Right?

What am I thinking, he needs to be stopped; he needs to die.

Adrenaline confronted and twisted the hate I'd been suppressing the past weeks. My hand clenched and my body stiffened, but Angel, completely oblivious didn't detect my change of face.

I wanted to hear the thump of his lifeless body hitting the floor, the assurance he will never hurt another innocent forever.

I bit my lip, swirling the drink in my hand as I listened to him guide her woozy body away from the bar. My breathing caught as I let them slip out the door.

I shifted in my seat to get up, but held to the black counter of the bar. The weight of the regret of my decision pulled me back down to my seat.

I would be shattering the world I created for myself, the delicate glass bubble that encapsulated my happiness.

"Angel," I said restrained, "I need your car." She raised her eyebrow "Why?"

"Please?" I held out my hand. She tilted her head, "How will I get home?" I ground my teeth, "I'll come back later, please; I need the keys now."

Her eyes grew suspicious as my patience cut violently short, "I'll drive you wherever you need to go."

"No." My hand trembled, the need to hunt rising.

She crossed her arms, I glanced at the door. I can't argue this, not enough time. "Fine, we need to go now." She jumped up and strutted out the door waving to her friends "Bye!"

I pulled her along, "Please Angel, hurry!" My eyes scanned the parking lot, combing through the shadows, desperate to find it wasn't too late. The couple entered a black compact car which silently purred to life.

I pushed Angel into the driver seat and I hopped into the other "Follow that car!" I demanded.

Angel slowly turned the ignition on and pulled out carefully. My anger and my sense of hurry shot through the roof.

Through gritted teeth I pleaded to her, "Please! Angel, we can't lose them!" She looked at me with cool, and unfazed collection, "What is your problem Moogie? Why do we have to follow them?" My fists balled and I agitatedly begged Angel to just follow without explanation.

Over and over we argued as she started complaining uncomfortably, I kept my same answer the whole time, "I'll explain later, please, just keep going!"

She huffed out a sigh and irritation struck through her face, "Fine, but this is kind of stupid, just following random people."

She kept a steady pace; obeying all the traffic laws, stopping at lights, occasionally letting other drivers cross in front of us. "Is this like your old boyfriend?" Angel guessed.

I wanted to bang my head into the dashboard. When we reached the stopping destination I instructed Angel to park slightly hidden under a droopy willow tree about a house away.

I dialed Joey's number on my cell phone, "Joey, I've got one and he's got a girl, I'm outside his house right now but I can't go in. You need to get over here, now."

Joey's preoccupied voice replied, "I'll be there in fifteen minutes, are there any other ones in the house?"

I bit my lip, "I don't know," Angel and I watched the people through one of the widows, the guy disappeared and reappeared with a baseball bat.

Angel looked at me confused, "Moogie, what is he-" He swung the bat at the girl's head and she dropped to the floor. "Ohmygod,

Ohmigod, Moogie, Ohmigod. What just happened? Moogie?" Angel's voice dropped into hysterics and her hand gripped my shoulder for support.

Her sharp, neatly manicured nails dug into my shoulder as she nearly burst into frantic tears, a pit of anxiety twisted my stomach "Joey that girl is going to die in five minutes, can you send another slayer?"

"No, all the slayers are at that northern Arizona coven hunt, it's just us."

I stared at the window the guy just dragged the girl's unconscious body from. I murmured softly and calmly into the phone as I stared at the house, "She's going to die."

Joey's voice grew severe and worried, "You don't know how many are in there, most don't travel alone and you know it, is the girl worth losing your life over? I'm driving over right now; I'll be there in fifteen minutes."

I stared at petrified Angel, babbling and panicking the entire time, and then I looked at the empty window. Her knuckles shown prominently as she tightly gripped the steering wheel; the moon illuminated her sharp cheekbones and alarmed face to a ghostly white showing an unnerved, frightened child. Everything I feared became apparent in her face, I failed.

"She's going to die, Joey, there isn't enough time." And I shut the phone off.

"Angel, if you see anything wrong drive out of here as fast as you can, and don't call the police under any circumstance."

Her eyes darted to mine fearfully, "Why, what are you-" I slipped quietly out of the car and raced over the fence into the backyard, with lightning speed and uncanny strength I leveled the backdoor under my foot and charged around the small, untidy house. I sped forward, dangerously armed with my hatchet.

That scummy cannibal was exiting a small closet sized bathroom and he had scarcely enough time to see me. I silently charged and sliced his skull into binary allotments.

My adrenaline pulsed and my heart thumped hard into my ears as I dropped back and wretched my hatchet out of where his head used to be. Oily spray and red goop splattered my nightwear and wetted my hands; I stared at it in the barely glowing lamplight in the cheap little hallway.

I kicked the distorted body askew and stepped into the bathroom. The girl dangled upside down, her feet tied to the shower curtain rod. She slept unharmed a foot away from knives and a bucket.

The house was spotless of any other people and when I finished sweeping the area I returned to the girl.

I washed my hands and then untied the girl. I gingerly carried her, keeping my arms away from my bloody outfit, she didn't stir until I exited the front door and was halfway putting her in Angel's car. "Moogie?" I glance at Angel, she stared at me agape, "Wha-wha, your clothes, b-blood, blood on your c-clothes!" I shushed her, "Angel, it's alright, please, don't do anything irrational."

Tears dripped down her face, "What did he do to her? The blood-" she raised a finger to point at my spattered clothes "Angel, I'll explain everything soon, okay?" She continued to gawk at me frozen but forced herself to nod.

Joey arrived minutes after, I smiled at him triumphantly, "She's okay, I'll take her home, can you clean up?"

He nodded and looked over at the car, "Isn't that Angel's car?"

I looked over at the car too, "Yeah uhh-" His voice turned steely and restrained as he drew his face back to mine, "Is that Angel in the driver's seat?"

"That's why I called you, I didn't want to expose-" Joey shoved me hard and his voice escalated in fury, "You just blew our cover in front of her?"

"I-I" I stuttered and looked at the car again, shifting from foot to foot in the leftover adrenaline. "Yeah, that girl was going to die. I-I had to act. And I trust Angel, she won't tell anybody." He ran his hands through his messy hair, deep in thought. "You take that girl home, I'll take care of the house."

I pulled my eyes away, ashamed, and started back to the car. Oh no, what have I done?

8
Evaporate

I commanded Angel to drive back to the bar, keeping my focus ahead of me. I gripped the armrest, wincing at the fuming internal regret. You idiot! You pathetic piece of worthless flesh! I crossed my arms around my stomach, my hands clutching the fabric of the sides of my shirt.

The moment the house disappeared from the rearview window Angel opened her mouth, "Are-" I interrupted her, trying to keep my voice steady. "Not in front of the girl."

Angel stayed silent, her breath caught at my curt tone. Throughout the car ride back, she kept looking at the unconscious girl sleeping in the backseat. I stared straight forward, hating myself for my neglect.

She woke up while we traveled back to the nightclub, still drugged; she acted in a loopy manner asking about where she was. Angel continued driving, fretful at what happened tonight, I alleged a basic story about seeing her at the club and then on our way home we found her passed out in an alley.

She bought the story, forgot it, and asked where her friends were. Then I let her out of the car and she ventured back into the nightclub, completely unfazed.

Angel stared at the girl in awe, "You're just going to let her go?" I turned and looked at Angel. "Yes."

She looked at me and then looked at the road, and she spoke in a flat, disconnected tone. "You killed the man. His blood is on your outfit."

I shook my head, realizing I needed more time to figure out what I am going to edit for Angel's explanation.

"Not now, when we get home, I'll need a shower, and then we can talk."

I met my eyes up with Angel's. My ultimatum was not negotiable. She bit her lip, the tears welling in the corners. I pulled away and looked out the window.

I ruined her, her childhood, her innocent youth. Why did I do it? Why did I crush my happiness? Angel was the only escape from my misery, my job, my life.

My tormented feelings made me dig my fingernails harder into a clench, I was on the verge of hyperventilating.

The girl I saved won't even remember me, she'll live an oblivious life, never contribute anything to society... And I chose that over Angel? A stranger for the light of my life?

I tried to rearrange my expressions to serious, still hiding my face from Angel. My breathing returned to an inhumanly slowed pace. My arms and body were caked with dried and flaky sweat and blood spots. The make-up encrusted on my face made it stiff.

What a mistake, Angel is going to be changed forever, I failed. I utterly failed to hold on to my two lives. Why couldn't I just let one human go?

Any other slayer could, nobody is as stupid as me. Slayers slay because they can, because they know that the ones they hunt are evil, monsters, but nobody ever worries about the collateral damage. But I have to help the little people, it is always the little people first.

Nobody even cares!

My eyes shifted to Angel again. I knew how she felt, completely filled with ignorance and questions. I was her so many times, sobbing and alone. This world doesn't have saviors.

I smiled to myself without humor; I guess that is why I do it.

The girl's body upside down appeared in my mind. She'll get to live another night. Nobody will have to grieve for her loss. Nobody will have to suffer pain like mine. The expense of my current happiness seems a fair trade.

When Angel arrived at my house my creaky bones grudgingly took on my weight and carried me to the door.

Angel trudged behind me, and I tried to not look back, I didn't want to see her horrified and judging face. Nor did I want to see the expression she will have when I show what lurks underneath the fake, teenager façade I always wear.

I carried myself cautiously, as before; my expression was fully controlled again. I returned to my old state of being, preparing myself for the rest of my life's misery.

The house was dark, I flicked a few lights on and commanded Angel to wait in the living room. After disappearing upstairs I carefully peeled off my clothes and placed them in a plastic bag, I'm going to have to burn them. Next I dropped my hatchet into a disinfectant solution I kept in one of my cabinets.

As a ghost, I drifted through the upstairs part of the house performing my normal cleaning rituals, showering, removing left over make-up, checking for wounds. I watched the multicolors sluice out of my hair with the special remover I kept next to the shampoo.

I need to burn my identity, and move out. It would be too risky to be with Angel after I tell her what I am. I can't seem to edit the truth, I wouldn't know how to evade it. She has seen too much.

Leaving will be enough though, nobody will believe her if she told anybody.

Fifteen minutes after I send Angel home, I should be gone. The house wouldn't trace to me, I just needed to take a few things.

I would need to evaporate, again, just like water on the sidewalk. In Arizona water disappears without a trace in a matter of minutes, it is as if the water never existed. It only stays in the minds of those who witnessed it. I will only be a weak memory to Angel one day.

I finished my shower and looked like a normal child again. Short, straight golden hair, clean jeans and a T-shirt, soft, rounded features; I was almost disgusting to look at.

Will I say goodbye to Angel? Knowing her now, the best friends we are, leaving is going to be very hard, harder if I tell her. I wasn't just a friend, I am her best friend.

I pulled out my massive make-up kit and slapped on pseudo age to my face and stared at the clean white door that led to the hall. There's nothing else I can do to procrastinate. I glanced one more time at the mirror, then left.

She listened quietly, asking questions here or there. When I finished my story I felt slightly relieved, she didn't run away screaming. Although, I did cut out some of the more deplorable parts, like the deaths from the diner and the other bigger mistakes from the past six years.

Angel had a very thoughtful look while absorbing this. After a pause she summarized my story, "So, your dad worked on this virus that made you immortal and drink blood?" I nodded and she added "And you're going to spend the rest of your uh, existence, hunting and destroying anyone like the murderers who killed your family until you find them?" I replied, "Yes."

Angel nodded "And you are like them? But with your dad's modified version?" I replied solemnly "Yes." I twiddled my thumbs and swung my legs back and forth.

"But you are a slayer? Those are people who hunt others like you?" Angel mumbled. I nodded, and she shot another question. "Why don't they kill you?" I looked up, "I don't exactly know why, pity maybe, I guess I'm just enough like them." I answered quietly.

"What it's like?"

"What?" Angel's intent stare met my thoughts, "The virus. How are you different from people?"

I thought for a minute, and then said, "I feel more alive, the vision is so much sharper, almost as if looking through a magnifying glass at everything. And my hearing, I can listen to the smallest movements, similar to this seemingly quiet room, it's filled with undetectable sounds to you but to me this is almost a jungle." I smiled, "I'm always listening to the air-conditioning systems, it drives me crazy."

I paused, and started again. "My hunger for blood is like nothing you have ever felt before. When I starve, I lose control. My world is flung upside down and I want to kill everything in sight." I heard Angel intake quickly, her eyes were so wide.

She then said "Blood, inhuman senses, immortality, is everything like the myths? Can you run faster than a speeding car? Why do you walk in the sunlight?" I shrugged "I never really tried to test any myths, I know what I know, and I'm still sort of human, I guess, so lore like garlic and fangs are probably formulated by imaginations."

Angel exhaled slowly, "Do you know how long you can hold your breath underwater? Do you even breathe?" I shook my head "I told you, I don't focus on that stuff, and uh yes, I still breathe, sweat, my hair grows, and so on." She looked at the refrigerator, "How much blood do you drink? Can you eat human food?"

"I don't need it every part of the day anymore, I drink it around once every day or so but the others consume a massive amount every few days. And their kind can't eat substantial human food, they end up just barfing it back up less than an hour later. But the modified version of virus that I have is closer to being normal enough to accept food."

Angel tilted her head "The blood, where do you get it?"

I half smiled at my intelligence, and the easiness of the answer. "Unlike them I can drink pig's blood. So I just waltz into the grocery store down the street and in the meat section I order the blood."

She shook her head. "That doesn't make sense! Why would they just give you the blood?" I leaned back comfortably in my chair, "Normal people do it all the time. Some special recipes require pig's blood, like German Blutwurst or in America they call it blood sausage. I just bring in a recipe list and they will get me what I need, no questions asked."

The conversation ended then and my lighter attitude sank. My eyes drew to my hands, time is up. I held my breath, "It is late, we'll talk tomorrow, okay?"

Angel analyzed my pained expression, she was taking this so calmly, so trusting that I was doing something right.

The corner of her mouth twitched, "I feel like if I leave, I will never see you again. It is a stupid feeling, I know." Her breath caught, soft and silky, "But promise me you won't leave?"

My mouth fell slightly open, her small tone so heartbreaking, her crystal eyes pleading. I blinked, feeling the tears come, "I'm sorry, this is all my fault."

She looked at me and tilted her head, "You save people, don't apologize. Nobody should stand in your way, nobody else can do your job."

She shifted and put her arm around me, "Even though it seems scary and I know I was completely panicked, I see now. You don't have to leave me, I want to help you, I want to save people. No more parties, no more getting drunk and acting stupid. You could train me, and we could save people together."

"What?" I stared up at her surprised, "You want to what?" Angel, in all seriousness repeated, "I want to help you hunt."

My mouth fell open, "You-you could die." I whispered, Angel shrugged, "You could teach me how to be careful."

My hands gripped into fists, "This isn't like anything you've ever done before, once you start you can't get out, even if you do find a way to leave, it emotionally ruins you." Angel nodded, "I know, but I still want to help you." I shook my head, no she doesn't, she doesn't.

It's a horrible life, perpetually slapping the face of death, while the unlucky fall around you. It is a countdown, only made for those who wouldn't care if their only light of existence is snuffed out before they've had a chance to live.

Slayers are the dying, running to embrace ache and unhappiness for a cause unworthy and thankless.

"No." I answered certainly. I shook my head, the tears drying. "Moogie, I want to help you, I want to stand by you."

I shook my head again, with the same certainty. "No."

"You know you can't be like this forever, one day it will be too much. You know you need me. And, and..."

I saw the future of what she meant, she could see the failure I was. She wanted to save me.

"Is this really what you want to do?" My voice weak, so unsettling.

Her tone and face never changed, "Yes."

9
Independence

Angel stayed in one of my spare bedrooms the rest of the night. When she woke up at around 10 AM, she left to work a shift at the ice skating rink. I left soon after to go work at a flea market with Joey.

I laid back on a hot metal chair with my feet propped up against a plastic bucket and picked at my nails while people crossed by our stand to browse the merchandise.

Joey had forgiven me for the night before, and I told him about my conversation with Angel about how she wants to be a slayer. I don't think he caught half the words coming out of my mouth though, the whole time he was half staring into space, half fiddling with whatever trinkets were in his reach.

I stopped my ranting about how I couldn't figure out why Angel didn't run away screaming her head off and I watched him. It took him a few seconds to realize I wasn't talking. He put down the spoon and looked up at my slightly irritated expression. "What's wrong with you?" He closed his eyes and leaned back, "My girlfriend just broke up with me." My mouth fell open, "What?" He shook his head, "I thought everything was normal, and when I came home last night I got this letter!" He pulled out a crinkly, over folded paper and handed it to me.

Joey had opened and closed, folded and refolded this poor little piece of paper, and it was halfway ripped and taped back together, he probably ripped it in anger and then stopped midway.

The contents contained a clean, hand-written cursive paragraph with the words "Dear Joey" taking up four lines before the hand writing shrank back down to one line spacing.

I quickly scanned the paper, it said in gooey girly language that he didn't do anything wrong and that their love just wasn't right. She met somebody else, and she hopes he'll find somebody that deserves him properly one day.

I read it a second time, and looked back up at him. Joey was now intently focused on picking the calcium off a fork. "What the Hell is this?" He dropped the fork and threw his arms up in the air "THAT'S WHAT I SAID!"

His explosion drew the attention of several onlookers and embarrassed by his outburst he returned to his intense fork-picking.

Keeping his attention directed at the fork he mumbled "All of her clothes were gone from my house, I rolled back the security cameras to make sure she wasn't kidnapped, and she had packed everything up and put the letter on my desk completely by herself."

I shook my head, his voice grew angrier while saying "I watched her get in an open top red convertible with another guy and then kiss him while they drove off."

I could see the bags under Joey's eyes as they twitched from lack of sleep. Then he smirked, "I got the guy's plate number though." I handed the letter back to him, "You know if you kill the guy it won't make you feel any better." He nodded, "I know, I know, but maybe that shiny paint job on his car and tires should be redecorated with my knife." I shook my head, "Let's just go take your anger out on somebody who deserves it, how about a hunt tonight? Doesn't that seem more fun than keying some idiot's car? And it is good for the community!"

The corner of his mouth twitched up. Then his cell phone buzzed, he shook his head, "I bet that text is from her-" He opened and loaded the holographic interface. I watched his facial expression drop and his body grow ridged. "It is from my cousin, Arnold." His mouth dropped, "Oh my God, Moogie, they got them."

"Who?" I asked. "Jonathan and Marit. Do you remember that coven bust in Vegas? Arnold's gang just finished. They found passports and I.D.s that confirmed it. The search is over Moogie, Jonathan is dead."

I half stood up. The phone buzzed on the table again, I snatched it up with my lightening reflexes. Arnold's reply was short.

```
We finished the raid twenty minutes ago.
Sending pictures now. If Moogie wants to see it in
person she has twenty-four hours to get to this
address.
```

Below was an address for a house in Nevada and a few pictures. Joey snatched the phone back, but leaned over to let me see the interface better. He clicked on the first picture.

A tall, black-haired man with chunks of flesh missing from his face, arms, and body was laying on the floor. Next to him a girl much smaller with that familiar lava red hair laid just as ripped up. The fuzzy images from my past matched the bodies of the dead. Bits of flesh were torn through, bullet holes cut into their figures. But I knew these were the murders who killed my family.

My eyes fixed on the photo, I couldn't move, the thoughts and feelings aroused in the pit of my stomach were overjoyed, relieved. They didn't die by my hands or feel any torture inflicted of how I wanted them to, but they were dead.

"I need to see them." I said quickly,

I looked up at Joey, his eyes met mine, "Of course, you book our flight, I'll clean up the shop." In less than an hour we were driving to the airport, the time blurred by, and I couldn't remember boarding the plane, or most of the flight. The only thing I could hold onto was the crushing need to examine every pixel of the pictures.

Joey fell asleep with his arms crossed and head on the side of the plane, next to me. I sat straight, tapping my fingers impatiently on the arm rest.

I couldn't believe it, no matter how many times I told myself they were dead I couldn't grasp it. For six years their images damaged me, all of the nightmares, the lonely crying, it was all I ever thought about when I ended someone's life.

A million times over I day dreamed about what I would say, how I would act when I finally would meet them, how I would make them pay.

I remembered asking Joey countless times if the other slayers ever found any sign of them. He always reassured me that he has everybody keeping an eye out and I would be one of the first to know.

How could they be dead? Is this just a sick dream to give me hope? Is it a mean prank? These people ruined my life, and disappeared. How is it that they just get killed one day, and appear on Joey's phone as bodies? My mind wandered for hours in the possibilities of doubt.

The plane touched down and startled Joey awake. We rented a car and followed the GPS on Joey's phone to a rich neighborhood when the house came into view.

Surrounding the house I saw black vans with the letters FBI on the side, yellow crime tape surrounded the perimeter of the house and men and women in oversized blue jackets with the letters FBI printed on the back worked in and around the house. "Joey, turn around, cops, turn around now." I hissed.

He smiled and shook his head, "You haven't seen Old Mr. C do a job yet have you?" I looked at him, "Those are slayers?"

"Yep, Mr. C is celebrating his ninety first birthday. He decided he was too old to be sneaking around at night, and he was going to go in no matter what, so everybody put their heads together to try to find a better way to raid this coven in broad daylight. This was the best idea." We fell silent as Joey parked the car. I could hear Joey taking a deep breath and tightening his expression.

Out the window I watched the figures at the faux crime scene. My loose muscles and normally innocent expression tuning cooler, less open. I centered my head slightly down and shifted into my unreadable glare.

"Do we need those jackets too?" I asked, "No." He said emphatically. We left the safety of the car and ducked under the crime tape. A bulky guy with dark brown hair and sun glasses jogged over to us.

He shook Joey's hand and nodded to me, his tone distracted and neutral. "Glad you could come, I'm Arnold. Before you see the bodies Mr. C wanted to talk to you." I nodded and followed Arnold through the door.

The other slayers around me stole glances my way. I didn't know any of them, but all of them knew exactly what I am.

These strangers have the predisposition to detest me, all they are looking for is the slightest mistake on my part to give them a chance to slaughter me. I feared them more than the creatures I risk my life to hunt.

The oldest man I had ever seen limped my way from the living room. He, as everyone else, wore an oversized FBI jacket. Instead of sunglasses he wore wide rimmed glasses to aid his sight.

He glared down at me, his under bite made his face set in a grungy scowl below his wrinkles. Conscious of his equal abhorrence to my small figure, a shiver shot through my arms, I battled my instincts for flight.

But tensely I stayed still, unnaturally still, holding my determined expression. He could never will me to cower on the outside, my doubts will only live in my mind.

Mr. C slid his eyes up to Joey, "George and Arnold need your help, go be useful." Joey nodded obediently, "Yes sir."

And he left without a moment to spare, and although my facial expression didn't change, I realized my vulnerability with my friend and protection fleeing without a second thought.

Mr. C cleared his throat, "Little lady, now I don't want to see you getting all delicate about the bodies." I tilted my head down in understanding, and took the insult without objection.

The surrounding sounds caught my senses as whispers left the mouths of a few slayers behind me, "Heh, how many necks do you think she has sucked on?" one said, another conversation buzzed, "She's just using poor Joey to get to us, but I'm not fooled." Two men carried some of the furniture out of the house, "I don't know why Joey would even consider dating a creature like her, she's sterile! I mean the nerve..."

My head twitched, as I unconsciously tried to shake their conservations out of my head. Mr. C eyed me suspiciously and started along down the hall. I followed, my quick and light step opposite to Mr. C's thumping and dragging.

He didn't look like a great-grandfather, or the scandalous man that he is accredited to be. He was a gruff old man, dressed in clothes out of style decades before. He made his way up a set of stairs alone.

All slayers, if they get to be that old, seem like him. One shade or another. I always wondered what it would be like to be his age, to let so much time pass.

The rooms at the end of the hall were cleaned out, the rugs were spotless, and all of the furniture had been cleaned out. On the left there was one closed door, his rough hand encapsulated the door handle and turned the knob.

The room, as the others, was scrubbed spotless, no furniture, the rugs were white, but in the middle of the floor a sheet of plastic had been laid out. On top were two bodies, their ripped organs were strewn out, and blood pooled in different indents of the plastic. I stepped into the room, it was silent in here, the only noise I knew was the occasional wheezing of Mr. C's breath.

I circled the bodies, they were ripped with bullets and signs of decomposition, their smell made Mr. C's eyes water. I knelt down next to their bodies. My breathing had stopped, and another breath didn't have to be taken for another minute or two.

I remained unnaturally motionless, gazing at Jonathan's face. My stillness fit in the silent room, time stopped ticking. Mr. C and my dangerous surroundings seemed like a mere glance in the distance.

Jonathan was without words, he was without love, he was without life. After all the fettering, the worrying, the doubts of my life, now acceptance engulfed my thoughts, the price was paid. I am free of him, and so is the memory of my family.

Then the stillness passed, new air entered my lungs, sound of creaking and commotion from downstairs grasped the corner of my attention. Another wheeze from Mr. C reminded me of the clock the slayers were on.

I looked up at Mr. C and stood, the fear and the paranoia of my current situation bringing me to my internal feet. "I want their heads." I said stolidly. Mr. C's expression didn't change, "George!" He shouted. A man with light brown hair, looking almost identical to Arnold materialized, "Yes sir."

"I want these heads detached, cleaned, and wrapped for this little lady, can you handle that?" He barked, antagonizing the young man with his challenge. George, in slightly disgusted, cold expression met my neutral face, "Yes sir."

Joey and I caught a plane back home by the end of the day. I now had a suitcase in the belly of the plane.

"I think he likes you." Joey said slightly amused, we were ourselves again. I leaned back and closed my eyes, "I'm just glad nobody tried to stake me." Joey snorted, "A stake? Nonsense, if they wanted to kill you they would use their custom crafted machetes."

I nodded, "Of course."

Joey looked out the window, "So, what are you planning on doing with the skulls?" I smirked, "They are going to be candle holders on that vanity in my room."

"Do you want to celebrate?" He asked. I smiled at his simple ways, take someone down, clean up, and have a beer. Repeat.

"No, we still have work to do."

10
Ready, Set, GO!

A few days later I started training Angel everything I knew about being a slayer. We moved all of the furniture against the wall in the living room and relocated the big screen TV to clear a wide space, I left the thick rug in the middle of the room as a crash pad.

I started teaching her little things like how to punch, and the right places to get the maximum damage or a certain outcome. Then I taught her how to avoid getting punched, with various parries and side step combinations, and we moved on from there to different types of kicks and when to use them.

Days flew by as I taught her the uses of an opponent's off balance, defensive stances, and how to get people on the ground. She was a quick learner, and we moved to grappling and arm bars, then how to escape them.

On the earlier days of training she didn't take me very seriously. She would comment on how I was too small or not strong enough to execute a certain move. After a while I grew tired of all the lip and retorted in a childish tone "I'm much stronger than I look." And she challenged me to an arm wrestling match.

"This will be good." I rolled up my sleeve and dropped my elbow onto the table. She looked smug, I have thin, short arms in contrast to Angel's long, finely defined and fit arms; I wonder how many times a week she goes to the gym, three, four days?

The first match I slammed her hand into the table so fast she didn't have time to blink. We argued and she completely denied it as a legitimate win claiming she wasn't ready. With the second round I slammed her hand onto the table faster than the first time and she called for another rematch.

I put my arm out for the third time and she jumped up and grabbed my hand, pushing with all her might to throw my arm down into the table. I didn't even budge. Then, with all my might I slammed her hands into the table so hard she shook them out after the match. I leaned back and smiled at her flabbergasted expression, "Do you want to go train now?"

As the training continued, my teachings escalated from her learning moves to applying them in fights to shifting quickly and fluidly from one to another. I would have her attack me and then we would switch positions. Most of the time our fights would end with me choking Angel until she lost consciousness for a second or two. In the beginning it was rare for her to land a blow on me, even if I was leaving weaknesses wide open for her to take advantage of.

After the sixth choke out in one session she stood up, looked down at me and glared with her arms crossed. "This isn't fair! You are a super person; I stand no chance against you! How do you know I'm not perfect on these moves and you're just too fast?"

I shook my head and opened my mouth to retort back, but after a second I just smiled. I found my cell phone and quickly sent out a small text. Five minutes later Joey appeared with a giant grin smacked wide on his face. Angel raised her eyebrow, Joey was at least four inches shorter than her, if she doesn't want to fight me, she can battle Joey. Angel scoffed at the challenge and slowly rose to fight him.

They circled each other cautiously and Angel advanced to attack, Joey instantly took advantage of the opening weaknesses and used her weight against her in a counter attack. Angel landed on the ground with a thud.

Joey choked her out swiftly and efficiently. Because Joey didn't mean to teach or go easy on Angel he took a few seconds longer to let go of the choke which completely subdued her. Angel was out cold. We stood over Angel and watched her wake back up "What-where am I?"

Joey put on a dead serious expression, "Angel! You don't remember anything? You were in a coma for two weeks after that car crash!"

Angel's expression turned to shock and her body froze until she noticed where she was. I tumbled on to the floor in hysterical laughter, and Angel's expression turned from confused to fuming. Joey was laughing at her too, almost as hard as I was and she shoved him to the ground angrily.

I tried to get up but I just tumbled back down, cackling and coughing after she stomped her foot like a child and spat "It's not funny!"

We roared and Angel stormed off to the kitchen. "She is so going to hate you for this."

I gasped and tried to assuage my hysterics. "Alright, fun time is over, let's get back to work." Around five minutes later she returned with something behind her back.

I raised my eyebrow, "What's that behind your back, a knife?" Joey snorted. She tilted her head and smiled deviously, a stripe of fear set off through me.

I watched her twist her arm and produce a tall blue cup. Even my eyes and reflexes didn't move fast enough as Angel threw the contents of the container at us. I froze with my arms up in attempt to shield myself. Joey and I were completely drenched in water, and Angel was on her butt laughing at us faster than you could say "Angel no!"

We started moving into fast and more complex fights, some lasted longer than thirty seconds, others ended after forty-five. When we would finish one fight I would instantly hop up for the next one, but she would take a while to get back up.

Angel always needed a break for something, bathroom, water break, lunch break, sometimes she would just be out of air. Joey was like this too; when Joey and I hunted he was always shoving some sort of snack or fast food take-out item in his mouth.

At first I never really noticed weaknesses like that when it was just me and Joey, but spending almost everyday with Angel all day I never realized how slow and needy people were.

A few times I failed to remember to check the time and Angel and I would spend more than seven hours training. Angel didn't whine much about physical exhaustion, but one day, after a particularly long section she watched me casually pick up the couch and move it back to its original place. "You know those myths about your kind?"

I shrugged, "Sure, most aren't true, you know that." She leaned against the wall, "I was thinking, maybe we could find out which ones are accurate." I picked up the TV and carried it back into the room, "What do you mean?" She shrugged, "Can you run faster than the speed of a bullet? Can you stop vans going forty miles an hour? Can you jump off a building and land perfectly fine on your feet? Does any type of sunlight hurt you?" I stood with my hands on my head and exhaled slowly, "Mmm, I don't know." I looked up at Angel's tired expression. "How about we take a break and test some of those myths tomorrow?" She smiled, "Sure!"

Angel basically lived at my house now, rarely was there a time we didn't see each other, and everyday she strolled right into my house and I made her breakfast or she would wake up in my spare bedroom next to the study and start the coffee for the day in the kitchen.

Soon magazines, newspapers, and mail addressed to Angel appeared at my door step. Three different papers would arrive nearly everyday, then fashion magazines, gossip papers and the occasional piece of junk mail would appear. I didn't know they were Angel's at first, I never read who they were addressed too, and I started reading them. Half the stuff in the fashion magazines completely confused me, why would a girl be worried about if a text ended with a smiley face or not? What is a Vutton?

All of the articles were confusing and written as if the author thinks they are entitled to the world to wait at their hand and foot. I would take the quizzes in the back too, most would end with the magazine telling me I am a complete idiot and I need to get a life or go back under the rock from which I emerged from. It utterly baffled me. In my frustration I sought outside help to decode this foreign language.

When I worked the flea market shifts with Joey I would give him the magazines. He would sit with his feet propped up on the table wearing his usual raggedy clothes and some form of hiking boots buried in glossy, teen-age girl magazines. And every time he would finish one his expression never failed to be bewildered, and even with his infinite knowledge he was still stumped with why any form of T-shirt is suicide, but colorful sports bras are the new formal wear. Though he did manage to identify that Spade is apparently a designer, not a shovel.

Then one day Angel found me reading one of the magazines and she exclaimed "Oh! You're the one taking my magazines!" And after scolding me about respecting her privacy I was only permitted to bring in the mail, and she had to read them first.

At one point of time her clothes integrated into my weekly laundry washing cycle when I noticed an entirely new laundry basket next to the washer and dryer. Then my spare bedroom door adopted a sticker of a pair of Angel wings. It looked odd being a glossy white sticker against the old, hand-carved wooden door, but soon another sticker appeared under it: Angel's Room

Today we were up early to beat the weather. At around seven it was already in the high eighties, a sure sign of the sun's enmity of mid-June and all those who aren't smart enough to stay in the air-conditioning. Angel had picked me up in her exhausted but still hanging on white Cherokee and we drove to her old high school; it should have been mine too.

On the drive over she explained to me "I looked up what the world records are for the fastest and strongest people in the world." She handed me a binder. "I want to see how close you are to them."

Inside the binder was page after page of things we can do. She had neat blank sheets of paper in each section made for recording. In the back I even found measuring tapes, a stop watch, and a few pencils and pens. I was shocked, "Who helped you make this? It's so organized."

She smirked "I did it myself. I wanted to make sure we tested you right." I shook my head "Why aren't you in college? You are smart enough to attend." Angel sighed "Everyone thinks that, but I don't want to become a doctor or an accountant. I want to live my own life." I shut the binder and looked at her, "What do you want to be?"

Angel answered as if she rehearsed it until perfection, "I'm going to be an actress, and I'm doing it all alone. That's why I work at the ice skating rink, I'm going to earn enough money to buy a ticket to California and get enough for an apartment to live in for the first few months." She looked at me and tacked on "Oh! And on the side I want to help you save humanity from evil."

I snorted, she glanced at me for a second, and her expression was dead serious. I leaned back for a moment. To be famous; huh, definitely not on my agenda.

I wanted to object, but my life is worse. I'm spending it killing people. I guess her aspirations aren't that out of the question.

When we arrived and the car's air conditioning systems turned off, Angel and I were defenseless against the torrid air and the dust that instantly clung to our arms and legs. I chose to wear some old shorts I used to wear in seventh grade. They fit perfectly, and it still looked relatively new, the shorts were shorter than where my thumbs hung when I put my arms down, and the pockets stuck out being longer than the actual length of the legs of the pants.

I surveyed the familiar track, across the field was the elementary school; I noticed the empty rundown playground and a rush of nostalgia and memories came back to me. One in particularly stood out. My family was walking the dogs; I took Lilie to the playground and tried pushing her down the slide. She, of course, flipped out and accidentally fell off the slide onto the woodchips below. I felt guilty the whole rest of the day.

I turned the memories off and tuned back into Angel's voice. She was bent over spray painting the ground talking about the strange world records people hold. I was about to object to the graffiti lines when she looked up and interrupted me "You should be stretching! Start here." She pointed at the wet line, "Then run as fast as you can all the way to there." She pointed another line.

Back in the beginning of seventh grade I remembered doing something similar to this. Angel opened her binder and pulled out the stopwatch, "My time for the hundred yard dash was about 17 seconds. I guess that's average. I believe you can finish this in about ten seconds or less."

I shook my head "You can't know that, I might be just as slow as I was before." Angel looked at me with narrowed eyes, "Why are you always doubting yourself?" I stopped and stared at her, even in jeans and a T-shirt Angel stared me down so very queen-like, keeping an almost aura of authority over me.

I shook my head and stepped up to the line. Doubting myself, how could she know? I can hold a perfect poker face when I play Texas

Hold'em with Joey's dad and the other slayers, but somehow Angel knows my exact internal conflicts?

I drew back from my strains of thought and looked up into her crystal blue eyes saying plainly and unemotionally "I only doubt myself because I don't believe in most of these myths."

Angel rolled her eyes and shifted her weight onto one hip "You are the most boring mythical creature I've ever met, Moogie." I smiled and rose to a lighter voice "I'm the only mythical creature you've ever met. So I'm the most exciting too."

I felt like such a kid, getting ready for her first track try-outs. Angel jogged over to the finish line and shouted "On your marks" I dropped into the running stance. "Get set," I looked up, and stared directly down the lot, "Go!"

The adrenaline surged through me, giving my feet an exhilarating gush of new power as my feet pushed off the hard gravel. Scenery blurred into a tan haze as I impelled at swift speeds towards the second line. I didn't take three breaths before I flew passed the finish. Angel was more excited than a toddler jumping up and down getting presents. "Wow Moogie 10.22 seconds! You should be in the Olympics!"

I lightly brushed rocks off my shoes and calmly looked up at Angel. Angel was extremely proud of her guesses, and we tested the hundred yard dash a few more times. As an hour passed, the suns rays blowtorched us and with enthusiastic vigor. I wanted to drop dead like bed bugs in this temperature and call it a day, but Angel, with perspiration dripping down her face pushed forward for more testing and minimal breaks.

After the second trial of the four hundred yard dash, Angel decided to turn in and eat lunch back in the car. I reveled in blissful air-conditioning.

Every other day we tested something different or went to a new place. On the off days we trained, moving on from hand to hand combat to weapons training.

One time we went to the gym and I bench pressed an easy 250 pounds. I lifted the front of Angel's Cherokee a few inches and pushed it around a little.

I also can hit baseballs nearly out of the batting range, (They would go further except there is a giant net surrounding the place) and pitch ninety-five miles per hour fastballs. Another day we went to the public swimming pool; I'm pretty good at most of the strokes but still no Michael Phelps. I can hold my breath under water for nearly eight minutes and complete a mile in four.

Weeks passed by quickly, my life seems to orbit around Angel once again. After each day I felt productive and guiltless. I worked with Joey and hunted with him on my own and during the days there was a new project or subject to cover with Angel.

On a dry Tuesday in September I took her out to a shooting range and I taught her how to fire a gun.

She could spot and name every brand of shoes a girl owned with just a glance but somehow she couldn't shoot the broad side of a barn if her life depended on it. Through the day I ended up spending most of the time trying to get Angel to stop shooting with her eyes closed. We made great progress.

After that we invested weeks on just the subject of guns, how to put them together, take them apart, load unload. I taught her where to carry them, hold them, where to keep them in her house, and how to use them. Ironically, her anti-gun friends would sometimes call her up while she practiced taking apart and loading one of her pistols, I would hear in the other room a conversation that sounds like this: "Hey Sierra," 'click' "What am I doing right now?" 'click, click, click' "Oh you know, boring stuff." 'chink' "No, I can't go out tonight sorry." 'clunk clunk' "See you later."

We shot a variety of guns, from double barrel shot guns to nine millimeter pistols. She loved them like a pair of shoes.

My shooting wasn't bad, I usually brush up on it monthly out of habit, but when I'm out hunting guns aren't the best weapons for close contact. Especially around the public where everybody else carries guns too. It is a universal rule for slayers, don't use guns for common hunting. They make too much noise; if the shells are found near the victim by the police then slayers are more at risk of being caught. It also gets pretty messy, blood spattering and all.

I remember hearing a story a while back about a slayer that used a gun in Phoenix hunting in an alley. At the sound of the shooting, several pedestrians pulled their guns out and blew him away. That's Arizona.

I like to keep my brain solely in my head, so I use a quiet and equally deadly hatchet on the majority of hunts.

But I do use guns. Usually in strange situations like if I'm on a big hunt, if I'm assigned sniper duty in the group hunts, or we suspect the other side has guns. Bullets don't inflict that much damage, a shot that could be fatal to normal humans might end up being just a wound that would heal up in a matter of weeks. Head wounds are still fatal but the other hit spots aren't as reliable. Hatchets prove to be useful in the accuracy category too, that's why I usually stick to my hatchet, when I'm decapitating the head of somebody I can be sure they are dead.

Soon we moved to knife training, and I taught her all the places you can kill somebody in one swing or thrust. Like the indent in the back of the head, one plunge with a small dagger in some places can make the body completely shut down.

We moved on to using odd tools like sticks, bats, boards with nails (which in my opinion is one of the most dangerous things that can ever be wielded), glass shards and bottlenecks, and anything else that can be improvised.

One of the most used subjects I taught was how to utilize the hatchet. You can't just go up to somebody swinging like a mad person, you have to be precise, if you overshoot or miss, and the thrusting power you meant to bring down on your victims might just end up in your leg. I showed her how to grip the handle so her hand wouldn't slip. We would go out to the middle of the desert and bring watermelons and cantaloupes. I taught her how to rush the fruits and split them in half, or in other ways. The first time we did it she was so concerned about not missing the watermelon or dropping the hatchet that she forgot to swing.

Then we moved onto other techniques I've used in chases, how to tackle someone, how to hop a fence. When I was a first time slayer I didn't realize you weren't supposed to sit on the fence because your pants get caught and ripped on the chain links.

Angel was ready by mid-October. Joey discovered a house with two of them inside and we were the only ones in town available for the hunt. We staked-out the house in my favorite new car. I leaned back in my seat sleepily; the moon had just risen, illuminating the silent street blue-white. The night was perfect for my eyes, not too dim or too bright, I could absorb every aspect of the street. Joey was sitting in shot-gun and Angel was in the back watching the plan Joey was laying out for the attack on the house. I knew his plans like the back of my hand but Angel kept enthusiastic attention to Joey and his diagram.

With his newly updated phone that ran on fast, cutting-edge technology our holographics were efficiently running at a quiet hum that I was pretty sure nobody else could hear except me, and the little building he had pulled up was detailed up to the nines.

Joey had pulled up a loose diagram of the floor plan for the house we were about to raid and explained the plan. "We're going in through the back, over the gate at this fence, and then we'll enter through this door. If we split up, you're with Moogie." He pointed with his green plastic stylus at a small door in the back yard. Angel grew wide with an excited smile. "Are we going now?" Angel hopped up and down in her seat excitedly. Joey gave me a slightly amused look as she wiggled with excitement.

Angel, Joey, and I exited the car and swiftly moved under a window to watch inside. We were in the side yard peering into the only uncovered window in the house, a young woman in a polka dot apron with her hair done up as if she was the housewife-next-door was bustling around the living room with a vacuum cleaner. A man dressed cleanly and sharply exited the living room and disappeared up the stairs.

I smiled at the sight of them, this young, seemingly innocent couple, the ones that manicured their garden, chatted with their neighbors, and waved to the kids walking down the street from school were cold-blooded killers, with the most disgusting ways of living. My smirk widened at the irony of my position in all of this.

We ducked down and followed Joey onto the back patio. After producing a lock picking kit and fiddling with the door for about a minute we penetrated through into the kitchen. Joey signaled us to go upstairs while he took care of the girl.

I let Angel lead the way to the top floor. All of the doors were left ajar except one, I flattened against the wall to the right and Angel was on the other side. With her hatchet ready and as determined as me, she threw open the door and charged inside.

I trailed in behind her and my senses captivated the room. The male was standing in a bathtub dressed in thick plastic gloves, an apron, and rubber boots. As Angel brought down her hatchet onto his head, he was slicing the neck of a young lady who was strung upside down, duct taped and struggling.

The girl's eyes widened and she thrashed around while blood gushed everywhere, he had been holding the girl steady before, but as he dropped to his knees with Angel's hatchet wedged in his skull, she freely jerked back and forth in panic. I jumped onto the counter and reached to cut the tie keeping her upside down.

Angel, taking a few moments longer reached over to the girl and pulled the duct tape off. The blood splattered all over the bathtub and all over Angel's shirt and slacks. She caught her when I cut the binds and I kicked the man's body out of the way to make room on the floor for where we are going to place her.

My hands inked red as I tried to seal up the wound, her right artery was slashed open and leaking astronomical amounts of blood. The girl gripped my leg weakly and gasped for air. Her tears dripped down her cheeks and mixed into the blood, "H-help! Please. Please! I don't want to die."

I leaned on her neck harder; Angel held the girl's hand and was on the verge of tears herself, "Moogie! Moogie! What's happening? Please! Moogie! What do I need to do?" I ignored Angel's panic, wishing she would go away and stop frightening the girl. I turned to her and commanded, "Go get towels." And Angel sped out the door.

"Look at me!" The girl turned her frightened eyes to me, "You are going to be alright, the police are coming and nobody is going to hurt you anymore. What is your name?"

"Eliza," I kept her focused on me, "Tell me about yourself, do you have a family? Sisters? Brothers?" She started rambling in between gasps and tears, "I-I have a little sister, sh-she's turning four in a week, and-" Angel brought in the towels.

Joey appeared in the doorway and interrupted the girl, "The rest of the house is clear, are you guys okay?" I nodded and Joey crossed his arms and leaned against the doorway, his facial expression was calm and collected. Almost unemotional.

I drew my attention back to the panicking girl, "Don't worry, you're going to be fine, we do this all of the time, you're going to be all right." Eliza looked up at Angel, tears streamed down Angel's face. "I'm sorry, I'm sorry.

Angel's hysterics frightened the girl, so I tried to keep her focused on me. "It's alright; everything is going to be alright."

Eliza wept quietly and less as I tried to sooth her.

Seconds ticked by as I had the girl talk more, my legs were completely soaked in her blood, she was fighting to breathe, and I could feel her slowing down. "Where is the ambulance?" She whispered drowsily. I lightly shushed her, "Don't worry about it. Don't worry." I looked up at Angel, "Hold the towel for me, please."

I gave up and shook my head at Joey. Angel didn't notice, she moved into my spot and continued to hold the girl's neck, continuing to assure her I knew what I was doing, and she would be fine. Eliza reached up and weakly stroked Angel's hair, "You're so pretty, just like an ang-" Her hand dropped into the pool of her own blood.

11
Please?

Angel's expression when we cleaned up the bodies shown so lost, traumatized. When we drove home she only stared out the window silently. I pulled into the driveway and she shot out before I could say anything, disappearing for the rest of the night.

I sat at the kitchen table and mindlessly searched through the jewelry I had picked up from the house.

My thoughts weaved in and out of dread and regret. The pit in my stomach pulled lower, what have I done to this poor girl? Why was I stupid enough to even consider allowing her in to my world? She was a child. A healthy, beautiful, clean child. And I had to go and mold her just like me. I finished separating the necklaces and started cleaning and polishing the gems integrated into the gold bands on the rings.

The sun rose, I didn't know how many hours had passed, and golden rays beamed through the circular glass window place high above me. The light shined on the silver diamond ring I was cleaning, it emanated rainbows around the darkened room.

I stared at the iridescent stone, then put it down and climbed the stairs and down the hall to Angel's room.

I leaned on the door frame and hesitantly tapped on the door. No answer. I tapped again, and entered her messy blue room, posters, pictures, and magazine cutouts were tacked scattered and unorganized on the walls. The place looked old with the antique furniture, but out of place with the bright clothing and make-up littering the floor and draping over the wood frames. Angel, curled up on the corner of her bed, her wavy, scarlet hair fanned out on the deep cerulean pillow and her soft snowy face, laid vacant.

I stepped lightly over to the foot of her bed and leaned against the bedpost.

"I couldn't save her Moogie. I did everything right, everything you taught me, and I couldn't save her. Why? What was wrong?" I could feel Angel's susurrus voice saturated in anguish. "Angel, sometimes, they don't make it. Our methods are not immaculate, and training can only do so much."

"What do you mean?" I traced the wood carvings on the bed post, "This job isn't always going to be how it seems. We won, you might have saved thousands of people, people that you will never meet or know. Those nasty people last night would have continued killing in the future, and-"

Angel shot up and bellowed, "But she's dead! Don't you get that? Gone! The future doesn't matter, it's what happens now that matters. That girl just died! Why are you and Joey so unfazed? You lied to that girl and let her die!"

Tears dripped down her cheeks as she continued to shout in a cracking voice "You guys just stood there watching, it was if you saw this everyday!" My eyes fixed on her and I kept a calm expression. "Angel, Joey and I have been doing this for years, losing a person or two is not uncommon. It happens."

Angel gaped at me; I met her eyes and then tilted my head down and counted the fibers on my sock. The truth of a slayer is starting to nip at Angel.

Angel wiped her tears away, but more replaced them, "You lied to her, you told her everything was going to be alright, and you knew she was going to die. And you said the police were coming and an ambulance and-" Her sobbing broke her sentence and made her words incomprehensible.

I bit my lip and risked a glance at her, "Yes, I lied to her; I knew she was a goner from the first moment I saw him slit her throat."

"W-well why didn't you call the police? They could have saved her. Isn't that their job?" Angel cried softly.

I shook my head. "No Angel, we never call the police, they are not on our side. And they can never do our jobs."

"Why?" She asked, bereavement and distress lining her tone.

"Think about it, they can't just waltz into houses and arrest people. Even I didn't know if the people we just killed were not normal until we saw the girl. We just look for certain traits in people and go by that. The police need cold, hard evidence, not suspicious traits. The girl would have died, and her murderers would have continued to walk in the sun. No doubt in their minds that they would never be caught and punished for their crimes."

Angel focused on twisting her hair around her fingers while listening to my speech. I continued, "I know it doesn't seem right that we have to play judge, jury, and executioner, but we have too, because nobody else can. This is a life completely contrary to the one you were raised in, and it seems like we are the bad guys, but we are doing the right thing, always remember that."

Angel stopped twisting her hair and looked up at me, she wiped away her tears, "Come on Angel, this isn't good for you, let's get you outside, a pretty face like yours shouldn't be stuck in here."

She took a deep breath and leaned off the edge of the bed, I watched her silent expression for too many long moments.

My mouth twitched up, comfort trying to reach her. "Don't worry Angel, reality will adjust for you, and I will be here if it doesn't."

The dial on the clock spun roundabout faster than I cared to remember, soon we were past the end of a windy autumn, and slipped into the lowest temperatures winter will allow here. No snow, no clouds, no rain, we always had dry, clean weather. The vast sky lit my world differently, still sharp and bright but not quiet summer yellows. The sidewalk became a different white, the trees, roads, and houses became muted, shady, but not somber, I always felt serene; this is the only time of year that my hate is ever slightly lessened.

Angel and I trained for hours, twice as hard, but included new subjects, I taught her how to chase and run away. We worked on her lying skills, and I showed her tricks on how to conceal blood on her clothes or patch up wounds. We'd hunt every night. She never broke down like the first time, rather the opposite. Something flipped her, she now led the way into combat, the first to kill, and the last to leave.

Her vigor and adaptive efficiency for killing struck pride in me, and shock into Joey. At the end of some hunts Joey would comment on how he had never seen someone so ferocious in a fight, and I agreed.

She almost never hesitated, her actions sometimes became rash and sloppy, but her explosion into a fight usually caught her opponents off guard. Angel's tactics soon surpassed mine; her skill was like no other.

During training one out of four times she would win the fight. I sometimes had to rely on my only advantage, my speed and strength to escape from her clutches. Joey even lost a few times to her when she started calling rematches against him.

Angel's attitude lasted all day, after a hunt, she would bounce around and bug me to train with her. She didn't know how to turn fighting-mode off. But as time passed, she soon became almost herself again, gaining some control over her emotions by mid-December.

I noticed this as she gradually took up her usual old habits again. She returned to reading her magazines of glossy covers with air-brushed faces, piles of those had stacked up in the corner of her room. On her dresser where Angel spent hours grooming herself and decorating her face, I noticed before the make-up had relocated into a drawer and her hatchet and gun which she cared for until they were spotless had replaced the main space.

But as time progressed, her blush, eye-shadow, and lip gloss returned and lived next to the blood-stained cleaning rag she used to scrub her hatchet.

She started wearing her fun clothing on non-working days, and she cared for her hair instead of slicking it back into a pony tail or a braid for convenience.

By mid-January she was entirely different in such a surreal sense, she soon became programmed as Joey and I to be always conscious of the surroundings, but also she learned when to relax and start a routine. I never did that. She never carries a bouncy, care-free expression as months before. I had extinguished her innocence and lit a different desire that burned white hot inside. But somehow she retained her old self; I knew this especially when she returned to her three newspaper ritual.

Everyday she would snatch up the mail from my hands and remove the New York Times, the Arizona Republic, and Variety magazine. After flipping through each and dissecting any part involving the entertainment industry, she moved on to searching the Arizona Republic's ad section for cars. One in particular, a cherry red 1977 Pontiac Trans AM with a giant bird painted on the hood.

Everyday before opening the paper she would tell me "Ooo Moogie! I bet today I'll find my T-bird!" And everyday she would be dismayed to find one wasn't there.

January melted to February and then to March, April and warm eighty degree weather rolled in without the showers.

On April thirteenth, Angel's birthday, I smiled at the New York Times paper when I picked it up off the front porch in my flannel pajamas.

Angel, half asleep, was dressed in a bathrobe with flaming cats, and a worn T-shirt and pants. She still snatched up the papers and started flipping through them.

"Today will be the day Moogie, I can just feel it."

When she flipped through the Republic and found only last week's silver mini-van as the highlight of the ads she shut the paper and exhaled in slight disappointment. I smiled half-way, "Hey Angel, why don't you look in the New York Times? I bet they would have it in there."

She rolled her eyes, "Right, because we definitely don't live a thousand miles away, and we have the time to drive out and bring one back."

I shrugged and lightly sang,

"You never know."

She looked at the newspaper and picked it up. After flipping through the horoscope and looking through the funnies, she opened to the car ads.

Her mouth fell open,

"Moogie?"

She showed me the paper and pointed to the middle ad. The ad was red rose bordered and in the middle were the lines:

Angel, roses are red, violets are blue, this isn't a T-bird, but Happy Birthday to you.

-Moogie

Angel squealed with delight and hugged me. "You remembered! Ohmigod, it's in the New York Times! How did you do it?"

I grinned wider seeing her smile glistened with happiness. She then rose from the table and disappeared upstairs to return a minute later with a pair of scissors, her car keys, a glue stick, and a small, hot pink box with a handle.

She plopped back down onto the table, threw open the box, and removed a locked little book decorated with stickers and glitter.

I stared at the ingredients with my eyebrows up to my hairline as Angel started explaining, "Ohmigod! This is soooo special! I'm going to keep it forever." Angel then moved to picking through her key ring and singling one out which she used on the locked book. After opening the book she cut out the date on the New York Times and the ad and glued them into her little book.

She then held it up to me and said, "See?" I rolled my eyes and shook my head, "Okay then," I glanced at the clock, "Come on, time to go to work." I slowly got up from the table covered in this arts and crafts project. She grabbed my hand, "Can we stop by the gas station? I need to get another one, I accidentally cut up an article on one of my favorite bands."

Her mood didn't falter all day. When we worked shifts at the flea market, she basically shoved the second New York Times paper down Joey's throat explaining over and over what happened at breakfast.

After mauling Joey she continued to tell anybody within listening distance about the ad. Joey got so tired of her freaking out the customers and scaring them away he let Angel take the rest of the day off making some excuse that some labor law somewhere says because of her birthday she doesn't have to work.

With no priorities or jobs I took her out to the best bakery ever, deep into the jungle of stores at the mall, and I ordered Angel a giant half-raw cookie dough cake with gooey marshmallows melted and spread in the middle.

We sat in the busy food court where TVs constantly played music videos that you couldn't quite hear and a merry-go-round constantly moving at the corner of your eye.

I loved being here, this always felt like the place to be, it was my favorite hang out spot when I was a kid.

We were making our very best attempt to consume this gigantic cookie without throwing up all of the rich, thick frosting that covered the top when Angel stopped.

"Remember a few months ago when we were talking about how we are the only people that can hunt, and normal people can't find them?" I shrugged, "Yeah. Why?"

"Who are 'we'?" She tilted her head; I swallowed and took a sip of my drink. "Slayers, there aren't many of us, but we are out there. Most are usually families, it's a very narrow crowd. Nearly every slayer is related someway or another by marriage or blood."

Angel raised her eyebrows, "Why?" I put my piece of cookie down, "Think Angel, slayers are hard to make. It took you months of training, and you panicked the first night you found out what I was and what I do. A slayer's life is a strange one; we go around and kill other possible murderers that we have never met before, and trying our hardest to evade society and their rules while still trying to deal with human nature. Wouldn't it be better to be raised into it? You would know nothing else. Besides, who would you trust to help you carry a dead body across town?"

Angel had been chewing the same piece of cookie in her mouth the whole lecture. "But I'm a slayer and you're a slayer, and we were never raised like Joey, and I've taken bodies all over town with you."

I shrugged again, "Our case is different, we are family, in a sense. We're just one in a million I guess." Angel took another bite and asked "So everybody is related. What about marriage, do they marry their cousins?" I laughed, imagining Joey saying I-do at an alter to his short, angry cousin Mary.

"It's complicated; marrying is a problem with outsiders, you have to be really sure they are the one because if outsiders can't cope with the truth, they endanger the identity of the slayer. I've heard of some that live double lives, others that quit altogether, and some that end up working out just fine after a blunt reveal. One time I heard the spouse found out and she almost went to the police, the slayer was so scared of going to jail he shot her."

Angel's eyes widened, and I continued on, "But some slayers take a different option. There are two big slaying families with many unrelated branches that have a life style like this as slayers. The relations aren't very similar. But basically American slayers are grouped as the Dollies or the Miltons. They don't marry their first cousins, but it is pretty common somebody has the same great-grandfather or something."

Angel shook her head, "That's really weird." I shrugged, "Yeah, but things usually work out. There are other families; those are the strange cases like me, sometimes a widowed husband or a family-less person." I downed the soda I brought in Angel's gigantic purse, while she asked, "Joey, what family is he from?"

"Joey is in a branch of the Milton family." I scrutinized at the details of my cookie's frosting design trying to remember Joey's family tree, he explained it to me one time all the way up to the first in the family slayers, who started in eighteenth century colonial America. I started elaborating on who they are, "Let's see, in Arizona I know several Miltons, Joey, Joey's mom named Miranda, Joey's dad named Charlie, Joey's older sister, Sarah, I haven't met her in person, but I've talked to her on the chatrooms. She's really prejudice against me for what I am. I think she moved out a few months ago to somewhere in Canada. Joey's grandfather had a brother, uh, Mr. C, I've only met him once, he's really old, and lives with Joey's parents."

Angel fed back to me who I just talked about, and I continued with my speech. "North of here I've met one of Joey's twin aunts, uh, Candice and her kids George, Arnold, and Mary. The rest of the family lives elsewhere in the United States. Other than the Milton family in Arizona I know a few Dollys, most keep to themselves, and a few drifters have come through town a few times following ghosts of leads."

She didn't have anymore questions after that, and we were basically done with the cookie, so I cleaned up and we wandered through the mall looking at all the clothes and jewelry in the windows.

At one of the stores we stopped at Angel searched through lines and lines of shiny black knee high boots, I rolled my eyes as she showed me one. It had laces instead of going up straight, they wrapped around the boot so to tying it seemed impossible.

In the checkout line I absently picked through the candles in a wire basket next to the cashier. Angel selected a few of the cinnamon ones and purchased them too. "What are the candles for?" I asked as she handed me the bags to carry.

Nonchalantly Angel mused, "Those creepy candle skull things in your room have bad smelling candles. When you do that funny ritual of lighting them the smell makes your room unbearable." I smiled, "What funny ritual?" Angel rolled her eyes, "Moogie, you are just so mysterious sometimes."

I played mix and match jewelry at one the vendor stands with Angel. "Ooo, look at these diamond rings! Don't you think they would be great with that necklace?"

Angel held a pair of earrings against her wavy, scarlet hair, "Moogie, I was wondering if I could ask you something else." I hung four necklaces together for a comparison. "Requesting permission to request permission is slightly redundant, don't you think?"

Angel looked sincerely confused. I smiled and quickly changed the subject, "What do you want to ask?" She nodded then opened her mouth, then closed it and bit her lip. I returned to analyzing the necklaces while Angel tried to formulate her question.

She blushed and said "Over the last few months I've realized something." My eyebrows rose, "Does your revelation have anything to do with your hair, because yesterday you spent three hours on it-" "I'm serious Moogie. And it was two and a half." I giggled, "Well tell me then!"

She bit her lip, and stood quietly staring at the mirror still holding the earrings. "We've been friends for a very long time, and, and-" She stopped, then started again, "I've never been so happy in my life Moogie, and I want to keep being a team like this going on forever, wouldn't you?" I shrugged "Sure."

We were quiet again for a few long seconds, "Moogie? Would you make me like you?"

I furrowed my eyebrows confused, "What do you mean? You are like me." She put the earrings down, and reluctantly answered in a softer tone, "To live forever, I want to, uh, share your virus."

My mouth dropped open and my voice turned to steel. "Excuse me?" Angel turned around and looked directly into my eyes pleading, "It's just-"

I put all the jewelry down and glared. The world dropped into a gray blur, people melted into the wall, the rumbling conversations of the people dropped out of my radar. I only saw Angel's dark hair contrasting with her pure serious white face.

I crossed my arms with my nails digging into my skin, "How could you ever ask something like that?" Angel's eyes closed, "I know what you are thinking, but really, what is going to happed twenty years from now? Thirty? You'll be you and I'll be so...different!"

I turned and stormed away from the stall, Angel and her long stride kept up. "We need to think about these things! I know you hate it, but really, what's going to happen when I grow old? Die?"

My hands balled into fists, "That's what you are supposed to do!" Tears welled up in her eyes, "Moogie, you don't have to be alone forever, you don't have to punish yourself like this. It wouldn't be a mistake, I promise you." I could barely keep from exploding into a giant ball of fiery anger. "No Angel, no way."

She didn't bring it up for a while after that conversation, but it was always in the corner of my mind.

One mid-January night I couldn't stop thinking about it, Angel had brought it up again and we had a horrible argument on the way home from an unsuccessful hunt.

She told me she didn't mind outliving everyone. I argued she will never have children, she said she didn't need them, she would live forever instead. Reason after reason she justified what I argued, then would elaborate on how easier life would be with her like me.

She would always try to stay cool against my vehement incantations of reason. I knew the underlying facts though; her words of truth stung my conscience along with the crisp cold air to my nose.

Alone, I will be alone and miserable, but that's the way everything should be. Alone, it rings in my head over and over. Alone. I can't ruin her humanity, I just can't; she has to understand.

We were drifting through the dozing city, the bars were closed, the shop lights had no more zestful attract. The day was done. Nobody except the occasional homeless person occupied the streets or sidewalk, shadows of familiar sounds preserved the background into a city silence. Angel and I disrupted the sleeping metropolis with our presence, we didn't fit, and I always felt at this time the urgent need to leave where I didn't belong.

The car was parked in a faraway garage because we hadn't found immediately close parking at the beginning of the night; as we started down the dimly lit streets I was getting the feeling this will take a while.

My head was stormed with stress, and my body felt tight and strung. We lost ourselves in the argument, striding angrily through our city, taking robotic turns, barely keeping our eyes out for the garage. Soon I knew for a fact we weren't in the right place.

"Angel, where are we?" She looked up confused, "Don't change the subject, I'm not going to let you be evasive on this one." I shook my head, "Seriously, I think we made a few wrong turns." She looked around her, "Yep, looks like we're in the suburbs. Anyway-"

I shook my head and interrupted her, "I think if we go down there we can shortcut back to the street we need to be on."

Angel angrily spun on her heel to the direction I pointed to and we dipped back into the argument.

We strode swiftly and again blindly on the never-ending sidewalk in unrested discussion of her mortality until we reached a canal. As we crossed the bridge I looked away from Angel and peered over the side. The water was low and caliginous, I could see outlines of small fish zooming around, trash built up on the large concrete sides.

I remembered this bridge, and the countless times I've crossed it to return to the city.

Something was off this time; I could almost feel the wrongness. Angel's conversation made me so uneasy.

As I listened, a grumbling noise arose greater suspicion of how right I was. It sounded under me, almost trying to be hushed. I leaned over and glanced down under the bridge. Three homeless people appeared into my vision. I quietly signaled for Angel to look over. She glanced over the side and shrugged.

One was asleep on the ground and two others seemed to be deeply involved with each other. I looked closer; one wasn't dressed like the other two, clean, and expensive.

The oddly dressed kisser let go and wiped her mouth. The other slumped to the ground.

Oh no. I hiked up my skirt to remove the hatchet. Angel picked up on it and quicker than I, she disappeared over the other side of the bridge.

Moments after, my feet dropped onto the hard concrete where the street light barely seeped over. On the other side I glanced at Angel entering a fight with the woman.

I paced into the other direction, the shapes of the bodies on the ground were motionless, both dead. Then I scanned the area to find evidence of anyone else besides her. It seemed to be just her, and the two homeless people had their esophagus completely detached from their bodies. I shook my head, I had noticed on the news days before, bodies were found just like this thrown into Tempe Town Lake, which is a long freeway trip away from here; it's nice I got to solve that mystery.

After that I casually glanced up to see if Angel had finished before I went to search the woman's purse by the bodies.

I froze, Angel was a limp mound on the concrete, dark, thin blood leaked out of her head, her scarlet hair sprawled out, I couldn't tell how much red was her hair or the blood. It quickly threatened to flow over the ledge into the canal.

Looming over was her opponent, a richly dressed woman in white leather, shoulder length dirty blonde hair frizzed slightly. Her sharp, manicured nails wrapped around the wooden handle of Angel's hatchet; I watched a smile creep up her face as she raised it to deliver a finalizing blow.

My mouth dropped and out came a half shriek, half cry. She turned, startled by the sound, and gained focus of me. Adrenaline sped the time up; I felt my mind rapidly react to my surroundings.

A blur rushed squarely to my face, in split seconds my eyes gazed at it when I threw my shoulder left. The icy blade of Angel's hatchet nearly skimmed my nose when it passed, and then behind me I heard it splash into the racing midnight water.

My eyes darkly slid back to hers as I returned to my previous stance.

My knuckles tightened around the handle of my weapon. Fear and shock illustrated itself into her features, dissolving her cocky irritation; she drew back and tensed defensively. I could see she hadn't met a peer like me in a while.

That anathema invoked the rage that welcomed me into the real monster I deny to be, and it passionately yearned for her annihilation.

With steps careful and precise, she prowled closer to me out of the soupy, aurulent light and through the shadow made by the concrete bridge. I circled around the opposite side and crept to her.

Somehow the world lost all sounds, what remained was the slow, deliberate breaths I took and the swish of canal water reverberating across the length of the bridge.

We had stepped close enough to be dangerous now, and her arms rose bent in front of her, ready. I raised my hatchet and brought my other arm up, ready. She slid left and in a flash rushed to block my hatchet arm as I swung down on her. At the same time she landed a powerful roundhouse kick that slammed me hard into the wall.

The handle of my hatchet slipped through my fingers and rapidly spun away from my grasp. Instantly she drew her attention to my lost weapon and started toward it, I sucked in a breath and hurled myself at her. My nails dug deeply into her ankle as she pulled forward. She lost all balance and her slim, strong body plummeted to the ground with a thump. She kicked and yanked and clawed to get the hatchet, but with all my might I jerked her back to me in one pull.

She flipped over in defense but I already had a strong choke hold over her.

She struggled and gasped, I had her. Her arms crossed in front of her face, grabbing her elbows. With this newly formed weapon she smashed the crooks of my elbows and I immediately lost my hold and collapsed.

The second I let go she flipped me over and bashed her fist into my nose. Pain daggered into my head.

She drew back for a second punch and to avoid it I rammed my head into hers. It ended with a large cracking sound and we separated. Black spots blotted my vision and my head spun harshly. I crawled and stumbled, my hands and knees scraped the rough, cold concrete and blood splurged out of my broken nose. My body willed me to the glistening hatchet almost in arm reach.

The blade was barely hanging onto the edge of the concrete, teeter tottering from ground to rushing water. My finger could almost touch it, but behind me I felt her claws rip into the muscle of my legs. "No!" I screeched. And with the tip of my retreating finger I touched the blade and it slipped into the water.

Behind me I felt her let go, but only because her claws had sunken into my back as she leapfrogged over me in attempt to catch the hatchet. Her hand clasped air as the metal disappeared into the bleak water. She turned and her hand swiftly tried to grab my head, I had almost no time to bring back my arms to fully defend myself and barely caught the arm that was seizing my jaw.

With both hands I pushed on her arm. Instinctively I grinded my teeth into her soft skin and she pulled back. I threw an elbow into her face which knocked her off my back. I advanced to attack her vulnerable position and she landed a kick straight into my stomach.

I shot backwards into the wall, the dizziness turned to a migraine. My soft hands trembled as they scraped and stung while I pushed myself back off the ground.

One foot, then two, I returned up. Blood dripped all over the ground around me. I looked down at my feet, or the woozy image of my sneakers, my head and my vision fogged, handicapping me to the point of not being able to stand straight.

My opponent wasn't any better, arm bleeding profoundly, hunched and feeling her neck. We started to circle each other all over again. She lifted her arms into a defensive position.

With a burst of fury I roared a sharp "Aye!" and rushed her. Startled by the noise, she froze and I grabbed her white leather jacket and dropped to the ground, throwing her over my body.

She smacked onto the ground and I jumped on top and picked up her collar. I balled my hand into a tight fist and drove four punches into her face. Each end with a hit so hard her head banged into the concrete with a snap.

Excessive blood pooled around the back of her head and dribbled out of her nose and mouth. I saw her front teeth were knocked in as she gasped for air, and I got off and grabbed a fistful of her fair hair. She cried out in agony as I dragged her across the ground over to the ledge of the concrete three feet away from Angel. She kicked and struggled, scratched and twisted; but it was strenuous and weakened.

I quickly lifted her head into the air and with new, livid strength thrusted her head into the corner of the concrete. Crack! I picked the bleeding girl's head and brought it down again, and again, and again.

She stopped struggling, she didn't breathe. Her skull opened in the forehead, I could see her brain slowly oozing out along with all of the blood. My entire body was soaked, but I hadn't touched a drop of canal water.

My fist had balled so tight my nails had broken the skin of my palms. I slowly peeled my fingers out of their indents into the muscle of my hand and let her hair slip from my grasp.

I sucked in the crisp cold air deeply. The blood from my nose still leaked and I attempted to wipe it off. My arms carried more gore and dirt to my face. The leg she had ripped into had skin shreds hanging off the sides.

I violently shivered; I didn't know from what, the adrenaline, the cold, or the metallic sweetness of all the blood, but my weakened body quaked as I lugged myself up.

I wavered as I stumbled to Angel's twisted side, my right leg was almost dead, any pressure put on it punished me with a surge of white hot pain. "Angel." I whispered. I reached for her warm neck.

She didn't move. I felt a very slow thumping in her neck. "Angel!" I tried shaking her. She didn't wake.

I struggled to my feet, "I'm getting the car!" While I staggered up the rounded concrete hill and back to the top of the bridge I glimpsed the mess I made.

It was a massacre.

I pushed my muscles agonizingly forward, sometimes collapsing to the ground overcome in cold or pain to climb back up the bridge. And then I managed down the streets.

The garage was completely empty, I held on to the railings as I pulled myself up the ramp, the blood from my hand stained the rail like dirt.

I found my car; with euphoric relief leaned against it and dragged my feet over to the driver's seat. My car brought me to my destination in a quarter of the time it took for me to get to the thing.

I tripped and sped back down to the base of the bridge and dropped to Angel's side. She still hadn't moved. I picked her up, and with some sort of miracle I carried her up the slanted hill, across frosted grass and into the front passenger seat of my car.

Carefully I reclined the seat back and strapped a seatbelt into her chair. That's when I noticed one of her knees was swollen and bruised to a deeply dark plum color and twice the size as the other one.

I sucked in a breath and ground my teeth together with my eyes closed. "No." I shut the door and limped to the trunk, and grabbed the whole box of trash bags with a roll of silver duct tape.

With another painful trip to the bottom of the bridge I pulled the bodies together and I moved them into plastic bags, then double bagged those bags and sealed them with tape. I slung them up to higher ground and surveyed my crime scene. All over the concrete drying blood and human flesh pieces from the fight scattered under the dark bridge.

My body sunk to its knees and I threw off my blood-soaked sweatshirt. After balling it up I dunked it into the sharp, icy canal water until it was completely saturated.

Now with an improvised sponge, I lifted out and dropped the wet heap onto the concrete. I put my weight on the sweatshirt and squeezed all of the water out, then I pushed the sweatshirt through the watery blood on the concrete, the sweatshirt started mopping it up. With the leftover chunks of flesh and blood I couldn't mop up I scooted it into a pile and shoved the pile into the water.

When the sweatshirt couldn't hold any more blood I held my breath and dunked the sweatshirt back into the painful, icy water.

Little by little the brown floor resurfaced and the crime scene ebbed away, I couldn't feel much of my hands when I finally put the wet bundle of sweatshirt into the trash bag.

When the concrete looked decent I picked up the woman's white leather purse and carried myself up the cold, popcorn concrete for the last time. In complete exhaustion and fatigue I lugged the body bags into the trunk. Then, pulled my body into my car and shut the door.

My trembling, numb hands attempted to put the key into the ignition, missing a few times at first, but I finally forced it in and started up the car.

My leg hurt too much to press the pedals so I turned the car onto autodirection for home. It sped down the freeway at the exact speed limit, not faster or slower, and I leaned over to examine Angel.

I listened for Angel's coming-to, first a grumbling sound, then a few whimpers; I fixed my eyes on her troubled expression. Angel's eyes were still closed, but she was twitching and jerking in pain until they shot open.

Piercing shrieks that shook my very core electrified the car. Curses, prayers, verbal gibberish escaped her mouth. "Angel!" Tears wettened the blood dried on my face. "Angel, it's going to be alright, Angel!"

"My leg, oh God oh God oh God! Fuck Fuck Fuck Fuck! Moogie! Moogie, it h-hurts! MOOGIE!" I grabbed Angel's hand, "We're almost home, it's going to be alright." She twisted and scratched the chair, thrashing her head around and sobbing, I burst into a flow of tears. "I'm sorry, I'm so sorry."

I fumbled around the dark floor of the car until my fingers molded themselves around the leather purse. I ripped the handle clean out of the stitching and stretched my body against the restraining seatbelt to give the leather to Angel. "Angel, bite down on this. Please." I said and I shoved the leather in her mouth. She still moaned and wept, but it helped, though her eyes glazed and blinked out waterfalls of tears. Blood stained the car and continued to drivel out of her face, head, shoulders, and stomach.

My hands balled into fists and broke the scabs from the wounds earlier. I held her hand until I could hear the creaking of the garage door being opened; my car was pulling us into it.

I pushed the door open and shivered hard, but pushed myself to rise. Using the car as my support, I scooted over to Angel's car side door. With a soft tug at the handle I opened it, "Can you walk, Angel?" She glared at me and twitched her head to the side, "Angel, can you grab behind my head?" She reached over my shoulder and I scooped her into my arms, a raucous shriek escaped her mouth and startled me half to death. The leather fell from her mouth and I stepped over it, half dragging myself and half dragging Angel through the door and into the house.

I shifted and stared up that daunting flight of stairs that lead to the bathroom where my medical supplies were, I shook my head and moved on. Her tears or blood, at this point I just can't tell soaked my shirt and clung roughly to my back.

The draining room had been cleared and cleaned up; I could fit her leg into the sink as a substitute for the bathtub. Angel wailed as I placed her on the chilly metal counter.

Careful not to bend it, I brought her leg across the sink so the swollen knee cap was under the faucet and flipped the sink on to wash the dried blood off her leg. In between howling she let escape broken words like "Moogie! Cold! Hot! Stop it all! Wait, fucking wait!" I slogged out of the room and shut the door, the room apparently was sound proof, because the only screams I could hear where the echoes bouncing around my head, but I didn't think about that for long as I focused on crawling up the darkened stairs.

The bathroom held all of the answers, I threw open the medicine cabinets. One of the hinges ripped off and the mirror shattered to the floor, leaving a brutal ringing in my head. I pulled off all the pain killers and sleeping drugs I could find.

I clung to the rail on the trip back down the stairs, wincing in agony as I tried to be excruciatingly careful carrying all the medicine in my shirt lifted as a pouch. I tried to put as little pressure on my leg as possible while keeping the rail under an unbreakable grip.

On the counter opposite to Angel I spilled all of the bottles out across the surface. They all pinged and tapped tauntingly as they rolled around. I shook my head, trying to make the sickening metal clanking sounds go away, and I shivered again.

I stretched my arms and lifted all of the bottles upright and glanced at their labels. I unscrewed the caps of the pill bottles with strained fingers. With a strong dose of numbing, knock-out drugs I shoved them into Angel's shrieking mouth. "Please, swallow these, please, please, everything is going to be alright, just swallow these." She twisted to the side and shut her mouth, she gulped and whimpered. I turned to her legs and tested my hand to see if the water was too hot. It would take at least twenty more minutes for the sleeping drugs to kick in, and ten for the pain killers to start.

I exited the room again, trying to block out her cries as I made my second pilgrimage to the bathroom. I stumbled and kicked through the broken shards of mirror until I reached the end drawer of the marble counter. After flinging it open I lifted out its contents, a little fishing tackle box. I numbly flipped up the latches and scanned the contents inside.

Upon reaching the middle step too quickly on my way back down, I tripped and tumbled to the floor. The box opened and out came all of the little tools clanging onto the tiles. Pain attacked my bad leg again in a wave of fire, it forced me gulping and gasping to prevent the screams and sobs out of me. I shoved my arm sleeve into my mouth and back bit down, as the pain eased to a rate I could withstand, I rolled over and pushed back up.

After gathering the tools one by one, scissors, a curved needle and string, hydrogen peroxide, gauze, alcohol packets I had stolen from a hospital, cotton balls, and tape, I returned to Angel and her horrible fit of suffering.

Angel rocked side to side singing and crying to herself. Her good leg had been angrily attacking the rim of the sink with kicks and stomps. Fingernail scratches marked up the counter, and I could see dents into the counter as I watched her slam her fist into the metal rim.

Every thud, every sound rang twice through my mind, racketing and making me flinch. I counted the seconds, waiting, wishing for the medicine to spread faster. Angel's singing and screaming ripped hard shivers in my spine and bones, only two minutes had passed. "Angel, I'm sorry, I'm so sorry. Please, I'm so sorry."

"It hurts," Her voice assuaged to a whine, then ripped back to the shrieking. I grabbed my head and closed my eyes, Angel, Angel! What have I done to you? The four minute mark passed and her agonizing sounds still didn't pass.

She cried out, "It's not working!" and jerked and twisted around. I tried my best to sooth her, but my own slight sobs were breaking the sounds. Soon she started growing loopy, verbal gibberish spewed out of her mouth.

I listened to her broken conversations with people I didn't know, stories I couldn't follow, and curses mumbled to the point of just being another incomprehensible sound.

Passed fifteen minutes she stopped thrashing and banging, I leaned over her and tried to start fixing her. Every wound I touched ended with her flinching. I had turned off the water because the dirt and blood had disappeared entirely from the bruised patch on her knee. I couldn't see what was wrong with it, just that her knee was almost triple the size of the other.

Her head wasn't seriously bleeding, it never quite was, but the left side of her face and her right shoulder had three open wounds across them. Both attack marks vaguely matched the back of my torn up leg.

Between her shrieks she informed me of something about her stomach broken, and she couldn't turn. I cut her clothes with the scissors from the tackle box and discovered the big blackish spots along her rib cage and lighter scratch lines across her stomach.

Twenty-five minutes passed, her sobs had converted into heavy breathing, and she stopped crying and flinching. The sleeping drugs had kicked in; she'd be out for hours. I tried to diagnose her leg, my verdict drew a blank.

I started shuffling around for a splint, the splint will be used to hopefully make her leg straighten and stay fixed, sometimes if body parts are bent while they are broken they heal the wrong way. In the dining room I started to my table and chair set, held my breath, and grabbed one.

In the empty garage space next to my car I painstakingly dragged the chair out, lifted it above my head, and threw it down with all the might I could conjure up. Shattering instantly, I dropped down and picked up the pieces I needed.

"Sorry chair." I mumbled sincerely. With the straight stick pieces I tied them on each side of Angel's leg, which looked like it could keep her knee straight and I moved on to the rib. Again, no idea.

Her stomach scratches weren't deep, and I knew they would be able to heal fast. I cleaned them, and then decided they couldn't be covered by a large bandage. In the tackle box I shifted through the tools and then closed the box. She needed something to cover her wound, I closed my eyes, opened them, and started towards the kitchen.

The contents of the middle drawer under the countertop contained the answer to my problem; I picked up the superglue tube in the far back under the birthday candles and returned to Angel's side.

Blood had returned in the scratch wounds, I placed the tube down and wiped off the blood again.

I unscrewed the cap and pinched the tube slowly across the first wound. Red appeared under the gel but didn't leak, I wiped and glued the other scratches next. By the third scratch, blood had seeped through, ruining the first glue line.

I shivered; my hands shook as I returned to the first line.

After letting them sit for a while, I reapplied lines and let them dry while I moved on to the shoulder.

After pouring Hydrogen Peroxide all over the wound, and then gagging at the idea of pouring that much on a wound, I selected my next instrument, the curved needle and thread. With a knot tied onto the end of the string I hooked the point into the soft fabric of her smooth skin. Gently and carefully I tugged the thread through the hole pierced and transferred it under the other shredded skin.

The point made a pricking sound and I watched it pop up the other side. As I pushed the needle through the cold under of her skin, blood stained and dribbled down my hands. I pulled the needle up and joined the two pieces of skin together.

Then I broke a hole into the other piece of skin, and tugged. My hands warmed as I slowly tugged her skin back together, piece by piece. I almost let the needle slip a few times if my hand trembled too roughly.

When the third opening on the shoulder was sealed and tied I moved onto her face. Her glowing, snowy face had a gash erupting from her beauty. I touched it with a disinfectant wipe and cleaned it the best I could with the cotton balls and disinfectant.

Her head had been scratched, but not bad enough to be serious. With hands still shaky I dabbed the scratched up wound lightly, and then decided to clean the rest of her hair. I gingerly turned her around so her head faced the faucet; slowly and cautiously I turned the faucet on and scrunched her hair under the running water.

"Angel, everything is going to be alright, you'll be pretty, and clean, and perfect all over again. Don't you worry one bit." I repeated it to myself over and over again. Dust, rocks, and blood swirled down the sink as I spoke softly to her. My finger combed her scarlet strands countless times after it was clean. I gazed at it, clutching it as if it were treasure. Then when I decided her hair was washed properly I retrieved a towel from the other room and dried her hair.

Her wounds were done bleeding everywhere, my improvised operations were finished, I gingerly lifted her into my arms and carried her upstairs and into her bed.

Angel, sleeping and still, dressed in new, clean pajamas and her hair, dried and fresh strewn out on her pillows reminded me of a sculpture, and I counted the breaths she took for a long time. Her chest rose and fell, occasionally they weren't in the right rhythm and I'd feel panicked, a breath would come too soon or take too long. I wondered if

I was imagining her alive and breathing; so I'd get up and lean close to her soft face, and listen to the intake of breath.

Her heat and warmth radiated against my stiff and cold body. When my marauded leg couldn't stand the tension and weight any longer I'd pull away, and my bones would creak and grind back to sitting down on the stool I had brought out from under her vanity.

No thoughts crossed my mind, no planning for the next step occurred in my busy brain, no sense was made; I watched her, and only her.

Time dissolved, I lost track of the moments, the seconds, the minutes. The room showed no evidence of helping me find it, so when I allowed myself to remember my own wounds needed to be tended to I emerged from the little room confused, thirsty, and fatigued.

In the bathroom I splashed and rubbed my half scabbed leg and scratched up back, I didn't see much to do. The warm water relaxed the back of my strained and ruined muscles; I would be limping for a few days. I closed my eyes and deeply inhaled the warm, moist steam, I focused on the rush of the clean, endless water pattering on my arms and legs. The golden light made the disappearing blood shimmer and shine rich and crimson. The color ripped my mind back to the concern of Angel.

I turned the faucet down and lightly dabbed and dried my leg quickly, and then with some disinfectant from the cupboard I started haphazardly bandaging up the wounds. When all the bandages were slapped on my mind drifted to medicine to make the final aches and pains go away.

In the cabinet where I accidentally ripped the door off, I retrieved a pill bottle with the pain killers of the same brand I gave Angel. I opened it and shook a few into my hand.

Angel will be waking up soon, the other bottle might run out. I tipped the pills back in the bottle, and put the bottle back on the shelf, I have no idea how long she will be like this. My leg doesn't hurt that much, I guess, in a few hours it will be ignorable pain, and after that just an annoying burden.

I felt relatively clean after that, my hair wasn't quite combed, mud caked under the crescents of my nails, I could taste dirt and grime in and around my mouth, but I had fresh clothes, so was clean enough to survive the night.

Back in the bedroom I slowly took all of the painful pressure off my feet and back onto the stool. She then startled, twitching and nodding back and forth, whimpers escaped her red lips. Has it been six hours already?

I dropped to my feet and gathered her next dose of drugs, behind me I heard her cries start. "I'm sorry," I whispered back.

She was wide awake now; her sky blue eyes twinkled with tears. I lowered my hand grasping her pills; she caught my forearm, weakly wrapping her white fingers across my skin, and then meeting directly into my eyes, with focus I hadn't seen before.

I winced seeing the depths of her agony, what I have done to her. Her hand trembled when she released me from her grip. I pulled back, helpless and petrified.

She went under again after suffering minutes of her scorching pain. I returned to my chair. Her face, twisted in tortured sleep, circled my brain longer than any other sound, phrase, or idea tonight.

I closed my eyes. My erratic heartbeat thumped and beat into my ears, this was my fault.

12
Not Turning Back

I stayed by her side, my thoughts taunting my conscience; the room soon grew too small, suffocating even. I retreated to the kitchen when I lost my last free breath.

Over the cold metal sink, I searched hopelessly out the window for help. Moonlight shined down on my hands, the window pane emanated cool air onto my warm, sweaty face until the window fogged up with the condensation built up from my breath; dawn is coming soon.

Logic and reason couldn't help me, my emotions betrayed me, my will power and motivation is nowhere insight. Any collection of pride and dignity to stand up left and could not be traced; Angel's crumpled figure replaced my reasoning, my beliefs, and my thoughts.

This is my choice; I had the power to prevent it, all of it. The selfish abomination I am, the death I bring, I plagued her with this appalling life.

My lovely Angel, I'm sorry, I should have left you alone. That was my greatest blunder, I didn't think, I didn't understand. I just didn't want to be alone, I would trade anything to undo Angel's pain.

The tips of my fingernails scratched the metal, I ground my teeth. The regret twisting and knotting my stomach, my breathing quickened, the cold truth shivering under my skin.

I want lifetimes upon lifetimes of loneliness, please, just save Angel, return her to her old life, before everything I have done to her.

I held my breath, hoping my wish would magically come true. That for once in my life, somebody would save me as I did to so many people.

The silence buzzed in my ears. Nothing happened. The calling in my head made no difference to the world around me.

I blinked, watching the drain of the moonlit metal sink. I sealed her fate; I lied to myself and pretended this wouldn't happen. I believed I could be stronger than the strongest.

I should have known, it is too late now; it will always be too late. She is changed forever, and I will undergo consequences of my actions.

I need to do what is inevitable; I need to follow through the passageway I chose. I made the decision to pull her in my world by climbing back into her car window.

Forever immanent, ceaseless my covenant.

I let go the tight grip on the sink, and pulled on an overcoat before making my way out the house.

The doors to the convenience store by the auto shop were just being unlocked when I pulled into the parking lot. Everything was quiet, no cars at the intersection behind me, no bells ringing at the grocery store to my left side yet, the silence was waiting for me.

I carried a limp, but with my weight I shifted around to minimize it. My biggest concern was breaking the wound open, I could ignore the pain.

The overly lit convenience store drove my eyes crazy, the linoleum tiles I moved on reflected bright light off of its glossy surface and at the mirrors above.

Everything made my eyes want to close, or cover them with something very dark. I shuffled over to the health care section and examined the shelves closely.

The plastic, official looking labels blurred together, I ran my fingers across the smooth textures of the fine, colorful cardboard boxes.

Soon my finger tips felt bags of cotton balls and miscellaneous items, then the bottles; then they came across a box of packaged syringes. I took hold of the sides, and lifted the box out of the white wire shelves.

As the cashier scanned my one item she looked at my half decent, half wild attire. I smiled as warmly as I could force myself to do and she asked me in a slightly fearful voice "What are you going to do with these syringes, might I ask?"

I paid with a credit card, "I like to scrapbook, and when I glue the smaller things into my pages I end up getting sticky if I spill too much. The syringes work wonders when I'm only trying to get a tiny amount of glue out, and my last bit broke last night."

She exhaled in apparent relief and smiled as I moved on to the sliding doors, "Have a nice day!"

The scab on my leg had broken open and soaked my socks when I checked it in the car; I huffed a sigh and got out to get the medical kit in the trunk.

"No!" In the trunk I found three large, thick trash bags taking up the majority of the space. Blood had sunken into my socks, and the back of my pant leg stuck to my skin.

After a half-ass medical job on my leg and a trip to deposit the bodies at the local dump I returned to my home. The sun was warming up the frost touched grass blades in my brown, dying yard.

My house looked different in the daylight, I could see blood drops, and muddy footprint stains tainting my neat white tiles.

The iron-cast lamp molded with flower patterns hung over the dining room and dimly illuminated the table, my new operating table. My body slumped into a wooden chair. I placed the items from the kitchen cupboard onto the surface along with an old, empty pint-sized Mason jar I found originally in the draining room. I also set up my box of syringes, dumping them out and picking up one of the needles, and found a rag, some hydrogen peroxide and a bandage.

I positioned the Mason jar under the crook of my arm and rested the side of my elbow on it.

My fingers pinched the needle steadily, and I slowly slid the ice-thin needle into my soft artery. Blood flowed through the needle quickly and dropped into the jar.

My eyes drifted and closed for brief seconds as I watched and felt the red, gel-like liquid trickle out of my arm and rise to the near top. I managed to pull the tiny metal thorn out of my sticky skin and seal the wound with hydrogen peroxide and a small bandage.

The lid screwed onto the heavy jar and I cradled it protectively on my way to the bedroom. At the counter with all of the drugs, I picked up her usual dose and clutched it in my hand. With the jar in one hand and the pills in the other, I dropped back down onto the stool set in front of Angel and watched her for the remainder of her sleep.

My eye lids crept down, dropped and fluttered at hearing Angel stir, a slight pain in my neck left present in my mind. She moved and started whimpering again, fear and adrenaline rushed to the pit of my stomach, it hasn't been six hours! Has it? My leg bandage from not so long ago had dark, crusty stains soaked through.

Angel groaned and I shot out of my chair to treat her. I fed her the pills and unscrewed the jar, "Angel,"

She looked at it drowsily as I pushed it to her mouth "Angel, please drink it." I lifted her head to it. "Please Angel, just drink it." Slowly she put her lips to the rim and I tilted it towards her. She sipped a little, pulled back, and spilled some. I caught the jar before it spilled onto her lap. "No Angel, you need to drink it, I know it isn't good tasting, but you have to drink it." I pleaded. She turned her head back and faced the jar again.

"Please Angel." I croaked. Soon she put her mouth to it again, and slowly but surely it disappeared into her mouth.

Her eyes fell to a close again when she finished and I returned to my stool, more agitated than ever, but soon I drifted back to sleep by her side.

The fire spread around me, all I could see were piles and piles of bodies. Some from my past, others from my present, I was in a warehouse, a familiar feeling warehouse. The eyes of the bodies followed me as I sought to find an escape, their judgmental stares burning into my stiff back. Guilt and pain ebbed from the pit of my stomach to my right leg. I called out to the bodies.

"I'm sorry!" in hopes they would release me from the pain. My palms grew heavy with a sticky red gel, I crushed it in my fist, and it spread all the way up my arms, latching on as I shook my arms to get it off.

"You will always have their blood on your hands." A voice inside me croaked.

I turned around, I found the opening to escape the fire, and Jonathan's back darting out. I launched into a sprint to chase Jonathan, ignoring the voice, reaching for my waist to retrieve my hatchet.

My foot splashed past a pool of blood coming from a woman with brown hair, I almost didn't notice. He disappeared behind tall shelves and I followed, on the other side I found two skulls laying on the floor.

My eyes fluttered open, no more fire, no more bodies, no more voice. I took a deep breath and closed my eyes again.

She stayed asleep for hours; the sun changing as it peeked through the curtains was the only marker of time. She slept the day, and never woke, so I didn't feed her more pills. By night time the wounds on her stomach were merely lines; her elegant face still had scabs tearing though. I couldn't see a difference in her leg.

The sun abandoned me, and the moon never arrived, I waited without any need of their help. Nearing midnight I saw her blue eyes look into mine. She blinked, and then opened her mouth, "Moogie."

Careful not to put any weight on her shoulder she pushed herself up. I jumped up and half way reached out to help her. "Where does it hurt?"

She took a deep breath and started examining herself. "My shoulder, my knee." She reached up and touched her smooth, scar less face, "I remember her scratching me here and feeling it hurt a lot, did it already heal?"

I nodded, worry swept into her eyes, "How long have I been asleep?"

I relaxed slightly from my tense position and brushed some of the long scarlet strands out of her face to behind her ear, "Um, twenty-four hours." She tilted her head and I pulled back to adjust her knee, "Twenty-four?" I nodded again, "Yes, and I called you in sick at the rink today, you can go back to sleep, everything is covered here."

She looked down at her shoulder, her sleepy face broke into sorrow, "I couldn't beat her; she was so fast."

I sat down on the bed next to her, "It's alright now, don't worry about it. Just get some sleep; do you want some pain killers for the shoulder?" She shook her head, I've had enough of those for now," She rolled her shoulder and winced, but kept a quiet tone, "These are going to be scars, aren't they?"

I shook my head and smiled, "No, you'll heal up just fine Angel, in a couple of days you'll be just like new." She looked up at me, "What? But-" She froze, "Last night? Did you? Am I?"

I nodded. She lifted her hand in the air and examined it, whispering to herself, "But I don't really feel that different." Her voice grew, "How did you do it? I don't remember much from last night."

"To catch my virus I fed you a pint of my blood, it's enough of my virus to properly propagate in your system without any serious problems."

Her eyebrows pulled together, "Why a pint?" I answered her in a quiet tone, "If you had consumed anything less, you would have fallen seriously ill, and if you didn't get any more after that you would have died."

I heard a quick intake of Angel's breath, but continued speaking. "I didn't know if I had given you enough at first, and I was really worried when you didn't wake up, but you started rapidly healing like me. I've never done this before; I've only read about this in journals."

I risked a glance at Angel, her eyes stayed intently on mine, and she quietly mumbled in a confused tone, "Journals?"

"Yes, my father's science notes."

I hesitated, but continued, "My parents were the scientists who discovered this condition was caused by a virus. They spent over fifteen years trying to understand this thing, and my father kept pages and pages of detailed notes about what he discovered about them. Back in the early nineteen nineties, he and my mom were the most advanced geneticists in the world, absolutely brilliant. They were approached by a private company that had discovered some people were immortal; they wanted to create serums in which they could commercialize the superhuman qualities and immortality.

I stopped and watched Angel, she nodded for me to continue on.

"The original virus came with set backs, people wouldn't be able to eat, and only could survive on human blood; consumers would face sterility and the strong urges to hunt and kill normal humans for their blood. They hired my parents to figure out how to isolate just the favored characteristics into a serum they wanted."

"Were they successful?" I shrugged, "Not really, I mean yes, they did succeed in finding out the components of how the virus changes people, how it makes them immortal, but they weren't able to properly isolate all of the desired qualities from the setbacks." Angel's fine eyebrows furrowed together, "How does the virus make you immortal?"

"From what I've gotten in my father's journals, the virus is something called a retrovirus, and inhabits nearly every cell in the body, it also consumes red blood cells, either ones from outside ingestion or dead or dying cells preexisting in the body. After consuming red blood cells it creates chemical byproducts, my mom was able to identify 38 of them. The twenty-fourth imitates the enzyme Telomerase Reverse Transcriptase, or TERT, which has the effect of lengthening things called Telomeres in chromosomes." Angel interrupted me quietly, "You lost me, what does that have to do with living forever?"

"When a cell divides, these things called Telomeres shrink, when the Telomeres are gone the cell malfunctions. After enough cells fail you die, this is called the Hayflick Limit."

Angel sat silently for a moment, "Oh, so this byproduct from the virus lengthens the Telothingys so when they divide, the cells stay at whatever state they are in."

Angel's eyes drew to the floor as she grasped the ideas, and then she started asking more questions. "You mentioned they weren't fully successful. What do you mean?"

"My parents did come out with a prototype of a modified version of the virus, which is what I have; and you now have." The last part of the sentence I slightly flinched at.

"But you said they worked on this for over fifteen years, why is there only one new version?"

I nodded at her confusion, "They had many failures, tons upon tons of ideas were tested to create a different virus, but all the other ones turned out to be unstable and would malfunction, killing the experiment subjects. The virus I have doesn't lose any bad qualities, it just weakens everything," I thought about the statement, "No, I take that back, our virus can handle food." I smiled, glad to have such human qualities as eating.

"Why?" I looked up at her, "Why what?" "Why can we eat and they can't?"

"The original virus digests differently; the acid in a person's stomach is no longer produced. The virus can pull all of the nutrients the body needs by breaking down the blood itself. After leaving the stomach, the blood will then be absorbed by the intestines, and sent across the body, so the rest of the virus that's hiding in every the cell will be fed by the nutrients that were generated by the blood. Anything other than liquids and blood won't be able to be broken down, and will be rejected by the virus. We can eat food because our virus is weaker, although we still don't have acids digesting; the virus just lets the food pass through."

We paused for a few seconds until she broke the silence with another question, "So, if your virus just lets everything except human blood pass, why do you drink pig's blood?"

"Pig is so close to human that our modified virus seems to not know the difference between them. I guess it pulls sufficient nutrients. The original can tell the difference though, and will reject anything except human blood."

Angel closed her eyes, "I guess I see why we are immortal and can eat food, but why are you so fast and strong without even trying?"

"Um," I racked my brain to try to remember the notes. "When you exercise, your brain sends chemical signals out to the muscles being used to tone themselves up and build into a stronger condition. The sixteenth byproduct compound from the virus has the effect of making muscle cells operate at its top capacity at all times. This is because the byproducts are constantly releasing chemical signals to imitate the ones from your brain. No matter where you are or what you are doing your cells will be constantly toning themselves to be at peek physical condition. Imagine; you could lie on the couch all day and be in better condition than the best athletes."

She smiled at me when I finished, then looked at her leg, "When this thing heals up, we are definitely going to race." I smirked, "Your butt will be unquestionably kicked into next Tuesday."

When the sun rose hours later I opened the curtains to let the first light in. Minutes after Angel started blinking hard, "Whoa! Look at all this detail, can you see this?" Her eyes swept the room, "Eww! Is my room really so dirty?"

Her eyes darted to mine, I nodded, "The hearing will get on your nerves though, especially outside in the city." "Hey, Moogie, is there's a chance you could get me something to eat? I'm starving." I nodded and pushed myself up. "Yeah sure, what do you want?"

She stared at the ceiling, "Um, I don't know, whatever is fine."

"Alright, I'll be back in a minute." And I trekked out of the room and down the hall. Before heading down to the kitchen I made my way into the bathroom and hopped up on the counter. A new bandage was applied to my quickly recovering leg and I checked my other wounds, all were pretty far along in the healing process. After a little cleaning and some new bandages I started into the kitchen to prepare breakfast.

For Angel I cracked a couple eggs and scrambled them, and for myself I dug out a zip lock bag of blood. I poured out the liquid and ran it through the microwave until the blood heated up, and then brought Angel's breakfast to her room.

She jerked the eggs out of my hands and started shoveling them into her mouth. Her fork immediately slowed down after the fourth or fifth bite and swallowed them slowly.

She stopped chewing and put the fork down, "Moogie, these eggs don't taste right, are you sure they are cooked?"

"Yes," I took a bite.

"They taste alright to me." She stared at them and I sipped from my cup, her head snapped to it, "What's that?"

"Blood-oh" I handed it to her, "Sorry, forgot." She timidly looked at it, and then looked at me, "Do I?" I nodded and took the plate from her.

"Food doesn't taste very good anymore, not like blood." I said, my feet swinging over the floor.

Slowly she put it to her lips and tilted the cup, her eyes rolled back and the sip turned into a gulp; she guzzled it down quickly, spilling some down the indents of her mouth. She handed it to me, shaken, and pleaded for more. I stepped down to the kitchen and pulled a few more bags out. She polished off six more, each going down faster than the other. When the sixth bagful was polished off she wiped off the drips leaking down her face, and licked them off her fingers.

Angel was completely absorbed in herself, lapping the blood off her hands. It took her a while to notice I was sitting in a chair beside her.

Just as I had predicted, Angel's leg healed in a little under a week. My wounds evaporated and Angel's shoulder reverted back into its even, unscathed state.

School was in session on the weekdays, it was a Friday afternoon when Angel and I drove to the high school's track to race. In the corner of my eye I could always see a fleeting high schooler in the distance, our line from months before had disappeared, no doubt from the hundreds of feet trampling over it all year. Angel didn't draw another one, but instead declared the field goal post in the grass field was the same level as the finish line before.

We weren't going to time it with a stop watch; it's just a battle between us.

I shrugged out of the sweatshirt I was enclosed in and positioned myself on the line, Angel, dressed in sneakers and hair pulled back into a thick ponytail with a white band holding it in place stepped into position on my right.

I started the words,

"Ready,"

"Set,"

"Go!"

We both launched out, Angel's long figure pulling ahead by a foot, then two, I heaved further, but then it was too late. Her long legs were already past the invisible finish line, I hadn't even reached them yet.

I sucked in the cool, dry air, and put my hands on my head, I'm winded, and Angel, hopping and dancing around with newly erupted vigor smiled gleefully with pride. There is no doubt in my mind that she won. She had won.

Days slipped by while we tested everything all over again, every category, every race, she was always better. If I could bench press 250 pounds she could do 300. Her batting broke the nets at the batting range, and made major league baseball pitchers pale in comparison with her blazing fastballs.

In everyway she has become an impeccable creature, she has everything.

The world quickly flipped back into a routine, she still led from the front, finished with record setting fights, and is more useful than ever. We can clean houses in half the time as before, and every situation we get in, nobody is babysitting, if somebody was lagging behind, it would usually be me.

Blood drinking isn't a problem with her, she never struggled with the taste, open wounds affected her in the beginning hunts, when a victim would be bleeding or somebody we killed leaked out an exuberant amount near her. But she learned to hold her breath and ignore it. She would even run errands and work at the ice rink with friends, I couldn't be worried less.

Even with this new efficiency, our relationship never changed, we laughed and talked. Her not being a normal human anymore did take some getting used too though. Habits and changes that I took for granted, or forgot to tell Angel ended up being strange lessons she had to learn on her own and deal with.

For example, Angel has less of a need for sleep, that meant waking up before all of her favorite TV channels and stores opened, and lack of appetite, large quantities of labored over food ended up in the trash, and wider spread breathing patterns, they kept making her uneasy when she would not breathe for a few seconds. We tried to do routine things like eating and sleeping anyway, and a few days after, she got into the groove of her new life. Although, she did learn some parts I hadn't even considered.

I usually buy a precooked chicken from the 'on sale' part of the store along with whatever groceries I needed to restock the fridge. On Wednesdays, which is a big workout day for her with three rink shifts, her daily work out at the gym, and whatever hunting we do at night, Angel usually busts out that chicken and gobbles it up for breakfast and lunch.

This Wednesday, while I was dressing up for a night out hunting, Angel rushed downstairs screaming my name, "Moogie! Ohmigod Moogie!" Instantly I was on my feet, hatchet out, "What Angel?" "Moogie, please, it's in the bathroom!"

I charged upstairs, full adrenaline, and kicked the bathroom door open. Nobody was there. "Angel? What kind of joke is this?" Angel still looked like jackrabbit after you fire a gun next to it, and in hysterics she cried, "It's in the toilet!"

I held my breath, "Ugh, it's going to be a snake." I cautiously crept over to the left side of the toilet and threw the lid open. Nothing was there except a pink, tube-shaped turd sitting in the middle. I looked at it and looked up at Angel, "What?"

She wailed, "IT IS PINK! It looks just like the chicken I ate, except, all chewed u-up." I relaxed, reached over and pushed the toilet handle, the evil pink poop swirled down the drain and disappeared. "It's alright Angel, I freaked out too, it's because your body doesn't have any more acid to break food down. The normal human food we eat just ends up passing through, untouched. And it comes out the way you put it in. Come on, let's go hunting, it will make you feel better."

After a few weeks she got the hang of being a completely new being, small things she didn't have to learn reminded me of how I did them the hard way. Especially my addictions, I will never let her fall into the paths I walked.

The first Friday passed, Angel's mood bounced from delighted to ecstatic with her new life. "I want to change the world Moogie, I want to do everything!" She rambled for the fourth time today. At the corner of my giant bed I sat cross-legged, flippantly cruising the internet and half paying attention to her, "Yeah that's wonderful Angel, how do you want to change the world now?"

She flipped over and rolled a few times on the majority of my bed, "I don't know. I-" Thump. I looked over, Angel had fallen off my bed, I giggled. "I meant to do that!" she lied quickly.

My attention returned to the computer as Angel sat down at my vanity, picking up one of the skulls. She reached into one of my drawers and pulled the lighter I kept there. The flame clicked from the lighter and she held it to the mostly used cinnamon candle.

"Mhm," she contemplated with fake seriousness, "How shall I change the world?"

She thumped her hands on the vanity and blew out the candle, "Let's go out tonight!" She nearly flew out of my room and down the hall; I listened to the beeping of the telephone dialer and Angel's voice chatting excitedly. Within ten minutes she returned to my room, and made a flying jump back on to my bed. "Guess what?" I peeled my eyes off of the screen and looked into hers, "The zombie apocalypse is coming and there's going to be a gigantic party about it?"

She shook her head, "No goofball, well kind of, I found out almost everybody on the planet is going to this rich kid's house tonight for this monster party, so get dressed, we're leaving in an hour."

Angel and I took the entire hour to get dressed, I threw on black slacks with a white blouse and a tight over jacket spotted in black and white, on top of the jacket I added a shocking red belt that slung sideways around my waist and never moved. I leaned over my bathroom counter for about fifteen minutes applying an electric lipstick shade to match the color of my belt, and smoky eye shadow with matching mascara. I couldn't do too much with my newly cut chin length hair, so I quickly brushed it and removed any stray golden strands and popped in some onyx earrings. I jumped into some black 3-inch pumps and trotted downstairs to wait for Angel.

The sovereign queen of grandeur beauty materialized and glided down the stairs in a dark, ocean blue plaid mini-skirt and an all black swoop-neck top. Where the normal sleeves ended at her shoulders, the right sleeve had fabric all the way down on her wrist but in shreds, almost as if a tiger had ripped through her arm. Blue stilettos raised her already six-foot-three stature higher and her scarlet hair indented slightly with a black hair band in it. Her dark lips pulled into a smile as I watched her figure descend the stairs.

"Ready to go?" She purred, and we stepped into my car, scrubbed clean of any traces of blood and dirt. Angel entered the invitation directions to the navigator and we started to the party at the rich kid's house.

The place we arrived at was nearly a mansion. Tons of people slung out into small dispersed groups everywhere, I could see kids in high school lettermen jackets to older college guys and girls. Everybody in the world had attended. Our usual group emerged from the sea of people and swept us away. But before leaving the chaotic living room I scanned the area for the snacks and beer.

I noticed wedged between a group of letterman jackets and the corner Joey leaned boredly against the wall.

"Hey Joey!" I jumped up and waved at him. His head snapped up to the sound of his name and his eyes locked on mine. A grin spread across his face, "Angel, look who's here-" I turned around and Angel and her group had disappeared. "Angel?"

Outside in the backyard Angel was deeply immersed in a conversation with a very plain looking boy.

She didn't even notice I wasn't there, I tilted my head confused, "Hey Moogie, it's a nice party isn't it?" I shrugged and turned to Joey, "Yeah, I guess. Where is the beer?"

Near the brick fence of the backyard, behind the pool and next to the grill, kids of all ages orbited around a couple kegs. With a red cup in my hand Joey and I returned to his corner. Strategically, it was the best view of the entire house, not only did it have a wide scope of the front door and the backyard but the view also covered the stairs and a little outlook of the wide screen TV in the other room.

"So what are you doing here?" I asked curiously, Joey raised an eyebrow. He pulled out his phone and pushed the power button, a little holographic interface pulled up his inbox and he opened up the first message:

Big party 2nite, every1s gonna be there luv to have u come.

-Angel

And attached was the address at the bottom from what looked like a picture taken from somebody else's invitation.

I blinked, "Huh, I guess she forgot to mention it." I looked up at him, then reached up to feel his coffee colored hair, "Did you gel it?"

He pulled away, shook his hair out, and fixed to its original position. "Yeah, and I still feel underdressed." I snorted and examined his apparel, "You're fine, you only look a little bit on the greasy side." He shoved me and I shoved him back chuckling. Joey was wearing what looked like the cleanest jeans I had ever seen him wear, a crisp white shirt, and slightly worn leather jacket. "So these are all the people you like to party with." I sipped the watery beer, "Nah, I have no idea who most of these people are, I recognize that clump of people, and that group in the backyard has the majority of Angel's crew." I said. But I couldn't see Angel.

Joey and I observed the rest of the people and tried to guess who they were, most of the kids were standing in their little groups, half-assing in conversation.

After I noticed this, I realized they all acted as if they were waiting for something. For someone or something to click party and fun mode on. With Joey we did the exact same thing, we did small talk, more words would come out of our mouths but they didn't mean anything, it was just to pass the time.

We eventually broke off from our corner and drifted from group to group, Joey and I could always recognize familiar people. Joey even mentioned he took college classes with some of them. I knew the people a little, but I've never had a genuinely fruitful conversation with any of them, so I have not the slightest idea if I liked them. And I can never recall having fun with any of them specifically.

The most exciting thing that happened before the sun went down was a few kids started playing the piano, various pop songs, then classical pieces, then a few songs that the piano players improvised when they ran out of material. Again, everybody seemed lonely, still waiting for something. Loud pop music played in the background, people were everywhere, I couldn't understand why everybody, including me acted like this.

Even the most talkative centers of attention didn't immerse themselves in enjoyment. Maybe I just wasn't drunk enough. I finally decided to share my observations with Joey, and we returned to our surveying corner, he assessed the kids, trying to grasping at what I said. I was right. "Maybe we're just not drunk enough." He mumbled, I shrugged. "I don't know," Around ten minutes after the sun went down Joey and I wandered around the parts of the house we hadn't explored.

The basement isolated us from the noise and the music upstairs; it was cool as I stepped across the smooth concrete, each step making a sort of click under my pumps. Dusty boxes towered high to the ceiling, furniture covered in white sheets arranged around the room into whatever convenient spots they could fit into.

Under one of the sheets I could see an outline of a very square loveseat, I clicked over to it and pulled it into the middle of the room; two boxes sat on the thick cushions, I picked them up and flopped on the couch, Joey mirrored me and I opened up the box.

I found some old CDs and a dusty, half-dead boombox. Joey leaned over and put it on his lap, we poked and turned the little knobs until we found how to insert the CD's and make it play music. Staticy, stale music started thumping out of the massive speakers. "Whoa! I can't believe my dad would ever lug one of these things around, how did people survive dealing with music this way?"

I shrugged, "Imagine, CDs only had twelve songs, and only by one artist! Weren't they supposed to be small and portable? That was just forty years ago." I pulled out my phone and compared them, the thin square in my hand had unlimited music storage and built in speakers.

I got up from the loveseat and prodded through the boxes, one of them held an old black and white pin stripe fedora that looked like it hadn't been worn in ages. I picked it up and shook the dust off. It fit on my head perfectly; I spun on my heel and waltzed back to Joey, slowly running my fingers across the rim of the hat. In an over exasperated and stuck up voice I raised my chin up in the air and said "Don't I look just so posh?" And then posed with my hands on my hips and shifted to my right side.

Joey snorted, "There's a spider coming down on your left." I jumped back and flipped the hat off my head. Joey cackled, "Very funny." I huffed.

The boombox player warmed up and sounded cleaner, though staticy sounds still drummed from the massive speakers. Joey stuck the boombox on the floor and we started flipping through the CDs. I recognized a few from the nineteen nineties, some I even remember listening to and singing to on my parent's tape player. The majority though, was a lot of synthesizer dance and pop music from the eighties.

I popped in "Greatest hits of 1983" and bobbed my head to the goofy computer sounding music. Joey shook his head amused; we briefly jumped from one song to the next. Even though it sounded ridiculous, each hit seemed to have an interesting beat or tune or theme, half the voices sound as if a live, imperfect person sang it.

They didn't sound like processed mush, and it didn't sound very sharp like the voices I usually hear on the radio. We popped open Joey's box which contained music across the board, and soon my mocking laughter silenced.

Joey's laughter quieted too at one point. I stared at the ceiling and we stopped flipping to another song every ten seconds, when CDs finished we'd open up another case and popped it in. We went through a mixture of nineteen sixties music until the nineties; sad, happy to loving and hating. But sometimes they dug into different emotions, ones

I only really heard superficially on the radio, melancholy, aimless, wondering.

Occasionally I would recognize a certain riff from something newer and realize the new one had been a remake; I couldn't believe so many lyrics were remakes.

"Do you think anybody ever listens to these things?" I looked at Joey; he was on the floor stretched out with his hand behind his head. I took a deep breath, "I don't know, wait, I have an idea. Let's bring the music upstairs."

We grabbed a couple of the better dancing CDs and carried everything up to the living room. The kids stared in awe as we brought up the huge, odd machinery into the clean, crowded living room. I leaned over and turned off the polished modern pop that was streaming through the house speakers. I stuck in "Best dance music of 1986" CD, which was one of my new favorites, and twisted the knob to nearly full blast. The house shook with the scratchy synthesizer sounds and I started dancing to the thunderous music.

It was just me and Joey, the other kids seemed apprehensive. The song played halfway through and Joey and I continued to dance without anybody else. Joey spun me a couple times and I tried to twist and jam without looking stiff. Joey was a natural at it, and I felt slightly jealous. The first song ended and the only ones dancing were Joey and I, the eyes of the crowd continued to beat down on us. "Moogie! I have an awesome idea!" Joey shouted over the music as the next song started playing. "I remember this old party game my Dad talked about doing when he was younger, I've never seen anybody play it before but I know the basic outline of the game, it's easy to do."

"What is it?" Joey grinned, "BEER PONG!"

I snorted at the thought of it, still conscious of the crowd around me. Joey didn't seem to notice them, I looked oblivious to them also, but I think we both were just good actors.

"Well how do we set it up?" Joey and I squeezed out of the ring of kids that were surrounding us and some followed curiously to see what we were going to do next. I helped Joey carry a waist high table outside, "What next Joey?"

Joey had retrieved the keg and brought it near the table, and he set up cups filled with beer on both sides of the table in a triangle. He handed one to me, "All we need to get now is a ping pong ball."

I looked around, and ended up venturing into the tool shed, I found a golf ball, but it felt a little heavy. The other sports equipment didn't look promising for a ping pong ball until I found a baseball chewed and stripped of its outer skin. It looked like a ball of yarn with shreds of white leather around it. I picked through the strings until I found the light rubber core.

The ball was slightly bouncy, not too heavy. I dropped it back and forth in my hands and then washed the dust and dirt off of it. Joey explained the rules to me and I let him go first. He landed the ball right into the leading cup, "Ugh," I mumbled as I picked it up to drink the cup.

Joey grinned, then his expression changed to slightly concerned, "Wait, doesn't it take twice as much alcohol to get your kind drunk?" I guzzled the watery beer down, "Yep, and that's why I'm going to totally kick your butt, so just pick out a lampshade now." Joey crossed his arms, "That's not fair, I'm only human." I rolled my eyes, "Fine, go find some hard liquor and I'll do a shot along with the beer."

One lock-picking later, Joey and I were deep in a game of beer pong, a large circle of people appeared around us, cheering or booing every round. Joey's excellent aim and reflexes were neck and neck with mine. He beat me, but I was one cup away from getting him.

When the game ended, I traded my spot in for a place in the audience. The spectators listened eagerly to Joey explain the game a second time. The night progressed and I cheered and booed and laughed with the crowd. I ooed at the near misses and hollered at the wide overshoots.

The games weren't as fast as when Joey and I played, normal kids were not good at all.

Game after game passed, different kids played against Joey. When he stumbled away from his end of the table, his winning streak stood unbeaten, he fought bravely and with a lot of beer.

Everybody high-fived him and slapped him on the back when he tripped over to me, he was the most popular kid of the night. I slapped him on the back too, and we wandered over to the chairs by the bonfire cracking in the corner of the backyard. Joey slumped into one of them and I pulled up and chair next to him. The fire was warm, and contrasted against the dry, cold air.

I leaned back, closing my eyes and listening to the final song on that album I had put on earlier in the night.

When the final music notes played in the echoic ending, somebody else turned on the modern pop again and the same scrubbed voices filled the house and backyard.

"Tonight was fun; I wonder if there are any other games we could play." I glanced at Joey when he didn't answer, "Joey?" Joey was out cold, "Hey," I poked his shoulder, he didn't wake up.

"Eh, you deserve a little rest." I mumbled, and got up to watch the current Beer Pong games. The night eased away from me, I checked on Joey a few times, he was still out cold. It looked like he was done for the night.

Without any friends, acquaintances to talk too, I wandered the house to find entertainment. I got to play on the newly released completely-immerse-yourself-into-the-game simulation machine that somebody's older brother brought in halfway through the night. I didn't remember the name but the experience was mind blowing.

I put on this hand, arm, leg, and head gear and walked into a tent that was set up in the backyard. A guy next to me entered the same way. An introduction showed me as a supernatural investigator taking a case to hunt the undead. Why does that seem slightly familiar? It then simulated a very detailed haunted house and around me zombies emerged from everywhere, a laser gun appeared in the air and my hand rose to grab it. The game made me feel like I was holding a cold piece of metal in my hands. Adrenaline rushed through me. The guy next to me grabbed a gun for himself and we fought through the course against the zombies.

I could run, jump, and crawl anywhere I wanted. If a wall was there I ended up bouncing off of it without pain.

It was my job without the soreness, or possible death sentence looming over me. If only my real job was like this! My partner ended up dying, taking me with him. That was definitely a first for me.

Through the whole game I could almost believe I was there, but the gear wasn't built to form fit me, more a basic mold of armor to fit the majority of bodies, and through the game some of it fell off. We had to pause several times to get it back on.

I didn't see Angel almost the entire night, glimpses of her here and there, but mostly she was hidden by the posse that orbited around her.

The first time I really caught a good look at her, the night was winding down, and I was sitting against a tree by the bonfire surrounded by half of Angel's cronies. She and the boy from the beginning of the night laid on the living room couch while the rest of her friends circled her. She smiled and rested her head on his shoulder, occasionally whispering to him or playing with his scraggly brown hair.

The girl next to me, I think her name was Taylor Moseline, noticed who I was staring at and chatted with me, she always looks for ways to flap her mouth and I guess it's my turn to endure her company. The gum in her mouth crackled loudly and fit with her high obnoxious voice, "Yeah, Angel and Thomas are totally getting back together. They've been all over each other all night long." I looked up at her, "They've been together before?" Taylor blew a bubble, and popped it, I flinched.

"Uh-huh, back in high school they were like sweethearts sophomore year, everybody wanted to be them, we were all convinced they were going to be a celebrity couple or something. You know all famous and fabulous and stuff." "What happened?" I half whispered. She snorted and the crackling escalated "He dumped her, he said 'You're just too needy' In front of everybody, I was there, of course, it happened right in front of me on my way to Geometry. Angel was completely ripped up for like two weeks."

I brought my knees up to my chest and rested my head, "Huh,"

Before Taylor could jump into another topic I stood up, brushed myself off, and mumbled some excuse about my beer needing to be refilled. My head cleared as I stepped away from the bonfire, the night air waking me up.

I ventured through the glass door and by the couch, "Moogie," I looked down at the voice. Angel's blue eyes were glaring at me. "I keep hearing that you're the idiot who turned on the bad music."

My back stiffened, "What?" "You heard me, the music was stupid, and everybody is making fun of you. Do you know what that makes me look like? I brought you here and you go and fuck up all the music."

She leaned forward, I took an involuntary step back, startled by her angry tone, "Angel, the music is fine, I'm a little tired, let's just throw in the towel and call it a night, alright? Come on." I reached over and took hold of her elbow; she instantly pulled away. I stumbled backwards and the beer in my hand spilled all over my white jacket. Angel looked at it and glared as she stated very frankly, "No."

I looked around and found not only her friends, but several other people staring at us. I turned and left to the bathroom to try to wipe the beer off my jacket. When I shut the door all of the chattering and party sounds muffled and was replaced by the annoying buzzing of the light above me.

My jacket had become hopelessly stained a yellowish color, it had sunken into my blouse underneath. I leaned my head against the mirror and closed my eyes.

When I left the bathroom minutes later Angel had disappeared from the couch. I drifted through the house, tired and miserable, hoping to see Angel's scarlet hair.

She was nowhere to be found. I looked everywhere, and after determining she wasn't in the house I went back out into the biting night air to my car, and obtain my cell phone to call her, it was gone. I jogged up and down the street incase I had parked it somewhere else, gone.

Back at the house I warded off some kids armed with markers about to graffiti Joey's face and shook him awake. "I need to borrow your cell phone," I grumbled and out of his back pocket he handed me his phone.

I dialed Angel's number, it went to voice mail, "Hey Angel, call me when you get this." I hung up and tried again. Then I called my own phone, straight to voicemail, I hung up. "Angel," I whispered into the phone, "Where are you?"

Joey gave me a ride home in his car; when I returned to the house there were no signs of Angel or my car.

1 day. 2 days. 3 days passed and Angel didn't turn up. I paced my house, called all of her friends, called her phone, then called mine, she was gone. I couldn't sleep, I couldn't hunt, I couldn't function. I waited, feeling every second tic by. Scenarios passed through my head of what could have happened, I remembered about a year before meeting Angel watching the news about a lose serial killer who shoved people into

their own car trunks to abduct them. I did that to one of my victims a little while later, and they didn't even have a second to retaliate.

I dreaded the idea of her disappeared, this is so unlike her.

At eleven fifty-four, six minutes until noon, Angel stepped into my house; she had a rosy smile on her face and wearing stale, wrinkly clothes from the party.

I watched her from the living room recliner as she took off her shoes and quietly tiptoed upstairs. At the second step she stopped. She straightened up and turned to my direction.

"Three days, Angel. Three entire days." My fists clenched together, "You left me alone, without a car, no call, no message, not a trace." She crossed her arms, "You were fine, Joey was there with a car." I stood up. "You left me, you ditched me." Angry tears welled up in my eyes, Angel's eyes became icy and bitter, "We're adults, you don't have to know exactly where I am, and you're not my mother. Why are you so mad? It was just a couple days I-"

My voice escalated, "Angel, you abandoned me!" She marched back down stairs saying in a haughty tone, "Obviously you aren't ready to have an adult conversation, I'm going to go and hope you have your act together later." She reached for the door handle and I grabbed her arm, "No!"

She did a counter combination and I ended up smacking into the foyer table, breaking it. "Fuck you Moogie!" And she wretched the door open and stomped out.

I burst into full sobs, splinters of the shattered table dug into my back and I could smell the blood from the pieces cutting into my arm. "Angel wait!" I cried, but I knew she was already gone.

13
The Slippery Slope

Everything stung, even after I pulled all the splinters out. Cold numbness entered my arms when I put ice on it, but I could feel my mind numbing with it. I forced myself to unstick the make-up on my face, took a long shower, and went to bed.

I didn't care about the time, I strung a blanket up on the curtains to blackout any leaking light. My mind swam with confusion, what did I do wrong? Why does she hate me? The more I obsessed about it, the more I loathed myself.

Sleep reluctantly came to me, fatigue did, and stress as a blanket wrapped me into a ball of misery. What should I do? Those words floated in my mind without a solution, drowning my conscience into sleep.

Dreams passed, more of the same I've always lived with.

The blackness of sleep subsided and my eyes opened to the sounds of plates rustling downstairs. I threw on some old jeans and a T-shirt, and my bare feet squished into the thick carpet as I crept out of my room. Night had fallen but most of the house lights had been turned on.

I silently stepped downstairs and peered into the kitchen. Angel, freshly showered with plain clothes was bustling around making herself a glass of blood.

I stared at her, after heating it up she picked up the glass and went through the doorway I was standing at. "Hello," I said, "Hi." She replied absentmindedly and went straight to the couch to watch TV.

I leaned against the doorway and stared at her, she didn't look back; she didn't say a word. I didn't bring any subjects up either, and life continued.

Thomas started showing his face more often, sometimes when Angel and I would dress up to go to bars or night clubs for a night of hunting and Thomas would appear at the door. Angel would leave with him, and they would go to other bars and night clubs to have fun, ditching me and my hunting jobs.

I always objected, but she would flick her wrist, brushing my words aside and say the fleeting excuse of "We wouldn't find anything, they are all gone, this area is dried up."

I spent most of my nights alone, waiting at bars, just like in the beginning. I never believed Angel about everyone being gone, but I didn't find any evidence to prove her wrong.

Angel stopped spending time with me, I saw her everyday, brought in her mail, but then she would leave to the ice skating rink for one shift and return at midnight. It was a world with and without her all at the same time.

Cool, mid-February winds blew through my door. When I stepped outside, I checked the mail for anything important like bills, and pulled out Angel's newspapers and magazines. I gathered a cup of blood for myself and left to my study.

Thin, peaceful silence filled the room as I propped my feet up on the desk and leaned back. Angel was already gone for the day, so I was just going through the motions of my normal routine. I glanced around my quiet room, old, almost untouched.

I picked my feet off the table and started going through the pile of mail I'd accumulated. It was a mixture of old to recent papers I had stuffed in a box to sort through later.

I paid the electricity bills, the cell phone bills, the water bills, and made the escrow payments. When that was finished I tossed them to the side and started through the junk mail. News, news, Wall Street, news, ads. Each paper I gave a cursory glance through and dropped them into the garbage. Next, make-up, dresses, celebrities, shoes. Nothing worthwhile in there, and I pitched the old magazines into the trash.

Next I flipped through some ads, Spa, construction, solar panels-wait, Spa? That looks like a good deal. I folded that one up and stuck it in my pocket.

I threw the rest of the ads into the trash and picked up the next newspaper, this one was the local one, dated a few days ago, with the front headline as The Renaissance Festival Is Back! Right under it stood a picture of a huge crowd going in and out of stores dressed as Renaissance people.

I stared at the headlines, "The Renaissance Festival." I whispered to myself. My fingers slowly folded the newspaper up and I glanced at my calendar.

My back smoothly slid into clean, black leather seats, and my car affectionately purred when I sped down the straight, grid-like neighborhood and peeled onto the freeway. The sharp machinery reacted in precise and instant movements to the lightest of commands, the machine installed above the radio lit up and asked in a robotic tone, "Good morning Moogie, may I assist you in finding a destination today?" I smiled, "No, I know exactly where I'm going."

This was my favorite place in the world. Through my teenage years I had nothing, no house, and little money. Working there was a life saver. I traveled with the Renaissance Festival all over the country and got a fresh start, a new life. It's high time I pay a visit to all of my friends.

I pulled into the dirt parking lot and drifted with the crowd to the ticket booth. "One ticket Nance." The old teller looked up and croaked, "Moogie?" I smiled and she handed me a ticket, "Glad to have ya Moogie."

The pale blue sky opened into a vast cool canvas as I merged into the crowd entering the front arches. The town crier noticed me and removed his hat while bowing deeply, "Tis our lady Moogie returning to us!"

I smiled and curtsied in the knee length skirt I was wearing, "Sir Paul, thou appears as fine as a fresh colt this morrow."

Obnoxious jesters and people dressed up in pirate costumes and droopy rag dresswear wandered amongst the tourists wearing shorts and T-shirts.

Bells rung, people shouted in front of shops to beckon tourists away and to their expensive jewelry or Northern Renaissance themed apparel ready to be sold on the spot. I recognized nearly everyone and I ended up chatting with many. I feel at home here.

After wandering and window shopping I headed for the weapons and armor store. The blades twinkled in the small light there was inside the dark room. Each grand and heavily polished blade made my sporting goods store hatchet seem petty and inconsequential. In the end of the shaded store a desk with an old cash register stood and next to it was a hastily painted eighteen or older to buy sign hanging on a rusty nail.

A very thin and pale guy with dark, ash brown hair sat behind the desk at a counter with his back turned to me. He was hunched over and surrounded by little tools, tinkering with something I couldn't see. He was completely oblivious to me standing in front of him. I grinned, and pulled out my hatchet.

Careful not to cut anything in half I slammed it face down on the desk, and it emanated a loud thump.

The guy jumped and nearly fell out of his chair, I cracked up as he hurriedly scrambled to get up, "Welcome to-"

He looked down at me and squinted, his mouth stopped rambling his lines. "Moogie!"

"Hello Andy."

He still looked slightly confused and still startled. "It's good to see you." Andy smiled at me, and then walked around the desk to give me a hug. "Wow! How long has it been, years? You haven't changed one bit." He ruffled my short hair, then looked down at the counter. He picked up my hatchet, "Well, what is this?" He ran his finger around the blade. "It's a very, um, sturdy piece of metal. A little bit worn, needs some sharpening, do you want me to buff it up?" He said this as he was reaching for a few tools over the counter.

I shook my head, "No thanks, I uh, lost the Tanto you gave me. And I was wondering if you could make me a new one."

Back when I first came here he was the one who showed me the ropes, I ended up being the girl who did everybody's chores or was a back-up stage hand, Andy's shop was no exception. It seems like I've manned the front desk for more hours than he has.

When I was ready to strike out on my own, I needed a small weapon to start off slaying. Nobody here knows what I am, or what I had wanted to start doing.

In Andy's world, it makes perfect sense to carry around small Japanese swords for self defense, so he was happy to make me one before I left. I loved the Tanto, but the first fight I tried to use it I accidentally lost it. I've had to make do with the hatchet ever since, it's sufficient in my work, but I miss the Tanto.

He stopped and handed the little hatchet back to me, "Of course, all steel in my shop is in need of a new home. A new Tanto is definitely in order. Hey, remember that battle axe design I came up with a while back? I completely revamped it and it's selling like crazy now, do you want to see the new one?"

Andy and I browsed all of his latest and greatest creations, he gave me a full tour and background for each of the new blades he crafted, and we caught up on each other's lives.

"How is living your own independent life working out? Are you planning on coming back anytime soon? Everybody misses you." I shook my head, "Nah, I'm still out changing the world."

Everything was almost the same as when I had left the Renaissance Festival, their bubble never changed.

"Have you seen Bethany yet?" I shook my head, "Not yet." Bethany is Andy's wife, when I first got here Beth was just a hopeless crush for Andy. After a few encouragements and a quick shove on my part I helped him get the courage to ask her out. They've been happily together ever since.

Even though he doesn't know my real name, or who I am, he was the only friend I had for a long time; I consider him and Beth almost my family.

"Moogie, do you want to see some of my plans for engraving handles?" I looked up from the crystal studded two handed sword I was drooling over, "Yeah!"

He smiled and turned to the back of the store, but at that moment a group of teenagers waltzed in and pulled some swords off the wall and started swinging them at each other. "Ugh, I have to go, how about after closing time you stay for dinner?" I nodded and left Andy to his shop.

The crowds were good this year, very chaotic and filled with happy customers, some of them were dressed in cheesy, Chinese knock-off Renaissance outfits. Yep, just as I remembered it here.

I drifted, admiring the new shops that opened up while I was gone, then I parked myself under a hunched tree and listened to a canorous and gentle song tapped out by a girl and her harpsichord.

When the song drew to a close a few couples sitting near her clapped, I found them slightly amusing because some looked awkward clapping with a giant leg of mutton trying to be balanced in one of their hands.

On the stages I noticed a few acts had changed drastically; others had the same lines I've heard them recite hundreds of times.

Some have adapted to the future, like releasing videos or having web sites they advertise during shows. One act even had a robotic skeleton instead of a puppet.

At the show after the belly dancers, one of the singing acrobats, who also happened to be one of the managers, spotted me in the audience and started serenading an improvised song about Moogie, the girl who doesn't like it when you moo her name. The song ended with "And if you ever read M-O-O-G-I-E off a piece of parchment." The other acrobats ooed as the song slowed down, "Then please, please don't moo, like a, COW!"

They all flipped and danced as he belted out "Moo!" And all jumped off stage to take their bows.

I gave them a standing ovation, and the singing acrobat bowed low as his cape spilled onto the dirt floor. He looked up and winked at me before exiting into the stage room cleverly disguised as a castle.

Through my wandering I caught sight of the large roasted pig in one of the concession stands; the butchers chopped and cut slices of juicy slabs of rare meat. Around me people gorged paper platefuls of the succulent pig. My head grew fuzzy; pig.

My mouth watered as the scent carried me to the lengthy lines forming around the stand. I had to restrain myself from snatching the pig from every person that left with a piece. I nearly lunged at a five-year-old that walked by with a particularly bloody chunk.

The server, a fat, jolly guy leaned over the counter and bellowed "What can I get for ya?"

"PIG" I moaned, mesmerized by the smell. The server squinted and his eyes grew, "Moogie!" He roared happily. He turned to the back where the chefs cooked, "Another pig slab, plus extra for our favorite little Satanist!"

I heard a voice in the back shout over the crackling of the cooking fires, "Moogie is here?" "Yup." On the counter a good chunk of meat appeared and along with it came a little paper cup of pig's blood. I paid and smiled warmly before taking them away.

The chefs always made fun of me when I ordered meat with the blood on the side in a cup. I used the excuse that I liked to dunk the meat into the blood for taste. They always joked that I would take the blood back to my evil lair and use the blood for strange satanic rituals. I'm glad they don't know the truth.

After lunch I continued on and reached Bethany's shop. It was at least twice the size of most of the normal shops and completely packed. Dresses were strewn everywhere, varying from small to large, conventional to ostentatious, some I recognized to be patterns I've helped tailor. To the far left of the shop Beth worked the cash register in a large blue dress. It went well with her light blonde hair pulled into a white bonnet.

Beth noticed me and waved, I stood there open mouthed at her big, pregnant belly.

Another worker took over the cash register and Beth waddled over to me. She nearly yelled in the loud chaos of the shop, "Hi Moogie! I haven't seen you in forever!" I started saying in an almost equally loud voice, "Andy didn't tell me you were pregnant!"

She paused, "What?" I pointed at her stomach. She nodded, "Yeah, I'm pregnant, did Andy tell you?" I smiled, "Congratulations."

Somebody tapped Beth on the shoulder and she had to help a customer. I waited a while, wandering around the shop, a girl in the corner waved her arms frantically to get an employee's attention, but the crowd was so packed in there that nobody noticed to help her. So I stepped in and did my old routine, first helping her choose a certain style or fitting, then worked in if she wanted any accessories. When that girl finished another older lady tapped my shoulder and I helped her fit a dress, then others wanted help, so I continued.

I finally got a break after the intercom sounded about the joust starting in a few minutes. Business shrank to the point Beth's helpers could easily take care of it. Robotically I wandered into the back area and sat down, easing the weight off my heels. The employees knew me and didn't bother to shoo me away, although one asked me why I wasn't in my usual costume.

I found Beth resting on a bench with her nimble fingers fixing buttons on a toddler size dress. I sat down with her and said "Now we can finish that conversation."

She nodded, and we gossiped like it was any other day, some I had already heard from Andy, but it was nice to hear her talk. She tends to treat me as if I was younger than I am, even though it irritated me in the beginning I always feel more genuine around her, I don't exactly have to act strong or know all of the answers.

We chatted through small talk; Beth is six months, three days pregnant and due this summer. And we talked about what the baby's name is going to be.

I pulled an unfinished dress from the back and worked on it next to her. We sat in comfortable silence, occasionally commenting about the fabrics and the different materials she has, I listened to the joust from the stadium near the rock climbing wall a few stores over.

I could hear the actor's voices project through the massive speakers, and smiled at the acting. I knew all of the jousters, when they practiced their scripts they would sometimes yell at each other fiercely with their lines and then go "Wait a second, I think I got that wrong."

I remember watching them practice fighting but not actually hitting each other, they kept props to make blood squirt out and when they stabbed each other the blades would collapse and looked rubbery. Everything ended with the chanting of "Long Live the King!"

The intercom came back on; the voice buzzed "The festival is closing in fifteen minutes." Beth looked up and said "Is it closing time already?" She looked down at me "Why don't you stay for dinner, Moogie." I laughed at the second invitation, "I'd love too."

The other employees closed up shop and Bethany and I strolled back to her trailer, the sun was gone by then and the moon was a small silver disk tonight. Fires cracked and danced bright everywhere, groups of people huddled around them eating simple dinners.

Andy's trailer, one of the ones in the far back stood plainly and simply like the others. A fire pit in front held its own large flames. Andy was sitting on a camping chair staring intently at the handle plans from earlier; I noticed three chairs set up. I offered to help prepare dinner, but Beth shooed me away to go talk weaponry with Andy.

We ate chicken and rice for dinner out of little tin plates, in between shoveling mountains of rice in his mouth Andy showed me sketches of different handles he's been doodling all year. My favorite was a metal dragon in which the eyes are polished emeralds, and the wings have pearl inlay. I know most of his ideas will never be made, but it was fun to pass the time dreaming them up. Then dinner was over and Beth went to finish a few costumes she didn't get to do earlier, and it was just me and Andy.

"That hatchet, do you think I could look at it again?" I nodded and took off my leather holster to hand it to him.

He looked at the holster, "Wow, did you make this yourself Moogie? It looks, um, interesting."

"Yes, the hatchet didn't fit in the holster for the Tanto, so I improvised and tried to make a new one based off of the one you made me."

"Oh! Well, it's very good." He sniffed it, "Did you use dental floss to stitch this together?" I nodded, "Yep, and I got the leather from this purse I bought at the thrift store."

"Uh, Moogie, it isn't leather, it's a substitute. You know, it looks kind of loose fitting, and the seams are a little frayed, I could probably tweak it a little." He got up and stepped inside his trailer, then reappeared with some tools.

"Dental floss was really creative, and it looks like it works, but I usually use nylon." Andy started on my holster, in five minutes it looked a hundred times better. Andy moved on to the hatchet, "I can see why you would choose a hatchet, it looks durable, but don't you think it's a little heavy?"

Andy pulled out a little square magnifying glass and scrutinized the end. "This blade has been used, a lot."

I froze when I heard his intake of breath, "Um, Moogie? I, um, there is blood on this."

I glanced at the blade; Andy's voice was hesitant, as he looked at my shocked expression. "What happened?"

I knew I should have scrubbed it again.

My cheeks grew warm as I started measuring my next moves. I looked down and kicked some dirt, feeling his eyes on me, "Are you okay?"

My eyes stayed strictly on the ground, I pushed little rocks and soft dirt into a pile with my sneakers. "I'm, uh, fine, I guess, it isn't anything really. I just, um," I tripped over my words. I should have had some stupid story to tell him, but nothing came, I had pushed all the stress behind me, and I couldn't find my way back.

I concluded my stuttering with "I don't want to drag you in to the matter, don't worry about it."

"You can tell me, and you know whatever it is I'll be here for you." I bit my lip at his response.

I shook my head, focusing on my mask. But then words started falling out of my mouth, "I um, kill people, Andy. There are so many, but I keep telling myself that they all had to die, I mean, I-they are bad, but sometimes I wonder if I am doing the right thing." I paused, he didn't say anything. My voice grew softer.

"There are so many of them."

I closed my eyes, "Sometimes I have a hard time telling if I picked the right one, it's scary to watch someone die, and there isn't a hindrance of restriction to keep me from doing it again." I knocked over the pile of dirt and smoothed it out with my shoe.

"They had to have been guilty one way or another, right? Or they could kill in the future. It's what they are, not what they've done, but I don't know if they have already killed. Maybe it's just-they're surviving like you and me. Am I just as bad? What if they found other ways not to kill?" I stamped the smooth dirt pile with the sole of my shoe, realizing I'm spilling out everything. "Am I really doing the right thing?" I looked up into Andy's eyes "Or am I just as low as they are?"

He was dumbfounded by my bizarre speech. "What? What do you mean surviving, why would they kill in the future? Who are they?" My voice grew to a whisper "People, people infected with a special disease."

I continued explaining, about what I am and what they are, the fire light glowed a deep orange in the starless night, and it almost felt like a dream. Little by little everybody disappeared into their trailers, but Andy and I stayed quietly talking. I think I cried part of the way through, I never really told anybody about my doubts, my head ached and my mouth tasted dusty in the desert night.

With everyone else I pretend, why is it with Beth and Andy that I stop trying to be tough, strong? I felt such embarrassment and regret crying to him, the one person I could have left out of my dangerous world. And he never told me I was wrong, nor tried to judge, he listened.

When I finished, Andy stared into the nearly dead fire, frozen, aged almost ten years older. I watched him closely, waiting for his reaction. He shook his head and wiped sweat off of his forehead, "What's next? Werewolves and shape shifters? Aliens?"

The tension eased off, and he started trying to grasp what I said. "You need the Tanto to hunt murderers? You've known about these people for how long?" I repeated and answered all of his questions, I didn't spend any effort on censoring or side stepping anything, my naked speeches felt unfamiliar coming out of my mouth. But I could feel blending in with the regret and awkward stress some feeling of relief.

Not long after I heard Beth moving around in the trailer, then the lights went out, our indicator it was getting much too late. Andy looked up at the lights and I got up and stretched, Andy rose too. "So you need another Tanto." His voice seemed off, yet matter of fact. "I could probably make you a new one by the end of the show here in Arizona." I smiled, relieved at his forgiveness, though I could see the change in his perception of me. I destroyed my kid-like face, he knows I'm not the Moogie he used to know.

"I'd like that very much." I said, my bittersweet tone trying to convey my gratitude in his acceptance. Andy handed the newly repaired holster and hatchet back.

I picked up the chair, helping Andy gather up everything. Then Andy stopped. "Why don't you stay the night? You can sleep on the pull-out couch and we can talk more tomorrow." I looked up, "Really?"

Andy smiled, I nodded eagerly, and Andy gathered the chairs and hauled them inside. Before I went in I pulled out my phone and dialed Angel's number. "What Moogie?"

"Um, I'm not coming home tonight, I-" Angel's haughty voice interrupted me, "Oh, so you can run around and go to strange places without me but I can't." I shook my head even though she couldn't see me, "No Angel, that's not-" On the other end of the line I heard a click and the phone went dead, her anger startled me, I closed the phone and went into the trailer.

The couch was pleasant; I've slept on it before. I ended up staring through the tiny window on the metal door nearly the entire night.

The sunrise woke me after a long night of trying to sleep; I wandered outside and watched the night turn into the ever-bright day. It's time to start the world all over again.

At around seven I heard rustling in the trailer, feet shuffling. Beth turned on the stove, and Andy came out yawning, I said good-bye and good-luck with the baby and I started on my long drive home. The sky trailed a light blue as far as I could see.

The freeway was wide open going away from the Renaissance Festival. Through the drive I just enjoyed the beautiful day. I turned off the radio that played the over processed voices, and flipped the switch to make the window go down.

My car pulled silently into the garage and I stepped out. Guilt made me pale from the consciousness of the words I said from the night before.

Why do I do this? What is happening to me?

Back in my house I meandered over to the new foyer table and dropped my keys back into its rightful bowl, then I shrugged out of my light jacket and placed it in the coat closet.

Occupying the space where I usually keep a line of sweatshirts I noticed a worn, dirty, unfamiliar, leather jacket twice as large as Angel's clothes hanging in between my blue and white sweatshirts. I reached over and picked it off the line. Never in my life had I seen this one, where did it come from? Thump, thump, thump. I listen to heavy footsteps descend the stairs and clomp closer to me.

The door swung open to the closet I was in and staring at me slightly surprised was the tall plain boy from the party. He looked much grubbier now, hair tangled and stuck together strangely, bags under his boring brown eyes.

My expression must have been just as surprised, we stared at each other. He broke the silence, "Um, my jacket." He pointed at what I was holding; I pulled it off the hanger and handed it to him. "Uh, thanks." And he closed the door to the closet. After hearing that door click, I heard the front door click.

That meeting was the most formal introduction he ever gave me. Thomas started appearing at the house very often, and everyday that boy entered my house he would track mud caked boots everywhere and I would be on my knees scrubbing it off when he left.

Everyday he came now, and everyday he stayed a little longer. I now saw Angel almost twenty-four hours a day, but felt more alienated then ever. After our first strange meeting he had a certain attitude around me, he looked at me as if I were...different. I am different, but not in the ways he was judging me.

Thomas was decent to me most of the time, not exactly polite though, and has no respect for rules and order. He constantly looked down on me with a strange expression; he spoke slower to me than he did to Angel when I tried conversations with him. He also addresses me as the roommate. He doesn't know my name, even after I've told him over and over.

Not only am I just the roommate, Thomas regards the house as if it is Angel's house, and one time asked me how much I paid rent.

Sometimes I would walk into in the living room and he would be parked in the middle of my expensive couch watching football on my TV dressed in a greasy, mechanic uniform and dripping in sweat with his grimy work boots on the coffee table. Chips would be crackling in his mouth along with a beer staining rings on my coffee table. He reminded me of a myth I once heard about a silt monster from the local Lake Pleasant.

In the few times Angel ever talked to me now, the subject would only be about him. Angel obsessed about him; he was God of her non-religious ideology.

I disliked him even more at night, and after keeping me away from sleep with thumping and sounds I wish I had never, ever heard, he had the audacity to stay over and demand breakfast the next day.

Angel's room adopted a king sized bed to replace the small twin sized one. Angel and Thomas soon started spending most of their days up there.

Weeks passed, I once watched Thomas accidentally break a few dishes and didn't bother to clean them up, another day they decided to take my car for a joy ride without telling me.

I had to ride public transportation and arrive at my shift for the flea market twenty minutes late, making Joey late for his college class. When they returned my car, it was caked in mud, littered with trash, and a dent was in one of the side doors.

My house lost the clean luster I spent so much time taking care of. Everyday trash or dirt or stains appeared, the counter gained a coating of oil and the dishes started stacking up. Even after I ran everything through the dishwasher, it felt like another couple plates appeared as I turned my back.

Old newspapers littered my now dirty coffee table, and magazines always seemed to be jammed in the couch. When I entered a room, I usually exited with a piece of trash.

On one occasion of trash duty I picked up a week old newspaper dated April 13th, in the ads section a hole was torn where I had placed Angel's birthday poem.

The power bill is through the ceiling now, I'm certain the neighbors loathe us because they're constantly up all night arguing or screaming or playing loud music. They never can turn the damn lights out when they leave the room.

At about four in the morning one night Angel and Thomas were playing music and the volume was turned up to the max. The door bell, a small whisper compared to the noise, drew me out of my pleading with Angel to turn it down. Standing at the door in a blue suit, a badge, and a belt with a gun was a tired and angry looking police man.

Not only were the police coming to my house on my top ten worst nightmare list, but facing one made me want to turn and run away as fast as I could.

I stared at the handcuffs and the gun on his belt as he started talking about a noise complaint. I held a steady face and nodded in understanding, he gave me a warning.

When he left, I turned and unplugged the stereo. "WHAT! Moogie! What are you doing? I was dancing to that!" I glared at them, "Didn't you just see who was at the door? Angel look at me." I barked.

She crossed her arms, "Turn it back on." I crossed my arms in response, "Moogie," she growled, "Turn the music back on."

"No." Then Angel kicked the coffee table, it flipped over and shattered at my feet. Angel's eyes grew wide with fear and she grabbed Thomas and ran upstairs into her room. I chased her, and rammed straight into the door Angel shut in my face. "Angel!" I screamed, and threw my shoulder into the door. "Angel!"

The door didn't open, and I could hear the sound of Angel laughing.

14
At the Festival

Less than a week passed, and the very late April weather warmed and beautified my lawn into its former glory. Angel carried on ruling my comfort until the day I received a call from Andy, his voice extremely enthusiastic as he said "Hey Moogie! Your Tanto is almost done. It was so great seeing you, and I was wondering if you wanted to come up and stay with us for the last part of the show. We only have two weeks left before the show ends and then we go up to Washington, and then to the East coast until next year." I was flattered by such a nice invitation, "But I don't have any costumes." I stated.

Andy laughed, "When has that ever held you back? Beth will loan you some clothes, come on! It will be like the old days!"

The more I pondered it, the more I liked the idea. "Sure!" I grinned, "You're the greatest Andy." and before I could change my mind or look back I was at the festival.

In the back parking lot, I jogged to the manager's office to get signed up for my job back.

I sat in one of the uncomfortable waiting chairs outside the manager's office, the door was closed and I could hear angry voices arguing.

After around five minutes of sitting outside the office the door finally opened and out came the manager and another guy I didn't recognize, the back of his shirt said security. "Yeah, we found Nicky making out with one of the drummers for the belly dancers, again, I'm sorry for firing them on the spot, I didn't realize we were short on silent fairies." Both men stopped talking when they noticed me, I smiled, "Hey boss, I was wondering if I could get my job back for the last two-"

The manager threw his arms in the air, and waved his hand, introducing me to the security guard, "Problem solved, Moogie will be Nicky's replacement until we can get the new girl in a few days from now."

The security guard looked at me, "She looks a little old, Nicky was only thirteen." The manager replied "Eh, I bet you'd be able pull off looking thirteen if you stopped wearing all that mascara, and just stuck to the sparkles and stuff fairies wear." I shrugged, "I guess-"

"Then it's settled!"

The security guard looked like he wanted to object, but he decided against it and turned to leave. "Uh, Moogie is it?" I nodded, "Your shift is from four until six, you know how to do all that fairy stuff?" I nodded, "Okay, I'll show you where Nicky's costume is."

After retrieving a little electric green plastic laminated thing, a new installment for security at the festival to identify who actually worked there, the security guy walked me to one of the costume holding areas, where he pointed out which costume was mine. He soon left me out on a call from his walkie-talkie.

I pulled out the costume and tried it on, it fit perfectly. Spinning around the full length mirror by the door I smoothed the creases of the fairy wings embedded with sparkles and adjusted the torso part of the costume. I wonder what that Nicky girl looks like.

When the costume part looked like it had enough of my fidgeting I leaned closer to the mirror and examined the details of my make-up. It looked a little on the old side, I wiped it off with the back of my hand. Then I removed more with some wet toilet paper from the bathroom, after the majority of my make-up disappeared I examined my not-so-dark-eyes-anymore and looked at my plain, underdeveloped face. "Let's hope I don't look too young for the part." I mumbled to myself.

I pulled off my fairy costume and stored it for later, keeping the little green laminated thing, and started to Andy's trailer. Beth and Andy, looking just the same as weeks before welcomed me warmly.

I put on a hefty dress and wrapped my now shoulder length hair into a braided halo before leaving with Andy and Beth, also in costume, to the workshops. I checked myself in a mirror in the trailer, the image reflecting back at me looked eerily familiar. I felt like I was transported back in time, back before Joey and Angel, when I was a lost adolescent.

Angel, out of one of the pockets I pulled out my cell phone and dialed Angel's number. The phone rang out and went to voicemail, "Angel, um, I'm going to be staying somewhere, for a while, I'll probably be back in about two weeks, sorry for the short notice. Don't worry about me, okay? Bye." And I hung up.

I held my breath after the telephone call, wondering if she would have worried about me.

Everybody prepared for a new day as I followed Andy to his shop, different perfumes and the smell of meat filled the dusty air; people stepped on their crates, fixing the final touches on their costumes. Doors opened, signs went up, and smoke filled chimneys.

From Andy's shop I could see the gates pulled open and the public entering in droves under the great arcs.

Andy's shop remained dark, Andy, Andy's assistant, and I were hoisting some of the swords onto the hooks for display, after that I quickly strode into the back room and brought out the eighteen or older to buy sign before the first batch of rowdy teenagers entered the shop.

At one point of time the customers eased down to where one of us could handle it, and I found myself idle.

I played with the small daggers in the display case, fixing and adjusting the blades to make them reflect light; they looked so exquisite with their beautiful handles and decorations, sparkling and twinkling behind the glass counter.

After the weapons shift I moved on to Beth's shop.

I was on mending duty with Beth, she had taught me how to sew, and we've made many dresses together.

Not only did we make dresses, we put twine, ribbon, and little gems all together to make crowns and bracelets. I helped decorate shoes and rings, I put together sewing kits for people to bring home, and I recorded the amount of fabric left and calculated how long it would last before we had to order more.

It was a Monday, and Mondays here at the festival meant lots of kids on field trips from school or day care. When my shift as a fairy came I put on my outfit and fixed myself as best I could to look like a woodland fairy. One of the other girls dressing up like a fairy, which I didn't recognize, loaned me some of her make-up and sparkles, and I picked up one of the large pouches at the door that was filled to the brim with little circles of blown glass.

They were cute little clear stones, and when I left the dressing room I immersed myself in the fairy act. I frolicked and danced around the area, smiling and waving at people entering the festival.

I had to be quiet the entire time, so I would wave my hands and bow to the little children, using body language to greet them. Sometimes they would grow shy, and hide or cry, others smile, showing little teeth and big gaps with hints of new growth. Countless times I would drop to my knees and hold out my hand, the little fingers of nervous boys and girls would slowly reach out to take the stone from the palm of my hand.

Nearly all of the little glass stones, had passed from my pouch and into a little girl or boy's hand. Sometimes the babies were too scared and I would show my dismay they wouldn't take the glass.

I relished in the returning children's excitement, they knew who the fairies were, and I sometimes would turn to find a little girl or boy lightly pulling my dress to get my attention. They would smile and wave or jump in excitement.

With my quick slight of hand tricks I would sometimes slide the stone into their pocket and then shrug implying I didn't have any. Then I'd pat myself where my pockets would have been and pointed to them to do the same. They would discover it in sheer shock, and would jump up and down in excitement. Zooming back to their parents they would be saying something like, "Mommy! Daddy! It was magic! See? Look!"

Half the week passed and the entire festival knew I was back, being the girl whose job is to be flexible and be able to help out everywhere meant I worked varied jobs everyday. I sometimes worked the back of the food stores, filling up the ice boxes, and then other times I would be with the face painter doing non-complicated doodles on people's faces, occasionally I would be filling in for somebody collecting money at the games or running a vendor stand, and now and then I just walked around being an obnoxious character to add to the scenery.

On Saturday one of the women who stood on the crates to rile the crowds up at the final joust fell ill and I ended up taking her spot.

Her job was to get everybody in the audience to cheer for one of the jousting actors during the show. I stepped into the giant square arena and looked around for my crate where I'm supposed to stand. My buccaneer boots clumped through the hay and across the dusty ground.

The arena was set up with a wooden two-story high building in the northern side. All throughout the building people in regal costumes sat representing the royal court, and above it all was a balcony holding two thrones for the King and Queen. It was the best seat, overlooking the entire area.

Under the balcony, making the rest of the perimeter of the arena were giant boarded stands where the audience is dispersed across it eating nearby vendor food. A few feet out from the last bench is a dirt walkway, after that another ring is enclosed by a wooden fence.

My side, the northwestern corner, was packed. Although I was slightly afraid because I hadn't done this before, I stood my ground and screamed and yelled in an English accent for the crowd's attention. My group was on the side for the pirate, and we were allied with the southwestern corner and enemy to the two evil jousters on the right corners.

I headed the crowd chant, they stomped their feet and whistled. In the southeastern corner the lady's entire group stood up and blew raspberries at us, I laughed and orchestrated my crowd to react and we warred with quirky comebacks and name calling.

"Alright, now to Evil Sir Vincent's lot!" I shouted and everybody stood up and pointed at the other group shouting in unison "You Suck!"

The Northeastern which we had just insulted, reacted with the entire crowd mooing my name. I put my hands on my hips and commanded my crowd to stand up and say "What's that I hear?" And they would put up their hand to their ears, "Are those COW-ards?"

Betty, the commander of the right northern crowd dropped her mouth open and started shouting to the crowds for the next comeback. On the Southwestern corner, the crowd turned to the northeastern corner and they shouted in unison, "Ooo! You got burned!"

The crowd shouting battles ended when the trumpets sounded, alerting us peasantry to the King and Queen and the rest of the Royal Court arriving. They went around the ring and I urged my crowd to cheer for them louder when they passed by us. When they finished they went into grand and wide wooden doors opening in the large northern building.

Then, surrounded by elegant people in flowing costumes, a carriage was led by two pure white horses. They were decorated with the royal emblem and fresh flowers woven into their mane.

The open carriage held two people with golden crowns atop their head. The woman, old but graceful waved and smiled, and the man held a serious expression of authority under his snowy white beard. When they passed us I urged my crowd to stand and show respect saying loudly but serious "Bow low! Tis our Majesties the King and Queen."

And I dipped into a low curtsy as they passed.

The King, when he appeared at the balcony gave us a speech and our announcer came into the ring to introduce the jousters. First came our pirate, I threw my arms up and everyone stood up and cheered when he rode by us.

We cheered for the good jouster and booed at the two evil jousters when they circled by us.

I half watched the joust; my job of keeping the crowd was hard enough. Through the fights I helped people up the stairs, carry drinks or snacks, and kept the bored children sitting in the front from making too much noise. I love tending to my peasants.

It was the last day of the Renaissance Festival, and the magician needed an assistant. Luckily it didn't involve sawing or being dunked underwater, my only job was to pretend to be an audience member volunteer, and then let the magician hypnotize me.

I settled down on one of the benches in jeans and a T-shirt with my hair hanging loose. I watched as the real audience dropped onto the benches grasping snacks and babies and maps. Their skeptical but interested faces watched the announcer introducing the magician.

The magician emerged wearing a microphone and a navy blue overcoat, his burly voice bellowed through the speakers, "I may look like an ordinary man, but I must assure you I posses in these hands," He held out his big paw-like hands, "extraordinary power and magic." And with the flick of his wrist a paper mache dove appeared in his hand.

He then placed his other hand over the bird's head and lifted it to find a live snow-white dove had replaced it.

I could feel the crowd draw into an audience, they were no longer paying attention to their phones or electronics. He had a show.

The show progressed easily through acts, all more entertaining and exciting as the ones before. Soon he announced about a half hour in, "Not only can this magic manipulate nature, but it can spread its power over you, any of you. So how about we get some volunteers?" My hand shot in the air and I waved it around a little bit. He pointed to me, a boy in the front row and a girl in the middle.

We got up to the stage and sat down in the chairs a backstage person provided for us and we were each handed a microphone I smiled and bounced around my seat excitedly and the magician asked our names and ages, the boy was Josh and was twenty-five, the girl, Caroline, said she was nineteen. My name was Tracy, and I was twenty-one-years-old, just like my driver's license states.

He then pulled out of his endlessly filled pockets a gold watch. "I have cursed this watch to make people succumb to my power."

He exhibited the watch to the public with a sweeping gesture. "Once my lovely volunteers catch their eye to it, they shall become whatever I want them to be. No matter how outrageous." In a lighter voice he added, "And they're all eighteen, so it's legal!" The audience ruptured into a light laughter but grew serious as he started the watch.

Slowly and evenly he rolled his wrist back and forth pinching the gold chain's end between his fingers, all three of us followed the watch swinging back and forth, back and forth.

The rhythmic ticking grew louder and softer as the watch sung towards me and away. I stooped my back down slightly and slumped my shoulders gradually as he mused "You are getting sleepy now."

I let my eye lids droop and he purred softly, "When I snap you shall fall asleep." The ticking wrapped around my brain, and so did the calm breathing of the girl next to me, Caroline. When I heard the magician's almost inaudible snap, I let my head drop on Caroline's shoulder with my eyes closed. Caroline's head laid on top of mine, and I could feel her warm neck pulsing heat and soft warmth on my skin. My mouth watered, but I didn't reveal I wasn't asleep.

"Tracy, when you hear this sound you will be a cat." I heard a whistle blow. "Caroline, when you hear this sound you will start singing holiday carols." I heard a bell ring, "And Josh, when you hear this sound you will be madly in love with the lovely old lady named Rachel in the front row." I heard behind me a recorded sound of a scale of notes on a harp being played. The audience broke into short laughter, and then quieted.

"Alright, now wake up." He snapped his fingers again. I let my eyes bounce open. We all straightened up in our chairs, and looked up curiously to the magician. He put a little silver whistle to his lips and blew. I jumped in my seat slightly then dropped out of it and onto my hands and knees.

"Meow." I uttered in a slightly whinny tone, and then stretched like a cat, pushing my hands forward and my back up. I slinked around the stage and rubbed my head up against the leg of the chair. Then I uttered another meow, the audience applauded impressed and I continued as he picked up a bell and rung it. Caroline, who was staring at me with a bewildered expression, made me almost break out of character and start laughing.

She started into "Jingle Bells" and then to "Winter Wonderland" and then to "Silver Bells" while I meowed and started licking the back of my hand. My hand tasted disgusting, although it did have a hint of orange flavor from the soda I spilt on myself earlier today.

Josh then stood up. "What are they doing?" He asked in a slightly scared tone, and the magician pressed the play button on a small remote. The recorded harp sound played and his head snapped to the old lady in the front row. "I love you!" He cried and jumped off stage; I patted around the stage and rubbed up against Caroline's leg. Caroline was in the middle of "Rudolf the Red Nosed Reindeer" but was soon being droned out by Josh's cries and pleads for the old lady to love him back.

The old lady was startled by Josh on his knees next to her, holding and rubbing his face on her hand.

Then the magician snapped and we all collapsed and closed shut our eyes. The crowd applauded vigorously cheering and wooing. It abruptly stopped at the sound of the magician's voice sounding, "Tracy, Caroline, Josh, when I snap my fingers again you shall wake without memory of any of this happening."

The final snap from his fingers brought my eyes open, I stared at my place on stage and tried to keep a confused expression on my face. I stood up and brushed myself off, while Josh and Caroline did the same.

He proudly stepped to us, flaunting his cape in the air and bowed to the audience. "Hello Tracy, how are you feeling?" I spoke into the microphone, "Umm, kind of strange, first I was in my seat and then I was on the floor. And my mouth tastes like dirt." The audience applauded, "And you Caroline?"

"My throat hurts, it feels like I've been talking or shouting something." The audience applauded again, "Josh? How are you feeling?" Josh looked at his hands, "I-I don't know." A smile crept up on the magicians face. Magic is a powerful thing; it can change your identity, functioning, and beliefs into such different things. Give it up for our lovely volunteers," we all stood up and returned to our seats while the audience clapped.

I stuck around for the rest of the show, even though my acting job was finished. The last segment of the show was advertising, he makes kits and things for minor magic tricks. He also sells a video for demonstrating all of the magic items in the kits, but that is separate. He also sent around a basket for tips because he doesn't charge admission.

I slipped through the exiting crowd and to the backstage. I didn't really have much to do after this job, so I chatted with the magician, and he was packing up for the day. I bid him good-bye and watched the other act moving into the backstage.

They were the belly dancers, and I had seen their routine more than any other group. There were six of them, all had their own color themes but still coordinated with the other girls. They were all bigger than me, so much more curvy and beautiful.

I watched them set up like an excited band groupie, "Are you sure you don't need an extra dancer?" I said to the lead belly dancer, Sarah, a very round and heavy woman. But all at the same time she was important and alluring, she glanced up at me, "Oh, hello again Moogie. I didn't see you there." I looked up at them, "Are you sure I can't be a dancer? I learn routines really fast and the stage has room for seven-"

Sarah shook her head, "Moogie, again with this? I told you, one the most important parts of belly dancing is having something to shake and jiggle." She pointed at my stomach, "Moogie, you just have nothing to shake." I crossed my arms and leaned against the wall, dismayed once again.

"If you like, you can beat the drums for us instead, it doesn't take much, you just have to keep the beat with the other drummers."

I felt slightly confused, "What? No, you can't just beat on a drum. Don't you have to know something?"

She shook her head, "Not if you're a back-up drummer, and one of our back-up drummers had been kicked out last week, come on, you can use his drum." She swooped me into her side and basically shoved me along enthusiastically to another room filled with a bunch of people rushing around with instruments, tuning, playing, and talking, it was the band that played the songs for the belly dancing routines.

"Hey guys, I found your new drummer until Bud gets his job back." Sarah, said in a deep voice, I smiled as a few stopped to look up at her, then one looked down at me, "Wait, you're that girl that fills in for everybody, weren't you just acting like a cat in the other show?"

I shrugged "Yeah," The band guy shrugged too, "Okay, good enough for me."

Somebody shoved a drum in my hands and a robe to match the other back up drummers. The band was about ten people, and they chaotically ran around backstage until I heard a voice say, "Five minutes until show time."

I stuck with the other two back-up drummers and they taught me a little about rhythm. I learned the basic parts for each of the songs the belly dancers dance too. The robe was way too big but I didn't stand out, we sat crisscrossed in the back on little cushions without drums in front of us.

The singer and lead for the band was an old stick-like tan woman with a crooked nose and an accent I couldn't quite place. She announced the dancers one by one, and I watched them gracefully emerge and dance onto the stage. They had a small audience, mostly composed of a group of dorky looking guys dressed in strange futuristic clothes and matching utility belts. They carried little communicator devices and plastic ray guns. I recognized the outfit, every year we get a group of strange people coming in dressed up like people from one science fiction show or another.

Andy always knows which show they dress up from, and he is constantly talking with them. I, on the other hand, have not the slightest idea what science fiction shows are big or what they dress up to be.

When one ends up being a customer I usually pretend to be confused and ask them if they are from the circus. Sometimes they play along, and other times they laugh. One time a customer flipped open his communicator and started talking into it, pretending to record observations of me, the Renaissance folk.

These geeks were deeply fixed on watching the belly dancers, especially when they started their first song routine together. I beat on the drums like the others; it was easy, the drum made different sounds depending on how hard I hit it, where I struck it, and what part of my hand I used. It took a while to get it to sound like the other two, but soon I was easily keeping up with them.

The song ended and the dancers finished into a final pose. Strident applause with hollers and whistling came from the group of geeks, and the belly dancers drew into a star formation with one girl in the middle as the next song eased into the atmosphere.

We played about seven songs, each belly dancer had a beautiful solo, shaking and swaying, jingling the little bells and coins sewn onto their outfits. Their quick bare feet stepping fluidly on the dark wooden stage, flowingly making their curves sensuous and aesthetic. Rain droplets pitter pattered halfway through the performance on the stage. None of the girls faltered dancing through the puddles. I held my breath, fearing they might fall, and they still held so much fatale.

When the dancers took their bows I had barely noticed an hour had passed, the drummers rose with me some of the last to leave, bowed and exited backstage with the rest of the band. While we were packing up, one of the back-up drummers, a tired looking guy with a brown and heavy afternoon shadow came up too me. "Hey, good job up there; you can catch on pretty good." I shrugged, "I guess it's my job." The drummer smiled, "My friend and I also work up with the gray hound rescue, and since Bud has been gone there's an open volunteer spot, do you think you'd want to help there too?"

My mouth dropped open, "Really? I love dogs! You can count me in." In no time I was out of my funny robe costume and back into another one of Beth's old dresses with my hair pulled up. The gray hound rescue has been a main attraction at the Renaissance Festival for as long as I can remember.

They don't really have anything to do with the Renaissance time period, but I don't think anybody cares; these dogs are probably some of the happiest dogs on earth, hundreds of people from all over the United States come to pet them every single day.

When I stepped into the little pavilion, half of the cute gray hounds were laying down taking a nap next to a fan blowing back and forth across their bodies. A few of them were getting their bellies rubbed by toddlers.

Around the damp pavilion floor were a couple of chairs, all except one was filled with smiling people holding the dog's leashes. It was quiet and peaceful in here, with the dogs lying around, and muted light, it felt like naptime.

I carefully stepped over to the empty chair next to the drummer and sat down, the drummer said in a quiet voice, "She's the one in charge; you'll want to talk to her to get assigned a dog." I nodded and looked to where the drummer was implying. A wrinkly old lady with strands of salt and pepper gray hair spilling out of her loose bonnet dosed in a rocking chair in the corner of the room.

I made my way over to her and she raised her sleepy eyes at me, she noticed my little electric green laminated card and said a tired voice, "Are you the new replacement? I meant to send out for one earlier, but I don't remember if I did." I fidgeted with the seams of my dress, "Yes ma'am, I am a replacement, but I didn't come from the manager's office."

"You may take care of Macy, Lacy, and Baby. Make sure their water is full, their leashes are in the corner dear." I looked back and walked over to pick up the three leather loops connected to the leashes on the corner post of the pavilion. All three gray hounds were dressed in little harnesses, and in the middle a number was sewn into it and their name at the top. I smiled at the funny outfits, and then took my place next to the drummer.

Gray hounds were tiny animals compared to Lilie, but their gray coat and black spot resembles my dog's fur. I daydreamed about my favorite dog in the world, her beautiful spots, smooth fur coat, her lovely brown eyes, I miss her.

People of all ages pet the dogs, asking their names, the older people who worked there full time knew the full names and backgrounds of the dogs. I listened to the older people talk about Macy, Lacy, and Baby.

These were retired racing dogs, similar to the others. When they barely pass their prime for racing, the gray hounds are dubbed useless and the majority of the dogs are put to sleep. The rescue is all about making a home for them to live out their final days or find a good family.

The afternoon passed calmly and lazily with the dogs. The rain and clouds progressed away from the festival to shower the freeways, and I watched the sun slip quietly out from over us and down. When late afternoon was struck by the sound of trumpets, the pavilion startled awake.

All of the dogs rose and stretched; some of the people did too, Baby, who had been curled up asleep all day, barked hoarsely and wagged her tail. In the distance the King and Queen and their court appeared with the trumpeters. I looked at the drummer, "What's wrong with the dogs?"

My question was answered when the inhabitants of the pavilion rose into a mass. The dogs bounced around excitedly and Lacy lightly tugged on her leash as everybody started outside to join along side the

King and Queen's open carriage. The drummer smiled, "Don't you know? We are part of the King's Royal Court!"

I looked down at myself, straightening wrinkles and brushing dirt off the bottom, quickly I fidgeted with my hair to make it less conservative and more important. It wasn't much of a change, but there was no time. I was to be in the court now!

We reached the great arches leading into the arena. The trumpets played the crowd screamed, I stepped in pace with the rest of the gray hound group.

The dogs led me along, they knew the routine. As I absorbed all around me, the entire arena lit up in a different way. I didn't see the crowd control or the backstage men, I saw the arena, I saw the people, I felt new, and excited.

When we made our way following the ring the dogs tugged more excitedly to the wide doors that lead into the grand two story building.

The back rooms where the jousters stood idle and the horses were fed I watched the stage hands in T-shirts throw everything together. We moved in a mass up the wooden stairs and into a plain looking room where the dogs pulled me next to the window. Right under the window sill a long oak bench with a cushion underneath it stood and the dogs hurried over to go lay down.

I took a space on the bench next to the happy dogs parked on their cushions and folded my arms across the window sill with the leash loops at the crook of my arms. I leaned forward and surveyed my view; seas of entertained faces filled the stands. As the King and Queen rode by I watched as the crowds rose and fell creating one large wave. My high up angle caught new detail I had never seen the thousand times I've been in this arena.

The window had a perfect view of the ring, the crowd, and beyond the arena I could also see the edge of the rest of the festival. Up here it was an entirely different world.

When the King and the graceful Queen disappeared into the two-story building I caught a glimpse of them going up the stairs we passed through. Then I listened to the King's speech, I've heard it a million times, but never did I listen to the words. It was a good speech, and I found myself chanting with the crowd for our king.

My eyes stayed only out the window, the background workers and their sounds of taking care of the show cloaked into oblivion.

Then the joust began, the horsemen rode out one by one, distinctly individualized. The first was the pirate, a bearded man in brown leather stitched together with a dirty maroon fabric. His grimy brown horse trotted around the ring gathering boos from the west and cheers from the east, he settled in a corner where crowds went wild for him. Then emerged from the gates a dark chocolate horse and its rider, a skinny man with bronze hair rode angrily and quickly out with traditional metal armor and a shield and emblem of green and black. His horse passed by boos from the east and received cheers from the west, he settled in the southwestern corner.

Out next and decorated in blue and white knight armor a blonde long haired man on a gray steed rode counter clockwise from the first two. Waving and triumphantly going around the ring. The southeastern corner went feral in screams and praise for him, this crowd had been the loudest so far.

Finally, a midnight horse whinnied for the world's attention as a knight in coal black armor carrying a shield with an emblem of black and red loped around the ring, far bigger than the other three horses. It drew hateful boos from the eastern side, polite applause from the southwestern corner, and from his corner the northwestern corner a deafening drum roll of feet stopping and beating the floor of the stands.

Each gave a speech, the jouster from the southeast spoke of winning this for honor, to prove good will always triumph over evil and long live the King. He beat his blue chest plate in respect for the King.

Then the southwestern jouster rose to address the crowd. He angrily called out for bloodshed against the southeastern jouster, pointing at him and fervidly cursing him for killing his brother and prophesying that revenge shall be had. The blue and white jouster defended himself with the reason that he was merely defending himself. I sniggered at the irony, history was repeating for the good jouster, to defend himself for defending himself.

The knights argued until they were silenced by the loud, dramatic steps of the dark northeastern knight. He took off his full helmet to reveal a head full of slick black hair. He laughed and called the bickering jousters fools, and then stated in a striking speech, that how pitiful that these are considered knights, and blood shall be spilt for his entertainment, as this is but one more battle against weak cowards he shall clash with.

The dark knight unsheathed a black iron sword and pointed it to the King. In a razor sharp voice and a scowl he called up to the balcony "This blade shall be stained once again in the blood of the unworthy! This is for Thou!"

The pirate hopped up casually, boot buckles jingling, he was holding a mug of beer and burping and swaying drunkenly, and he roared to the crowds a great speech cleverly disguised as a call for a peasant revolution and representation of the people, and the good jouster jumped up and helped him off the wooden stage saying in a confident and noble voice, "Good man, thou art drunk, these swashbuckling and outlandish ideas are fun, but let us return to the real world, the games!"

It started with the jousters on horseback running and catching rings, showing off excellent skills. Then the battle started, everybody fully shielded. The pirate, still acting slightly drunk had resisted accepting armor saying "They are but just restrictions to my winning." Then they were off, the pirate killed the revengeful guy, and the good guy was killed by the dark evil knight. Then it was down to the pirate and the dark evil knight. The pirate cheated and pulled out a gun and shot the evil knight at the last minute.

We applauded as the jousters took their bows, and people started exiting the stands, the final closing time was beginning.

I walked with the dogs back as they went with the other dogs to get dinner and go to bed as the crowds left for the final time. The sun kissed the sky goodbye, and I made my way to the real armor store to help close up Andy's shop until we can take everything down tomorrow.

"Guess what?" Andy belted excitedly as I entered the store, "You finally learned to tie your apron in the back by yourself?" Andy stopped, "I only needed your help those two times," he shook his head out of that thought, "I have your Tanto." He pulled out a little pouch with a crisp looking handle and placed it on the counter. I picked it up and examined it. "Oh my," I breathed at the blade. The handle, carved beautifully into a delicate swirl formed perfectly with my fingers as they removed the blade from the pouch. I found myself staring into a crystal clear mirror, evenly dawdling slanted until both sides joined at a painstakingly small needle sharp point.

Andy watched me, and quickly smiled as I looked up at him, "It's gorgeous," But Andy still looked agitated, something at the tip of his tongue.

"Moogie, follow me, I have something I want to show you." I carefully slid the blade back into its holster and went with Andy into the backrooms. "I was thinking about the Tanto, and what you were going to use it for. And I realized you probably would run into or already have run into problems carrying around things similar to knives. When I finished your sword I realized it would be really useful if you had a disguise for your weapon."

Next to the office, piles of unloaded crates and boxes stacked up, he picked one of the crates and showed me the inside of one of the boxes. I nodded in consent to his words but was confused as to where he was going, so I urged him on.

"I looked for an everyday object nobody would question you about. I came up with numerous ideas, screw drivers, crutches, canes... But none seemed to fit." He opened the box "Then a couple weeks ago I had to run to town, on my way out I saw a cop smack somebody in the head with a flashlight." I laughed, "How very violent, that inspired you?"

Andy removed a black flashlight out of the box. "I bought this off the internet, and then started modifying it." I took the flashlight and examined it closer, then mumbled "Um, what did you do to it?" I clicked the button to turn it on. The flashlight didn't come on.

"It looks like a broken flashlight, I don't know how it would be able to disguise the Tanto though, how did you modify it?"

I handed the flashlight back to Andy, he twisted it around his hands idly as he explained "Originally I was thinking I could hide a different weapon in it, but it couldn't hold anything except a small dagger; but I realized that wasn't enough. What if the weapon isn't always the same length?"

I shook my head "What does that mean?" Andy dug around in the same box and brought out a small metal tube and handed it to me.

The tube could have easily fit into the handle of the flashlight. He explained "This is a baton." He took the metal tube and flicked it forward. Almost like a telescope, linked metal shot out, and the result was a stick the size of a full length sword.

I laughed, "Are you saying make a baton that I can flick out of a flashlight?" He nodded, "Yes, except I would make a kind of contractible sword you could use based on the baton idea."

And Andy turned the end of the flashlight to the floor and pressed an unseen button with his thumb. He raised it in the air and thrusted his arm down. Instantly a blade shot out and clicked together creating a full sword. I stepped back. "Oh my."

I couldn't see the indents where the sword parts contracted; it didn't look like a baton at all.

In one motion Andy tapped it on the floor and turned it upside down, the smallest blade went into the next and that went into the next as it quickly was brought back into the black flashlight. Andy smiled shyly at my completely open gape. "You can put it in your purse or put it in this little leg holster like the one you made. I-"

He broke off his sentence when I hugged him, "You're the greatest person I've ever met." He patted me affectionately on the back and I let him go, "I call it the Flashsword, because it will always come out in a flash and out of a flashlight."

He launched into an explanation of how he made it, and where he put the button so nobody else except me could see it without looking closely. He talked about the springs and the collapsing part; I listened to him with wide eyes glued to the stunning creation. He would flip it out and show me the different sections of the blade and what he did to it. The burnish blades had a manner of elegance in which the Tanto could never reach.

He let me hold it on our way back to the trailer, I didn't feel worthy to own such a work of art, but I knew I would be wielding it for the rest of eternity.

The sun stretched as I did the next morning, ready for another fine, hard-working day. I dressed in my old normal clothes and met Andy and Beth to help take down their shops and load everything into the crates and boxes before hauling them out to Andy's pick-up truck and shipping container that he's been transporting around the country for years.

The day inched through; I watched my little Renaissance fantasyland slowly be stripped back into a ghost town, transportable rides were disassembled, vendors' carts rode into the back of trucks and trailers, collapsible things were deflated, and tents were taken down.

The smells of the food and animals that mixed with the roasting air reverted back to the average, dusty desert air. All of the magic was being packed up, ready for transport to spread beauty on the next area.

The entire day felt like a long sunset. When the sun left the grounds and the cars started to drive away I bid Andy and Beth goodbye. I returned to my polished black vehicle, wearing the clothes I had brought two weeks before.

The car purred awake from its long nap, and the familiar robotic voice asked me if I needed help going anywhere. "No, I'm just going home." And the voice quieted. I followed the line of cars until we reached the freeway; I took the open, solemn road back to the city where as the loud, rumbling train of the Renaissance Festival took the opposite way.

Their figures retreated quickly as the moonlight settled in and I sped along the nightly expressway. My fingers gripped the steering wheel feeling flexible and used from all of the needlework I did with Beth, the car's air conditioning tasted fresh and cold, opposite to breathing the warm dust mixed with magic.

My teeth set on my bottom lip, regret set in my stomach. I could go with them, turn around now and travel the country forever with the festival. It would be easy freedom. Life would be so quiet; I could have that magic my entire life with a family that accepted me. It would be so fulfilling.

My eyes though, stayed locked on the lonesome road ahead of me.

15
Disappointment

When I pulled into my driveway at nearly midnight, the yellowed lights shined inside the windows all throughout the house. I stepped into the heated foyer room, calmly shrugging out of my purse and sweatshirt and hanging the sweatshirt up next to the row of Thomas's jackets.

The house echoed sounds of Angel and Thomas somewhere being loud; it filled the rooms and removed the serenity of a quiet house. I absently meandered into the kitchen and filled a well-beaten coffee mug with some blood and popped it in the microwave for a few seconds.

The sounds around the house rose; I could now discern three voices down the hall. Who is the third?

It was coming from the draining room, as I turned the corner the voices heightened as I came to the door left slightly ajar. I pressed the cool metal and the door swung open with a loud groan.

Angel, and Thomas stood over a man beaten and battered, duct taped to the chair. The man was blondish and old sobbing hysterically; under the bruises I could see he was Ben, my neighbor across the street. "What-"

Angel rushed at me, hastily shoving me out of the room, "What are you doing back?"

"I-"

Angel angrily prodded me down the hall, "Look, everything is under control, we'll dump the body by our-"

I stopped and cut in, "Angel, what are you doing to the neighbor?" my hostile voice and eyes met her irritated ones. "Moogie, look, he deserves it. He was totally telling the whole neighborhood lies about us being white trash and sent me this stupid letter and-" My voice shot up, "Angel you are torturing the neighbor what are you thinking? We don't just kill-"

"Hey!"

Thomas protectively stepped in front of Angel and shoved me, "Don't talk to her like that! Who do you think you are?" He shoved me again before I could regain my balance from the first one. I reacted and threw a punch into his stomach. With faster and better reflexes, he caught my hand with one of his. I felt instant pain shoot through my elbow as he roughly twisted my arm behind me and shoved me into the living room.

My head spun as I slammed halfway into the couch and the end table, I jumped up and darted slightly staggered to attack him. With a cocky smirk he caught my kick and threw me into the wall. I knocked my head and tried to shake out of the rush of pain and adrenaline, Angel's slightly amused voice announced proudly, "Oh, by the way, I turned him."

Thomas rushed at me and picked me up by the shoulders before I could scramble to my balance and threw me with angry force into the flat screen TV.

With glass digging into my skin I desperately pulled out my hatchet, but instantly he lunged for it and wretched it out of my hands and hurled it into the mirror across the room. Suddenly, he turned back and grabbed my neck with one hand and raised me up before shoving me into the wall.

I scratched and gasped while staring into his cold, hungry brown eyes. "You are so stupid, bossing Angel around all the time like she is your pitiful side kick, she told me everything. You are the weak one, you are nothing and you constantly try to bring her down with you." He loosened his grip slightly as I started blacking out, catching only his words as I tried to suck in as many breathes as I could.

"Angel and I deserve to do what ever we want; they are all just stupid humans, who cares if they die? They're all just weak sheep. If you can't see that then you are even more spineless than they are!" In his irate speech, spit from his mouth splattered in droplets on my face, he stood taller, looking down at me and I slid down to my feet, his hand still pinning my neck into the wall.

"You are such a horrible person, forcing Angel to suppress her nature, it is our world. And you-"

In one fluid motion I reached to the back of my waist band and removed my forgotten Flashsword, my thumb pressed the little rubber button and the blade glided out. In a swift exert of my final energy the sharp blade swooped through his neck, penetrating the viscose skin and exiting silently, without an impediment of mercy, adorning his filthy hide with a delicately thin ribbon of crimson.

His grip lost and his body sank right as his head toppled left. I breathed the warm house air with new life as I stepped over his body.

I paused an instant, rolling my aching shoulders, and calming down.

The tip of my blade marked the tile as it rhythmically dripped drops of fresh blood. I spoke softly, but gravely. "Angel," her eyes slid from his body to mine, seeing my composed expression. "In life, we are neither superior nor inferior to any other human being. He," I tilted my head to the bleeding skull with skin sitting upright on the floor, "He, has become the human race's utmost enemy in the truest sense, if you become what he has, I will end you."

Angel's eyes glowered into mine, and a scowl pressed into her lips. With her arms crossed and her head bent slightly, she turned and tramped lividly up the stairs, and after making a few rustling noises she returned downstairs and disappeared out the front door, the old oak slamming behind her.

I wiped the blade off on Thomas's clothes before collapsing it with steady hands. My ears picked up muffled sobs in the other room and I turned to Ben's direction.

When I stepped into the draining room I looked down at his tied up state. He was bleeding, his eyes were half closed, but his chest rose and fell in a heavy wheeze. He looked at me with a purple and red face streaming wet with sweat and tears.

It reminded me of the time when I was little, maybe ten or eleven; a crow had been fighting something in my backyard. I went out to investigate and the crow fled. On the ground lay a baby bird, it was frantically struggling to breathe.

Ben attempted to talk in between the fight for his breaths, "Moogie!" His arms pulled at the duct tape and his fingers curled and uncurled. "They, they-" blood mixed drool slid out of the corner of his mouth and down his chin.

I remembered the baby bird's head was bleeding as a strip of skin had been ripped out of its head, and I watched confused as it wiggled and flailed its wings.

And then my father came out. He bent down and stared at the bird with me.

Ben said in short, staccato words, "I need to call the police. Moogie please help me, I need to go to the hospital."

The bird soon stopped flailing and closed its eyes its chest rose and fell quickly, fighting for life. I turned to my father and asked "What should we do Daddy? The bird can't fly away." My father looked into my eyes and said "Honey, this is your choice, you scared the crow away. Its life is in your hands now."

I watched the tiny bird, contemplating its fate. If I left it alone and walked away the ants would start eating it alive, and the bird would die slowly instead of the crow's swift death. If I tried to save it, the little bird would most likely die of infection, and that would be a slow and painful death too. Then I realized what I had to do.

I picked up a stone nearly twice the size of my fist and raised my hand in the air to crush the bird..."

The little bird didn't make a sound, its eyes were closed. I don't know if it knew what had happened. When I gently lifted the rock back up, seeing the crushed body made me instantly regret my decision.

Maybe I could have saved it, maybe if I nurtured it long enough and disinfected it everyday it would have returned to health.

I stared down at Ben's eyes, and smiled, "Don't worry Ben, you're going to be fine, everything is going to be all right. I gently caressed his face, wiping the tears off his swollen cheeks, "You are going to be fine, and everything can be cleaned up and fixed. They won't hurt you again." His breathing slowed, calming, the stress leaving him.

I stepped out into the hall, in one of the closets I picked up a stack of white towels and carried them into the draining room. With one of the towels I silently cleaned his chin and face.

Ben isn't a bird; he isn't something that needs to be put down.

I placed the towel down and cupped my hand around his mouth, shutting it from making noise. My hand felt under the folds of the towels, the Tanto's smooth handle clasped in my hand.

The point of my Tanto pierced the tender place just underneath his rib cage traveling straight through his heart. The blade, so sharp and smooth, probably went in without him feeling it at first. It reminded me of Teflon, I twisted it to rip his heart open wider and it let him bleed out more rapidly.

His eyes grew wide, and his head flinched, I stared into his frail, pleading eyes, "I cannot let you go Ben, I'm sorry."

His life streamed down the handle of my blade and past my wrist, drizzling down my shirt and pants and spilling into a puddle across the floor.

I felt his lips under my hand try to form words, my hand lifted. But before he could utter a final word, his jaw slackened and was unable to convey anything except a slight twitch. I watched the light leave his eyes and his pupils dilate into black disks. I had taken everything, his life, his memory, and I snuffed out his final utterance. The spark disappeared, and did not return.

My survival is constantly at stake, and the risk is far too great, he is not a bird, but he can chirp.

16

Time and Poetry

In cleaning up Ben's empty shell I had to cut his binds and peel him off the chair, his warm blood wetted my hands and clothes before later turning into a cold paste. My shoes squeezed out blood footprints through the tile when I went back into the living room, carrying Ben's body over my shoulder in biodegradable trash bags doubled over.

Thomas was folded up and placed into another set of bags; his head went in after. I sealed them both tightly with tape before putting them in the corner of the room.

My clothes were put into a bag for the burn pile; my heavy shoes went along with it. The Tanto was tossed into the sink where I filled up a disinfectant, and I had to tug at the hatchet a few times before it came out of the wall; it had gone straight through the mirror's back.

The wide, thick rug, along with the couch, and the TV were hopeless, the mirror was added to the throwaway pile too. I'll have to strip the couch's outer blood spattered fabric and burn the rug before dropping the rest off at the dump.

In the draining room, Ben had been tied up in one of the dining room chairs; I added that to the burn pile.

After a shower I threw on some clothes and took the two bags to the trunk of my car. I drove and turned a few streets until I came across a lower-middle class looking neighborhood and turned into an alley. At one of the middle dumpsters I got out and threw the huge lid to the dumpster open. In the trunk I grabbed one of the trash bags and pitched it in. The lid shut and I drove on to another alley to toss the next.

I wasn't worried about anybody finding the bodies; dumpsters have always been a common method for serial killers and slayers. Joey even takes them directly to the dump. The oceans upon oceans of trash filling our cheap deserts can successfully swallow bodies into oblivion.

What I was worried about was Angel's method of kidnapping Ben. I had not the slightest idea if anybody had heard her or seen her. Did any security cameras pick her up? I turned streets and passed through dim pools of light illuminating the open road.

Is my beautiful house compromised? If somebody had seen Ben kidnapped would the police have already been to my house? If I run away now I will certainly look guilty when somebody notices Ben being gone. Staying at the house might be my best option. Or is my attachment to this place possibly blinding me to something?

I bit my lip as I pulled back into my garage. Ben's body in the bag drifted through my mind, I'll never see him again, nor will his friends or grown up children. It was so easy; I merely tossed him into the trash, and he differed from no other garbage bag. No ceremony, no last rights, or allowance for grief over his body. He's gone with the leftovers of yesterday's meal.

He didn't deserve it, no matter how much he pestered the neighborhood with his overly annoying advice that he forced everybody to endure and smile through, the torture and death penalty should not have been his price.

What was the point in taking his life? Why did Angel do it? He wasn't hurting anybody physically, he was just irritating. Memories of his selfish and gossipy acts flashed through my mind, his nosiness and judgmental looks made everybody hate being around him.

But his life, the one life he had to spend on whatever activities he wanted ended in hours. He was cut short, and he was no less than any other human in the neighborhood.

I stepped into my house, the night was nearly passed the dead, and I could feel the fatigue pulling me down.

The house was in shambles, not only the living room but as I noticed the rest of the house suffered neglect from the two weeks I had been away.

Dust trekked onto my fingers as they drew across the tables; I saw muck in the cracks and corners. Trash and broken glass littered and my feet felt specks of the products of erosion carried under soles of footwear. This was all my mess.

When the sun shined and then passed by my windows I had finished cleaning up the draining room and was mostly through cleaning the tiles in the living room. I felt deliriously tired from the entire night invested into cleaning.

I almost missed my cell phone ringing, thinking it was just my imagination. When I pulled up the holographic screen to the inbox I found one text message.

```
You ruined my boyfriend, so I just ruined
yours. Fuck you Moogie
    -Angel
```

Attached the text were ten pictures.

I scrolled through them. The ten pictures were in crude lighting, and were vulgar snapshots of Angel having wild sex with Joey. My mouth was to the floor; my mind was now burnt and scarred with the images. Angel, what are you doing?

"So I ruined yours."

Did she kill him? I startled at the thought, dropping my cell phone. Scrambling down to pick it up I hit my knees a little too hard and fumbled the phone.

After grabbing it again, I hit his number on speed dial and impatiently let it ring.

How could she be so mean? What if he is dead? How could she do such a thing?

The thoughts screamed in my head, the confusion, and the betrayal. Angel's betrayal. Why would she spite me like that?

After two and a half beeps it picked up, "Joey?" "Hey Moogie! How are you?" Joey's light voice sounded perfectly fine, I let out the breath I was holding, "Are you okay?"

"Yeah, better than okay actually, why?" I straightened, and then leaned against the wall, "Um, well," my voice cracked, and I felt hot tears coming out of my eyes.

"I think I need to call you back later."

And he muttered a slightly confused "Okay." before I turned the phone off. I broke down in sobs the second the line went dead.

Weeks stagger, sometimes slow and agonizingly quiet or fast and lonely. I didn't think about time the way I did before.

Angel didn't return, she just vanished. The police at one point of time went on a half-ass tour of the neighborhood to ask questions about Ben, when they reached my house I sat quietly in my study. They knocked for a few minutes, and then gave up; I never heard them come to my house again.

The police are constantly following up on fruitless trails for disappearances, people can vanish and not a trace will be left. So much life has been lost for years, and the police just can't comb through every case.

It isn't just because they don't see a trail, but the work can pile up and cops are just like any other humans. Most cases lack even a glimmer of hope, more like a folder in a database. And as this system lets so much slip through the cracks, it leaves others with the opportunity of the forgotten justice and punishment.

There will be no retribution for the crime against Ben.

The winter was just as any other year; I had worked a hard summer, my kill average dwindled though. For most of them I traveled to the neighboring states, or the edges of Arizona. Most of the time I worked alone, but I did join many group hunts. I had money, stability, travel, and vast amounts of time.

The house was spotless; the rooms gained a new wardrobe, dressing in some of the better furniture money can buy. But every night when I finished my busy days I always stepped into a quiet loneliness. This loneliness could not be drowned; no trinkets, television, or projects have ever been able to subjugate this emotion.

The holidays came, I decided to take a break and drive to northern Arizona where I had a plot of land and a trailer. It was a secret place, and nobody except me knew about it, I had purchased it after the first time I had been robbed. It was my safe house.

The plot was in the middle of a forest, near a dirt road, and it was one of the few places my cell phone did not get reception.

Up in the woods the air was dry and cool. When I was younger, my family would come up to play in the snow at a resort north of here, the ground always seemed wetter and colder then.

I stepped out of my car and threw on my winter jacket, then I squished my feet into a pair of winter hiking boots.

Endless snow covered the ground ankle deep. Old tree trunks gripped unseen ground and stared down at me, I was a mere child to them, nothing more. Their evergreen leaves and pines balanced pure, glistening snowfall; I felt slightly ashamed when I ambled to the trailer, stirring and melting a path across the timeless expanse.

What I carried to the trailer in my left arm was a baby tree, and in my right a sealed PVC pipe filled with gold inside. Not only is this my safe house, but I take some of the surplus money I built up throughout the years and bury its worth in gold around the lot. This was one of my only ways to keep money in one place without needing to worry about losing everything to a compromised identity.

With the gardening tools stashed in the corner of the trailer I dug a hole in the northern section of the lot. This area had several other young trees planted from previous years, and after the hole was big enough I planted the time capsule and placed the tree over it.

The tree is a marker to where the pipes are, they are slightly different from the local trees, but can still blend in with the forest. When they grow up the roots will protect the pipes from metal detectors and other treasure seekers if any come across my lot. If I ever need one of these pipes I will have to cut down the tree and uproot the stump, so I'll only take the money when I desperately need it.

In my crouched stance I pushed dirt and snow mushed together back to the baby tree. The snow and earth muddied up the thick gloves I was wearing, and the wind behind me whooshed passed my newly chopped short hair. The strands brushed my upper neck and under my jaw line, I shook my hair back and dropped into the snow.

The dark green pines watched me as I discerned the muted gray clouds that outlined and over lapped the others. White specs receded from the sky, sometimes the winds spun and the pieces swirled and fell into a new direction. I saw them into twisting patterns and new paths, and the wind made the only sounds.

When the tools were put away I surveyed the other trees to make sure they were alright and turned my back on them to go home. When I returned to my car I reversed and the wheels pulled away. My final view of the lot disappeared, and I returned back to my city.

2019

Roses are red, violets are blue, cake is great, and I would love to eat some with you.

Happy Birthday Angel

-Moogie

I stopped and stared at my desk, the thin sheet of paper stared straight back. I reread the text of my New Years Resolution, I had never written one until this year. I know they aren't very useful, and nearly everybody forgets about it about a week after it was made, but this year I made one.

By mid-February the one list item I wrote did not come true.

Nor was it conceivably fulfilled in March or April.

On May fifteenth I decided to take it back out for reevaluation.

I traced the scribble words with my fingertips, the dark indent of the paper where I had carved it in during January still reflected the pain I put in it:

> 1 Get a Life

It should have been an easy task, but a year has passed since Angel left me and I still feel the same as the day she left.

I folded the piece of paper and placed it back in the drawer attached to my desk. Today, I will find a way to move on.

Some way. Maybe a distraction?

Like what?

I don't know, a friend?

Who would be my friend?

The dead?

No.

A slayer?

And let them kill me when my back is turned?

Would Lilie be my friend?

Yes.

Both sides of my inner monologue agreed synonymously, the thought of getting Lilie back excited me.

I paced around my room. Lilie, how to get Lilie. The Lilie embryos are still in the cryogenic stasis case at my old house. I know for a fact the lab is the safest place in the world to hold my highly illegal embryos, and there is no chance it would have been opened while I was gone, but somebody else is living there. I expect that I can't just waltz back into my house after a decade and climb back into the lab.

I tried to scrounge up the memories on how to create Lilie, I didn't remember much, the journals I barely understood the first time seemed foggy in my brain. Reading all of the books down in the lab could end up being a bad idea, but I need to go through them again. If somebody found out I had them I could go to jail for a very long time, I need to find a way to read them and be able to get rid of them instantly.

Maybe I could digitally copy all of the pages from the journals, and then delete them if they are threatened to be discovered.

How do I scan them? Copy machine? I imagined sneaking into an office at night, only to be discovered and thrown in jail for breaking in and scanning papers.

My imagination failed in being anymore creative or plausible, so I tried humanity's substitute for approachful thinking.

I surfed the internet using different keywords to find how to quickly copy several books in an estimated couple hours I would have the house to myself.

Most results that pop up and occupy the first few pages ended up being discussion forums or irrelevant websites.

A few forums I skimmed suggested manually flipping pages and taking pictures, other suggested the incredibly unoriginal copy machine idea, and other said just download the reading material off the internet.

With all of these ideas being of no use to me I tried new keywords. The internet was blanketed with ad farms, pop up ads, and viruses that my computer's firewall blocked instantly after I pulled up a new window.

I wandered through cyberspace, occasionally getting sidetracked with a video or an interesting article.

On my fourth set of keywords I dodged six pornography websites that involved girls wearing books and stumbled across two similar ideas, the first website was an instruction page that involved bifurcating plywood or cardboard and setting up lights that shined down on the divided pieces to get the highest quality resolution.

The other website suggested a much simpler idea, with instead of a v-shaped holder, the book is flat on a sheet of paper, but the photos don't have the best quality.

I decided, since I'm going to be looking at these documents for possibly the rest of my life on an archive quality disk, I'd want the best quality pictures. So I started on the v-shaped holder.

For the materials I wandered around my garage, picking through the basic power tools I owned and I accumulated the other needed supplies for my new project.

The garage was a mess, most of the stuff was from the previous owners and various shelves had boxes and boxes of junk I never bothered to search through.

I have absolutely no experience with putting things together either, the last piece of construction I had to do was when I was doing a favor for a friend and I had to put together a music stand.

The instructions and materials all came together in organized little bags clearly labeled and clearly divided in a box. I sincerely thought I followed the instructions religiously.

When the stand was finished it was put together backwards and I accidentally scraped up her tile floor. Mechanics are not my forte.

After printing out my website instructions and sufficiently scrutinized the picture until I thought I understood it, I moved on to the first step: make sure all materials are insight.

I reread the step several times and said it aloud to myself before counting each word. Why oh why am I being such a moron? After coming to peace with my idiocy I read my second instruction.

I picked up the boards, they were a little rough and my thumb pricked on a splinter, "Ow!" I flinched and dropped one of the boards and it fell to the ground, too quickly I lunged down to the board and dropped the other.

Both clanked angrily on the tile and made my ears ring. "Grrr," I hissed and stomped on one of the boards, it snapped in half. Regret dropped in my head and I picked back up the unbroken board.

I swept the splinters and the rest of the broken board off to the side with my foot.

I scoured the garage for another board. The plywood shelf from the funny curved bookcase seemed pretty similar to what I needed. I carefully removed the paint cans and pulled the shelf down. Slowly the bookcase leaned forward and fell over. The rest of the shelves fell out and clattered on the floor as I jumped back, startled by the noise.

I picked the shelf back up and stacked the paint cans next to it. I looked at the useless shelf and shook my head, who would build such a stupid shelf?

The book holder took a while to put together the first time. The clamps to keep the glued boards from sliding off one another had some sort of prejudice against me.

I continually tried shoving it against the boards, but the clamps slowly scooted off. If the clamps didn't go on like the instructions said the holder would be crooked, so over and over I shoved the clamps on.

The bottoms of the boards had been shoved so much the glue smeared and I needed to have an all new line of glue applied.

I gave up on the clamps and tried duct tape next, that failed, and then I moved on to becoming a human clamp. I pressed them together with my hands and sat for a while, the glue oozed out the sides and dried on my arms and on to some pieces of my hair. My arm started falling asleep and I decided for another alternate.

I shoved the paint cans from the funny bookcase against the holder, although it looked awkward and I once again punished myself for my fatal moronic mechanical skills it seemed to dry and set in place.

I watched it nearly the entire time, and I peeled the glue flakes off my skin, every piece pulled ended up dragging along some hairs and a little skin. My arms felt raw by the end of the sitting.

I contemplated on whether to paint it when it dried, but my splinter filled fingertips pleaded otherwise.

When the stand was finished and the glue was dry, I tested how well it held by putting a book from my study in the holder. I set up the lights and the tripod to hold the camera and started flipping through the pages.

The pages seemed good quality, but I realized I'm going to be flipping thousands of pages. To try to be faster and more efficient, I started researching possible page flippers.

Back on the internet my first set of keywords were flipping rig, and when I searched, I found myself going through sailboat websites. Apparently flipping rig translates into a flip sail rig. Before moving on to the next set of keywords, I glanced through all the pictures and links one more time in hopes of finding what I wanted.

At the very last line of pictures I noticed a particular plywood boat that looked like a big ugly box. I peeled my eyes off the holographic interface and looked down at my weird shelf, is that a boat?

I switched over to my phone's identification scanner and held it over my shelf and watched the phone try to name it.

The phone beeped positively and a smiley face appeared on the screen before fading into the results. Yep, my incredibly ugly shelf is an incredibly ugly boat. I would have never guessed.

Back to the internet search engine I tried a new set of keywords; if I don't find it in here I might need to consult the dictionary to find more words.

I tried another forum; the conversations always seemed to dwindle into the users calling each other idiots regardless of the topic. At the very bottom somebody with an unreadable username suggested somebody smart should just build a gadget or software to instantly scan a book as you flip through the pages. The comment was posted a year ago.

I pulled out of the search engine interface and went to the gadget and game store that I never bothered to look through.

The worthless uses for these things go on and on. Some gadgets involved launching imaginary rotten fruits at people by tapping into the camera on the phone. My favorite so far is the random word generator; it encouraged people to say words and definitions in public places.

I remembered a while back talking to a bank teller and she answered one of my questions by giving me the definition of asphalt. I didn't understand it until now.

Scrolling by a training gadget on how to play the piano properly with your toes, I stumbled upon a gadget that scanned books and recreated the pages on my phone.

With glue attaching loose strands of hair to my cheek from the plywood holder project I held my phone over a test book and watched the program work like magic. The page appeared with every word clearly defined on my screen, ready to be read with confidence.

Sometimes I just have these anomalous days.

The night came and I left to stake out my old house. My gloved hands touched the aged backyard lawn while I balanced myself to crouch in waiting for the owners to leave. I had hopped the fence in the alley and I hid in the darkest corner of the lot. The house looked different as I scanned the backyard from my hiding place.

All the grass had been replaced with dirty red clumps of gravel, and tan and dirty green weeds sprouted long stems throughout the rough yard. Occasionally, if the invasive fibers grew too thick they crossed and tangled together into bushels. All the trees were pulled, no longer were there colorful citrus to shine in the dusty dawn light. The paint on the house had decayed and faded like the mascara stains on a girl's cheek when she cries.

The finer details of the house were unkempt, windows were dirty, and weeds clutched the outside faucet. The trampoline was rusted to a fragile state, and if a particularly strong gust of wind blew, it might just collapse. The pool's dark green murky sludge held a dead bird floating in the middle. The house seemed to have lost all the warmth and invitation, a feeling that only a decade ago I felt from it. This building was an empty shell; alien to its former self.

A half hour passed and the two people inhabiting the house escaped out the garage and to their jobs. I tried the old key in the door with hopes of not needing to pick the lock, but the key wouldn't fit.

I walked around the side, there was a door leading to the laundry room, which lead into the living room. I remember nobody ever went through that door, I tried the key there. The door clicked unlocked, I guess they don't use it either. I was in.

The laundry room didn't change much except cleaner, and it smelled like chemicals. I glanced around the house a little to make sure nobody else was home before climbing down into the lab.

It looked the same, the strange machines, the work table, the bookshelf, and the embryo case. I cleared a part of the work table and pulled the first book off the bookshelf.

On my phone I turned the gadget on and flipped quickly through the pages, the scanner worked, and on the screen I could see the pages being reconstructed virtually. A full book was copied and saved after a few rounds of fast page flipping, and I moved through the first volume within ten minutes.

I quickly scanned the longer volume set, occasionally stopping to read a paragraph or two that caught my eye or closely examining a picture. This one contained various research notes and descriptions on the virus and its mechanics.

After finishing and replacing the final volume on the top shelf, I ran my hand across the ledge. I found a medium sized leather pouch. I stretched and pushed up on my tip toes to get a better grip on the pouch and my fingers inched it out of the place it was wedged into.

I released the latch and found it held a number of drawings and letters that looked scribbled on with my father's handwriting. Along with the papers there were two palm-sized journals. I couldn't scan the journals very well so I took the pouch with me.

After a couple of snapshots of the strange machinery around the lab I unplugged and picked up the embryo case and headed out.

Halfway home I stopped at a computer store and purchased a back up battery system for the embryo case.

At home on the dining room table I grinned at my case. Everything had run perfectly as planned, with the case plugged in, I opened the brilliant insides to check that the embryos lasted through the trip. My soon to be Lilies in their test tubes aligned perfectly as I knew them years ago.

I picked up the receiver to call the next breeder on my list. How many am I going to have to go through to find the right dog?

It has been a few days since the idea first came to me, I ran through the books again and with the bare minimum information refreshed in my mind I tossed the unopened pouch into a locked drawer. After scouring the local newspapers and the internet, I had procured a long list of breeders to pick and choose which would be the one to carry Lilie. I tried the next breeder.

Yes! This dog was in heat right now, so I invited myself over to go meet the owner, and I was on my way.

I nearly died of anticipation as I spent an hour driving to get there. The house was out in Buckeye, Arizona's rural area; I didn't mind, I would go to the moon and back for Lilie.

I met the breeder at her house; of course, when she saw me the first thing she said was "You're a lot younger than I thought! Are you even old enough to do this?" I looked at the sky; internally kicking myself for forgetting my make-up today and I turned and smiled up at her. "Ready?"

Inside the house it was very tan, tan cabinets, tables, chairs, even the lights seemed brown. Most of her furniture was a Cabana look and her walls were a pasty white. Not my taste, but I can see she put a lot of effort into it.

She showed me around the house and then brought me to the backyard, I noticed three small children staring up at me behind a swing set across the pool. I leaned over to the lady and asked "Do you want them seeing this?" I nodded over to the kids.

"Oh they're fine, they've already seen the real thing and they're used to this artificial stuff." I shrugged and opened the suit case, she went to go tie up the bitch so it wouldn't run when I tried to impregnate it.

I advertised myself as someone who does artificial insemination on Great Danes; it's popular with bull dogs and other animals that have hip problems, and it's a lot cheaper than getting a stud. The wonders of artificial selection are going to bring me my dog.

I'm doing this job because the Lilie embryo needs to be inserted in a dog's womb to grow. I have to get it in somehow, so I hid the embryo with the sperm and I'm going to shoot it all in at the same time.

All I have to worry about is getting the embryo attached to the mother and not rejected.

I pet the bitch and tried to calm her down while the breeder got the choker chain around her neck. Then I made sure it was on right and the dog couldn't move much, although I don't keep scars, bites really hurt. I put on gloves and started the procedure.

First I inserted a tube inside the dog; she flinched and tried to struggle. One of the kids jumped up from their hiding place and tried to hold the dog after she started whining. I mumbled to her, "It's alright, don't worry honey, your almost done." And grabbed the next thing, a syringe without a needle, and put that in the tube.

I pushed the sperm in until all of the white disappeared before I pulled the syringe and the other tube out. There, all done!

When everything was loaded back into the suitcase I released the dog from the choker chain. The three kids surrounded the dog and gave her bits of food and tried to comfort her. The breeder lady paid for my stud fees, which covered the money I spent for buying the dog sperm and I left giving her my cell phone number if anything went wrong. I also paid her back some of the money so I can have first pick of the litter.

I drove home feeling satisfied, I'm going to get Lilie back, and nothing will get in my way.

July poured into August with monsoon season, and in the beginning of fall the breeder contacted me. The gestation period was finally over! New Lilie would only be a car ride away.

With my first clone, after the dogs are born, buyers pick out which one they want and the breeder would tie a ribbon around it. When the dogs are ready to be weaned the buyer comes back to buy the dog. All I need to worry about is getting a ribbon on Lilie before anybody else gets theirs on my dog.

The breeder, Alison, was waiting in the shade on the front porch when I arrived; I hopped out of the car and jogged over to the steps.

Alison's kids were inside playing with the newborn puppies. Scooting them around, picking them up, putting them back down; I worried the newborn puppies would be hurt.

I dropped to my knees next to the kids and started grouping the puppies. They weren't fast enough to escape the baby pool they were trapped in, or be able to move from one side to the other without taking an hour. So they easily stayed in the sections I put them in. It's amazing they start out so helpless, yet become so massive and intimidating.

I looked up at Alison, "I'm the first to pick from the dogs right? These are all of them?" She nodded, "Yep, you have the pick of the litter."

I went back to sifting through the puppies, several were completely black, or completely white, only three out of the fourteen were remotely close to what Lilie would look like.

Maybe she was born missing a few splotches, and her gray patterns weren't there yet. I quickly checked the puppies one more time. It was still only down to these three.

The first had white paws and a white neck like Lilie would, but her stomach and back didn't have any splotches, just one solid color. The second had the wrong head color, white with black spots, and I moved to the last dog. It couldn't possibly have been Lilie because it was a boy.

"Are you sure these are the only dogs?" Alison nodded, "Yep!"

I blushed, the agitation sinking in my stomach. Failure is always there, and now I wasted another embryo. I took a sharp breath to keep from bursting into tears. The little dog in my hand squirmed as I stroked it. I put it down to let it wiggle around blind with the others.

One of the kids looked up at me, watching the change in my expression, I caught her gaze and her eyes darted back to the dog in her hand.

What is she hiding?

I continued to look like I was examining the puppies; my apathy towards them escalated by the millisecond.

Then Alison left to use the bathroom and I pulled money from my wallet, the green paper captured strict attention from the small eyes of the children. "You and I know there is another dog, could you take me to her?" she looked up again, first at my face and then at the money.

The little boy to her right leaned forward and snatched the money while whispering, "Down the hall and the first door on the left." I smiled, and left the baby pool.

The mother dog was sitting inside a brown weaved basket in a white pillow, and a small gray puppy with a green tied ribbon was asleep, fragilely curled up next to her pseudo mother. I dropped to my knees and gasped.

"Lilie?"

"Lilie Ann McClair?" I reached over and picked her up, the dog had the same yin-yang pattern on her neck with small white paws from my memories.

"Lilie!"

There she was, in my hands, alive, real, and tangible. Behind me I heard Alison's steps. "No! Anything except her." I looked up and shook my head, "I can't believe you would lie to me, we had a deal!" Alison shifted her weight, "Well, uhh, you see my friend helped me deliver these dogs and she wanted this one really bad. She already paid more, and I'm losing my house-"

I shook my head, and the small creature wriggled in my hands as I stared up at the breeder from the floor. I wanted to punish her, knock the breeder down and make sure she didn't leave without a few scars.

But then Lilie would never be mine. I changed ideas.

"I'm more than willing to double what she's paying in cash right now." Alison's eyes grew wide, "Uhh, well-" I interrupted her, "Cash, right now, in your hand."

She looked at me; I could see the desperation in it, money is always more valuable than loyalty, especially in this age. "Alright, let me make a call."

I only caught snippets of the conversation over the phone like "Cash right now" and "What about the other one?"

Instead of eavesdropping anymore I turned back to my dog. I cradled Lilie while stroking her soft head with two fingers. It trembled and whined, blind like the others. Her coat had a few splotches, one shaped like a heart and another splotch looked like a tiny diamond.

I never was more sure about who this was now than anybody else on this planet. She was undoubtedly Lilie, my princess, my dog.

I stayed next to her until Alison got off the phone and pulled out the paper work. She tried to not look at me after I paid and signed the papers, ashamed that she was caught.

When the eight weeks passed I returned to Alison's house. It was different, half the furniture was gone, and the rugs, which I thought couldn't look any whiter, looked cleaner than ever. Boxes stacked everywhere; I quietly followed the kid who had let me in to the dogs.

They were all kept at a corner of the backyard that was sealed off by a chain link fence. They seemed over crowded and with only one bowl of dirty water that a pup was sitting in the middle of. Worse, it must have been a hundred degrees outside. I flinched as the dogs barked at me in their horrific pen. What was she thinking?

The kid pulled out Lilie, her massive paws offsetting her not fully grown body, and she was bleeding on her left ear.

I bent down and tried the collar I brought Lilie, she flinched and shied away, trying to break my grasp of her unnaturally thin build.

"What did you do to her?" my mortified voice whispered. The kid shrugged, "She snagged her ear on that." The kid pointed to a broken piece of the fence, "A lot of puppies do that." Alison came outside and noticing me, she exclaimed, "Oh! Moogie! Uhh hello." Her voice edging on fearful.

Lilie whimpered, panting and wagging her tail. With my strength overpowering the puppy, I scooped her up and left as quickly as possible. Lilie is finally rid of her horrible problems, it was all I could think about.

On our way home she vomited on my backseat, I let the fearful dog into the house. The first few steps she soaked in the quiet and dim environment. I watched her as she sat down in the middle of the foyer room. The little puppy stared wonderingly up, first at me, then at the stairs down the hall, to her right into the living room, to her left the kitchen.

I silently sat down next to her, and then I stroked her back. She hiccupped, and then laid down. Her gray muzzle tucked into her paws.

Being on the floor I examined the house from her perspective, it seemed bigger, spacious, even silently frightening. I pushed myself up from the floor and she looked up, questioning my actions.

I smiled, "Do you want to see the house?" I didn't wait for an answer, I just started the tour. "This is the living room. I don't spend much time here anymore, but it is a nice place to entertain guests."

I turned back to look at Lilie, she had followed me, and I continued on. "This is the kitchen, and this is where I will feed you."

I reached over to the unpacked grocery bags on the counter. I removed two bowls and peeled the stickers off. "See?" I showed them to little Lilie. Lilie's brown eyes expectantly looked into them, and then looked up at me.

I nodded, "I'll feed you twice a day." I leaned over to the sink and scrubbed to bowls, I set aside one and filled the other with water. "It will always be in the corner right here. I'll clean and refill it all the time."

I set the bowl on the floor for her and stepped over to it. She prodded her white paws over to the bowl and lapped it up with her dark pink tongue.

I sat down on the kitchen tile next to her, she seemed exhausted.

"Are you okay, Lilie?" She startled and looked at me, I felt her stomach, ridges from her ribs felt like upside down stairs, and thin fur stretched across to protect the bones. I let her return to the water.

Her ear was swelled and infected, I treated it the best I could, and then I took her upstairs to give her a bath. She kept jumping out and going to the tile, I kept catching her and almost inhumanly fast I scrubbed the desert dust off of her.

I wiped her down and she shook, her legs trembled. The surprise and fear from the bath made her want to leave. I dropped down, and clutched her in my lap as I leaned against the bathtub. She whimpered as she tucked her head under my chin and I rocked her back and forth.

"Everything is going to be alright. I love you, and you will love it here. I know it is strange, but I bought lots of toys, and your own bed for you, but if you don't want to sleep in your bed you can take mine." I kissed her bumpy gray head and continued to try to sooth her. "I want to take you to puppy classes to train you to sit and roll over, and we'll have lots of fun. You will see."

Her gargantuan paws pressed against my legs, she was so big already; if she grew anymore she wouldn't be able to fit in my lap.

Two days passed and she didn't change. I showered her with treats, toys, and new water every ten minutes. She barked and wagged her tail only a few times, she mostly looked sick and depressed.

When I remembered Lilie as a young child, she was the opposite, jumpy, happy, and constantly taking and chewing on my stuff. This one acted so docile, she was sluggish except when she was afraid. I called Alison begrudgingly and she just said coolly "Oh, she's just getting used to the new food, nothing to worry about!" and then hung up the phone quickly.

I still continued to watch her every move; she looked so sick. She kept throwing up everything I fed her and refused to do anything except lay on the cool tile next to the water bowl.

On the fifth day I called Alison again, and she brushed it off saying it was the environment and Lilie will get better in two weeks.

My puppy harshly coughed and had diarrhea, she hiccupped every time she grew frightened, and most of the day she slept.

I didn't leave my house for two weeks, and I wasn't apart from her for more than ten minutes. I nearly forgot any life outside my home. Her state declined rapidly, the throwing up, the diarrhea turning bloody, her lethargy and apathy for food, I felt destroyed on the inside.

My stress and fear grew. Every time she fell asleep I would panic that she would not wake. Sometimes my fear grew irrational enough I would jolt her to consciousness and keep her from returning to sleep.

Lilie's wellbeing slipped away and I and my erratic emotions couldn't control it. I dialed Alison one more time, "Hello?" "Hi, this is Moogie again; my dog still isn't feeling well. How are-" Alison interrupted me, "It's probably Giardia, a parasite that causes Diarrhea and throwing up. Nothing to worry about, it's just something the dog has to fight off."

She hung up the phone right afterwards and I went back to watching her every move. When I would pet the scruff of her neck it stayed bunched up, and her eyes were sunken in. She got to the point of not even being able to stand up and walk around. Even with what the breeder says, I have to take her to the vet; she's losing to the parasite.

I carried my dog to the car and then to the vet. A few people stared at me carrying the abnormally large dog so easily, Lilie threw up all over the floor and the vet ran some tests on the vomit. She also took Lilie into another room while I had to stay out in the waiting area.

The place made me uneasy; I hated labs and offices like these. But that didn't matter now; I grabbed a magazine and tried not to think about it. Even mindless celebrity gossip didn't occupy me; I tried focusing hard on the newspaper.

The doctor that took Lilie came back out, "She has a disease called Parvo." I looked up into her eyes, "What's going to happen to her?" The doctor sighed, "I hooked her up on an IV and some antibiotics, but all we can do now is to wait and see, Parvo isn't something to be cured with one medication."

At home I didn't do anything; I couldn't sleep. At one point I glanced at myself in the mirror, dark circles ran under my eyes, my hair and make-up looked dire, and I hadn't changed clothes in days. It almost looked as I had lived on the streets again.

I showered and cleaned up a little, fixing my shoulder length hair, it needs to be cut again.

The sight of her little puppy tail not wagging or lifeless eyes kept flashing through my mind.

The house was so engulfing. Too big for me, much too empty. I wandered the hall upstairs; I passed by my room, by the study, Angel's untouched door, my hand using the wall for a support. I came to the end, to the door with the plaque that said playroom.

I turned the stiff knob, returning into the rooms with the faded walls. The furniture was gone; each piece separated and auctioned off years before. I went to the corner by the window and sat down with my knees to my chest.

I closed my eyes and leaned against the wall. The preserved air in this sealed corner of my home tasted in my mouth.

Nearly five hours later I received the call from the veterinarian's office, when I arrived the receptionist seemed lively and bright. "How may I help you?" I checked in and sat in the waiting room for the doctor. I calmed down and tried to clear my mind.

The doctor leaned out of her office and read off her clip board. "Tracy Herald?" The doctor smiled at me and asked me to come into her office. I smiled back and followed her.

She offered me a seat and pulled out my file. "Your dog is the Great Dane, Lilie, am I correct?" I nodded "What's the verdict, Doc?"

She smiled at me again, except it wasn't warm or comforting, "She didn't make it through the night. I'm sorry; it was too late to save her."

18
Letters

My grieving brought me to seek an answer to her death. I had called Alison to tell her what happened to the dog, and one of the kids had picked up the phone.

"Hello?"

In a dead, soft tone I spoke into the receiver. "It's Moogie; may I speak to your mother?" The kid paused for a moment, and then answered, "No, she's got important stuff to do." I sighed, "Alright, tell your Mom that my dog has died of Parvo-" The kid interrupted me "Not another one!" my voice stopped.

"What do you mean another one?"

The kid seem distracted when she said, "Well, all the other puppies died except for one, which went to another lady like you." She paused, sudden fear in her voice. "But don't tell my Mom I said it! Blame it on my brother; he opens his big fat mouth all the time!" The kid hung up.

My joints locked with the phone to my ear, all of the puppies are dead?

I brought the phone down and stared at the dial pad. She knew and she let her die. I quickly dialed Alison's cell phone next. "Who is this?"

I stayed silent a moment, cold blood freezing my body. "Hello?" Her voice trembling slightly.

I took breath, "My dog is dead. She was killed by Parvo, she contracted it because of your poor handling."

She knew who it was on the other line, her voice hastened. "I-I don't know what your talking about."

Her defensive voice raised, "It wasn't my fault, and no refund, I'm sorry you can't take care of your own dog. The contract says after two weeks the dog's heath care is not my problem."

I laughed humorlessly, "You killed my dog over money? You knew what was wrong and tried to weasel your way out of the consequences?" My tone stayed at a dangerously calm line. The next moment I heard a click. She had hung up.

I gripped the phone and raised my arm to throw it across the room. I stopped, turned and picked up my keys and my Flashsword, the phone slipping out of my hand.

Her selfishness killed a piece of me, and the only way to exact the favor is to scar her. My car sped down the freeway as I decided which of her children will die in front of her. She deserves to die, she has innocent blood on her hands.

My small fingers gripped the steering wheel, the car's voice beeped, "Moogie, I am afraid you are passing the speed limit by twenty miles per hour. It is advisable to slow down for you and the safety of others."

"No!" I barked at the computer. It did not answer. I leaned forward and noticed the compact car on my right. Three girls were in the backseat laughing. I let off the accelerator.

"I know, I know." I mumbled to the computer. The needle ticked back down, my grip loosened.

I looked down at the Flashsword, my mind slipping back into numb mourning.

Hurting her won't make Lilie come back.

This is not going to be a precedent I will set today. Just because she harmed me doesn't mean I should end her life, I will not murder. I am not who I hunt.

I set the course to return home, the gripping guilt vacuuming me into sorrow.

It is time to start letting go.

2020

Roses are red, violets are blue, it's your birthday today, so happy birthday renewed.

-Moogie

July 20, 2020

My car endured the slow traffic on the freeway from the airport. It seemed like the entire Phoenix population had decided to take the same freeway section as me, I didn't mind. I stretched and yawned, I'm returning home from a huge hunt in New Jersey, and the plane ride from the east coast was long.

I haven't come across any jobs in Arizona for nearly a year, and the rest of the country has plenty of slayers everywhere. All over it seems like there is not much to hunt anymore.

I pulled into my garage and went into my long waiting home; I closed my eyes and listened to the silence. Being with slayers is like hanging out with pigs, they are earsplitting, vulgar, smelly, and incapable of using anything that resembles an eating utensil or a napkin. All the traveling I've been doing made me appreciate the home I love so much.

The house's familiar feel refreshed my memories, the drafty feeling of the living room, the overall unusual stillness, always cooler and somber.

I carried in my travel bags to my cinnamon smelling room and started unpacking; everything needs to have New Jersey thoroughly bleached out before I can use it again.

When the travel bag emptied I zipped it up and carried it to the top shelf of my closet and jammed it back in its place. I stood back and examined my walk-in closet, everything was so tidy and familiar, I hated traveling to the other states. Nothing came even slightly close to Arizona. Everything had to be humid and muggy or the skies had to be overcast and rainy. My stomach always turns when breathing their air.

I looked back at the suitcase. Nobody needs me anymore; this had been the first successful hunt of any sort all year, and we had a surplus of slayers with little room.

The times are changing; hunting isn't as it used to be. It seemed all anybody could think about was the dying profession. Slayers chattered and worried about income the entire time, how the work has been gone for months. I agreed with them. Every night I ventured in hopes of finding just one kill, and I always ended empty handed.

It was odd, watching the people I've worked with in such dispute. Their entire, multigenerational livelihood is coming to an end.

I left the closet and sat down at my vanity; from my drawer I removed long scissors, careful, I evened the edges of my hair. It had gotten so long, passed my shoulders, it offset the sharp makeup I was wearing.

My odd appearance set my jaw. What kind of people are they?

I put the scissors down as it was trembling in my hand, my hair was short enough now.

They are parasites, when the host dies they die. I saw none of them rejoicing, celebrating humanity cleansed of a horrible race of creatures. Income, is that what they worried for? Is that all they cared about?

I shook my hair and combed it, my appearance had returned to a dark and satisfactory glare.

They shouldn't even be considered humans, they have just as much apathy for human kind than the ones they hunt. They kill and take. I shook my head. I never chose this life; I was pulled into it by Jonathan.

My memories of confused and deprived childhood resurfaced. I had hatred, it was unlike any other. I had a noble cause, I remembered the original retribution I dealt.

I didn't hunt because slaying was in my heritage; no it was that my family died in vain.

I never dreamed I would grow up like this.

My eyes trailed down to the skulls, the old red candles fused onto the top of the craniums. I smiled at them, calming, and picked one up. The yellowed bones felt heavy in my hands.

These skulls and their long gone brains cause me no more grief. I picked up the other skull and carried them to the study. In the top drawer I found my letter opener and carefully started picking the wax off the skulls.

I was conscious of it, it hadn't been so natural then. I had compressed state of mind, I've lived such an eccentric, masochistic life...

The globs fell little by little. When they were cleaned off, the candles completely removed, I set them aside.

I held the letter opener in my hand and stared at it. My thoughts tumbled over and over slowing on my judgments of the slayers. A rush of regret and realization folded in my mind, I shook my head, no, but what have I become?

I'm a robotic killer, just like them, this pretty house and my expensive furniture is paid with blood. I don't want vengeance anymore, I want money.

I dropped the letter opener from my hand. It sharply clattered on the wood desk pinging and piercing the silence. When did this fall into daily tedium instead of vengeful justice?

I scrutinized my memories, why didn't I stop? A blush warmed my cheeks, I am just as stupid and prejudice. I'm a killer. I'm an awful killer. I take and, I murder!

I stood up and paced the down the hall. I'm so stupid, I'm so ignorant, this is not who I am going to be when I die! Today I will change. I lifted a trunk from under my bed and started putting my weapons away.

It is time to move on. Finally put these memories behind me, I've spent so much time here. Justice was dealt a very long time ago. Murder, death, this is not my livelihood; this is not the person I will be when I die. I will never call myself a slayer again, I will not slay.

The weaponry around my house started to fill the trunk, guns, knives, everything except my Flashsword, and the Tanto. Those are special, they don't deserve to live in a trunk to be forgotten.

I closed the case, and a feeling of obligation left me. For a moment I could feel myself in the future.

I returned to the study, optimistically energized.

I could finish school; grow up my mind where my body will always fail me. I turned and opened up one of my locked desk drawers, pulling out the very top folder. Inside were admission forms and brochures for different colleges and veterinary schools, all I need to do is fill them out.

Being a veterinarian was always a dream of mine, and it was shelved the day my family died. Under that folder I pulled a binder of sheet music, pages and pages of dots I never came to understand.

I could be a serious violinist too, or maybe a music teacher. Under that folder I brought out the final item, the leather pouch from the lab.

Maybe I could learn to understand what I am.

I flinched as my phone started ringing in my pocket. In a slightly irritated voice I answered to the unknown number. On the other end a tired and disheartened voice sounded into short, quiet bits of speech, "Moogie? Moogie is that you?" I blinked at the familiar voice. "Angel?" Angel continued, "Moogie, I'm, um, I'm in jail and I need you to come get me."

I stiffened, and asked seriously, "What is the address?" Her voice rose slightly, "Umm, 464 North Rexford Drive." I switched Angel over to speaker phone and entered the address into my GPS gadget. "Are you sure that's the right address? Because it seems that you gave me an address in Beverly Hills." Angel quieted into almost a whisper, "Um, yeah, it is." "Beverly Hills? Are you serious?" I exclaimed. "Please Moogie, it's only a few hours away. Please, nobody else will."

I set my jaw, looking back at my study, and then I reached over and picked up my car keys. "Fine." And I hung up.

By afternoon I was well into the California city, the sun held a fake-feeling light that bounced off the sidewalk a certain way making everything look almost opposite of my real desert. The tan, shallow-looking people laughed and passed by my tinted window.

I sat through traffic, witnessed homeless people eat out of trash cans, maneuvered through crazy drivers that would randomly cut me off and almost swerved into a pole when some people stepped out in front of me without looking.

When I reached the parking lot to the jail the air was surprisingly cool, with fatigue and irritation I marched into the crummy building.

The cheap tiles and occasionally flickering lights gave the uncomfortable room an angry atmosphere that made all of the dirt-bag looking people seem just as tired and rigid as me. I stepped to the receptionist and started the paper work to get Angel out. After the forms and other legal work had been taken care of a guard disappeared into another room with my signed forms and reappeared with a tall, tired red-head dressed no better than the people around me. She protectively gripped an envelope the guard handed to her; I noticed the outline of a purse inside. Her lips pressed into a thin frown and I turned to the receptionist. "Is that it?" The bored woman behind the glass clicked and unclicked her pen repetitively. "Next?"

I turned and she wordlessly followed me as I stepped out the door. In the parking lot I looked up at her, "How are you?" I asked, "Oh, I'm fine, everything is great here, have you seen the sites and the beach yet? California is so much prettier than Arizona, and it has the beach, and it never gets to unbearable temperatures." I nodded but internally disagreed. "How about you?" I shrugged, and answered her. "Never been better."

We dropped to a silence again, but by then we had reached my car, "So, what are you doing all the way out here?" Angel dropped into the seat next to me. "Oh, I'm getting an agent soon and I'm going to try the whole modeling and acting career thing. A bunch of my friends do it too and they sometimes take me to auditions with them, they said I could definitely make it with a little more time. "

"Ah, I remember when you told me about wanting to be an actress; it feels like that happened a million years ago. Anyway, where's your car?" Angel shook her head. "Um, I loaned it to one of my friends for a road trip and they um, accidentally totaled it. But they said they were going to give me a new one when they could afford it. And it only happened about a year ago, so..." Angel's voice dwindled and then quieted.

We were silent for a few moments; Angel picked at her nails and fidgeted uncomfortably. My hand held the key in the ignition. "Well, where is your apartment?" She shook her head, "The landlord was being a complete jerk, he said just because I was a few months late with the rent, even after I told him I would get him the money like almost the next day, that he had locked the doors and threw all of my stuff away. I haven't been able to get in ever since."

"Where do you want me to drop you off then? Isn't there somebody's house you stay at?" Angel closed her eyes, "Um, well, um, I sort of got kicked out last night from Carol's couch. It was completely unfair, I mean I told her I liked her ex-boyfriend and she didn't even really like him in the first place." Angel seemed to be talking to herself more than me now, "It's complicated." She concluded.

I gripped the steering wheel impatiently. "Alright, what do you want me to do?" Angel blushed and looked down, pulling on her tight dress, her cheap old make-up caked unflatteringly on her face. "I-I don't, know, um." She stopped herself and closed her eyes, "Can we just go home?"

I leaned back and stared out the window, "Yeah, we can do that. Let's drop by Carol's house and pick up your-" "No, Moogie. There is nothing left, it's gone, I just want to go home."

I stiffened at her tone, was she going to cry? I twisted my wrist and the car started to life, it greeted me and through the recognition software it greeted Angel by name. I pulled out and drove through the lanes to reach the one that led back to Phoenix.

We hardly talked at first, but if I asked the right questions she would give me quiet answers. California had not been nice at all. At one point of time she dug through her envelope, the flimsy purse inside had some make-up, enough money for about one bus ride and a few crumpled sheets of torn newspaper. When she placed them on the dashboard to look deeper in her purse for something I noticed the borders of the newspaper had little ink roses and familiar text. "Roses are red, violets are blue..."

We were well into the night and I drove on my familiar freeways with the windows down. The air was warm and familiar again. At home

Angel picked herself up and out of the car, and we entered my dark house. Angel immediately steered through her familiar surroundings and disappeared into her room with a pack of blood fresh out of the refrigerator.

I returned to my study and picked up my folders, the sheet music and the applications for veterinary school went back into the desk.

With the papers and two journals in the leather pouch, I tossed it up on my bed. After a long shower my body moaned and croaked to go to sleep.

Exhausted, I slid into my warm, thick sheets and picked up the first small journal. I flipped to the first page and sighed, the page was like reading a foreign language, I understood the small words, but the big ones were lost on me.

It doesn't look like I am going to do better this time around reading these journals than when I was thirteen. I shut the book and tossed it to the side, after digging through the pouch I picked up and opened the next one. And with one cursory glance I shut it aggravated, if I want to start understanding this I'll need to make a list of terms I need to look up.

In a final attempt to understand the confusing books, I scanned the pages with my phone identifier. The results were "object unknown".

Drowsiness pleaded for me to go to sleep, and I quickly glanced through the rest of the pouch, it has some papers with scientific drawings and not much else.

Wedged between the drawings I noticed a flash of color. I caught the corner and pulled into the light.

It was an old Polaroid picture, inside the faded yellowish frame the picture of a lady looked down, captivated by a small baby in her arms.

I turned it over to the back, and in elegant handwriting a small note was written.

David,

Our baby was born last night, the doctors informed me there were some complications in the birth and little Melanie will be the only child I shall ever be able to give life to. Your lack of honour to rise and stand up to your responsibilities is truly abominable. I want absolutely nothing to do with you or your appalling principles. You are a disgrace.

-Fiona Lela
July 2, 2002

I gawked at the name it was written to. How could this exist? Hurt welled as my vision blurred, David was my father's name.

I shoved the letter into the pouch and with all my might I chucked the heavy thing into the corner of the room. Feet grounded to the floor as my vision turned upright, my chest heaved, Pain had etched and carved the daggers now shoved in my heart. I found myself sprinting down the stairs.

I tripped, and caught myself on the rail. A liar, a hypocrite!

I opened my mouth to scream, silence remained in the house, waiting vindictively for me collapse and lose my sanity.

I would have never guessed my father, of all people would live such a double life. He is the reason I exist as I am, he taught me the very morals I cling to.

What was he? An oath breaker? What about loyalty? What of all the lessons? He was the first to put lives and fates of others in my hands, he was the one to teach me to chose the right way, not the least painful way.

I slammed my fist on the cold rail, it made me shiver, and it reminded me of the coldness of immortality, the curse he gave me.

I didn't cry, or scream, or let it go. I could feel it, a glob of confusion something else, I choked on it, for I knew it was something deep within me. It was something deeper than the memories and regret, of beatings I've repressed, of hate I've concealed. I let go of the rail and backed up, I looked up at the ceiling and closed my eyes.

I waited, my fingers still clenched, my jaw clasped tight. I couldn't fall to the ground, I wouldn't.

My father, me, what am I? My chin jerked down and left. Myself. My strained and religious morality.

I turned back to my room, I rolled my shoulders, and tiredness returned to the back of my mind. I bent down and picked up the pouch when I reached my room again.

The pouch's contents dumped onto my bed, and I took the crumpled letter. I unfolded the creases. I didn't know what to do with it.

Then I glanced up at the other papers spilled on my bed. All with the same paper.

Several envelopes addressed to a post office box from an address in London, England that I didn't recognize. And I could see half hidden pictures, more like the Polaroid wedged between complicated scientific drawings.

I laid them out on my bed and ordered the envelopes by date. The first envelope was dated nearly a year after the picture, I opened it up to find a letter in the same cursive.

Dear David,

I want to thank you for coming to meet little Melanie, she seems to genuinely like you. At first I didn't know what to feel after I saw you again, but I know now. I'm writing to assure you that I will not burden your family with the knowledge of my existence, and when Melanie is old enough she will understand this too. My dearest, I love you.

-Fiona Lela

A picture dated a while later after the first letter showed a smiling girl, her arms and body looked scrawny and fragile. She was posed to show off a little red dress with yellow polka dots and yellow puffy sleeves. They contrasted with her beautiful golden curls and mousy greenish-blue eyes. I recognized the dress, when I was about her age I had one exactly like it, and I never gave it away. I turned it over to the backside and read.

Melanie will not stop wearing the dress you sent her; she loves to make-believe it is the height of London fashion.

The next latest date was on another picture, nearly a year had passed. The picture was of my father holding the hand of the little girl, and the girl held half eaten candy and a grin broadly across her small, but more developed face. Behind them, Melanie's mother, and all around the background rides and booths themed in a carnival air. My father looked down on Melanie with a proud and satisfied expression. The only writing on the back said "Our day at the carnival."

Letter after letter I pieced together Melanie and my father's mistress's life.

Dearest David,

Tonight has been lonely, like every night, it is difficult to raise a little girl alone. I seemed to have forgotten why I'm writing this letter. I find when Melanie asks how long it will be until she can see her father again my replies will always disappoint her. But I know those special times you come on business trips to see us that I will not have to feel like I do right now, and believing that makes everything else tolerable.

With all the love I can conjure for you,
Fiona Lela

With that letter, another picture was dated the same day. It was Melanie, no more than four years old, wearing a faded blue sundress; she had her back to the camera and was sitting alone on a rocky beach, the waves crawled close to her feet and she looked passed them, slumped over, her body expression thoughtful but melancholy. I knew that expression. I knew the face she made even though I couldn't see it. My father sometimes had it, and I used to never understand why.

Nothing had been written on the back except the address. "Leysdown-on-sea, Kent, UK."

Several letters dated after those were from Melanie, she had drawn pictures and written small notes.

Dear Daddy,

I can not wate tosee you agan! Wen you com out I want to go to the ~~carvile~~ carnival with you again. And I want to get ice screams and fish and chips and play dolls after tea. I love you!

Form,
Melanie

Dear David,

Melanie positively adores the kitten you gave her. She has given him the name of Mr. Momo because of they way he meows, and they are the greatest of companions. We bought him a collar with a bell that she had chosen and he sleeps on the foot of her bed every night.

With love,
Fiona Lela

Several pictures after that included Melanie hugging and holding the cat, playing with him, and the last picture showed the cat curled into a crescent moon shape at the foot of her bed while she slept.

Dear David,

Melanie has returned from school crying again. The cruel children have been hazing her about being born an accident, and that even her father can't stand being around her. She doesn't know how to explain herself, and today she didn't want to go to the final days of school. I understand what I'm asking for is extremely difficult, but it would mean everything to her if you could arrange a business trip to come out. Just for the beginning of the third year of school or what you Americans call second grade, and take her to school with me similar to all of the other parents. This certainly will stop the rumors from the parents and the hazing of the children. And she can finally be happy in primary school.

Sincerely,
Fiona Lela

No letter had been dated after that, and only one picture remained. Melanie, Melanie's mother, and my father stood outside smiling and waving in front of a school. Sets of parents with children passed everywhere in busy crowds, not one child had only a single parent, and glowing little Melanie fit right in with them.

I didn't realize how long I had been studying the letters until the early dawn light cut through the small holes and cracks in the curtain. When I saw the light bouncing off the crisp letters and old photographs my body reminded me of how tired I was, so I gathered the writings together and scanned them into my phone before clearing my bed. Sleep snuck up and pulled me down until two past the afternoon.

"Angel! Angel!" I called out of my room as I started packing my clothes into a large suitcase. Angel appeared at my door wearing fresh clothes with a revived smile and touch of make-up on her face. "What?"

I stood up straight and excitedly half yelled, "We are taking a vacation to London!" Angel's eyes expanded, "You mean London as in London England?" I nodded, "Pack your bags, we are leaving, today!"

19
Names

Angel didn't stop talking about the fun we were going to have in England; she knew all of the fashion, and which stores we had to shop at first. She couldn't have been more energetically compliant with my adventure. "Do you have your passport?" I said as we pushed our heavy suitcases into the car. "Passport? Um, yes! No, I think I left it at my mom's house when I moved out."

I pulled out of my driveway, and the car's voice greeted me. I gulped, "You left the passport at your mother's house?" Angel nodded, ever since I can remember Angel has loathed her alcoholic and divorced parents. When Angel tried moving out to live at my house permanently her mother had a horrible fight and screeched at Angel to stay or never show her face again.

I pulled up in front of the low middle class home and kept the car in idle, "Do you have any idea where it is?" Angel nodded "It is under my bed." She took my hand, "We have to break in, I don't want my mom to know I'm here." I pulled away from the front of her house and turned the corner. "Are you sure she won't let you just go in and get it?" Angel shook her head, "No, absolutely not, she will call the police." I shrugged "Alright." We got out and cut through the alley to the backyard.

We darted across the small, shabby backyard where the landscape was hard dirt and browning weeds, as if we were back on a job, we snuck up to the one story house and Angel jimmied the window leading into her room. She gently slid the glass to the side and stepped in.

The room couldn't have been a filthier pigsty, dirty clothes everywhere, stains and old wrappers scattered here and there, the closet in shambles.

I watched Angel step down off her bed; she dropped to the musty carpet and reached under the messy bed. I kept watch, first scanning the backyard, then looking back to check on Angel in her room.

Then, in the corner of my eye I noticed someone stepping into the door way to her room. I hissed a warning to Angel.

Who stood before the room was not Angel's mother, but a young, chubby little scarlet haired girl. She watched Angel timidly as Angel jumped up and went straight to the window. The little girl waddled to the middle of the room where Angel had been milliseconds before. Angel, halfway out stopped and looked back.

"Oh." I heard Angel whisper.

She reversed into the room and dropped to one knee, leveling herself to the girl's eyes, "Don't tell anybody I was here, okay?" The little girl nodded, her curls bounced and reflected the afternoon light as Angel's hair did.

Angel stood up, "Do you want to help me?" The girl nodded harder, and Angel pointed to the bed, "My passport, a little book under there, is stuck and I can't reach to the back to get it. I really, really need it. Do you think you can get it?" She turned and dropped down to her knees before crawling under the bed. The girl backed out now covered in dust and waddled to Angel, clutching the passport. "Thank you." Angel whispered as the girl placed it in her hands. "Now stay quiet about this and don't tell anybody." The little girl nodded again, and spread her arms wide; Angel took a deep breath, "Alright." And Angel swooped the girl into a hug for a few moments and let her go.

Angel turned to leave and the girl opened her arms again, Angel looked back and sighed, "Okay, another one." And hugged her again.

Angel pulled herself through the window for the last time and I shut it behind her. While we hopped the fence and jogged back to my car I asked "Who was that?" "My little sister," She held up the passport, "We got it! We are going to England!" she sang.

Angel had never mentioned a sister. I opened my mouth to ask more, but Angel flipped the car radio on and started singing, changing the lyrics to "We are going to England!"

The plane ride was extensively boring and loud, I couldn't even hear myself think. We watched a few movies but the audio was so horrible I had no idea what was going on, though the story line just looked like a bunch of people on a quest to do as much self damage as possible. It seemed similar to what usual a cable television is, violent reality TV. Angel absorbed herself completely into the games on her phone, and we landed the next day.

Angel's enthusiasm and energy after all that flying could power the sun for days. I have no idea where she gets it. For the rest of the day she yanked me around touring the city, getting a hotel, and exchanging most of the U.S. money to pounds.

The next few days Angel and I did a Double Decker bus tour, and we saw the city and its wonders. I didn't realize London was so old! People drove on the wrong side of the road, there weren't as many sky scrapers as I expected, and roundabouts were everywhere, confusing me beyond all else. We goofed around on the subway system called "The Underground", getting lost, but it worked out because we got to eat fish and chips from a vendor.

We even spent a few hours at Stonehenge with a group of German tourists that kept giving us strange looks when we laughed too loud. And at the end of the days the only thing on my mind was the conversations I'm going to have with Melanie. What will I say? Will she be as I imagined her? Will she look like me? Will they like me?

The morning of the fourth day of procrastinating, as I call it, I finally decided to visit and introduce myself to my sister.

Angel was ready for more play out on the town and decided to take off when I told her I wanted to run some errands. I didn't quite know how to tell her about Melanie, but I don't have to worry about it right now.

The place they lived at wasn't far from my hotel. Before leaving I took my time looking at myself in the mirror. I wanted to show my newly discovered family who I really am. I left my million pounds of make-up off, and dressed like I would with my own tastes, comfortably casual, of course, I now resembled a child. I bit my lip, staying a few more seconds in front of the mirror and then tentatively started to the door.

I grabbed an umbrella while leaving the hotel because outside it was pouring rain, just like when we got here. I flagged down a cab and told the driver to go to 13 Miller's Court, on the back end of 26 Dorset Street. And away we went.

On the ride there the cabbie talked to me. "What's a little American girl doing all the way out here alone?"

"I'm visiting extended family." I said. "You aren't afraid of strangers? Well, you're very grown up to do this all by yourself." And then he launched into a story about when he was a child he was too afraid to go out with his friends to rock concerts because he didn't want to embarrass himself in front of strangers. I smiled sweetly and nodded, there was not much else to do.

I used to act so grown up when I was twelve, I just didn't understand how fragile childhood was. It sometimes makes me feel even better when I can drastically change the reaction from people with simple wardrobe tweaks, I can pretend to be a kid, but I can only pretend.

When the cab reached Melanie's house I paid and thanked him before turning my focus to Melanie's home. Rain poured so heavily I had trouble seeing the door before I was five feet from it. I buzzed the doorbell and an old brunette woman with graying strands gently opened the door. From her medium stature she looked down her pointed nose at me. My smile glowed brilliantly, I shook her hand. "Hi!"

She greeted me with a light English accent, stunned at my forwardness. "Hello little girl, how can I help you?"

I was already soaked and my clothes were stuck to my skin. "Ms. Lela? My name is Moogie, you don't know me but you knew my father, David McClair."

Her eyebrows knitted together, "Uh, excuse me?"

The lady's face drooped into a solemn expression, "No, I'm afraid." Then the lady stepped aside to invite me in. "It chilling out here, would you like to come in and sit down for coffee or tea?"

I stiffened, embarrassed and my smile dropped in a fixation. I stepped inside the warm and dry house, immediately feeling guilty for dripping water all over the carpet. She showed me to the sitting room and then disappeared to fetch the tea. I took a seat in the middle of the subdued blue room, the furniture matched with the light wooden frames. I politely waited, watching the rain drizzle outside the clear window pane. She arrived with a silver tea set, and a tray of cookies. I checked my frozen smile stayed and stopped myself when I realized I was swinging my legs.

"Do you like sugar or milk?" she asked as she poured the tea for me. I passed on both and she sat down after making herself a cup. She stirred, and I watched the steam curl and expand across the air.

"Moogie is a pretty name, I'm not quiet sure I've heard it before." I shrugged, usually when people comment on my name I shrug into a hard glare and tell them to deal with it; I sometimes forget it does sound strange to most people. "Is it the name your parents gave you?" She asked politely, I smiled, most people say instead, "Do your parents not love you or something? What kind of name is that?"

"It isn't my real name," I said quietly, "it is my favorite though."

She smiled, "I see, names don't always fit, my mother chose the name Brandy for me, but as time passed it became unpopular, and now I go by Mrs. B, and I'm more content than ever being called Brandy."

Our conversation silenced into discontentment though, and the lady's eyes didn't meet mine when she spoke again. "The previous owners of the house, your friend Ms. Lela, passed away a few years ago from a car crash. I purchased this flat from an estate sale. I'm sorry you weren't informed sooner. This tragic business should not come from a stranger." I digested her words, staring into my own teacup. "What?" I peeped, my voice so slight and thin.

She didn't look up. Afraid to see the despair on my face.

Mrs. B started to talk again, and I only heard muffled sounds in the back of my mind.

It is too late. I missed them by years.

I turned away and stared out the window. The light choked from my fixated smile, my eyes bore into the rain. And then a single unquestioned thought slipped in. How many times did Melanie stare out the window?

My head tilted down a fragment, such a poignant, immovable creature I had become.

They lived here, walked and talked in these rooms, cried and lived. More questions ascended and brushed my unquenchable mentality dam. Did Melanie have any friends? Did she just sit alone in her room all day, reading? Did she ever wonder if there was anything more than the dismal void of a world here?

The room seemed to expand, filling with imperceptible memories of what I had missed. I'll never know who Melanie was or if she would ever like me too.

The tea cup tipped and nearly spilled onto the rug, I didn't notice it until the hot water burned my fingers. I startled bringing the cup back upright, and the old woman silently watched me.

"I think I should go." I abruptly stood up pacing to the door; nearly out I stopped with my hand on the handle. I turned remembering my manners.

I tried to smile again, not remembering when I lost the fixed one; though now it looked half hearted. "Thank you for all of your help. It was nice to meet you Mrs. B." She nodded, "You be a good girl Moogie, don't lose yourself." And then I turned my back to venture into the rain.

20
Nowhere To Be Found

"I'm sorry Angel, I know, but-" Angel held a finger up to silence me. I closed my mouth, the live videochat wavered slightly on the holographics and the lagging made our call choppy. "Look Moogie," Angel's determined voice commanded, "We are not leaving England now, we still have another week and a half until we have to fly home, and we are not going to just waste money. You are not flying back home early. This is a vacation Moogie! Work will still be there when you get back. Nobody misses you."

I gritted my teeth, "Angel-" She crossed her arms and glared at me. My defeatist attitude folded under Angel's words. "Alright."

Angel smiled, "Thank You Moogie!" And looked off screen, trying to turn off the chat, "Stupid-" click. Neither of us has gotten used to the controls of holographic videochat yet, I'll figure it out sometime.

I glanced at the clock, only an hour has passed since I got back to the hotel. I found myself more homesick than ever.

I looked at the clock again, the numbers hadn't changed.

I stood up and dropped all of my wet clothes, meandering through the room hopelessly. Dressed in new unsoaked clothing I ventured away from the room and to the lift. The little box I stood in to get to the lobby didn't play music; the only sounds were the sounds of the machinery that raised and lowered the lift. Nobody else was with me, so I gripped the handrails and leaned against the mirror wall.

The initial shock was nearly worn off, mourning remnants soon evaporated into what fuels my drive.

How apposite, how clever, life to give me another hope, and, with all the grace and courtesy possible, even an offer of tea, exterminate it.

I wanted to blame somebody, I need someone to blame.

The floors ticked down rhythmically, I synced my breathing with it trying to focus on the choppy breath sounds I made.

And then I found myself fighting the yearning to scream, to rip my hair out and punch the mirror wall. It is always me, always my misery. Back flat on my heels I pressed the lift button back to my floor. Down the hall I returned to the hotel room, eleven B.

I slipped the key card into the door, fixing my eyes on the light bulb turning from red to green. I need to say good bye to my unmet family, pay respects to their graves.

With an older, business-looking suit replacing my current clothes I then went into the bathroom. After a meticulous make-up job my features looked professional, and I strapped on some high heels. I grabbed my umbrella again and called a taxi.

The cabbie took me to the county courthouse. I weaved through the crowd of men and women dressed in the same dark grey hues, the rain and the dimness made the world so drained of life.

Entering the official building, I had to file through an old metal detector. In the small bucket I placed my Flashsword, my shoes, and my purse to be scanned. Slowly then after I followed the next person in front of me, their grey business suit as colorless as all others. Security deliberated on my Flashsword as little as everybody else's belongings and I received all of my items back without a second glance. I wish I could have thanked Andy again at that moment, he is so smart.

I glided along the linoleum flooring as I passed into a line. Through several minutes waiting and fidgeting, a clerk became available.

The lady at the desk adjusted her glasses and looked up at me, "'Ello, how may I be of service to you today?" I didn't smile, my facial expression between anguished and somewhat dead, yet my voice stood demanding. "I just found out somebody I'm related to had passed away, I need to access the death certificate to find the location of where they are buried."

The woman's jaw tightened, irritated at my lack of common courtesy, and she reluctantly glanced at her screen, "We don't carry that information on the death certificate." "Oh." was all I could say before I could collect my thoughts into another question. "What about who the body was released to?"

"Yes, we have that information, what is the person's name?" "Fiona Lela." The tapping started on the keyboard, then her fingers paused on the keys, "Do you have proof of your relations with this family member?" I froze, "I-uh, it is back in America. I-I didn't know I needed any."

The clerk eyed me suspiciously, "I'm afraid I can't help you then." My breath caught, proof of identity? I just want to see the graves, or what ever happened to the bodies. They know who set up the funeral, it is on that screen. Isn't her job to help me? Shouldn't she be more useful?

I exhaled, "Please," my tone growing sharper, "I need the information." I enunciated gravely.

She cleared her throat, meeting me directly in the eyes, "No." My hands clasped into fists on top of the desks. "Give me the information." I growled. She straightened at my threatening tenor. "No." she said again. I leaned forward, "Look, give me the fu-" She cut in, "I will not stand bullying. No proof, no help." her tone sounded off, wholly without fear, a wall to slam into me.

My eyes trailed from the clerk to the grey security guards, I could lean over the counter, get the information before the clerk would scream. But security would haul me away, or arrest me; I have no idea where I would go.

I bit my lip and met the clerk's eyes, she smiled smugly as she noticed me sizing her up, and seeing the guards. She was conceited, knowing that she won her invisible battle. And her finger tapped the escape key once.

Fury replaced the fizzing anger which had long surpassed the numb mourning I entered town hall with, who does she think she is? I resisted the violent impulse to attack her, break the barrier of inferiority and authority, across the desk of fiefdom to show her exactly how safe she really is. She had the information!

I straightened up, glaring at her. In a cold, quiet voice I heard her say, "Thank you for coming in, have a nice day." Then she lean to the side and called, "Next!"

There was no shown reluctance to leave. The grey didn't end after I left the building. It seemed to have stifled the life out of the entire city, the cold gravitated me to the dark sidewalk in a way I never felt anywhere else. Nothing was light, and then without hesitation I found myself running back to the hotel. Fighting with all my might not to trudge or slump lower under the soaked world pressing on my back to fall.

I pulled off my depressing suit and sat on the corner of my perfectly made bed, my head falling flaccid into my hands. Who else would know the information?

I hate England, I hate it so much, I won't say it isn't fair, I know too well how the game of fair morphs those who partake in it.

I lifted my head up again, and then fell back on my bed. My soaked underwear and chilled skin hitting the soft, dryer-smelling blanket. What am I going to do?

Who would have seen their bodies? The minister, the grave diggers or cremators, the people working at the morgue to determine cause of death, close relations of the Lelas... My head swam with elaborate, inefficient ideas that wouldn't work in the time I had until my plane ride home. I just want to pay respects; this is supposed to be about letting go, not obsessing about something I couldn't have controlled.

I thrashed around my bed kicking and making the bed creak. No, no, no, no! I stopped and dejectedly laid on my side.

My thoughts returned to trying to be productive, instead of the tantrum I was throwing. The lukewarm air mixed with my breath, evening in taste as I stayed quiet, thinking.

My pondering weaved in and out of the hushed rain, and the sound of my low inner voice dwindled, thinning into a dark and shallow doze.

My eyes snapped awake, startled by hearing the usual silence. The rain had stopped, and I found Angel's comforter arbitrarily thrown over me, the blanket sort of covering my mostly naked body. I pushed myself up on my elbows and scrutinized at the clock digits and then at the window. Groaning I dropped back on the bed, night and morning joined in a time limbo that spanned through the uncertain city, the grey lightened but I couldn't quite recognize if the sun had risen yet or I wasted the entire day sleeping.

I stared at the ceiling blankly to let moments pass by, sometimes if I focus hard enough I lose ten minutes or so. The regret emptied my stomach, and after dawdling in thought I heaved the blanket on me to the other bed where it fell short and jumped into a pace.

"Melanie, Melanie," I mumbled, pacing. Who knows where you are? When you lost life, who noticed? Who cared?

My mind shifted, did anybody care? Why? Or did anyone pay attention because there was something in it for them? I looked to my wallet, who collected your money? There couldn't have been a will, I shook my head.

What would happen? I stopped, maybe it is time to pay the government clerks another visit, figure out the probate benefactors.

I made my way to the closet, the suit in the humidity stayed damp, but I put it on anyway. The sodden fabric made my skin cold but fresher feeling.

I stared in the mirror imagining how to sculpt my latest make-up façade.

I decided to lighten up, appear more youthful, and then I rearranged my expression from dead and serious to a more sympathetic and melancholy. I tilted my chin down and examined my face from new angles; the clerks would have a harder time saying no to a girl who needed help than to someone that demanded help.

Security hadn't remembered my face as I drifted with the indiscernible suits. And I watched my Flashsword dubbed as harmless as an envelope.

I wasn't ten feet from the clerk I had talked to before, now at another desk I spoke to the fragile looking lady in front of me. "Hello, how may I help you?" She asked automatic and with small energy. I forced a quick smile, and said tentatively, "Hi, I-well just discovered one of my family members passed away, I wanted to know if I could find the benefactors of the will or probate. I don't have any other way of finding them and asking about this sort of business." I nervously pulled my earlobe and hunched lower in my posture. The lady tilted her head to the side empathetically, and then she nodded "What is the person's name?" "Fiona Lela."

The lady typed something on her computer, "How are you related to her again? I'm a niece to Ms. Lela." I lied. "Huh," She said as she set intently on the screen. "Nobody is in here, except her next of kin. A minor, and she's on a trust."

That has to be Melanie! "Yeah, that's my cousin." I said, the lady tilted her head agreeing distractedly and tried searching a little bit more, I asked her "Do you think I could get her information? So I can contact her?"

The lady, looking disappointed, and shook her head. "I'm afraid I can't do that, because of how young she is, privacy laws." My mouth fell agape, again? But then I closed it, relief and anticipation filling me again, Melanie is alive, I will find her.

"Is there anyway you can point me in her direction? I have no other way of finding her. There isn't anything you could do?"

Shame reached her face, "I'm sorry miss, it isn't me, it is their rules. And my superiors are always watching. I'm sure you can find her by other means."

I rose and shook the lady's hand, grateful for her help, knowing I wouldn't get much else with sheer persuasion, and I clicked my heels right out the building.

With risen spirits I haled a taxi, and then I traveled back to the hotel room. Distractedly slipping inside the door I accidentally kicked something. Partially under my shoe I discovered black, lacy underwear. Instantly I shot out of the room and shut the door, and then turned to knock. "Hello? Angel? Are you there? Is anybody else in there that I might possibly not want to see without their underwear?" No answer. I shrugged and said, "Alright, I'm coming in; just don't say I didn't warn you."

I opened the door a tiny crack and cautiously stepped in, before entering any further I stooped down to pick up the underwear, into the main room the rest of Angel's clothes were aligned in a trail leading all the way to her messy bed. I sighed and shook my head, then scooped up the rest of her clothes, including her corset and stashed them back into her suitcase. I fixed her sheets and found myself doing other busy work while I contemplated the next place I should go to find Melanie.

My phone beeped on the table and I reached over to pick it up. Ugh, my phone automatically updates itself and constantly sends me emails about Angel's latest activity on her profile online. I've tried sending the stop-emailing-me text they always have at the bottom fine print of the email, but it doesn't work.

Angel loves playing on the internet. Especially so if there is a picture to be taken, she will upload it as fast as possible to all of her friends on her favorite stupid social website.

I shook my mind off of Angel and switched to thinking about Melanie, more than seven million people in London, how am I supposed to find one person? I deleted the update email and went back to straightening out the room.

Wait, I looked at my phone again, if Angel and every single one of her friends have a profile, maybe Melanie does too. Using the hotel computer on the TV and the wireless keyboard in the drawer under the TV, I searched through the night looking for Melanie on various social websites. Everybody in the world seemed to have one except her.

Melanie Li., Melanie M, Melanie N., nothing had her last name, nobody had a profile even close to what she would look like either. She might have changed her last name to match her foster parents or wherever she is. She might not have the same first name either! Where is she?

Hours flew like jet planes, the sun rose but disappeared behind more stormy clouds. My extensive search to go through every Melanie in England by social networking sites remained fruitless.

Angel returned to the hotel room several hours later, though I had lost track of time completely. It didn't help that I couldn't tell time by the sun either, with the sky sobbing its eyes out into the inhabitants of

England. "Hey," I mumbled. "Hey," She mumbled back, I ripped my eyes off the holographic screen to look at her.

Angel tripped inside and ripped the keyboard out of my hands, after tossing it to the side she turned around and flopped on me.

I cringed under the weight and tried to suck back in all of the air I lost, I could smell the stale alcohol emanating from her body, and her shirt was on backwards, her hair was a rat's nest, but she was rosy and smiling. Even as a mess her beauty surpassed any supermodel on her best day.

She kicked off her shoes, "How is your mission going?" she asked. "No luck," I answered, "What about yours?" She looked up, "Huh?" I smiled, "Your quest to find and hang out at as many parties as possible." I tapped the tip of her nose with my finger.

She smiled, "It is going completely awesome!" And she jumped up and launched into a mountainous story about Chinese food, socks, and all of her new friends with funny accents.

Angel stumbled over to the coffee maker and started some coffee. Then I watched her half drag herself into the closet, and then she moved onto the bathroom where she showered and returned with fresh clothes on. Angel filled a paper cup with black coffee and tripped out the door. "Bye, good luck with your mission thingy for whatever."

"Don't go driving if you're too drunk." I said plainly. Angel was already gone; I didn't think she heard me.

I spent a while more on the computer; some of the comments on these profiles are so engrained in texting language that I needed to find a decoder on the internet to decipher all of the confusing short hand.

I abandoned the social websites and started researching foster homes; which I knew nothing about. Soon I found the directions to the local foster home agency and dragged myself out of the way I had been sitting in for the past several hours.

Before heading out I checked myself in the mirror again, I looked just like I was hours ago, except with slightly stale clothing and faded make-up. With my brush I combed down the sections of hair that dried in a clump together from the rain and I wiped my face.

I revamped my outfit into something more comfortable, and my image reflected a little bit more child-like than my last outfit. With a few quick touch ups I didn't look quite like an adult as before, but merely borderline, it would do for now. I grabbed the umbrella on my way out and went down to the hotel lobby. I called another taxi and went to the foster care office.

This cabbie was silent most of the ride, and he addressed me with miss and madam the few times we did talk.

My feet splashed through water when I jogged to the front door. The building didn't look significant, and the lobby was empty. I went to the front desk where a lady sat clicking boredly on her computer. I leaned over the counter and said, "Hello, I'm looking for a kid possibly in your program. She's my cousin and I'm visiting from America." The lady looked up. "I need the person's name and proof you are related to them."

"Melanie Lela, and I have a picture of her family." I said, innocently I took my phone out of my purse. She frowned "No sweetie, I'm afraid that won't do." The hand down at my side twitched, pressing the button on the phone back off. I decided to act more on the kid-like side in my persuasive attempts.

"I haven't actually met her; ever since I was little I wanted to meet her."

My voice cracked slightly, "I used all of my money I've saved to come out to England. I just found out that her mother is dead and I've run all over town looking for her!" I started tearing up. "Any other proof would be back at home. And I'm leaving in a few days. I won't have time to get proof." The lady blushed and stopped clicking on the keyboard. "Please can you help me?"

She kind of rustled about for something, and avoided eye contact with me; I intently watched her trying to conceive the desperation I have. "Please?" I knew her face started into a guilty expression. "My boss would be extremely upset if he heard about this. You didn't receive this information from me." She stood up and said to me quietly, "I can't look it up on the computer; somebody is always watching it nowadays. I'm going to search for your cousin in the written records. Stay here." And she left the room.

I calmed myself down, bittersweet in my triumph; I felt remorse for my self degradation and playing a victim, there is no honour in being a cry baby.

I started wandering around the waiting corner. It was two basic couches and a few chairs spread evenly next to a fake plant and a rack of pamphlets. I stepped over and examined them, they all had new parenting and caring for children advice. I picked one up; the front had a picture of a small child on it. The title read: So You're a New Parent, What Now?

Another pamphlet had a few teenagers sitting around a table laughing, the title of that was Dealing With Teenagers And Their Hormones. I sniggered at the advice as I flipped through, it warned about the dangers of children and their false entitlement views along with the futility of trying to get teenagers to see the way you see. I put the pamphlet back and picked up the next one: Puberty and Boys. Before I could properly read that one the lady came back.

I returned to the desk, and said "I found Melanie's latest records, not long ago she was transferred to a group home under a woman I know." She took out a piece of note paper and scribbled down a first and a last name with an address. "Thank you so much." I smiled excitedly and took the paper.

On the other side of town I impatiently gripped my seat in the cab. Melanie will be there.

The rain lessened, though still pouring a nightly wall of water that greyed and sponged the color out of the city. Occasionally I saw a dark blob or two bundled in rain coats on the sidewalk, but mostly I watched the water stream across my window as I passed the urban blur. I arrived at a brownish-reddish brick building that reflected off of the constantly rippling mirror made in the sidewalk.

I stepped quickly to the building to escape the chilly morning air. As I entered through the wide doors, the hinges creaked; the place looked like what I imagined a boarding school would be. The tiles were a dirty bluish color and matched the dull light blue walls. To the right was a reception desk, and to the left were double doors leading to a larger room with long rows of tables. In front of me was a grand wooden staircase.

The wood from the handles shined on the staircase, polished by many hands and their oils, the corners and door had rounded edges to them. The place had seen many children pass through the system. I went to the reception desk, nobody was there. "Hello? Is anybody here?" I said as I peeked over the desk. The desk had a computer, an office chair, a cell phone, a dog bobble head, and some papers and writing utensils.

I leaned over the counter further to see what was on the computer. But at that moment I heard footsteps descending the stairs, I snapped back and looked up to where they were coming from. A plump, aged lady appeared; she had a plain black dress with a set of clunky pearls set tightly on her neck, and her grey hair was combed in a moderate bun.

She stopped when she saw me, I strode over to her with my piece of paper saying "Hello, I'm looking for somebody, and I was told to come here and talk to-" I looked at the little paper and read the name off. "Mrs. Nadine Cleaver." I looked back up at the lady. She stared down at me with narrow eyes, "I am she, who are you looking for?" "Melanie Lela. She arrived here a few years ago as an orphan," She crossed her arms and looked up in thought.

"Hmm, I don't think I know that name. Have you talked to my receptionist?" I shook my head, "Not there." Mrs. Cleaver looked over my head at the desk. "I guess she's still on her break. Follow me; I'll try to find this Melanie you speak of." We went through the double doors across the large room, then through more double doors, and then took a right. I followed her down a long hallway to the end door.

A plaque with the name Cleaver stamped into brass was mounted on the door. In her office I plopped down on the seat in front of her desk feeling like a child sent to the principle's office.

Mrs. Cleaver typed something into a computer, "What was that name again?" I patiently repeated and spelled the name out for her, "She was released a few months ago on her eighteenth birthday."

I sighed, "Do you know where she went?" "The notes say on her file she left early in the morning, almost unnoticed." Then she said half to herself "I do not remember her name, the only thing in her file was a disturbance about her and a cat." Mrs. Cleaver shook her head, "I don't know why I don't remember her, I used to pride myself on knowing the names of every child that steps into my door. My memory must be fading."

I looked down at my hands, "Are you sure there isn't anything else you can tell me?"

"I'm afraid not. Maybe some of the girls know her, they are on break right now, I suppose you could ask them."

I stood up and shook hands with Mrs. Cleaver, "Thank you very much." She showed me around some of the building and directed me to the girls' sleeping quarters before leaving me alone. Bunk beds after bunk beds lined up throughout the room, most of them were empty, but in one of the rows a few girls sat in a circle talking. They looked early teenagerish and I headed over to talk to them.

When I appeared before them the smallest girl of the four noticed me first. "Oi! Who are you?" The others looked up, "Hello, I'm looking for somebody, a girl older than you, she's blonde-" One of them cut into my description, "Who says we do know her? Why don't you just speak to the registration?" I shut my mouth and started answering that question. "The lady in charge has searched through the records already, she directed me up here to see if any of her friends know where she is." My tone turned tipsy to the impatient side with the rude little girls. "Now, do any of you know a girl named Melanie?" "No." They said in unison.

I took a deep breath, "Are you sure? She's blonde, bluish eyes, has a little cat with a bell on his collar named Mr. Momo-" The girls interrupted me with a gasp, "Mr. Momo!" one of them shouted. I nodded, "Do you know who I'm talking about now?" They all nodded, the girl in the middle spoke up while adjusting her glasses, "Of course we know who Mr. Momo is, he is the most wonderful kitty-cat in the world. We all used to pet him, and feed him with whatever food we could scrounge from dinner, and he would meow in the sweetest li'le way-"

"Yes, but what about the girl?" None of the girls seemed to care about Melanie, and they all launched into chatter about their favorite memories of the cat. After a few pleads I was ready to string them up and torture the information straight out of them, but I halted my anger when they quieted into a smaller chatter and the girl with the glasses started again. "We don't know where Mr. Momo is, one day he just disappeared and didn't return, but if you find him could you tell him we love him? Certainly he misses us."

"Do you remember anybody else leaving that day? Any of the girls?" The smallest girl stared up at the ceiling in thought, "Yea, that real quiet girl left too, Mr. Momo liked her a lot. Nobody knew her name, and she didn't really have any friends." All the girls nodded in agreement, and another girl cut in, "She just sat alone all day long and pet Mr. Momo. He loved to sleep at the foot of her bed."

"Do you know where she might have gone to? Did she have any posters or personal items left behind?" The girls shook their head and the small one answered, "No, her bed over there was spotless, it was nice because usually we have to clean up after they leave and make the bed fit for the next girl."

I leaned my shoulder against the bed post, "If you had just turned eighteen and could leave, where would you go?" The small one shouted "Paris!" Another shouted "South America!" The two in the back shouted in unison, "USA." I looked at them, "Where?" One answered "New York." and the other "Los Angeles." All had different dreams and explanations for why they wanted to go, I exhaled defeated and thanked them for their time.

I hit every step quickly on my way down the stairs, the tiles echoed as I clicked across them. The receptionist, now back in her seat looked up and said "Is there something I can help you-" I interrupted abruptly without looking at her, "No thank you." And I shoved the grand doors into the rain.

The dreadful little droplets pounded into my head and dripped down the back of my neck before I could put up my umbrella. I called a taxi and started on my long ride back to the hotel.

At the hotel room I stared at the blank search engine on the computer with my fingers on home row. The little bar stayed blank. My fingers couldn't type, there was nothing to find, and there are no more leads on Melanie. She's a ghost; I typed in 'Melanie the ghost' to the search bar and pressed enter. Internet porn popped up as the first result and I exited back to a blank search bar. Why can't Melanie be like everybody else? Why must she be different?

But I answered those thoughts the second they entered my brain, she is special, she is like me. Alone and different.

Where would I go? What would I do? Go to college? Try to make a living? I picked up the umbrella again and left the hotel. Instead of flagging down a cab I turned and walked down the sidewalk. My feet soaked stiff and cold in seconds through the puddles; I could feel my hair tangling from the rain which had hit it before I could get my umbrella up.

I didn't know where to go; I searched among the faces that surrounded me, turning corners and glancing into shops. None were Melanie, I saw children, adults, old people, and everything in between, girls that laughed and walked in sync with each other, holding hands. Old men that gambled and grunted at each other while they sat on steps. Delivery boys that sped by on bikes, nobody resembled Melanie. I went through a park where people took shelter under trees, or children played in the rain. The dismal rain continued to pour, who could live here? There is no life, no sharp points, no border to tell right from real. I wanted to scream. "Melanie? Melanie?" I whispered alone.

My phone buzzed, another update, after deleting the message I switched to my photo album. One by one I examined the photos of Melanie. I stopped at the one on the beach, then looked down at the address. "The beach." I mumbled, it was only a few miles away now.

I researched the address, it was located in the Isle of Sheppey, it wasn't connected to the mainland, more like a large island spanning a few miles wide on the far east of England. I turned down into the Underground, virtual moving ads smiled and winked as I passed through the long subway halls.

I followed the signs as they directed me to the line I wanted to take, Victoria station was where I wanted to go. Buskers and their echoing music sang throughout the halls, mediocre, but devoted.

A pleasant computer voice above me announced the departures, and the ever constant reminder to "Mind the Gap" between the platform and the subway train.

The subway wasn't fun to ride without Angel; everybody seemed to be skilled at not looking at one another even as they were face to face. People read tabloids, attempted books, and quiet chatter of various European languages were at the corner of my perspective.

It wasn't far after, the train from Victoria Station rode the majority of the way, my stop at Sheerness, a town only a few miles from the beach.

The day had ticked by, the rain hushed into a sprinkle. I rode a cab next. The little car drove along the northern part of the island, the road followed close to the beach.

I watched the tide, on some parts the damp grainy sand seemed flat and smooth, waiting for small feet to draw impressions on it, only then to be followed into jagged rocks. The ocean was just as gloomy as the city, it was a different, but still invoked the same stomach knotting I cringed from.

The road turned inland, I leaned forward, "Is there any more road next to the beach?" He shook his head, "Sorry kiddo." I nodded and leaned back, "You can stop here then, please." I paid and left the cab to find the weather also taking its toll from me, even with my shielding umbrella. But I journeyed, silently following the shore.

The tide was in, my feet freezing from sea water splash, I continued to glance at the picture, and then at the land comparing. I wandered, and time passed, I knew eventually I would get to the edge of the island where the town was. I wasn't lost, I'm never lost, only alone. Finding my way seems a silly phrase sometimes, because everywhere a person goes is their way, and it seems impossible to lose or find it, it will always be there. Destinations can change, goals, companions, and purposes, just never my path.

I stopped as I realized my feet were trudging on rocks again, I examined the photo, and then looked at the larger rocks. A few yards away one looked similar so I positioned myself as if I were the photographer.

Yes, this was the rock I came for, it was the picture, only now my eyes were the camera, and no little girl alights it, staring distant.

I looked all around me, up to the grassy hill to my right, left to the ocean, and behind me to the shore line I just drifted across.

I stepped over to it, then sat down and leaned against the rock. She wasn't here, I can find the places she's been to but the person is gone. I exhaled; my toes nearly numb and my neck growing colder with the goosebumps rippling under my jacket.

Humans are wisps, even I, an immortal being, just passes through the world. How many millions of years has this rock been here?

I will die, maybe young, like Melanie and the rest of humanity. Or will I go out in a car crash, I remember reading a story about a world war veteran dying from a car accident. He survived fighting on the front lines countless times, enemies all around him called for the blood of him and his fellow companions all the way to the end, yet somehow back at home a car ended his life.

I shook my head and tried to disappear farther into my jacket. I cringed at the cold, I'd trade Arizona summer heat any day to replace this muck.

Once again I winced, and I ignored the stress of my body the best I could. My hunger churned, my body still quivered, so I fixed my eyes to a point into the scene of the passive, freezing nature.

The wind chill reached to me and lamentingly brushed the tip of my nose.

Home, home is so far away, and every time I return I find myself obliged into venturing back out again. The sea washed forward, passing through the cracks of the wet rocks, and my feet suffered another cold rush of water.

I shook my head, it's time to go back to the hotel. Tomorrow will be a better day, I'll search elsewhere, college rosters, maybe I could get a job at the government and look up the information myself. That would mean another identity, and staying here longer than a few days.

I could start with local shops, try to figure out if anybody knew the Lelas, they had to have a routine somewhere. I just hope she didn't leave the country. My mind swam in plans, they would take time, I didn't mind very much. It was her mortality I would need to worry about though, each day brings new risk. Back to the hotel I started to go.

"She's not there," a voice murmured to me.

I stared across a grey misty beach; the sounds of the waves rushing the shore reminded me of cars zooming past.

"She doesn't exist," a higher voice whispered, I flinched at hearing it, my mouth sucking in the sodden air.

I walked along the beach, the greens and greys mushing together in a cold haze. I stopped, peering into the distance, my feet making no impression into the canvas of sand. Far away I surveyed a little girl in a faded blue sundress, her little figure not noticing me. "She doesn't exist, just like you."

My eyes cracked open, staring at the room illuminated by the chalky light. My nose and front of my face were chilled, I took a deep breath and stretched, the stolid air and hotel room taste filling my mouth.

My legs were in a tangle with the sheets, the comforter had been kicked to the end of the bed. I craned my aching neck to glance at the pale green clock numbers. I had slept merely five hours.

I sat up and shuddered at the unfamiliar cold on my warm back and turned to the side of the bed, stress made my bones creak as I pulled myself to my feet.

Melanie has created my nightmares.

I returned to the computer and continued searching through my list of nearby colleges. I came to the realization that this could take years, so I also had been half-heartedly searching for apartments. I clicked and surfed and typed, the list of colleges was a broad shot in the dark, and there were a lot.

Angel's cell phone vibrated on the table next to me. I picked it up and opened the holographic screen. Angel was texting me through somebody else's phone.

I lft fone on contr.

After spending a minute or two deciphering Angel's text I texted back.

I see that.

She replied quickly.

U R on the cmpter again Rn't U?

I texted back.

Yes, Angel.

Angel's reply was fast.

Imma go to this awsm prty, U wanna come?

I looked back at my list of colleges.

I have work, I can't party right now.

Plz?

No.

U need FUN!

I looked back at the computer again. I've got to find Melanie. Angel and her new friends are of no use to me except a distraction.

I tossed the phone to the other bed and searched. Minutes passed by and the phone stopped buzzing. I returned to the search.

On the floor I heard my phone go off, I picked it up and looked at the message.

Scientists say partying is good for you.

Angel's full English text caught me off guard.

I tld al my frnds u r cool n they wnt to meet u

I exhaled in irritation at her persistence, though she had won me over.

Where are you?

YAYYYYYYYY! 1 sec let me go fnd out.

Seconds later Angel sent me the address and a picture of her sticking her tongue out at me in front of a house.

I dropped out of my old clothes and threw on a jeans skirt that had patches of colorful bandana-like cloth randomly sewn around the front. I put on a plain green blouse with yellow snakes sewn throughout my shirt and slid on a loosely fitting jacket to match.

I sharpened my features with some make-up and grabbed my umbrella once again as I left.

The lawn was empty when I arrived at the house, it didn't seem like a party, but I could hear loud music inside. The only people I saw were three boys sitting on the porch steps looking pretty bored. I walked past them and went inside, the place was empty. Angel was in the living room with a beer in hand lying on the couch. "Awesome party," I said in a deflated tone, "I'm going to have to be very drunk before I'll start having fun. But I'll try." Angel glared at my sarcasm and pointed behind me to a door way. Through the door was the kitchen and inside there I found the fridge. I grabbed a beer, returned, and flopped on the couch next to Angel.

"Tyler!" Angel yelled and I jumped, startled. A young man sprinted into the living room. "This party sucks, where are all the people?" Tyler shrugged, "This party is pretty lame. But I know of a better one up the road." Angel stood up abruptly and knocked me off the couch, "Let's go then!" Tyler disappeared into another room and Angel and I went out to the front. The three people on the front steps stood up. "We are going to another party." Angel declared to them, their faces lit up and one of them answered "Finally!"

And as if the three were in a dog show, they instantly jumped up on Angel's command and faithfully followed her.

On the side of the house a garage door pulled open with loud clanking noises and a humming that stabbed my ears gracelessly. A green Mini Cooper rolled out and everybody tried to cram inside it. I jumped into shotgun while Angel's three friends got the backseats. Angel, because there were no more seats, decided to lie on top of the three boys in the back, rubbing her body all over them to get comfortable. I rolled my eyes up to the ceiling, now fully understanding why they are mindless puppy dogs.

Under my shoes I felt a squashy something; I made the mistake of looking down. A moldy pizza stuck to my foot and the greenish cheese slowly consumed the rest of my shoe after completely surrounding the sole. One of the boys pretended to throw up when I pried the gooey starch off and threw it out the window while the rest of the chorus sang "Eww!" in unison. Then I noticed the entire car's floor was filled with wrappers and moldy food.

"Ready?"

I finished the beer off and threw that out the window, "Let's go!" Tyler then turned on the radio to full blast with some whinny English rock song and we sped over to the other house, clearly past the speed limit.

Tyler ended up taking a wrong turn and we had to turn around twice, the rain cleared up by then, and when we arrived the sun was setting in the dim city.

At the house everybody in the Mini Cooper clambered out on to the front yard. People were everywhere, music thumped and blared from the inside, and I could see people jamming on the roof. Six days into the country, only Angel could find a new posse and a party like this.

Angel was the first person inside the big house. Everybody turned and recognized her, all shouting almost in unison "Angel!"

A tall, goofy boy emerged from the crowd to greet us personally. "This party is bloody fantastic!" he leaned over and planted a big wet kiss on Angel's mouth. He then turned to me, surprised I repelled him a little too hard and he went flying into a large potted plant a few feet away. His drunken expression was slightly irritated and he yelled confused "What the Hell!" But then he giggled and said "That's funny, huh huh."

I rolled my eyes, I am still not drunk enough. Where is the beer? The goofy boy squinted at me. "Whatever." I was about to set off to the kitchen and searched for real liquor when Angel pulled me to the side. "What are you doing? Stop ruining the fun Moogie." I grinned sheepishly and said, "Sorry, reflex. I'm trying not to inflict harm on anybody." Angel huffed out an angry sigh and said, "Just don't do it again." And Angel let go of my hand, ditching me in the crowd.

The band obviously had not the slightest idea how to play or sing, but nobody noticed. I felt like I couldn't breathe without inhaling somebody else's warm breath. Angel was long gone, her attention only to her entertaining friends, and I drifted alone through most of the party, my ultimate mission now was to find a place to sit and ride the rest of the night out.

Taking a break didn't turn out to be all that I wanted, I needed some sort of distraction, something to take my mind off my frustrated search.

After a few downed beers somebody found an old Karaoke machine and I watched Angel rise from the crowd and onto a table, she confidently serenaded the adolescents with an unrecognizable song.

I smiled and remembered Angel's horrible singing voice when we were kids. She tried out for the school play and for chorus but was denied both. When one of her favorite songs came on the radio she would start wailing out the words, I grew so tired of it that I started singing along just to drown her out of my ears. I was afraid of telling her I didn't want to listen to her voice.

But now, even as a drunkard swaying and slurring the words she sounded nice, beautiful, like an angel.

The song closed with a piano solo and Angel jumped down from the table, a sea of applause filled the room and a guy rose from the couch to sing the next song.

I snagged the seat on the overcrowded couch and exhaled in relief, finally a place for me.

Next to me on the right, a couple deeply entwined with one another, on the other side of me a guy completely absorbed himself into a social networking site. I looked at his phone screen again. The name of the site was: Valiant Vets Unite!

I pointed at the phone and said "Hey, I want to be a veterinarian, I'm already sending out applications to schools. What is it like?" His eyes grew wide and he shook his head, "Are you joking? Being a veterinarian is horrible, my sister is one and all she says is how she has to spend everyday in an office trying to diagnose weak, dying animals. Most of the time the cases are hopeless, because by the time they are brought in, it is too late. A lot die before you can figure out what is going on. They aren't like humans, and my sister spends a lot of time just guessing all day long."

I shook my head taken aback, first at the guy's long, intelligent speech, then at what he said. "What? But that doesn't make sense; I thought veterinarians were like, medically advanced." He shook his head, "Yeah, more advanced compared to the eighteen hundreds, if people then got a sick horse or something they just shot it. Look, what I'm trying to say is my sister hates it, everyday animals come in and die in front of her." He shook his head and leaned back saying quieter "Sometimes people bring in their pets perfectly healthy, and then ask her to quietly put them down because the owners lose interest and don't want take care of them."

I was struck disgusted, "Really?" I looked down at my hands and repeated the question. "Is it really that bad?" He nodded again.

"Why are you on a veterinarian social website anyway?" He looked down at his phone, his voice sounded like he was losing interest in me, dropping lower into a monotone. "It's a great place to find rich women. Duh." Our conversation silenced and I could see his attention fully back into the phone. I looked up at the ceiling, great; there goes my back-up career. I made a mental note to shred those applications to veterinary school.

The couple decided to take their slobbering elsewhere and a quiet girl, playing a slingshot game on her phone with holographic mode turned off sat down in their place.

Angel appeared before me with her hand on her hips, "Hey, we are finally playing bad oldies music on the karaoke machine, aren't you going to sing?" I shook my head, "No way, I hate singing, you know that. I'm utterly oblivious and tone deaf when it comes to singing in the right pitch." I slurred "utterly" into "oblivious" and it kind of came out "utterblivious" All the booze I've been drinking is starting to kick in. Angel shrugged and disappeared again into the crowd.

The quiet girl looked up from her phone and turned to me; in a low voice she said "You're an American?" I looked at the girl dumbfounded. "Yes! How did you know?" She smiled, "Your accent, so what is it like there?" I laughed at myself, duh, my accent, why didn't I think of that?

I answered the best I could, describing Arizona and the desert made me miss home already. We talked for a while; she seemed to like to listen more than she liked to talk, and I found I had a lot to say and describe. She enjoyed listening to my perception of the life in Arizona, and commented on how opposite it was to here.

I moaned in agreement, "It is too rainy here, too cold and mushy. Nothing is sharp, just a mash of blurring, drab, colours." My chagrin bowing my shoulders into a hunch.

"Why are you here?" she asked in a small voice, my vision fuzzy and my head far from all reason. I was so relaxed I almost answered, "To hunt diseased people that want nothing except to prey upon humans and their blood." But I caught myself on "To hunt". And silenced my monologue about the life I just retired from.

She raised her eyebrows, "To hunt what?" I shook my head, "Somebody I've never met before. And I don't think I'll be finding her anytime soon." She tilted her head, "How do you do that?" I stretched and leaned back casually, "I started out with a name, her mom's address, and a few pictures. The address was a dud, and everywhere else I've looked I only smacked into a brick wall."

"She must be special, traveling out here and living in all this discomfort to seek her out." I nodded, this girl has no idea.

She adjusted to face me better, "Can I see the pictures?" I shrugged "Sure." I dug around in my purse and pulled out my phone. When the holographic screen loaded I pulled up the pictures I scanned.

The girl examined the pictures one by one as she listened to me talk about the locations around England I've searched. Occasionally she commented, but seemed just as engrossed in the pictures as she was when she was playing the games on her phone. "And her latest home was this boarding school-like place. It seemed like all the girls there knew her cat more than they knew her."

The girl stopped on the picture of the cat and stretched the picture to zoom in on the cat. "Yes, everyone always likes Mr. Momo." She mumbled distractedly, I froze, and then her hand stopped flipping though the pictures.

I didn't move. She sucked in a breath and her eyes grew wide with alarm, and she blushed a deep red.

I couldn't answer. The people, the noise, the music all drifted into a far away background. My head spun, the golden chandelier above us seemed to illuminate her features better than ever. My drunk and relaxed brain snapped and counted the milliseconds again.

Her eyes matched mine; she didn't look like the girl in the picture, but like an older, stronger, more beautiful version of me. She didn't wear or need make-up, her golden blonde hair curled sharply below her shoulders just as mine did before I cut it. Her fair, healthy skin hadn't a flaw nor did her teeth stand crooked. I could see the uncanny mix of my father in her strikingly well. This was her, unequivocally and irrevocably her.

At that moment a guy soared off the table he was dancing on and slammed into the back of the couch. We were all jolted and my phone flew onto the floor. I launched forward to get it as it spun across the tile; it stopped when it bounced on somebody's shoe. That person noticed the phone and kicked it away from them sending it across the floor again.

I pounced on it and pull it tightly to me; I stood up to return to the couch. She was nowhere to be found.

21
Rain

The lights grew too bright, the room started shrinking, and a suffocating amount of people became extremely conscious in my mind. I searched the faces for hers, she was gone. I darted through the crowd, and out the front door.

The chilly night air hit me instantly and my fuzzy eyesight and senses focused again. It was a slap in the face to wake up.

Nothing had stirred, I couldn't see her. I spun on my heel and sprinted back into the house, through the crowd, I skirted by Angel's scarlet hair, "Where are you going Moogie?" I flinched at her derisive voice behind me, but continued to move through the kitchen door and to the backyard. A few people turned their heads from looking at the gate that led to the alley over to me. I could hear the final clicking as the alley door finished closing.

I dashed to it, away from the crowds and the light. My shoes crunched on the uneven rocks, the dark alleyways revealed no sign of Melanie one way or another.

I'm such an idiot! To hunt? She thinks I'm going to kill her. How could I scare her more?

I'm going to lose her, I'm losing my second chance.

I desperately started down the left side, adrenaline shaking me into a frightened sprint, "Melanie!" I wailed. I held my breath and tried to listen for her motion, footsteps, anything.

The terror pulled a pit in my stomach; I wanted to crumple to the ground. I bit my lip and fought the heavy breathing that could lead to the bitter sobs. I heard nothing. I looked ahead and found another fork leading deeper into the maze of paths. I turned in the opposite direction and called her name.

"I'm not here to hurt you! This is all wrong, I'm sorry!" I tried with my predator senses to find her, my eyesight couldn't do much, nor my hearing.

"Melanie! Please! I'm your sister!" I started to back up, my voice rising into a gravely shout, "Please, please, please comeback!" my voice cracked and tears dripped through the corners of my eyes. My hands balled into tight fists. I looked down and shut my eyes to listen again.

My feet stopped as I called in a lower voice, failing in hope, "Your father was my father in America, and when I lost him-" I choked back the sobs, and then tried again, "When I lost everyone I thought I was alone, and for a decade I suffered. But then I found my father's letters, I found you."

I backed against a fence next to a dumpster, my voice lowering even more, "You and your stories, your favorite dress like mine, the lonely days without a father, your first day of second grade when my father walked with you to school. I couldn't believe it, and I left everything for the slightest hope of finding you."

My voice struggled to say more, the words slipping quieter into the void of nothingness, "My friends transform into aliens, people I thought mattered suddenly change their minds and disappear in the blink of an eye. Anyone can disown me, and pretend there wasn't that special bond, but I know now that I have a sister, a sister!" I slid down the fence and shoved the tears off my face, my voice deflated with certainty of defeat. I was alone now, wherever she had fled to is certainly beyond earshot.

"I don't really know why, but I needed to find you, that somehow, somewhere you exist. And that will never change; you will always be my sister."

Small droplets of rain mixed into my tears as they splattered on my arms and legs, thunder roared and echoed as it followed a flash of lightening. The water pitter pattered into the dirt, and I couldn't hear anything except the rain. "I'm sorry Melanie," I said in a weak voice, as my sobbing lessened. "I only wanted to meet you one time."

The final strike of defeat notched into my soul. I looked up at the sky covered with dreary grey clouds, the tears hid amongst the raindrops, only I could tell the difference. Still I shunned disgustedly away from them, my signs of weakness.

I'm not supposed to cry, so why am I? It hasn't done me any good so far. I should be stronger; I'm not the little girl I used to be. I'm not innocent, and there was no empathy in my line of work, not in this life.

I pushed myself up from the dirt and rocks, the rain soaking my skirt and through my jacket. I bitterly ground my teeth together and brushed myself off.

She is too good for me, she shouldn't be near someone like me. Maybe this is the world trying to save her, it has done her no good her whole life, maybe this is pay back.

I slapped the side of my face to sober myself up and tried to stop the tears. I shouldn't be here, I shouldn't selfishly seek her out.

I would rather her stay alive than live half dead like me. This is for the best. Maybe one day I'll stop mulling over the life lost when I was a child, and focus on the potential of what I should become. Chases like this are holding me back. Grudgingly I pushed myself forward, and only four sober steps were taken.

"I've never had a sister before."

I stopped, my foot in mid step from fourth to fifth, and turned to the voice, Melanie had been sitting on the other side of the trash can. Her knees had been pulled up to her chest and her arms tightly wrapped around herself like I had been seconds earlier, her golden blonde hair spilling off of her shoulders and dripped rain water.

My thoughts evaporated, forgetting my doubts, and my mind flooded with true contentment.

She raised her head to look at me, lightening flashed and illuminated a brief smile on her face.

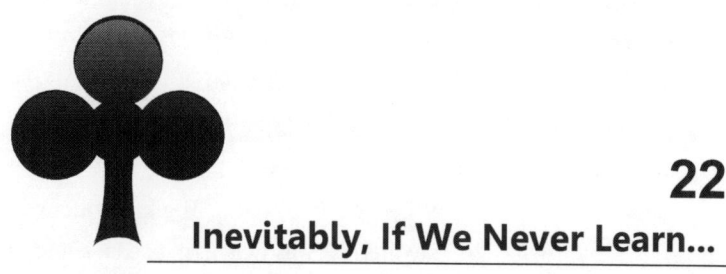

22
Inevitably, If We Never Learn...

The rain continued to pound on my head, Melanie stood up and straightened her soaked clothes. "I'm getting kind of cold, do you want to leave? I know a diner not far away." I looked back down the alley; the house party wasn't in sight. I looked back at her, awestruck, then gave a slight nod, "Sure."

I followed her as she expertly turned through the maze of alleyways until we reached a busy main street on the corner of an intersection. we entered an overly bright diner. Above the door we passed under a blue florescent sign saying Tom's Diner in loopy cursive.

We sat down at the counter and a man appeared to pour some coffee. He filled mine full but hers only halfway, distracted by somebody coming in the diner. I straightened and tried catch him "Wait," Melanie's eyes picked up from her menu, "It's alright." And the man kissed the woman while she shook out her umbrella.

Melanie's eyes drew back to the menu pretending not to see them. "My mother used to take me here after her job sometimes. It's one of my favorites. My old flat in Miller's court is just a few streets away." She picked up the coffee and looked at me. In a serious voice she said, "So, I have an American sister that I've never met before, from my American father that disappeared when I was in Primary school."

She laughed a little without humor, and sipped the coffee, but her face seemed confused while trying to comprehend it. "What happened to my-um our father? How did you say you lost him?"

I poured milk into my cup and stirred it in, "He died ten years ago, it was only a few months after he last saw you."

"How?" I looked away from her and fixed my eyes on the newspaper the man next to me was reading, the front cover headlined about some actor dying. "Um, he was murdered."

I heard a sharp intake of her breath, "What?" The blood drained from my face; did I really just say that? "It was two insane serial killers, a man and a woman, that wiped out my entire family. We were on our way to a family cabin when my dad needed to stop at his work to grab something. I guess I was lucky when the killers forgot to check the bathrooms where I had been hiding. They even killed my dog before disappearing for six years."

The man with the newspaper flipped through the horoscope and the comics, and I closed my eyes. "The police got them though."

I risked a glance at her, Melanie stared back wide-eyed, blatant shock painted her face. For somehow she thought she offended me. "I'm sorry." Was all she could manage.

I shrugged, trying to ease up conversation. "It has been years, I'm sort of over it now. At peace with the issue."

"It must have been hard, what did you do?"

"What do you mean what did I do?" I said, my voice lowering slightly. "Well, when my mother died I went to that halfway house." I didn't know what to say. Should I tell her the truth? No, of course not.

My voiced was detached and my face held a good liar's expression, almost completely collected, "I grew up drifting through houses, then before I knew it I was out on my own as an adult." To further myself from letting any misery show, I tried to lift the subject off of me. "What about you? You're mother died in some sort car crash right? Do you know anything about that?"

She nodded and then blushed, "I was there. We were on Westminster pier going back home, I was eleven. We had gone up to the steps and near the intersection when I spotted a vendor selling fish and chips. I love fish and chips, so my mother bought some, I finished and went over about a meter away and tossed the rubbish."

I watched Melanie's hand tremble as she put down her cup; she took a breath and started again. "My mother waited for me on the corner of the sidewalk, but in the middle of the intersection a car sped through a red light. Another car hit it."

Melanie looked out the window and watched a lady hitch up her skirt in the reflection from the window, her hair dripping wet from the rain.

"I watched my mother smile at me and behind her I watched the car spin out of control. And then, it hit her. I ran to her side and her head was bleeding everywhere, and I don't remember if I screamed or not but people started rushing over to me. The driver of the car got out completely unscathed, and the car was barely dented. He looked at me, and I remember his terrified face. And then he got back in his car and pulled away. I told the police the part of the license number I remembered but they never found him."

Melanie silenced again, collecting her thoughts, and I listened to bells chiming from outside before finishing the rest of my coffee.

Her hands shook, I remembered that feeling, knowing I couldn't control my life.

"What did you do next?" I asked. She looked up confused. "What do you mean? There wasn't anything I could do, the police couldn't find anything, he was gone."

She didn't seek revenge? I stared at the empty cup in my hands, sobered by her reaction. She didn't seek further investigation? Just follow the police and then take their word on the matter?

My puzzlement seemed to worry Melanie more, so I rearranged my expression to hide my surprised aversion, "Right, nothing you can do."

As I continued through the night talking to her, I realized she was nothing like me. Her intelligent, yet introverted mind made my head spin. She saw mass problems with the world, yet she wasn't angry.

My composed face revealed little of my opinions after that first slip up, and when she had finished her elaboration on our fourth or fifth topic I noticed the time.

"The rain has cleared up; we should probably get back to the party." Melanie nodded, and I silently paid before we started back to the house.

I broke our silence with one more question, curious to her odd reactions "When I questioned the girls at the halfway house you stayed at they didn't seem to know who you were. Why was that?"

Melanie shrugged, "They never asked my name, any time they ever wanted to talk to me they were looking to start an argument. Nobody really acted like anybody's friend there; they all just took turns talking about themselves, perpetually. And when they've told their stories they move on to praise themselves in front of the next set of listeners. The only deviations they ever made from their cycle had been when somebody started a quarrel with another about a frivolous comment or action. I didn't see the point of trying to be friends with them. So they ignored me."

I held my breath, once again baffled by her aptitude in observance, and further disturbed by her dissimilarity to me. Melanie was my opposite, yet genetically speaking she was more similar to me than any other living creature.

We strode through the cold, nightly alleys and turned corners while I listened to her grievances. "That must have been a lonely childhood." I replied. "But you have friends now?" She looked at the ground, "Not really."

"But those people at the party knew you."

"Those are just people," she replied. "I only know them because they attend the same university as me."

"What are you training to be?" I asked.

"A veterinarian." She replied. I opened my mouth to warn her about what I discovered tonight about that job, but decided against it. "What university do you attend?" She asked.

"I don't attend college." I said flatly, "What do you do then?" I didn't hesitate on my partially true story, "I flip houses with a friend for a living, we buy up old homes and liquidate the insides of them before fixing them up and selling them again."

We reached the back gate to the house. She stared at me, "You know, I don't even know your name, and you know everything about me." I smiled, "My name is Moogie, I am twenty-four years old, and I live in Phoenix, Arizona." Melanie smiled back, "It's nice to meet you Moogie."

We opened the gate back up and stepped inside, catching a few glances on our way in, and after we reached the heart of the party we were ghosts again.

She glanced at her watch, "I have classes tomorrow. Are you staying for long?"

"A few more days." I replied.

"Do you want to go to dinner with me tomorrow night? Hopefully have a normal conversation?" I grinned, not making any mistake of hesitating, "There is not one thing in the world I would rather do." We swapped contact information and she started to the door. Before opening she looked around at the messy chaos of the party. "Do you have a ride home?"

I shrugged "Not really, I was just going to call a cab." Her eyes brightened, "I can give you a lift back to your hotel. If you want."

I nodded, "Alright, but I need to grab my friend first."

Angel, completely checked out of the party, was on the couch where I had been just earlier tonight slobbering all over a boy I didn't recognize. After choking back acid reflux upon seeing her so deeply involved, I managed the words "Angel, it's time to go, the ride is waiting."

And as if pulling a suction cup off a window, Angel wrenched herself out of the boy's mouth and pulled out her compact to adjust her smeared make-up. "Okay, ready to go!" And didn't give the highly confused boy a second glance.

When we reached the door Angel turned and threw her arms in the air, before taking a bow. "Bye Angel!" the crowd bellowed in unison. "I bid you ado my lovely friends." She replied to her subjects.

She whisked out the door right behind me. Melanie waited patiently by her car, when I led Angel, I noticed Melanie raised her eyebrow, I smiled and raised my arm to signify Melanie, "Angel, this is Melanie, Melanie, this is Angel."

"Yes, I know you; we went on that shopping trip together yesterday with some other people." Melanie stated optimistically. Angel crossed her arms and tilted her head down slightly to look at Melanie. "Um, okay, then um, it's nice to see you again?"

Angel didn't seem to care enough about common courtesy to continue the small talk, and she looked at the car. "Can I drive? I've always wanted to drive different than the American way." Angel hopped up and down excitedly, "Please Mel? I'll be careful!"

"It's Melan-oh never mind, alright, just don't kill us." And she tossed the keys to Angel. Angel hopped into the right seat instead of the left to drive and brought the car into a low rumble.

I stepped into the back with Melanie and Angel pulled out. "This is so amazing!" Angel sang cheerfully. In a matter of fact tone Melanie surmised "Yes, it's nice driving on the correct side of the road. You Americans have it all backwards."

I rolled my eyes, "So what do you want to do tomorrow night? See a movie?" Melanie shrugged, "Sure, nothing like a thriller or action movie to fill your Wednesday nights." I shook my head, I have enough adrenaline rushes in my life, giant spiders and knife fights just aren't the same anymore. "What about that romantic comedy that just came out?"

Melanie smiled, "I already saw it."

"How was it?" I questioned.

Melanie giggled again, "There was this one scene and I laughed so hard I peed myself a little." I snorted, and glanced out the window. The chaotic party house disappeared in the dark line of industrial houses. We turned into a shopping part of town which I recognized as near my hotel.

Melanie and I chatted happily of our plans and she named her favourite restaurants around town. The car passed through traffic and water puddles from the rain earlier tonight, I watched the water swish and spray the glistening wet sidewalk.

Angel's phone buzzed in her purse and started singing one of the songs I frequently hear on the radio. I laughed, it was the rap song I loved to make fun of because most of the song comprised of a rap guy belting out the same monotone four phrases over and over again with a powerful drum beat.

Angel reached in to check it and Melanie pat the drum beat on her leg. "Ooo! Is it one of your admirers?" I mused...

23
Mistakes

July 30
August 1, 2021
10 hours later

The vivid lights over irradiated the room to my sensitive eyes, the chair I was agitatedly sitting in had fabric that rubbed roughly against my skin, and I hadn't slept since the accident. Angel sat across from me, just as serious as we unendingly lingered in the hospital waiting room for news about Melanie's state.

The car had hit Melanie's side. We crawled out of the broken windows after the car finished rolling, Angel and I walked away from the accident without a scratch. They took Melanie away on a stretcher.

A nurse leaned in with a clipboard and called out my name. I leaped to my feet and followed the nurse out with Angel tailing me. "How is she doing?" I shot. The nurse's eyes met mine with a grave expression before opening a pair of double doors.

"She's stable now, and she'll live, but I'm afraid I have some bad news." I stepped inside the long room. The hospital smelled strongly of dried blood, stale air, and metal. My mouth felt as if a tin spoon had twanged against my teeth. I shivered as the nurse led me down the room.

Doctors and nurses hurried from place to place, seven beds lined up along the left side of the wall with people hooked up to machines and IVs. Each had a curtain and a bedridden client. Secured to one of the middle beds in the intensive care unit I could see Melanie.

Her face wrapped in gauss, the side of her face that had been to the window was so heavily bandaged I couldn't see it. I could make out the outline of a body splint and leg splints under her blanket; she looked like a fragile, broken doll.

"Miss Herald?" I looked up at the nurse. "Miss Herald, your friend is, well, has been damaged beyond repair, I'm sorry but she's become quadriplegic. She will not be able to move anything except her head for the rest of her life. I'm sorry."

The blood drained from my face, and the noise of the room amplified. The clicking of metal, footsteps on the white tile, the lights buzzing and hiccupping. Everybody was breathing too loudly, chattering and thinking. No. No! Tears didn't come, but a swelling emptiness. My nails dug into the palm of my hand. Melanie's still, sleeping body filled my eyes.

It's all my fault, it's all my fault. I should have never come here, I should have never let Angel drive, Melanie, I am so sorry. My thoughts cringed at the invisible, insufficient apology.

Angel looked down at me and turned to the nurse. "Can we have some time alone?" The nurse nodded and pulled the curtain to shield us in with the sleeping Melanie.

"You look like a ghost." Angel whispered. I flinched at her voice, and pressed my lips together, I couldn't answer Angel's observation. She shook her head, "I'm sorry Moogie, it was an accident. But there is nothing we can do. I think we should go. Don't get worked up into one of those passive fits you have. You just met the girl last night."

I held my breath at Angel's selfish statement. Detestation of her filled my heart. I wanted to shove her, slap her around until she understood. But my fists stayed clenched by my side and I spoke in a distant tone. "Angel, she's my sister. She was my mission." Angel's face dropped, "What? But your sister is-"

I cut it angrily, "My full blood sister is dead, yes, but my dad had this affair, and well, she's the only person left in the world that is related to me." Angel stared at Melanie. Her ignorance ceasing at the statement. "Oh."

Melanie's chest rose and fell evenly, the only part of her that wasn't covered with bandages had an IV inserted in it. I placed my hand on her warm, exposed arm, the one she would never be able to use again.

I watched her for a moment more, silent, paused.

And then progressed forward.

"Angel, stand guard, warn me if any nurses are coming in." Angel stared at me, "Why? Are you going to put her out of her misery?" I stepped over to the hazardous waste bin, ignoring her question. Inside I dug around until I found a used IV bag and a syringe.

"Moogie, what are you doing?" Angel asked more urgently. I washed the bag off in the sink along with the needles for the syringe and IV. "Angel, just keep guard." I commanded as I washed the crook of my arm.

Conscientiously I let the used syringe glide under my pale, translucent skin. With a pull of the plunger I watched the red ooze extracted from my arm climb the tick marks on the syringe tube.

When I couldn't draw anymore I pulled the thin needle from my arm and slid it into the valve on the bottom of the IV bag. "Moogie, Moogie, that's a horrible idea. Moogie, stop-"

I again extracted a syringe full of blood. "Moogie!" Angel hissed. "No Moogie!"

I could hear Angel' desperation as I continued to ignore her, "This isn't right, just let her go!" She frantically whispered. Her words meant nothing, she had no right.

The bag filled with what I thought was a little more than a pint of blood, and I hooked it up to the pole that held the three other IV bags. Then I inserted the needle from my bag into Melanie's arm. Her soft skin punctured easily, but strangely lifeless, without a flex of notice.

A flow of red rushed down from the bag and through the malleable tube. It disappeared into Melanie's arm and I backed up. Angel's silent crying caught my attention and I turned to her.

But before she could say anything Angel stepped to the side to let the busy nurse enter the room, I froze, keeping my eyes away from the extra IV bag hanging on the pole. Angel snuffed back her tears and I watched the nurse pick up the clipboard and examine all of the machines, one by one she checked everything off.

I held my breath, tense, and my hand naturally reached to touch the Flashsword in my jacket. The nurse gave a quick glance at the IVs, then she took a look again. Oh no.

But the nurse returned her pen to the clipboard and checked it off. She glanced at me and nodded in greeting before putting the clipboard down and exiting our isolated room.

Angel resumed her angry glare at me, "You said we wouldn't do this! H-how could you?" I held my neutral expression and didn't answer her.

Her fits clenched and let go. I knew exactly what I was doing, making myself a hypocrite, no, only adding to the steep life of pure hypocrisy I led. I didn't need to look into Angel's eyes to see the double standard I played.

"I thought it was just going to be you and me." She breathed unforgiving.

She threw open the curtain and rushed out. I quickly closed it back, and stepped by Melanie's bed. I brushed her hair away from her face before settling in the corner of her bed. "Everything is going to be alright Melanie, you just wait." I said to the sleeping girl.

I stayed with her as long as they let me, monitoring the bag that would change her into the immortal I am.

I didn't see Angel for hours after that, and when I saw her again Melanie had been moved into a room more private than the ICU. My head was back against the wall and I was dozing when Angel entered. She looked brighter than before, and the anger had left her face.

"Hey." I said opening my eyes wider; in her arms I noticed she held a few bags of blood. "Look what I found Moogie!"

I shook my head, "No. Go put them back." Her shoulders slumped, and her voice begged in a whiny voice. "No! Pleeease? It is free and there is enough for you, me, and that new demon spawn you created."

I exhaled sharply at her passive aggressiveness and stood up, "No. We do not steal from hospitals. The blood doesn't belong to us, trust me, I have already tried that. It does not work at all."

She straightened up and shifted all of her weight to one side, and spat icily, "Fine." Angel marched out the door again, and I closed my eyes and shook my head.

"Moogie? Is that you?" My eyes shot open, "Yeah, yeah, it's me, Melanie." I flew to her side, taking her hand as she groggily came-to.

"My head hurts." She reached up to touch it, "I don't remember anything, Moogie, what happened to me?"

I held my breath, should I tell her now? Her drowsy eyes slipped down, for a moment, "Go back to sleep Melanie. You're going to be okay, and we'll have plenty of time to talk later."

And she drifted away again, I let go of her hand and settled back down on the chair next to her. What am I going to do? I can't let the nurses know she can move again, she wasn't supposed to heal. How am I going to get her out?

Break out? Ruin my current identity and have hospitals looking for Melanie? What happens when she gets hungry or wants to leave? Stands up in front of the nurses and tells them she is all better?

Angel returned and I relayed my thoughts and worries to her. Her first reaction was to nonchalantly pull out and adjust her make-up, and then she shrugged, "I don't know, and nobody has any guns here so we can't do a gangster escape and shoot all of the nurses that get in our way."

I nodded and mumbled in agreement, "Yes, no gangster escapes." Angel reapplied her dark, cherry red lipstick, "I have an idea!" She shut her compact and turned to me. "Okay, so when I was around fourteen I wanted to go to this party, but my bitchy mom didn't want me to go. So, I told her I was just going to go stay at this girl from school's house for a sleepover. But, when I left, I ditched the girl's house and went to the party instead, and my mom couldn't tell the difference."

A triumphant smile appeared on Angel's face, I stared at her dumbfounded, "Huh? What does that have to do with anything?" Angel rolled her eyes, "Ugh, why did I ever think you were a genius?" I raised my eyebrows, "You thought I was-" "Look," Angel cut in, "we need to get her signed out of the hospital right? So we could just tell the hospital people we are moving her to another hospital and on the ride there we ditch the second hospital and go home."

I paused, surprised at the plausibility of her plan. She truly was smart, I wonder what would happen if she honestly tried to apply herself.

I shrugged, trying to save face and acted nonchalant, "We could try, but how would we ditch the second hospital?" Angel frowned, "Hm, I remember my grandfather had a stroke in Phoenix that paralyzed him, and my grandmother wanted to transfer him home. They hired a professional medical transportation service because the hospital ambulances cost more. We could hire one of them to bring home Mel, the demon from Hell." I set my teeth on edge, "Don't call her that."

I researched on my phone the different transportations available and looked up hospitals in the area. After some paper work and a conversation with Melanie's doctor, along with a doctor from another hospital, Melanie was approved to be transferred and the next day we were ready to execute our slip through the system plan.

I confidently went with her as they pulled her stretcher into the ambulance service car I hired; Angel gladly directed the ambulance to Melanie's apartment. Before Melanie reached her house, I called the second hospital and informed them that we will not be checking in, and that we decided to go with another hospital. After confirming our identification, they promptly ended the conversation and I never heard from them again.

"But those aren't real! What are you talking about?" I patiently explained again, "We aren't mythical or magic, it's a virus." She still argued further. Melanie was fully healed the next day, and she panicked when she found her new sight and hearing. My scientific explanations didn't help the situation at all.

"I'm not going to drink blood! Not even from pigs."

I shook my head, "You have too, or you will die." She shook her head and paced around the room, "I don't want to be this, this creature of the night!" Angel snorted behind me, and Melanie broke into tears again.

I sat down on her bed, nearly two hours of explaining and arguing has left me mentally fatigued, and Angel and her snide sideline comments made Melanie more confused.

"Why? Why did you do this to me? This isn't fair!" Melanie covered her face in her hands, I looked at the floor guiltily; her reaction wasn't what I expected. "I'm sorry. It just happened."

"You should have just left me, I don't want to kill people or drink blood or anything! I just wanted to be normal. That's all I ever wanted!" Angel was doing her best to suppress her laughter, I wanted to slap her.

Melanie dropped on the bed next to me in defeat, "What is the point? The entire world is against me, and there is nothing I can do to stop it."

I exhaled and repeated for what felt like the millionth time, "Melanie, I'm so, so very sorry."

Hours passed, her starvation strike seemed to be slowly killing her and I couldn't persuade her otherwise.

"Melanie, it doesn't taste bad, I promise." Melanie crossed her arms and closed her eyes, "No," Angel, in worse temper than ever before, got up from the couch and pulled me into the other room. "If she doesn't want to eat, let her die. Why are you spending so much time trying to fix her? If she wants to die then let her, I want to go home."

I shook my head, "Angel, this is not about you anymore. We can't abandon her, and I am not going to leave, so you can help me or get out of the way." I started back out to the kitchen and called to Melanie, "What if we slip it in your food? You won't even taste it." Melanie glared at me, "Yes I will." I shook my head, "What do you eat? You are probably hungry right now." I asked.

"Bangers and mash." Melanie stated, and Angel scoffed, "You ungrateful little twerp, why can't you just drink it?" Melanie beamed a fumingly irritatant expression at Angel, "It's not strange, you just aren't sophisticated enough to wrap your small American mind around it."

I quickly searched on my phone to figure out what bangers and mash was, it was just another name for sausage and mashed potatoes. I put my phone away. "Angel, it's alright, Melanie, don't be so grossed out about the blood, okay? You eat it all the time." She turned to me, "What?"

I raised my hands, "It's the juice you eat when you eat bangers, and I'm guessing you eat black pudding too right?" She nodded, and by nightfall Melanie had finally eaten. Even though this skirmish was solved, it was the start of the battles I constantly fought to make her understand her new life.

I let pass the flight back home, my new residence became Melanie's apartment, England had involuntarily become my new home.

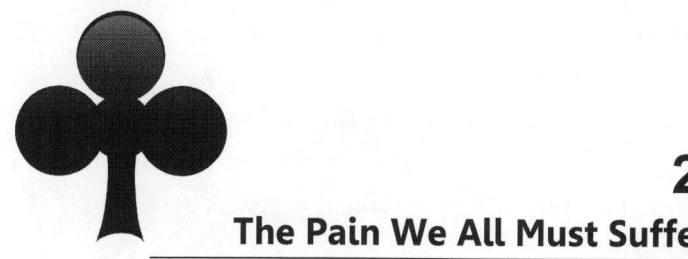

24
The Pain We All Must Suffer

Melanie extremely disliked her new life, and she made me conscious of it everyday. She acted like a lead weight every time I tried to get her out to learn. She refused to pick up a weapon, she plugged her ears when I tried to explain to her the possible situations she might be put in if Angel and I ever went hunting, I didn't know what to do.

Angel and Melanie bickered more than an old married couple, and they constantly asked me why I'm even trying.

The rainy August washed into a cold September, and then a colder October. Melanie begrudgingly stopped acting reluctant to listen whenever I mentioned anything involving her new life, and moved to just passive aggressively hating me.

Angel stopped blatantly complaining to me about the futility of my mission, and sought ways to be herself in this night and day opposite environment. Angel tries to escape the apartment as much as possible, I rarely see her. Most of my time is spent with Melanie, even though she resents me whenever I talk about immortality or moral, but we are friends when we talk and do other things.

I let the subject of Melanie's new life drop after a while, hoping she will be more open minded later. It was mid-October when I tried as mildly as possible to tell her again about this life.

I didn't think it would have much affect, but I was still set on making her prepared and more safe than sorry.

We were lounging around the living room one night, Angel was watching television and I was playing checkers with Melanie. "No! That is so fake!" Angel shouted at the TV. I glanced to find Angel watching an old nineteen seventies Kung-Fu movie. The actors were doing cheesy moves that didn't exactly work in real life.

"Well what would you do instead Angel?" Angel rolled her eyes, "First, I won't go monologing such a stupid speech, I'd have a much cooler one, but really fighting I would side step, sweep his knees and break his neck."

I tried imagining it, "No, that doesn't seem very plausible; if your opponent is equally matched they would dodge the sweep if they hadn't already killed you in your monologue." Angel stood her ground, laying on the couch, "Liar, the sweep works every time."

I shrugged, and sang slightly sarcastically, "Okay, whatever you want." Angel turned the television off, "Do you want me to prove it to you? Your butt hasn't been handed to you in a long time, I think it is high time you need to be reminded how your butt is properly kicked." I stood up, speaking the rules for Melanie's sake. "Fine. Whoever chokes the other out first wins."

Angel pushed the couch against the wall, and cleared a space for us to fight. Melanie stared wide-eyed, "What do you think you are doing?" I looked back at Melanie, "Training, I haven't done it in a while, and you never know when you'll be put in a situation to fight."

Melanie stood up, "What do you mean?" I shrugged, "Sometimes we have to fight unexpectedly." I turned my back to Melanie and circled Angel. "Are you ready?" Angel nodded and she made the first move. We fought several rounds, she got me a few times on the leg sweep, the sweep was a simple move, she would rush me and grab my shoulders. Then with her right leg she would swing it forward and catch my right leg from the outside, sweeping it forward. It would land me flat on my back with the wind knocked out of me if I wasn't careful.

Before another round started, I noticed Melanie had been watching us meticulously. I helped Angel back off the floor, and turned to Melanie. "Come join us, I'll teach you a few moves." I beckoned her over to us and she vigorously shook her head. "No, I have all I need watching from here." I pleaded with her further, "Come on, it will be fun!"

She shook her head and stood up, "You know, I'm really tired and I have classes tomorrow, I think I'm going to bed." And she disappeared into her room.

"Dammit!" I cursed, and lugged the couch back to the middle of the floor.

Roses are red, violets are blue, it's bloody fun to talk in an English accent, so 'appy Birthday to you.
-Moogie

May 6, 2021

It was an average Sunday night, and tonight like others we were all in our own worlds. Melanie was petting and baby talking to Mr. Momo, Angel was watching TV and I had just finished cleaning my Flashsword. It was spotless, and has been spotless for nearly a year now, but I check it once and a while because sadly these days I find myself picking pocket lint from the niches.

Violence was far from anybody's mind, Melanie, Angel, and I acted like normal people in their twenties. Melanie's main concern was classes, for Angel her social life, and I invested my days into learning and living all of the things I've always wanted to do.

As we took our permanent residence, I had some of the stuff from my home shipped out, my bass, my violin; Angel just bought new things for herself, constantly keeping up with London fads and fashions.

I knew a little more about my bass, but I wasn't very good. I had finished writing three songs which all sounded the same, and the lyrics were boring. Mel couldn't play anything and Angel's guitar was still at home, so I spent hours alone researching techniques online. I even bought a holographic computer training program, life-sized. And I still sucked. My music sheet reading skills were just as bad, and maybe it's because I have the education of a middle school kid.

Even Angel knows more than me in that department. I barely can figure out percentages or integers above the basics for paying bills and getting by, but imaginary numbers, radicals, slope, rational, irrational, what does this all mean?

I never told Melanie of my stupidity, she always acted knowledgeable, she knew all of the kings of England, and the Krebs cycle, and poets and authors. I always smiled and listened to her learnings from college classes.

She had essays and Socratic Seminars, which were sort of debates, but nobody is on a specific side, they just sit in a circle and discussed ideas. And she knew Latin well, and she could sew.

All the time we would talk, even though I lacked so much standard knowledge, I found some of the concepts she knew from classes I learned on my own and had given them different names.

She knew her home well, and we all would find time for trips to the beach when it became warm enough, and a few times we drove into the country to enjoy the castles.

Melanie was especially good at history, she could tell entire biographies about a duke or an important English artist.

When Angel would abandon me for the latest and greatest at the moment, I would stay back at home or go to Tom's Diner and talk to Melanie.

Sometimes I could finish her sentences, she was so quick at picking up fine details and concepts, she was so agreeable with me.

If I stayed away from death, immortality, and training, our conversations would fly with the hours.

Her voice was so even, and so familiar, just as the rain streaming down the window, it became a constant in my life.

Angel never objected to living like this, nights seemed longer. I felt apart from them, even though I saw them everyday, we weren't together as a whole, but pieces fused together, with me as the only common denominator. We were never simplistic; this was never how I would have guessed life to be like. I was closer to Melanie at times, or alone, which would happen often with Melanie's college life separate from us, and Angel had her moments.

After cleaning my Flashsword I planned on doing something like counting the money again, though I know how much we have down to the last cent off the top of my head. We were running out fast. I dreaded the idea of flying all the way back home to dig up a tree and pull out my emergency gold stash. It might be time to get a job, time to really get into the inevitable of conventional living.

It was only six o'clock, what else is there to do? I didn't feel like vegetating with Angel or playing my instrument. Before shooting down my next thoughts I blurted out, "Let's go out to eat tonight." Melanie's head snapped up from the cat rolling around on the floor. "What?" Angel looked up, "No."

I jumped up and snatched the keys, "Yes. I'm driving!" Angel held her breath and threw herself up; "Okay!" then shoved Melanie aside to get to the door first. "I got shotgun!"

Melanie crossed her arms, "It's my car. You guys are so immature! I'm getting shotgun!"

I dropped into the front seat, and Melanie somehow managed to pull in front of Angel to take shotgun. Angel groaned, "I called it!" Melanie stuck her tongue out at Angel, "My butt got here first, take the backseat." Angel ignored her, "Moogie! You heard me, I called shotgun first." I shook my head, "Just get in the back Angel."

She huffed an angry sigh and slammed the back door before settling in the backseat. 'You guys are unfair." I laughed, "Don't be melodramatic; unfair does not exist in my vocabulary."

We went to an older looking restaurant, on the way Mel and Angel fought over the radio stations, I couldn't tell the difference between the newer stations. We finally settled on an older station playing an old 2005 hit I regularly listen to. The restaurant was pretty old-fashioned, waitresses with note pads, in normal restaurants people have computer note pads that have all the menu items prewritten. Others don't even have waitresses that take your order, but a touch screen in the middle of the table with the menu items.

Our old fashioned restaurant had white linoleum flooring and very few items on the menu. I sat in a booth with Angel in the middle and with Melanie on her left.

The restaurant still had paper covers for straws too, Angel did the trick where she opened one end and blew the paper covering at Melanie. Melanie tried to counter but hers just ended up falling onto the ground. Angel laughed and I sniggered.

I can't even take them to restaurants without fighting. Melanie then turned red and picked up her spoon, and she threw it at Angel. With my quick reflexes I caught it and put it next to mine. Angel had ducked under the table to avoid the spoon and came back up with a piece of gum stuck to her hair.

I laughed as the waitress had come with the soups and salads right then giving us a strange look. Melanie had ordered a soup and without a spoon she looked at me expectantly. I, being the mature person in the group ate with two spoons, telling Melanie to eat her soup with a fork. Finders keepers right?

Halfway through dinner they finally stopped scowling at each other and stopped their retaliations. I was relieved; at one point Angel had stooped down to trying to drop French fries in everybody's drinks.

"I think it's kind of weird that we eat and we don't have too." Melanie said, making conversation. I shook my head, "Eating is a privilege that our kind usually don't have. After meals they have to make themselves barf it all back up within a half hour or they'll get sick. If you don't like eating, you don't have too. I will gladly eat anything you don't want." Angel dropped her fork, "That subject just made me lose my appetite."

I sniggered and started shoving the unsoda sullied French fries in my mouth off of her plate.

"I think its funny they call bars 'pubs' here." Angel said. I shrugged and Melanie rolled her eyes, and Angel started saying random sentences using 'pub' in it. "'Ello mate, care to frolic down to the pub and get a pint? I 'eard pubs are out of style in America, they call 'em bars."

Melanie huffed an annoyed sigh, her facial expression screamed out that she was taking it slightly offensive, and she countered acidly back with a fake American accent. Both were pretty horrible at it, slipping up and adding words neither would say normally and I decided to join in with a fake Russian accent.

My cell phone interrupted our pseudo-multinational conversation and I opened it to find the caller ID as Bill, an old slayer.

I glanced up at Melanie and Angel, both still annoying each other. I looked back down at it buzzing, my mood faltering.

No. I am different now. They are not who I want to be, I am not a parasite like them. I've got just enough to trace a new life and follow it, to do something good!

The phone buzzed once more, trying to coax me to it, if I did, I wouldn't have to worry about money for a long time. It would be quick and easy.

My head slightly jerked to one side, almost shaking my head. I turned my phone off and put it away. And then I relaxed. I looked back to my friends and smiled, trying to dip back into the conversation.

Melanie was sort of mumbling a half southern, half New York accent. I smiled and picked up my drink, it tasted bland and I stopped upon tasting a bit of soggy potatoes in it.

I looked at Angel, listening to her sarcasm, and then found I wasn't quite processing her voice. The seconds pulled longer, but I had long since stopped trying to clasp time and its lack of finite momentum. She was talking, words were forming, biting into the conversation, but I couldn't focus. And then it started buzzing again, I winced.

The little black box was off. I looked at my friends, ignoring me. And the sounds of the diner rushed into my mind. I knew the mindset of my past. Three couples in the back, the ventilation system heaved, my waitress was carrying shakes and one of them was going to fall.

The Flashsword hidden from sight waited on me. I didn't even remember putting it on...

My fingers slid down to the weapon, my smallest finger creeping closer to touch the rim. I pulled away as the cold metal shocked my hand.

A second later, after a crashing sound behind me, the waitress was on her knees scrambling to pick up the broken glass. I jerked my head again. Without looking I turned the phone back on and hit the buttons to reach Bill.

"Hello? Is this thing on? CAN YOU HEAR ME?"

"Hey Bill. What is up?" I asked, somber but neutral as Bill struggled with the videochat. He growled in his old gruff voice, "Don't address me like that, where are your manners?" I stopped, "Sorry Mr. Milton, how may I help you?"

He nodded in approval, and spoke to me in a slightly louder voice than usual, "I know you're out in err, England," He eyed me with a tired and angry face, "We found a coven out here and it's all hands on deck, we are getting close to making a raid big enough for the books, and we could use you as a sniper. Are you up for it?"

I nodded, "Yes sir, I can be out there by tomorrow, can you get somebody to pick me up when I arrive?" He glared at me, then nodded, "But you are paying for the blood stuff all on your own, I don't want ANYTHING to do with it." I nodded, "Yes sir."

And then the screen went black, I looked up at my counterparts. "We are going back to America."

They silenced, and then Melanie shook her head, "I'm not going." I pulled out money to pay for the food. "Yes, it will be fun! You have always wanted to see America."

Melanie held her breath, "But I'm not like you and all that stuff, I'm just Melanie." I nodded, "Of course, and you don't have to fight, it will be a simple job Angel and I will do, and you can hang out in the back. I know plenty of slayers that have wives and children that go to these things and just stay at the house. You will be fine."

Melanie didn't seem convinced, Angel then poked Melanie's arm with her straw and started bawking like a chicken, "Melanie's not a Melanie, Melanie's a chicken!" Angel taunted, "No I'm not!" she replied.

After glaring at Angel she nodded, "Fine! I will fly out to America with you!" I grinned and booked the flight for three seats.

Angel and Melanie fought more than the twin five-year-old boys four rows ahead of us. I tried to pretend to not know them and looked out the window, I couldn't see anything except full white clouds and black sea, the Atlantic seemed to be a smooth blanket, sometimes folding and straightening out.

The six hour flight across the Atlantic ended and we took two others, zipping across the states to land in Ponca City Regional Airport in Oklahoma.

I lugged my suitcase through the airport with Angel buzzing around the news stands and food courts; Melanie fussed with herself and kept dropping her purse and suitcase on the ground. Somehow we all managed to get to the pick up line in one piece and an opal colored minivan pulled up to us. "Are you Moogie?" the woman driver asked. I nodded, "Yes, you are going to take us to Bill's house?" She nodded.

And I opened the car door, Angel crossed her arms, "Seriously? A mom van?" I rolled my eyes, fatigued and tired of her poor behavior. "Angel, just get in the car."

Reluctantly she obeyed, I was the last to pile in and I took the seat closest to the door. Our driver pulled away, and glanced back at me, "Hello, I'm Carrie; you might know my sister Candice?"

I nodded, trying to compose a reserved face. "And this is Angel, and Melanie." I pointed to Angel shaking out her scarlet hair and then to Melanie, searching her bag. "Hello." They both said in monotone unison.

"Is this your first time in Oklahoma?" I nodded, "Yes, it seems much greener than I imagine it would be."

The town was run down, faded by rain, weeds sprouted in every corner, and all of the buildings seemed beaten and defeated. I couldn't imagine living here.

It was dreadfully overcast, and reminded me very much of England, except it didn't smell or sound industrial.

"How much rain do you get here?" I chatted, and Carrie easily conversed with me.

Carrie was middle aged and tired, her skin stretched over her knuckles like old gum stretched after it has been out of your mouth for too long.

Her faintly wrinkled face was hard and dry, without a hint of youthfulness. Her sister seemed the opposite as I compared Carrie to my memories; Candice always smiled and had laugh lines, she always had a special glint. I couldn't believe the drastic difference on the same face.

"How many other slayers are there?" I asked, she frowned and paused, "The children your ages are my son Nate, his cousins George, Mary, and Arnold, some of their second cousins, and all of Bill's boys.

My husband Joseph and I have been staying at the house along with my sister Candice and her husband Fred, Mr. C wasn't feeling up to it and Charlie didn't want to go either, their children were too busy so you won't be seeing them this trip. Bill's sister Sierra is here too, but only because she lives here now. I think a Dolly arrived this morning by the name of Jordan but I don't know how long he will be staying, and that sunny boy from Florida is also here, but he only talks to Arnold."

I stared out the window, trying to connect the names to the family tree, my body growing tenser and more stressed by the second.

England made my troubles so far away. The slayers had been a foggy memory up until now, and I realized how I let myself change and grow softer.

They won't see it though; I will make sure the slayers don't exploit my vulnerability.

We pulled into the towering wire gates leading into the mansion's inner yard; I entered the address into my phone for safe keeping, 901 Monument Street.

With a mental roster of which slayers are going to be at the house I started to dread them already. I only recognized the names from hearing gossip about them, and Candice with her children Mary, Arnold, and George were the only ones from Arizona.

Carrie pulled up through the driveway and dropped us off at the front door. Angel, Melanie, and I gazed at the beautiful house, even without sunshine to brighten the scene, I could enjoy its beauty. The manicured lawn with bushes and trees were pruned with meticulous care. The house was made of brown bricks and seemed aged, but not degraded and overall a modest mansion. I couldn't believe such a building could exist in the midst of this shabby little town, but in another way it seemed to fit no other place than a niche in Oklahoma.

After soaking up the sixty-five degree, slightly wet atmosphere I knocked the big handle with both hands and the butler answered. I planted a smile on my face and stepped through the front door, hoping the inside was just as pleasant as the façade.

"Given the circumstances and the amount of people residing in the house you three will be sharing this room." The butler opened a door to a room with two beds. I stepped inside, "Thank you." I said. And the butler was gone before I turned back around.

"I'm getting the bed on the right; you guys will share that one." Angel said lightly as she effortlessly tossed her gigantic bags on the bed.

"Why? You and Moogie are closer together; you shouldn't be too uncomfortable sharing a bed." Angel glared at Melanie, her pride obviously hurt that somebody had the nerve to stand up to her. "Do you really want to play that game? Miss I-share-half-my-genetics-with-Moogie-because-Moogie's-dad-is-a-pig."

Melanie growled and shoved one of Angel's suitcases off the bed.

I closed my eyes, opened them, and shoved one hand on both of their mouths. "These are some of the most dangerous people you will ever meet. Each and every one of them is itching to have our heads on a platter because they consider us just above the vermin they hunt. You are more than welcome to keep shouting and give them reason to kill us." I said this in a calm and serious expression, both of them silenced as I took my hands off their mouths.

"I'll sleep on the floor; you both can take the beds." They nodded to my proposition and unpacked silently.

Minutes later the intercom came on in the corner of the room. I jumped at the sound of Bill's voice propelling out of the speaker. "Now that everybody is here, late or not, all those who are going to do the job need to report to the dining room for briefing, and the rest can come for dinner when called."

I sniffed angrily at the insult about being late, what did he expect? He only called me hours before, and I flew out on the first available flight, we weren't late, but now everybody is going to think we were.

Melanie stayed put as I got up to leave the room. "Melanie? Come on!" She shook her head, "But the voice said-" I cut her off, "I'm not leaving you here all alone. And nobody will be able to tell."

People from all of the rooms materialized and started toward the dining room. Angel, Melanie, and I were a little ahead of everybody and found our seats at the table quickly. As more and more quietly took their seats I noticed Candice's family appeared. George and Arnold nodded to me and their sister. Mary tapped Arnold and whispered something to him. He nodded and she kept stealing glances at me.

William Milton Junior, or Bill as everybody called him, sat at the head of the table looking as important as ever, and I noticed the two seats next to him were taken by two men with dark brown hair. I didn't know which of Bill's four sons they were, but they looked very much like him.

Angel sat to the right of Melanie, and Melanie sat to the right of me, on my left the seat was taken early by a boy wearing a leather jacket with slightly tanned skin and sandy blonde hair. He contrasted with the rest of the people as they all had various shades of brown hair and brown eyes.

He leaned over to me, "I'm guessing you got prime seats with that super speed?" my mouth twitched, though I still kept composure. "You look a little on the deep fried side, shall they be serving you tonight next to the potatoes?" He snorted, though I could see he was just as tense as me. "Yeah, they probably would want my head on a platter, I guess I'll have to worry about that if they ever lynch you. They might just decide to take out all the birds with a stone."

"I'm guessing you're the Dolly?" He nodded, replying, "Yep, Jordan Dolly, and the only one that seems brave enough to sit next to you guys, you're Moogie, right?" I nodded. "Us outcasts have to stick together, right?" He nodded, "And when trouble comes we throw each other to the wolves and run away."

I smiled at the sarcastic truth, "That sounds just about right." He was playing the game just as much as me.

Bill cleared his throat loudly, "Is everybody here?" He said this, and glanced uncertainly at the nearest seat to his right, empty.

He picked up a folder and opened it "Alright, we'll start, a few days ago-" "Wait!" The doors shot open and a boy burst inside the room.

"Sorry, I'm here now." Bill stood up, "No Jerry, this meeting isn't for you." The boy, winded from sprinting stopped, "What? But I'm fifteen now! And this is one of the last big hunts ever!"

Bill's face turned red and he crossed his arms, "This meeting isn't for you! Go back to your mother."

He slouched, "But-" He looked heart broken at us, "But-"

Bill pointed to the door, "But nothing, go!"

The boy blushed deeply, and I could see he was about to cry, he was desperate, and then his mistaking eyes met mine. His tone icy with the final argument, "You tell the blood suckers the plan, you let them go fight. And they make all kinds of mistakes. But you deny your son? How could you?"

I had no pity for the boy as all heads turned to me; I felt the shift in the table, and keeping quiet I pretended not to be offended. But Angel stood up then, and leaned over to me, "I'm leaving. Melanie, let's go." And Melanie silently rose.

I kept my eyes fixed on the boy, and everybody watched Angel and Melanie leave the room. Not one word was spoken; tears started streaming down the boy's face. I hated him, and I loathed Angel for being so weak.

After Melanie and Angel left, he stomped out of the room, his footsteps echoing across the ceiling.

"Sorry for the interruption, my youngest son gets a little too excited sometimes." Bill avoided eye contact with me, and said no words further on the subject.

In the center of the table a little machine was propped up on four legs, and what seemed like a projector was installed in the middle. Bill clicked a button and a large holographic map appeared in the middle. I was seated directly in front with the best view.

"This is the map of the town we are in now. This is the mansion, and these are the six locations where people have disappeared." Bill stated this while one big blue dot appeared on the map and several smaller red ones were interspersed around the holographic scene.

"As you can see-"

"Bill?" George stood up from his seat next to Candice, "Are you telling us you don't know where the coven is?" Bills voice shook, "Um, well, yes. But-"

George crossed his arms, "You are telling us that you brought us all here so we could follow just a lead?" The temper in George's voice seemed to get shorter every word, heads turned to Bill, waiting for his reply like twelve-year-olds waiting for gossip.

"As you can see the evidence is all here, I mean-" George interrupted Bill, "You mean you lied to us to get us to chase some spectral clue? Bill, we all have leads in our own towns, and you know for damn sure if you aren't a hundred percent certain there is a coven here, then we can't stay and follow up with days and days worth of staking out and following people."

I agreed, growing madder as I caught on to Bill's wolf cry.

With George's point brought up Bill had lost us. Everybody started to rise and leave, George was right, Bill had lied to us. Bill frantically clicked through the holographic slideshow display until he reached a map of an interstate highway. "Wait!" Several dots appeared around the highway from the Winifred, Kansas until Ponca City, Oklahoma.

"Look, this is one of the larger covens, ever since the second disappearance here I've been able to track these monsters. They have been along State Highway 77, killing around the same amount of people in every stop, and, even the same kind of people. It looks like they are currently residing somewhere in here." Bill gruffed hard and quickly his explanation, it caught the attention of half the slayers trying to leave.

Eventually Bill's captive audience returned and he could continue his prideful leading. I hadn't left my seat, Basically all of the victims were young men and women, their bodies disappeared from parking lots, but their cars stayed at the original parked location.

When the meeting finally concluded Bill pushed himself up from the table and he made his way out. "Dinner will be served shortly." He grumbled.

Moments after, the intercom came on and Bill's voice boomed the permission for the rest of the guests to come to the dining room.

Neither Angel nor Melanie returned to my side, they were too afraid. The boy Jerry shot me a look of disdain as he took his seat close to the head of the table. A man much older with a beer bottle in hand stumbled into the room as the final few people sat down at the table. "I'mmmm here."

He took a swig and settled in the empty seat on the first right of the head of the table. Few watched him with disgust, I looked also, briefly. Unluckily, he caught my eye and glowered at me, "What are you lookin' at blood sssucker?"

I looked down and focused on my reflection in the fork. Servers appeared with silver plates. Before I dug in I noticed half the table watching me, I blushed, were we supposed to say prayer?

Jordan Dolly even looked down at me with the same expression. "You know, you don't need to eat or put on a show, or do you like to celebrate bulimia?" Jordan's puns didn't make me laugh this time, but I understood.

They really did take me for a full enemy, after the countless times I've explained the difference, after all these years.

Silently I ate whatever food was on my plate, it didn't take long, and I stood up, "Thank you Mr. Milton, I think I will excuse myself and turn in for the night. And I hope we can catch the killers ransacking your town."

My chair loudly echoed as I scooted it in, and the servants quickly dodged out of my way as I stepped to pass them.

Then another chair scooted and behind me I heard, "God damn blood sucker can't even stay to respect my Daddy's meal!" And barely missing my head by about a foot, the beer bottle from the drunk man passed me and crashed into the door in front of me. I stopped and swallowed, the glass shattered and almost like a mist, shards graced by my legs.

I didn't turn around, I didn't look at their faces; they weren't worth the plates they ate off of. With both my hands I pulled open the door and walked straight through.

25
Try Again

All I wanted to do was prove them wrong. Melanie and Angel had already finished packing everything by the time I returned to our bedroom. "We are staying." I commanded blackly.

"We are going to hunt by ourselves, I have the information about the leads, and we are starting tomorrow." Angel stared at me in confusion, "I thought this was just a job, not a hunt." I shook my head, "Bill lied to us."

"Then why are we bothering?" she asked, her voice so impatient. I looked up at her, "Why? This is going to be one of the last coven hunts out there, don't you want to see their faces when we are the only ones to find them?"

I turned to Melanie and said, "This is a dying game, a time in history that will be looked back on, we have the privilege of participating in it. And you guys just want to give up because somebody doesn't like you?" Their faces remained skeptical, so I tried a shorter approach, "It won't be dangerous for you, but you have everything to gain!"

Angel still looked at me uncertainly, and Melanie looked down at the ground. I held my breath, "Please?"

Angel nodded, and Melanie mumbled consent. All of us slept horribly, I would startle awake at the slightest sound, Angel sometimes got out of bed to listen to the door, and Melanie wouldn't stop tossing and whimpering.

I tried fixing the problem for Angel by barricading the door, and I brought Melanie sleeping pills. The sleeping pills were just a placebo though because most drugs don't work on us, nevertheless, Melanie stopped tossing and turning.

I wasn't going to let them give up yet.

Worst of all, when the sun rose the intercom came on with the piecing sound of a bullhorn. It startled us to our feet, and before I knew it I was holding the Flashsword out and ready. Then I realized where I was and put it away.

We didn't bother going down for breakfast, just headed straight for the door. Coming out from the hall Jordan appeared. He smiled at me, and I nodded to him as I put on my coat. "Getting a head start?" I nodded, and replied "Breakfast is for people with time."

"Are you going to need a car?" He asked, I stopped, "Yeah," I countered. He pointed to the key rack by my head, "That one on the far left is Sierra's; she isn't going out anytime soon, I don't think anybody would notice."

I flipped the key off the hook, "Thanks. Which one are you taking?" he pointed to one on the far right, "One of the servants is loaning me her car." He winked at me and reached passed me to take the key. I blushed at how close we were, but he didn't notice, and then he grabbed his coat and headed straight out the door.

Angel crossed her arms, "Who was that?" I shrugged, "Just a Dolly. We met at dinner last night while you were making your escape." Angel looked at the door again, "He's kind of cute." I shrugged again, nonchalantly. One of Angel's simply sinister smiles appeared, "Bravo, my seductress trainee, you got your first car out of an admirer, soon with a wink of an eye, a flip of your hair, and little more time learning from me, boys will be giving you the shirts off their back."

I snorted, and shook my head, but Angel seemed genuinely proud of herself. I looked at Melanie and giggled, she nodded her head in mock agreement with Angel and we continued out the door.

I checked the cars and found we all had to cram into an old Beemer that looked like it was welded from two cars. Surprisingly, it blended in very well with the other cars.

I drove through the streets, the image of the holographic map in my head as a reference. Most of the disappearances happened in mall parking lots, and a few outside restaurants. Like the other slayers, we decided to stake out, Angel dressed up and we were going to use her as bait.

"Ready?" I asked, Angel reapplied some red lipstick. "Ready as I'll ever be." She said. Melanie and I stayed in the Beemer, and Angel took the role of bait, strutting around the buildings. She was a flash of red against the soggy shades of brownish building and sidewalk. Yes, she definitely stood out, but in another way still looked normal.

Angel as bait has worked before, nobody has ever come up to me and put drugs in my drink, but I have lost track of how many times Angel has gotten slipped a mickey.

Unconsciously my eyes were drawn to her, she was the perfect bait, if I was the weak minded child I used to be, I wouldn't be able to control myself. She would have been my first choice to feed on.

It is ironic, given she is an unusually cruel slayer and takes pride in ripping the life out of who ever thought they were going to have her as a midnight snack.

Melanie was anxious; she looked guilty and awkward with her inexperience in stakeouts. I reached over and pet her hair. "It's alright Melanie, shhh, relax, nobody is going to attack us. If they do I'll end them before they can get to you."

She looked like she was going to hyperventilate. I shook my head, "Here Melanie, take this." I pulled my skirt up a little and unstrapped the leather holster on my leg. The Tanto, which I kept as a backup, was as smooth and new as the first time Andy handed it to me.

After Ben I had scrubbed it thoroughly, making every part shine. The piece was more of a work of art than anything else, and I found little use of it as the Flashsword always had taken the wear and grind of a main weapon.

Melanie looked at it in awe. "I don't really need it, for now you can use it for protection, later if you want to, I'll teach you how to really use it." I grinned at her speechless expression, and as she held it I found it seemed somehow better with her than with me.

Angel naturally walked in and out of stores, at certain time intervals she would go to the parking lot and walk around the cars, trying to find isolated areas where she could look vulnerable.

By the end of the hour she checked back in with me and dropped off three shopping bags. "What is this?" I asked.

Angel dropped the bags on the backseat, "I can't just walk around stores all day empty handed! They are props." I glanced inside the bag, "Expensive props, why are you dropping them off?" Angel exasperatingly sighed, "I can't go back into the mall with bags, duh."

I pinched the bridge of my nose, "Okay, whatever, did you see anything?" Angel shook her head, "No one except a few other slayers, it looks like two other groups are staking out this location." I closed my eyes, "Alright. Get back to work."

Hours passed Angel returned multiple times with lunch, way too many shoe boxes, jewelry, and three phone numbers from guys.

The entire day passed without luck, we returned to the mansion at half past four in the morning. All of us got about three hours of sleep before we started the next day's worth of staking out.

"I didn't know lying around made people so tired." Melanie commented.

A week passed and nothing happened, the staking out method was useless. As Angel returned again with another phone number, I turned to both of them and said, "We aren't going to catch anybody with some other slayer's method. Maybe we need to look at the situation differently."

Angel lean against the car, "What do you suppose we should do about it?" I wrapped my arms around the seat, and laid my head on the top rest. "Let's do what we do best, go to bars and night clubs, even in this desolate towns like this, they have entertainment like Phoenix and London." Angel nodded, "Yeah, and you know, I saw a bar over at that strip mall, let's head over there tonight."

I changed into one of my skimpy outfits that night, and Angel only did minor tweaks to her current outfit. Melanie, who had changed in the bathroom downstairs, appeared before us in a conservative pink polo. Her hair was clipped back and her shoes were so clean they glowed.

"Ready!" She said. Angel fell on the bed, choking and laughing, I bit my lip. I was afraid of messing up my dark, heavy mascara. "Um, Melanie, well, it is a pretty outfit, but, well, it isn't right for this occasion."

Melanie's cheeks glowed red, "Oh, I don't have any proper evening wear other than this." Angel's face was beginning to look like the color of her hair.

"You can always borrow some of my clothes, let's see what fits you." I picked out a new top for Melanie, and shoes that were not so clean that they squeaked.

I ruffled Melanie's hair up, and when she thought I wasn't looking she tried to straighten it again. Melanie shied away from make-up with the excuse they give her boils all over her face and I gave up. Melanie looked odd, but still outshined me any day of the week.

We left the mansion and I jogged ahead to get and bring the car around. At night the grassy grounds seemed different, almost tranquil, it reminded me of a golf course I used to walk on with my little sister as a child.

In the moonlight, we would collect all of the stray golf balls and build a nest. After organizing them by color we would play pretend for hours, trading, juggling, talking to them. I couldn't remember a night which we didn't find a new game.

I shook out of my thoughts and opened the Beemer door. Another car pulled in and parked a few yards away, Jordan exited the driver seat. "Hey!" He called. I waved and dropped into the Beemer, turning the key in the ignition. He came up and leaned into the window, "Hi, I haven't seen you all week." I shrugged, "I've been working, any progress on your side?" He shook his head.

"I don't think anybody is making any headway, it would have made it into Bill's daily reports. But I did hear that in a few days if nothing turns up, there is going to be a huge group search throughout all of the farm land around here. Are you going to go?"

I shook my head, "Nah, I have my own methods."

He looked slightly dismayed, "Besides being nocturnal, what are you doing out so late anyway?"

I smirked, "I told you, I have my own methods." And I winked at him as I pulled the car out to Angel and Melanie.

"What took you so long?" Angel moaned, "I had to stand next to that for a full five minutes!"

"Hey!" Melanie shot back.

"Leave each other alone, we have better things to do." I cut in. Obediently, they clambered into the car and we started to our next location.

In the strip mall a little building wedged in the middle had the name of the club in red flickering florescent lights; I entered first with Melanie trailing behind.

I didn't realize how much of a night club this not was. Everybody wore some variation of flannel and looked like you could scrape a coat of grease off of their skin. This place wasn't any bigger than any of the stores around them.

It was more like a bar than a night club, except the center was cleared out like a dance floor. A few people were dancing to the country music playing from the DJ's speakers. I planted myself on one of the bar stools and ordered a bottle of beer, Melanie did the same, and Angel dropped off her purse with me. "I'm going to dance." she mumbled, and blended in nicely with the people.

Melanie downed her beer quickly and ordered another, she shoved it in her mouth and I caught her arm. "Melanie, stop, we don't actually drink the drinks, especially when out hunting."

Melanie popped it out of her mouth, "Oh, good, I hate these bloody things anyway." I stared up at the ceiling, and then kept my eyes out for any suspicious activity.

The end of the night passed, and I could see everybody in the bar, no one did anything out of the ordinary except an older guy danced with Angel a bunch.

Angel seemed more focused on the guy than anything else in the bar, and Melanie decided to put all of her efforts to peeling the labels off her and my beer bottles.

Finally the bar closed and we were all kicked out. Angel happily talked to the old guy outside the bar and took his cowboy hat off his head and put it on hers. She laughed and waved to him good night.

"I'm glad one of us enjoyed themselves." I mumbled tiredly, "Shut up." Angel teased back.

The next morning I startled up by that stupid bullhorn and banged my elbow strangely on the wood floor I was sleeping on.

Angel seemed daily unaffected by the bullhorn, she rolled over and ducked under her pillow. Melanie pulled the covers over her head and both of them were still after that.

Still in my pajamas, I decided to go explore Bill's study and pick up another book, I had been reading half the time in stakeouts and I just finished the next book in the series I was reading.

I opened the door, and stepped out, "Hey Moogie." I jumped. Jordan, fully dressed in his usual leather jacket and jeans leaned against the wall next to my door.

Nobody else except us were up in the hall, and I looked at him confused, "What's up?" He looked at me, and said slightly nervous, "I wanted to catch you before you turned into a bat and searched the city for the coven." I laughed, and he continued, "Well, um I was wondering if you wanted to go out with me sometime."

I blushed and looked down at the ground, "Really?" was all I could reply. "Yeah, there is a movie theater a little north of here, and tonight is that big farm land search, so I was thinking tomorrow-"

"Yes." I answered; he looked just as shocked as I was. "I'll pick you up out front of here at seven okay?" I nodded and people started emerging from their doors, he started away. "Bye." And I waved.

I turned back inside and shut the door, "Angel!" I jumped on the bed and ripped the pillow off of her face, "Guess what!" she rolled over, "It's too early." she whined.

When Angel did wake up, I explained what happened and she shoved me. "No way! Why didn't you wake me up sooner?" Melanie was excited too, and offered to loan me clothes if I needed them, I shook my head, "Thanks Melanie, but I do own clothes other than the stuff I usually wear."

Date or not I still had to work, and by night fall we were out to another bar. The old guy was there again, in a pin stripe suit this time. He and Angel talked around half the night and I found myself once again the only person trying to look out for any signs of the coven members.

Then, with all the grace and sway of a true God, Angel stood up and walked along the bar table. The bar tender was too shocked to object and Angel clicked her heels over to where Melanie and I sat. "Excuse me everybody, but can I have your attention!" She called to the bar, somehow the music stopped and all eyes were on her.

She turned around and said something to the bar tender and he poured her a shot. "I'd like to give a toast to this young lady right here." Angel pointed to me, "After twenty-five years of life, today she was asked out on her first date by a smokin' hot guy!"

My face was redder than the hot dogs they served, and Angel, bright and confident as ever, raised her glass. "To Moogie!"

I stopped breathing, as all eyes were turned on me. Everybody raised their beers and hollering out in unison, hollering "To Moogie!" And Angel slurped down her shot. Finishing she hooted, and someone in the back shouted "Amen!"

The music flipped on again, and she hopped right down and ruffled my hair, "Good job baby sis." She said, and went back to the stool next to the old guy.

I didn't know how much I was going to be traumatized; nobody had ever called me into the spotlight like that. Of everything that has ever happened to me, that was one of the scariest moments ever. Only Angel could pull that off. She is the most amazing person that ever existed.

I smiled, knowing only that as fact. And I smiled also, because I realized what a future I have. I have Angel in my life, we haven't been close in these months but that will change. I will rebuild our relationship, I will fix everything that has ever been broken.

Forever isn't such a lonely place, my life isn't as it used to be. I don't really know what I will do with my life after I finish this job, but I know that it will be alright, because Angel will be in it.

"Moogie, why is Angel allowed to drink on the job?" Melanie asked confused. I looked up at her, leaving my thoughts, and grinned at her face. "Because Melanie, Angel has been training and building up a resistance to this stuff for years. While you were in primary school coloring, she was out night after night training extremely hard with all of the variety of liquor she could find." I held a serious poker face and Melanie took the answer seriously, though I was still shaking from adrenaline after Angel's embarrassing speech.

"Oh. Well that makes sense." I bit down on my tongue hard to keep from falling off the stool in hysterical laughter.

Angel came over to us with a beer in hand, "Did you like my speech?" I nodded and opened my mouth to answer her. Melanie cut in, with a curious and serious expression, "Angel, is there any chance you could teach me how to build up a tolerance like you have?"

Angel's eyebrows rose, "Huh?" I slapped my hand over my mouth to keep from laughing.

Both of them looked at me as is I was crazy. "What?" Melanie said, "What did I miss?"

The bar closed, and Angel kissed the old guy on the cheek before running to catch up with us. "Don't worry Angel, one day it won't matter that you are sixty years apart, because you will be over a hundred years old and he will be the young one." Angel plugged her ears, "Don't talk about that, I don't want to wake up one day and know I'm five hundred years old!"

I laughed, "Why? You'll still look pretty hot, it's just you'll be twenty times smarter than the average boy you date."

Angel laughed, "Yeah, I guess you are right, I will still be hot five hundred years from now."

We laughed and talked, and then we passed an old diner, "I bet they serve fish and chips in there, do you think we could go in?" I shook my head, "They won't be like it in England, but some good old American French fries sound good right now."

Melanie shook her head, "French are not-" Angel shrugged, interrupting, "Yeah, it's only two in the morning, who doesn't crave French fries at this hour?"

I turned around and parked the car. The moon had been covered by the clouds and the white luminescent diner looked cold, but not as cold as the air we were walking through.

Inside a couple sat at a booth by the window, and an old bearded man slept at the back of the room. Two tired young women sipped coffee at the counter, we decided to take the booth behind the couple, Melanie sat with her back turned to them while Angel and I faced them.

They looked just as tired as the girls at the counter, the waitress arrived with a smile planted on her face, but she looked fatigued too.

"What can I get for y'all?" I curved my hands to shape a circle and said, "A big bowl of French fries and three coffees." She nodded, not bothering to take it down on the pad she held in her right hand.

Angel adjusted her hair and fidgeted boredly. "Moogie?" she asked suddenly. I looked up from my quiet fidgeting, "Moogie, you know how Santa Claus has that white fur on his suit?"

I raised my eyebrows, "Yes?"

Angel twirled her hair, "When Mrs. Claus made it, did she have her little gnomes kill a bunch of baby seals or a polar bear to get them?"

Melanie scoffed at Angel, "They are not gnomes, they are elves."

Angel pretended she didn't hear Melanie beside her.

I shrugged, "I don't know," I paused, imagining what would happen in a polar bear versus tiny elves fight would be.

We left the conversation for future contemplation and Angel picked up the ketchup at the corner of the table and read the label, "Are tomatoes actually in ketchup any more? Or are they synthesized like the sugar?" Melanie opened her mouth to say something, but decide against it.

While Angel was seeking the ultimate questions of her universe on the back of a ketchup bottle, I examined the diner around me. Everything looked kitschy, genuinely retro, circa nineteen fifties. There was a high possibility that nothing had changed since the nineteen fifties, the entire city didn't seem like it moved very fast into the future. I wondered what I was going to look like seventy years from now, or five hundred.

Time seemed bazaar, I felt nearly every moment, yet when I stop to look back at my past I find it so far away.

I looked at the customers again, the couple seemed slightly odd, instead of plaid, the woman wore an expensive fur coat. Her hair on one side had shiny waves frozen in place no matter which way she moved her head. The sunglasses she held looked like a model's from a fashion magazine I read when I was a child.

Strangest of all she spoke in another language to the man across from her. "Hey," I tapped Angel, "listen to their accent, what does it sound like?" Angel stopped and shrugged, "Sounds like German." I nodded, "Or Austrian."

Melanie smiled, "I guess I'm not the only foreign person here." Angel returned to the ketchup bottle, and Melanie seemed to be sorting salt on the table.

I looked up at the couple again. The woman was watching me, like she heard everything I had said. I blushed and got up from the table, making my way to the bathroom.

In the mirror I adjusted my make-up and played with my hair. The woman then came in too, out of a little designer purse she found a lipstick and twisted it up. I turned to her, "Where is your accent from? I'm dying to know."

She looked at me, "It is Austrian, you had guessed right." I blushed, she heard me, though I thought I was talking in a quiet voice.

"It is pretty there?" I asked stupidly. Her lips pressed together and she smiled mysteriously, "Yes. Especially in the winter." And she turned and walked right out.

As I passed the table again I noticed something strange about their food, it had been cut up and scooted around, but neither of them looked as if they had eaten anything.

The Austrian woman had settled back down in her seat, the man asked her a question and I only recognized one word, "Clementina" as he first addressed her. The woman replied with a smirk and shook her head no.

Our French fries appeared and I carefully tried to look nonchalant. Angel, oblivious to the possible situation, dumped ketchup all over the French fries while ignoring Melanie's objections.

I pulled out my phone and started texting Angel and Melanie.

Don't say anything out of the ordinary, the couple isn't right. Something is wrong.

I sent it and Angel instantly got the message, her expression hardened and she didn't look up at the couple. Melanie looked up and raised her hands confused. But then her cell phone buzzed and she read the message.

She looked back up at me alarmed.

Melanie: What do you mean?

Moogie: The couple hasn't eaten their
   food, and they have already paid
   for the meal. Don't look.

Melanie: So?

Angel: U R rite, they R weird

Moogie: I think they are stalking

Melanie: What?

Angel: Yeah.

Melanie: I'm lost

Angel: Shut up Mel

Moogie: The Austrian woman heard our
   conversation, about   the
   accents.

Melanie: I can't see them, what are
   they doing now?

Angel: Who R they stakin?

Moogie: The girls from the counter.

Melanie: are you guys sure?

```
Moogie: Yes.

Moogie: Wait, the girls are getting up.

Melanie: The lady just asked the girls
   to help jump start their car.

Moogie: We need to follow them.

Angel: Whn?

Moogie: Now.
```

We hid behind the Beemer far into the parking lot and watched the girls pull their car up next to the couple's car. I leaned over to Melanie, "Do you have the Tanto?" She nodded, "Yes,"

I looked at her, "Pull it out."

The first girl opened the hood; she and the man leaned over next to it. The Austrian woman beckoned the second girl over to the trunk; she obediently followed. In one swift motion, the woman stabbed the girl in the neck with what looked like a syringe, picked her up, and placed her in the trunk while the other was completely oblivious.

Melanie's breath caught, and before she could take another the Austrian woman walked up to the second and hit her in the neck before sweeping her off her feet and carrying her to the trunk.

Angel had her phone out. "I'm calling the slayers." She said. "No!" I whispered and shut the phone.

Angel pointed, "But look, we can follow them back to the coven and kill the rest of them tomorrow night." I shook my head, "Did you just not see them? Those girls will die if we wait."

Angel looked back at the car; the Austrian woman had put the second girl in the trunk. She had lit a cigarette, took a few drags and put it out on the second girl's arm.

Angel looked back at me, and a knife replaced her cell phone, waiting for command.

I, in turn, removed my Flashsword and placed my thumb on the button. "I'll take the guy and you take the girl, Melanie, you stay here."

We both jumped out and rushed them. The woman took off instantly into a run and Angel veered away from me to follow her. The man stayed, cursing, and I swung my Flashsword. He dodged it and I swung again. The sword bounced against the concrete and the man charged behind me. I turned and side kicked him squarely in the stomach. He and I both shot back, me getting knocked onto my butt and him flying backwards completely off balance. The Flashsword slipped from my hand and skitted a few feet away. I wanted to lunge and get it but he regained his balance and rushed me again.

I jumped to my feet and dodged out of his reach. He turned and glared, he and I circled each other and I rushed and did a sweep on his feet.

He thudded to the ground hard and I jumped to pick up my Flashsword, I swung down at him and he rolled to the side. My Flashsword clinked off the sidewalk. Then I swung again and missed. His legs were to me now, and I quickly stomped on one of them.

He cringed in pain, his mouth dropping open to scream. I placed the tip of my Flashsword to his neck. Behind me Melanie screamed, "No! No! Moogie! Stop!"

Before she could finish her sentence I jabbed the tip into the soft fat of his neck. Blood coursed out into a puddle.

I turned to face Melanie who had left the protection of the Beemer, brain matter dripped off my sword. Out behind Melanie the

Austrian woman sprang from the bushes. She had a trash can lid in hand, and she struck a blow to the back of Melanie's head.

Melanie dropped to her knees.

The bitch continued to charge at me, I raised my sword and we met, the trash can lid as a shield crashed with my Flashsword.

Somehow she managed to punch me with the other hand, and shove me off. I swung again, this time aiming for the lid. It flew from her hands and she backed up.

I swung again, barely missing her stomach.

Realizing she was outmatched, she turned and sprinted away.

I started after her, but looked back; Melanie was standing back up. "Come on Melanie! Let's go!"

Melanie just stared at me. "Come on!" I called, looking back at the woman's escaping silhouette. I started back to Melanie's petrified side. "It's alright," I said.

I stood by and patted her on the back, "Are you okay? Did she hurt you?" Melanie shook her head.

Angel appeared, "I lost her." She said panting slightly, "I know." I replied, "She just escaped."

A minute later several cars pulled up. Nearly all of the slayers spilled out, and an expression of guilt distinguished itself into Angel's sharp features, "I'm sorry Moogie, I had to call them."

Several slayers sprinted to the car and others to the body. All of them were looking at me, and the goo dripping from my sword.

Bill strode over to me, his eyes narrowing. Before I realized what he was doing he back handed me, and I hit the concrete. "You stupid, blood-sucking parasite, why didn't you follow them?"

I tried to get up, and the old man kicked me in the stomach. I bit my tongue hard enough to make me bleed. "Two girls, back of the car, wouldn't survive." I gasped.

"Those were just worthless little people! Do you know how many others we could have saved?" His gruff voice was raised to a roar.

He kicked me again and I threw up blood. "Boss!" one of the slayers called from behind him. "I got an address! Let's go!"

He planted one last, hard kick into my stomach and turned away. "You are a disgrace to everything slayers stand for!" and he turned back to me and spat on my cheek.

I heaved and tasted another mouthful of blood. Then I made the mistake of looking up. They all watched me, Angel and Melanie too. Their faces frozen in shock.

Bill disappeared into a car, the slayers had already picked up the body and cleaned up the scene. They were starting the ignition to both the cars and the girls I saved disappeared into a van. I fixed my eyes on the concrete cracks my blood was filling.

The rest of the slayers piled into their cars and drove off, it was back to just Melanie, Angel, and I.

My eyes stared blankly into the concrete, I wasn't hurt very much physically, and the worst was probably a broken rib.

I picked myself up, my hand pressed against the cold concrete and stung as rocks poked into it. Melanie hadn't moved, neither had Angel. They were statues. I reached down to pick up my Flashsword and I closed it quickly.

They followed me as I returned back to the Beemer, and I turned the ignition. We didn't speak as I passed the corner, coming back to the mansion, they didn't help me as I climbed the stairs to our room.

Every breath I took shot a ping of pain through me, and when I reached my door I found a post-it note folded and stuck to my door.

I peeled it off and entered our room. Angel then spoke, "How did you know she had escaped when I hadn't told you yet?" I looked up at

Angel, "She was hiding in the bushes the entire time, and she jumped out and fought me after I killed her mate."

"How did she get away?" Angel asked. I dropped my purse on the floor next to where I sleep. "She ran." Angel's words started getting sharper. "Why didn't you chase her?" I looked at Melanie, "I was afraid of leaving Mel-"

"You idiot!" She shouted, I flinched at her voice, "You keep babysitting her! She is one of us!" I looked at her dumbstruck.

"How could you neglect your job like that?" I opened my mouth to answer her, but she started again. "Why do you care so much about her? If you wanted her to be safe then why did you bring her in the first place? You know she can't defend herself!" Angel shoved me, which hurt more than I expected. "You always think about her instead of me! I don't even exist to you anymore! You are always saying 'Melanie this' and 'Melanie that' am I not good enough to be your best friend anymore? She doesn't even want to be here!" tears streamed down her face, I looked at Melanie. She was far away in a corner, silent.

I looked back at Angel. She stared back at me, "I hope you are happy with my replacement, you-you don't deserve me anyway." And she stomped out the door. I held my breath, partially because breathing hurt, but I was speechless. The only thing I could do was rush into the bathroom and throw up again.

The post-it crumpled in my hand. I shut the lid and closed the bathroom door, I couldn't think, it hurt so much to breathe, and I couldn't bring myself to cry. I laid on the floor and stared at the ceiling. With my thumb I flipped open the note, in sloppy, half cursive handwriting I read the paper.

The date is off, don't talk to me, don't even look at me.

-Jordan Dolly

I crumpled up the paper and tossed it into the trash.

The intercom came on about an hour later, "Thanks to the mistakes made by one slayer today, we found evidence a coven of seven have fled and are nowhere to be found. Good night, and I hope we shall never experience such a loss again."

I rolled over and my chest stung. Seven, seven times the amount of people I could have saved today, and instead I chose those two girls.

I closed my eyes, two girls. What was I thinking? Why was I so blind?

The self loathing returned as clear as the aching daylight. No beer haze would ever lighten it, no friend could ever comfort me.

The hand of suffering tightened its grasp, bringing the physical pain of regret. And all of the action to sand down the lament and exercise of retribution could never make it go away.

The next morning the bullhorn startled me awake. I emerged from the bathroom floor and found Melanie asleep in her bed. The other was untouched. Angel's suitcase was gone too, and a pink letter was folded neatly on the pillow, I opened it and found it was written in eyeliner.

After all that we have been through you refuse to choose me, and I won't ever forgive you.

I found someone who actually appreciates me for who I am. He is not what I deserve, but Moogie, you and I are done. Fuck you.

-Angel

I pulled my eyes, not even attempting to claw out of the void, what have I done?

26
The Weasel

Melanie and I packed, she read the letter when she thought I wasn't looking, and made no comment. I dodged out the back door, and the servants gave me dirty looks as I passed through. I called a taxi from the airport to pick us up and although I didn't see anybody I knew they were there, waiting for me, the ultimate disgrace, to leave.

We rolled our bags into the airport and went through security, all of my weapons checked into the belly of the plane.

"You never said where we were going." Melanie said as I handed her the ticket.

I smiled, but half-heartedly, "We are going home."

The temperature was one hundred and five degrees outside and drier than England could ever dream to be. Phoenix didn't change at all, same smell, the same sky, the same almost-dead-but-still-hanging-in-there vegetation along with all of the foreign plants on the side of the nicely landscaped freeway. I missed it all.

Melanie stared out the window the entire time; I drove, absent-mindedly telling her all about the city. I wanted to cry again, but I didn't, one of the worst days of my life happened and I rolled over it in almost denial. I was waiting for the self hatred to make me implode into the mess I should be.

My mindless chatter turned into talking about my childhood memories. I was born and raised here; before I had been turned I had never left Arizona. I found myself trying to explain every bit to Melanie, to paint the best picture I could about how this place is so undeniably significant in my life. The entire time she stared out the window listening.

I took a detour to show her the street I grew up on, I pointed to my house, my elementary school, middle school, and the place where I was supposed to go to high school. We drove by the parks, and hangouts at the mall. I named all of the kids on my block I would sometimes play with, and Angel's house.

Then I showed her the bridge Angel and I fought against the esophagus ripper woman, and the places I hunted as a young slayer, all of it seemed so long ago.

I finished my small tour and we started home, my home. The straight roads I went down had looked different in the sky, at night when the buildings lit up each area was shaped into giant squares. It reminded me of a chess board with a perimeter of mountains. It was so easy and relaxing to navigate; I had no roundabouts to worry about, no sinuous streets or unlabeled dead ends to get lost in. Phoenix is beautiful.

The street sign was in view, and Melanie, so taciturn watched it, "Moogie." She said.

"Yes?" I answered.

She paused, something I never saw hesitated inside of her soft expression on such a grownup face.

In that pause I felt myself snap out of the haze in which I had spent the last hour or two in, self indulgently talking.

I looked up at her, she had such beautiful golden hair, it was the same shade as me, but somehow I never could stand to see it in my reflection. Years and years of violently cutting it, I stopped truly looking at and appreciating the pretty shade.

She couldn't look at me. Her voice was so politely prepossessing, and completely miserable. "I can't do this. I'm sorry, I don't belong here. I can't do it."

I braked and idled, paused into the silence.

"I'm sorry, I'm sorry for everything, America was such a bad idea and look what happened. Moogie, this isn't my place." Melanie's voice shook with tears, and I looked down.

I turned the car around and sped on the freeway back to the airport, and the lightrail flashed by.

We arrived back from where we came. Melanie shoved whatever tears she had away and turned her back on me with a short goodbye. I watched her as she melted into the faces without expression.

My hands were frozen on the steering wheel, I didn't grip it, there wasn't much strength in me. I looked back at the faces, trying to see her face in the people. She was gone, and I couldn't stop her.

I returned home again, a place I had rarely seen. It was unsteadily quiet, I rolled my bags in and carried them up stairs, the sixth and seven stairs squeaked when I stepped in the middle of them.

I unpacked, slowly hanging all of my clothes up, putting the shoes away by color coding them, and when I was done I showered and laid on my bed.

I couldn't make myself cry, there didn't seem to be a point. Crying only seems to matter when it is on somebody's shoulder.

Not much time had gone by, days maybe? And I found myself as a different person walking among the living. They are living here, people, it would be impossible not to in the sun.

I was colder though, my physical being fit into the temperature, and I found myself periodically stopping to acknowledge the heat and feeling dry.

I didn't cheer up, and I didn't get better, though a realization for the futility of my depression came in a sort of weather spawned epiphany.

This is what I wanted. I wanted that new life, that utopia of silence. But my past decisions were far away now, something about the beauty and good of normalcy seemed moot.

I found myself sitting crisscross on my bed, it was still light outside, but the afternoon was already coming to a close. My room still smelled faintly of cinnamon, but the candles on the skulls were long gone.

Imminence of eternity had settled with the dryness of the heat. And I wanted to cancel this dead awareness of time, this isn't how life has ever ticked by for me, I wanted to grip time like I used to. I would see it come and go, but I was actively running with it.

But that feeling of security was just a side affect of how I really was. No, it was something more because it wasn't just self satisfying. My past wasn't just death and time wasting; I was something sincere. I shouldn't have turned my back on it. I see it now. I wasn't a perpetual parasite, and I wasn't a self employed mercenary, I saved people.

My decisions are now and are again, I wanted to hunt.

BoJing: I'm saying Oklahoma will
                            always be remembered as
                            one of the last botched
                            jobs in the world.
New kid101010:   I can't believe we let
                            the suckers out of sight.
(AnnaBanana24 enters the chatroom)
AnnaBanana24:   Somebody needs to tell me
                            what Moogie did. I NEED
                            TO KNOW!

Sportychick93842:	Half the slayers were there, I'm so glad I opted out
Surfinscooter531:	You couldn't afford it anyway
Sportychick93842:	So? U were too chicken
Surfinscooter531:	No! I was busy
Sportychick93842:	Right, crying over your exboyfriend is definitely busy
Surfinscooter531:	I am not gay! And it wasn't about him
AnnaBanana24:	Will you please stop that stupid sibling crap? I NEED TO KNOW WHAT THE SUCKER DID!
New kid101010:	I was there, I came all the way up from Florida
AnnaBanana24:	AND?
New kid101010:	we all tried hunting this huge coven and Moogie found a few of them out stalking, she jumped the gun and killed one but let the other get away to try to save two girls. The coven then vanished.
AnnaBanana24:	I knew it. She can't do ANYTHING
BoJing:	She should have called for help, why didn't she?

New kid101010:	IDK nobody can ever tell what she is thinking
Surfinscooter531:	My brother Nate saw her at the mansion, stoic
Zombiehunter231:	A few years back, when we caught Jonathan, Mr.C made me cut off Jonathan's head so she could keep their skulls. We should have known not to trust her.
AnnaBanana24:	U guys TOTALLY SUCK! I mean what idiot would invite a sucker to do a slayer's job?
BoJing:	Bill
Mr. Cactus:	Bill
BluntBoy778:	That Milton guy
Surfinscooter531:	Half of us are Miltons u idiot.
BluntBoy778:	All of you guys suck too. I mean this is Storid all over again.
New kid101010:	Who?
(OakieBill enters the chatroom)	
BoJing:	Michael Storid, aka "The Weasel"
OakieBill:	Calling him a weasel, is an insult to weasels
Mr. Cactus:	He was the worst bad in even in my day

AnnaBanana24:	I heard sumtims weasel skins chicks and dudes 4fun
BluntBoy778:	He got minions too, they use voodoo potions on victims
BluntBoy778:	bfor he left a few yrs ago, skin apeared in the trash in NJ
BoJing:	Sure about that? Weasel is con-artist.
Surfinscooter531:	I thought he died 2 years ago
Surfinscooter531:	don't u remember?
Sportychick93842:	Idiot he escaped, I was there
Surfinscooter531:	No! he cummit suicide!
Sportychick93842:	That was his underlings!
Sportychick93842:	I helped with the OZ Coven raid he was in
Surfinscooter531:	Your r wrong! Idiot
Sportychick93842:	Don't make me fly to California just to kick your ass again!
Surfinscooter531:	I'll be waiting with a body bag to take care of you
Sportychick93842:	THAT A THREAT?
Surfinscooter531:	A PROMISE.

Bojing:	Cool it down guys, don't make me call your mom and invite her to the chatroom
Surfinscooter531:	You wouldn't!
Sportychick93842:	Anything but Mom!
Bojing:	Back to the subject.
AnnaBanana24:	Whr do u think he is?
Sportychick93842:	Slow boat to China is the only way to get out of OZ without slayer detection
BoJing:	If he was in China I would have known.
BoJing:	Any slayer near Asia is dying to kill him after the Shanghai problem
New kid101010:	What?
BoJing:	He knows not to come near China because all of the business he ran, draining and selling blood of young women. It was huge about ten years ago.
BoJing:	It took nearly every slayer in Asia and some in Europe to destroy that operation
BoJing:	Bill remembers it, he was a sniper then
OakieBill:	Yes, 2011, a horrible year to be anything except a slayer

BluntBoy778:	Where could he be then?
AnnaBanana24:	Slayrs lost him in 14th century, we only no of the thgs hes done
OakieBill:	Huh? 14th?
AnnaBanana24:	Yea, got writins in the diry of slayr from mid-ags
AnnaBanana24:	Saz he wipd out viligs nd viligs+ownd milons o slaves
AnnaBanana24:	Nbody can fnd hm
OakieBill:	Where is your grammar Miss Anna?
AnnaBanana24:	don't need it
OakieBill:	I only understand half of what you say.
AnnaBannan24:	4real?
OakieBill:	Why do you use numbers? It doesn't make sense!
BoJing:	Off topic!
BoJing:	We could talk legends all day, are we making any headway?
New kid101010:	Kind of, I didn't know any of this before. Has anybody tried finding 4sure what happened to this Storid guy?

BoJing:	Good question, are there any OZ slayers that know anything?
Sportychick93842:	There are seven slayers in OZ, we've searched and killed everything with fangs
Surfinscooter531:	They don't have fangs!
Sportychick93842:	It's a figure of speech, get it through your thick skull!
BoJing:	Don't start again
Sportychick93842:	sorry
Surfinscooter531:	She started it
Sportychick93842:	You r just as guilty!
Ontarionightstalker enters the chatroom)	
BluntBoy778:	o no
Ontarionightstalker:	Miss me???
AnnaBanana24:	Gt out TROLL!!!!!!
Ontarionightstalker:	How very polite, Anna, don't make me report u.
Swissguy99:	She will. She got me kicked out twice.
Ontarionightstalker:	Is that you John?
Swissguy99:	GTG…
(Swissguy99 leaves the chatroom)	
Ontarionightstalker:	What r u guys doing?
BluntBoy778:	Nothin u ned to no
BoJing:	We are still off topic
BoJing:	The Weasel, we need to figure out where he is

Ontarionightstalker: what a surprise, I knew he couldn't hide forever

Ontarionightstalker: Is anybody going to go find him?

AnnaBanana24:   How wud we do tht?

Ontarionightstalker: Simple, look4 clues at the last place we saw him

Sportychick93842:   TY DR. OBVIOUS

Sportychick93842:   We did that already, nothing, he just disappeared, Australia is clean

Sportychick93842:   It is so clean slayers go here on vacation and retirement because they know 4sure they won't run into the fangs

Ontarionightstalker: It wouldn't hurt to go search again, people do miss things

Sportychick93842:   Tons from all over the world have retraced his steps and found nothing

BoJing: She is right, all of my friends, including me, have gone to that site. We've read all of the records about the last fight in Australia too. Nothing.

OakieBill: Nothing is there

Ontarionightstalker:	Why don't you go then? If you're so sure why don't you check again?
BoJing:	Sarah offered a good point, why don't we listen?
Swissguy's wife:	She had a good point last time too, now my husband doesn't go on the chat here
AnnaBanana24:	Yea! Shes shotdown all of our ideas be4, she doesn't deserve to have a voice here!
Surfinscooter531:	yeah, and there is something wrong w/ that famly, I mean her brother was banging the sucker tht just bochedthe Oakie coven job
Ontarionightstalker:	I have nothing to do with those ppl
BoJing:	This is supposed to be a chat for everybody, I'm sorry she bashed your ideas, but the past is the past, we have a discussion to continue.
BoJing:	What happened?
BoJing:	Why is the trail cold?

OakieBill:	he disappeared, the last time we saw, nobody followed him or chased him fast enough
OakieBill:	Slayers today are so lazy
AnnaBanana24:	Hey! U hve no idea wht I deal wth…
Mr. Cactus:	I remember it like it was yesterday, he abandoned his coven and escaped with nothing but the clothes on his back
Swissguy's wife:	No, I thought he had a passport and flew out of there
Frenchmouse234:	No, we found all of his stuff
WWBD483948:	No, my sisters and brothers were there, he's magic
Spy49583950:	BS, he died
Moogie:	Are there any real accurate records?
AnnaBanana24:	OMG!!!!!! HOW LONG HAVE U BEEN ON?
Moogie:	The entire time. Are there any records of he last fight?
Ontarionightstalker:	Bitch! Get out of the forums.

```
Spy49583950:          You  shouldn't  eavesdrop
                      on us
Moogie:               I  just  want  to  find  him
                      too.
BoJing:               It  might  be  best  if  you
                      leave
New kid101010:        Yea   go   ruin   someone
                      else's life
```

I exited out of the chatroom and shut my computer off, my hands quivering in anger.

"Mr. C?" I scrutinized the holographics, Mr. C was on a video call with me, not twenty minutes after the I left the chatrooms.

"Yes, Miss Moogie." He leaned back and looked off screen then looked back at me, his rough bark was quieted slightly, "So you're interested in catching Storid?" I nodded, "Yes sir."

He coughed and let out an old wheeze, "I don't have many years left Miss Moogie, and I know not a person fit for the job of finding this man before I die. Nearly half a century ago my brother William happened across Storid, and Storid killed him. William's boy still has the journals that recollect the hunt written from William's hand, and no eyes have read it except William and his son."

My eyebrows pulled together and I gave him a confused look, old Mr. C then was thrown into a coughing fit I waited patiently for the man to finally stop, "Mr. C, have you seen a doctor for that?" He glared at me, "I don't need a doctor to tell me that I am dying." He looked off screen, and wheezed again, "Good bye Miss Moogie." And he reached to turn the button off. "Wait!" I said. He hesitated for a second, "What?" he gruffed.

"Thank you Mr. C." he stopped and tilted his head down and shut the call off.

I closed my eyes, pinched the bridge of my nose and then stood up. I packed my bags and headed out to go see one man, Bill Milton.

27
Bill Milton

May 21st, 2021

The mansion hadn't left my eyes for a week before I had flown back to the Oklahoma town where it lived. In a rental car I passed through the gates again and stood at the door.

I recognized the butler as his glare met my eyes; I guess he knew me too. He showed me up to Bill's study where I waited for Bill to enter the room.

He was fuming mad, a level of disgust I had never seen before rolled off of his rough face. "You have the goad to step back into my house uninvited after what you did? How dare you!" He roared and spat at my feet.

"Get out of my house!" I held my breath, "Sir-please sir," I squeaked, he picked up a book from the tall shelf next to him and chucked it at me. I dodged it, and held up my hands, "Please sir." He picked up another and threw it. The book spun in the air like a disk and I dropped down as it skirted the top of my hair. He pulled a knife from his belt and rushed towards me; I turned the other way and started for the door.

Before I could rip the door open and run I heard a scraping sound and a thump followed by a croaky scream. I turned to find Bill on the ground, the knife sliding across the floor while he was pressing on a bloody gash in his right pant leg. "Mr. Milton!" He was grinding his teeth to hold a scream. I rushed to his side.

"Don't worry, I'll go get help." His face reddened from holding his breath and the pain, and he grabbed my arm and shook his head.

"You need help!" He shook his head, "neither my sons nor my servants can see me like this." I shook my head at his absurdity but complied.

I stood up and opened my suitcase, below the folded clothes I found my emergency medical kit and pulled it out.

"Mr. Milton, let me look at it then." I said. He pointed to the doors. "Lock them." He whispered.

I jogged over to the double doors and shut them, and then locked them. Then I shut and locked the others. Bill let me look at the scratch, it wasn't deep, but it needed stitches.

"I'm sorry Mr. Milton, I'm going to need to cut your pants further," He glowered at me, I picked through the kit, "Sir, this would be easier if I took you to the hospital."

He shook his head, "Cut them." With the small scissors I had, I snipped the seams of the pants from the foot to the wound.

I poured some hydrogen peroxide and he flinched, and soon I was cleaning and tugging the skin pieces back together without a word.

I looked at him, "Can any of your sons help you back to your room? You need to lie down and heal." He shook his head. "No. I can walk, pain doesn't hurt Miltons like normal people." When I tied the last stitch, I watched him throw the ripped pants over his leg and prop himself up with the desk. He tried to put weight on the leg, but as he did he collapsed.

I caught him before he face planted on the floor and steadied him. It was effortless on my part because of the immense strength I have, but he seemed to realize the state he was in.

"It's alright Mr. Milton, I will not tell anyone about this. But you need to get back to your room." He let out an exhausted breath and I helped him limp to his room. I carefully made sure that no servant was watching, and he directed me quietly to which room was his.

It was the most ostentatious bed I had ever seen, I thought it to be fit for royalty. I laid him down on it and found some fresh clothes for him to put on later. After determining he was alright I turned away, determined to forget my little trip to Oklahoma. "Why did you come here?" He asked, his tone seemed calm, and didn't sound like a bark.

I looked back, "Your father had tracked Storid, and he kept journals. I believe there might be something important in those journals to finding and killing Storid." My eyes fixed onto my feet.

I risked a glance, his face had lit up again into a flushed red. His figure was ridged; the weight of my request must have been hard for him.

He looked out to his left, there a window poured in gray light, a blade in its holster laid on the table to his left also. I didn't know what he was looking at, his face became indecipherable. I counted the full breaths he took before he spoke again.

"My daddy was a good man. He was honest, and always took care of the family. It was a damn tragedy when he died and he must always be remembered that way, honest and noble." I looked up at him, and his mouth was pressed into a line, "I know you lost your family at a young age as I did, and you know what vengeance tastes like." Pointed to the floor, "Under there is a safe, pick it up and place it on the bed in the space to the left of me."

I hesitantly stepped forward, then stepped again, and again until I reached the side of the bed. I swallowed, and then bent over to the space under the bed. Underneath I reached with both of my arms to pull out the locked safe, barely tall enough to fit under the bed.

I carried it in my arms and placed it on the side he indicated.

He twisted the knob several times and the door clicked open. Inside were twelve journals, Bill's hand was large enough to pick up four at once and I leaned over to take them from him.

They were old, worn, and rough on my hands, "You have to return them right here when you are done, I don't want you leaving the house." I nodded in understanding and left to his study.

February 12, 1972

The chase has gotten me nowhere. I had abandoned little William Junior's birthday for nothing but a dead end. The coven Storid was supposed to be in was destroyed, and all records of his were left at the housing location. Even his car had been left there. I'm going to track down the coven in Arkansas to find more information, and then start on every identity he had left for clues to where else he lives...

March 20, 1973

Four new slayers joined the hunt tonight. Young Bill Jr. and his friends, Charlie, my sorry excuse for a nephew, God knows how my sister could ever have raised that bastard. Joseph, who acts like he is going to cry every time we shoot something, and Fred, I have no idea what he is, I just want to puke every time I see him. If this is the future front line for slayers-kind then I reckon our earth will be doomed by the next century. Anyway, they are taking the new lead on the stranger that came into town...

December 20, 1973

From what I've heard slayers are popping up like daisies! Seven new ones in Texas, six in California, one in Hawaii, Lord knows we don't need more over there...Four of the untouchable covens have broken up. More lone wolves than ever. I wonder if Storid is one of them...

July 6, 1977
(Afternoon)

I'm going to get him! All my life I've been waiting for this moment. I'm going to capture Storid.

Though I can only regret to say this is one of the most humiliating finds I have ever discovered. That bastard has been living not a mile away from my mansion, from my boys.

I had found him last night, little Sierra and I had a fight and she ran away. I sent Bill and some servants to go out to search for her with me, and I took streets I didn't usually go down.

Storid, as casual as a Wednesday night, was about to enter a home. He didn't see me, but by-God I saw him. For the past five years since I broke up his coven he has been living in a house I could see from my window.

That Son-of-a-bitch will pay for his arrogance. I'm planning on capturing him tonight at dusk. And I had some spare time to write before I finished preparing.

July 6, 1975

(Night)

Not a single soul knew I was out on a hunt tonight. I wanted this with the help of no one, because nobody can understand what this man has done to me. He lives in my town, kills my people, and lives within throwing distance of the most dangerous threat he will ever encounter. Who does he think he is? Who would be reckless enough to live in sight of a Milton?

I didn't want nobody to get the fame I deserved. When I reached his house I circled and entered in the back to find him and a girl had captured and strung a little boy, skinning him alive. It was a horrible sight, they would take patches and peel them off slowly, and then lick the blood off. I knew the boy too; he was a sibling of one of Bill's school friends. When both had their backs turned I jumped from my hiding place and stabbed the girl in the back of the head. Before he knew what was going on I hit him with the butt of my gun. I gagged, tied, and bagged him before carrying him to the trunk.

I took him down to the basement and set him on the chair. He woke up and started struggling. Almost getting away, I managed to knock him out again; I still don't know how he did that.

He woke up to find I strapped him down twice as much and he laughed. He answered my questions on which myths are real that I heard about him. These myths and things will be documented later, after I have done away with the body.

Then I told him how I was going to kill him. I told him my story and how I spent my life tracking him down, and I am about to make him understand.

This entry will go down in history forever; I hope the millions who read it and study it will know the strength and ultimate integrity of the Milton family.

July 7, 1975

_(2AM)_

He is gone, I turned my back when I was writing in my journal and everything went black. I woke up again and he had left, I have failed, and he took it, my pride and my joy. I can no longer live without what he has cut off. This is my final word, my family will avenge me.

May 22nd, 2021

I turned the page, it was blank. The sunlight in the window to my left was replaced with occasional moonlight depending on the clouds. The study was illuminated by slightly yellowed light bulbs and made the old, browned pages darker and harder to read. I couldn't tell how long I had been sitting in Bill's desk chair; I had been so absorbed in Bill Senior's story here in the journals. And after reading all of that, nothing else? He was so adventurous, never standing down in a fight, always filled with more pride and perseverance than any other slayer.

His father, John Milton, had the mansion built in the nineteen twenties for five and a half million dollars. John was an oil tycoon and a devoted slayer. Back then, slayers were strict on keeping into the family and John ended up marrying his adopted daughter and niece by his first marriage. Her name was Gertrude Dolly.

Throughout Bill Senior's journals he constantly talked about his resentment that his mother was a Dolly and how everyone else seemed to forget that.

Bill Senior's life ended up being volatile, at one point John Milton lost his entire fortune and oil company, the entire world believed it was lost to stocks, but really John had furnished an army of slayers to sweep Europe. The amount of bribes to keep people quiet, feeding, housing, and transportation to get the slayers everywhere seemed to add up and they almost had to sell the mansion.

Like his father, Bill Senior wanted to cleanse the entire world with his slaying expertise and Storid had been an upper priority. He was a meticulous observer when it came to Storid's life. He even had a sketch of what Storid looked like.

After losing Storid like that, how could Bill Senior just give up? He couldn't retire after a success like that, he almost had Storid.

The servants let me stay in the chauffer's quarters for the night, separate from the house. The servants knew what I was, or what they thought I was, and the next day they didn't prepare a breakfast for me.

I was too absorbed in studying the journals to care much, and when the sun rose I returned to the house and knocked on his door. "Leave." Was the answer called from behind the door. "It is me. Let me in before somebody sees me." I said. Silence after that, and I stepped inside. Bill was in the same spot as the day before. His arms were crossed and he was watching me. I put the books back into the safe. "Did you find anything?" he asked. I nodded and answered with another question.

"Why didn't he write any more? What did Storid take?"

His droopy face and mouth grimaced longer. He stayed silent, almost lost in thought. But Bill never gets lost in anything.

"Mr. Milton, why did your father not write anymore?" Another silence, and Bill's expression stayed the same as he looked into my eyes. "Storid drove him to kill himself."

"But why? Mr. Milton Senior never gave up." I said, almost to myself. Bill's hands pulled together in a fist, "Storid killed him, nobody could have lived after what Storid did to him."

I shook my head, "Why? What did he take?" Bill Senior couldn't have been talking about will or anything metaphorical, he didn't believe in souls or will, he only wanted to get his job done, and nothing in the mind was ever going to stop him from slaying.

I pleaded with Bill further, and he glared at me, his emotions seemed ripped with hatred. "No man could have lived on after what Storid took, how Storid violated him." He repeated, as if reciting lines. I shook my head "What is it?" I asked.

Bill's voice quieted to the roughest whisper I had ever heard. "Storid did something much worse than killing him; he cut off his dick."

28
Retracing

May 23rd, 2021

"Hello?" The voice on the other side answered, "Hi is this Chelsea?" "Speaking," She replied.

"I'm Moogie from America and-" "Oh! From the chatrooms!" she cut in.

"Yes, I was told you owned the library of slayer journals; I was wondering if I could go through some of the reports on when Storid was last seen." Chelsea laughed on the other end, "You know, you really do sound like a twelve year old, and yes I'm the library caretaker. Did you really try to save that coven in Oklahoma?"

I exhaled exasperatingly, "I was thirteen when I was turned, not twelve, and no, I was trying to save a couple victims--that's beside the point. Would you mind if I flew out and looked over a few of those journals?"

Her voice changed then, "Are you serious? Fly all the way out here to see my journals? Of course!" I smiled even though she couldn't see me over the telephone call.

We swapped information on when I was flying out and where she would pick me up. She said I could stay at her house. I'm glad too, hotels and their little extra expenditures burn a quick hole in my wallet.

May 24th, 2021

"Ugh!" I picked my leg up off the ground and threw it down. It started prickling again. I can easily kill somebody by bashing their head on a slab of concrete but I can't quite get the courage to wake and tell the fat guy next to me on the airplane to scoot over to the other seat.

I tried to adjust my body half shoved up against the side of the plane with the armrest digging against the side of my leg, and tried to get the circulation going again.

Although, he is asleep, maybe I could...

I got off my uncomfortable position and slid to where I was supposed to be. My body made an imprint on the stretched pillow made from the sleeping guy's fat and leaned over to push him into the other seat.

His gelatinous body jiggled under his bad Hawaiian button up shirt with cheese stains and knee length shorts. What a tourist. I was about to pull out a book and read for the next few hours but something stopped me. What was that smell?

Ugh, the rancid odor made it hard to breathe, I could hear the people around me gagging, and some adjusted to sit as far away from the smell as possible. I coughed and gagged, quickly getting up and running to the bathroom.

The tourist's S.B.D.s are not going to make my life any more pleasant. I put my hands down on the sink to steady myself as turbulence jolted me. This is going to be a long, long flight.

After four flights and what seemed like waiting forever to get my bags off the carousel I wheeled myself to the pickup line and parked myself by a bench to wait for Chelsea. After forty-five minutes and several phone calls which went straight to voice mail, I opened the holographics again to check my messages. My eyes crossed and my eyelids drooped, being jet lagged made reading all the much harder.

One message at the corner of the screen though, I opened it. A video message of a woman with a high ponytail and tanned skin said she had an emergency and had to leave the country. With her sincerest apologies Chelsea also added the locations of several hotels in the area to stay in until she got back.

I hailed a taxi and went to the first on the list; not caring where it was. When I checked in the bellhop immediately made my bags disappear. Black spots appeared in my vision and after the bellhop vanished with his tip I dropped into the bed and fell asleep.

Chelsea hadn't called me while I was sleeping, so I was at a dead end. I had no idea where she lived, and no other slayers were at home in the area. I don't even know if Chelsea will come back, I should really stop going to foreign countries on whims.

I paced across my room, what to do, what to do. Maybe I could find Storid's coven location and just go from there.

After half unloading my bags I emailed a few of my slayer friends, which I don't know if they actually are my friends anymore, or if they ever were in the first place, and asked about Storid's last sighting's address. No reply for an hour, two hours, three. I'm going to be fifty by the time I find Storid.

With nothing to do I ventured out to the rest of Sydney for sight seeing. The place was filled with things to do, beaches, parks, museums; and the weather was colder than Arizona's winter days, and being on the opposite part of the world this time of year is their early winter.

This place was dazzling. The sun shined with a different feeling here, not much humidity, though my hair was a little frizzy. It was almost night and day different than England and a little closer to Arizona than I thought. England would have been so rainy and dreary.

The place smelled like the beach, and I wore a light jacket and sunglasses while I wandered around with the other tourists. I reached the building that defined Sydney, the opera house, and stood gazing at the great architecture. My poor and insignificant figure beside it shrank. I imagined being the star to perform inside of it, so many people watching and clapping and cheering. I shook my head and started back to the hotel, the dream filed away for some other universe, some other time.

Chelsea returned on my fourth day in Australia. She told me she rushed out because of a huge scattered coven, which was more of an alliance than a coven because they didn't live together in California. They needed all the slayers they could get to contain and cover up the battle.

I wondered why I wasn't invited, and shrugged that out of my mind. Though, I was shocked I was moved lower on the priority list than Chelsea. Chelsea was the daughter of Carrie, and from what I heard, a slayer without really being a slayer. That is one of the reasons she lives in Australia and mans the only slayer library in existence; she is in the least dangerous place in the world. I guess that means everybody officially hates me.

Chelsea took me deep into the suburbs, her house didn't have air conditioning, but I heard most of them don't need it, and the walls were brick with a red tile roof. She showed me around, and then she brought me to her library. It was the only different color in the house, a brownish white. A table and a few chairs were placed in the middle on the room under an old-looking ceiling lamp attached to a fan. The rest of the room had shelves everywhere, books of all sizes, colors, and conditions filled the old brown shelves.

More than six or seven shelves spanned on both ends of the room, and aligned on the walls there were shelves that reached the ceiling.

I gaped at it while Chelsea explained, "My family has been documenting events for generations. We also store other journals from slayers outside the family."

- 367 -

She showed me to a row at the end. "These are my immediate family's journals," She pointed to a row of pink, frilly journals "Those are my grandmother's, she was a slayer for forty years until she died of cancer in 2007."

Chelsea fidgeted with her pony tail, "My brothers and I have electronic journals now, I'm trying to get everybody to start them like my cousin got everybody to go on the chatrooms, but some people have written on pages for so long they won't change."

We went into another row; most of the books here had been deteriorated to the point of falling apart. At the edge of the row at the last and bottom shelf laid a small computer. Chelsea picked it up and opened the interface. "Some books have gone through fires and floods, so to keep the text from being lost completely I have to bring it into the computer. That sometimes means hours and hours translating and typing and scanning."

Chelsea animatedly chattered about the books as if I were any other slayer. She eagerly explained all the details of the library, not considering if I wanted to know or not. I didn't really mind, I wasn't on much of a time pressure and I don't think she receives any guests to the library often.

Chelsea dreamily leafed through one of the books as she prattled on, "My dream one day is to make every journal online with categories and easy to use interfaces, so every slayer at all times anywhere can use journals and upload future ones. We wouldn't have to have libraries and keepers like me with the potential of losing everything, and I don't want anybody to die because of the lack of access to information."

She closed the book and slid it back into the shelf, and then shut the computer off. "Somebody is going to die because a piece of information was lost in a slayer's journal. It'll be my fault. It'll take years to get these online, maybe not even in my lifetime." She said, her expression now in definite dismay.

I nodded, listening to her saying her fears again, and she looked down at me, "Moogie you're lucky, even though everybody doesn't like you because of what you are, you get to live forever. You get to see life and when slayers will finally wipe out every last one of them."

My expression changed at that moment, she envies me? I shook my head and changed the subject. "Speaking of cleansing the world, I'm looking for Storid's last battle with the slayers." She jumped back to her electric self, "Oh! Of course!"

Swiftly, she picked unlabeled books off the shelves stacked them into my arms. After going through all of the rows on one side she moved to the other, and the stack grew so high I had to put them by the table to free up room again to carry them.

When we finished she pointed to every book individually, and told me which pages the fight started on and whose book it was. I struggled to remember them so I grabbed a piece of paper left on the desk and jotted the names and sections of every book I needed to read.

She finished and I looked up from the paper I was writing on, "Have you read all of these books?" She nodded, "All the ones in English, there are a couple in Latin, and the section over there is in Mandarin, and I haven't tried to learn the languages yet." She looked back at her books, pointing to the different areas, before she disappeared into her own little book world again I said, "Chelsea?" She turned around and looked at me again slightly off guard, "Yes?" she asked, "Thanks."

The journal of Arthur Joan Dolly

June 13th, 2014

I've finally got the information I need, "The Weasel", as everybody calls Storid now, had taken up a home somewhere around Sydney. I couldn't believe it! I had always pinned him as a private guy, owning a place out away from masses of humans. But Bess, lucky as she always is, stumbled on a few of his cronies taking their evening picks from a bar while she was out on vacation in Australia.

I couldn't imagine little Bess tracking them all the way back to their house and not getting caught, but I guess it doesn't matter now.

I'm planning an attack with every slayer I know around here to take down this coven. I called the Miltons in on this one too, that family has had a grudge against him since the early nineteen hundreds. Everybody is acting as if they are counting down the seconds until we attack.

June 28th, 2014
Evening

Tonight we will kill Storid, slayers from all over the world have come to fight, most comprising of older American Miltons, the ones I know closely are Charlie and his boy and girl, Sierra and her son Jack, and Sierra's older brother Bill Junior, and old Mr. C, who seems to never miss anything earth shattering. The older and less agile slayers were set as snipers, drivers, etcetera. Anybody young or healthy has to fight.

June 29th, 2014
Early morning

Our attack was successful; we discovered Storid's cars and all of his money and identities. But he managed to escape. All of the planning, my work, all has gone to waste! Those idiots couldn't snipe him if he was standing at point blank range! We had several casualties so I got stuck cleaning up while the others chased him. Somebody forgot to keep watch on the backyards and that's how we think he escaped, hopping fences. Pathetic. Everybody has been driving around looking for him, they've retraced his possible escapes everywhere, he's gone.

We've captured and are planning to execute all of the surviving coven mates, they were all young, freshly turned and that's all he lived with. He had three older, less dangerous ones taking care of the eight others, but nobody even close to his age seemed to reside with him. The three older ones had commit suicide as we started winning.

He seemed to keep everything to himself, all of his minions were blindly devoted to him.

They sang gleefully when we executed them in the end.

I even saw Storid! I could have shot him! But Jordan was wounded at the same exact time, and when I looked back he had disappeared into his house. After we raided the inside he had already fled on foot. He's gone. Just gone, disappeared into thin air.

May 26th, 2021

The afternoon light was shining in my face when I closed the final journal. All the accounts were nearly the same, Dollys, Miltons, even a few non relations, like an old guy named Dean and his younger brother;

all had one thing in common. They were all so cocky, acting as if they can waltz in and Storid will surrender, and then shocked that he got away. It seemed wrong, years and years of chasing him and these slayers think they have him? Who do they think he is? A kid born yesterday?

I picked up the map from the first book and the sketch from the sixth book. The sixth slayer was an artist who drew elaborate sketches of the scenes. The one I held depicted a scene with Storid running across a side yard. She was the only one who blamed herself; the others blamed the rest of the world for not getting Storid.

I looked at the map for a while, where would Storid go and live undetected for nearly half a decade? I closed all of the books and stretched.

Chelsea was more than glad to let me stay at her house for the duration of my adventure in Australia. I borrowed her car and drove over to the old house that Storid and his coven lived in. I turned the car off and stared at it from my dashboard

The house was large and old, the paint was peeling, and a tilted fore-closed sign stood in the middle of its barren, dead lawn. I tried to imagine it as it used to be. I checked the picture I took of the map and looked back at the lawn. Three cars would have been parked in front. Another would be in the alley; Storid would have been to the room left of the front door. I stepped out of the car and crossed the lawn to the inside.

The walls were vandalized and opened. No doubt people looted the copper pipes and stripped anything else from it. Furniture had disappeared, and lights were removed.

I stood where the three older ones killed themselves, and tried to put myself in Storid's mind. What would I have done? I looked around; in my sight I saw an upstairs, the kitchen, and another room to my right. I jogged over to the kitchen. I looked around again and then out the window. People would have been fighting in the backyard, and I imagined slayers trying to advance this way. I turned away and walked through to the right side yard.

A white fence confronted me, with one of the top boards broken off. I looked around. If I looked to my left and my right I would have seen slayers attacking me. I jumped up and grabbed one of the top boards of the fence, it then broke and I fell into the alley.

I hopped back up and looked back at the fence. Two similarly broken fence pieces now sat side-by-side. I picked the glass from the alley out of my hair and scanned the area. A black van holding slayers would be on either side of me. I looked ahead and hopped the fence into the neighbor's yard. I ran northwest of where I was standing and hopped back into the alley. Now I was out of sight of both vans, and off the road.

I followed the alley until I reached a fork in the road. By then the fight would have been over and the slayers would have been searching everywhere for me. I have no car, no money, and no blood. What would I do?

I stopped and surveyed the area again. A high school was to my right, while more of the neighborhood was to my left. Where would Storid go?

More cars and slayers would have been further down the neighborhood and I would surly get spotted walking. How would I get past them?

I jogged around the school. No kids were there, a car or two in the parking lot, where would he go? I leaned against the bike rack next to me. What would I do? I walked around a little more; trash was everywhere, papers, dirt, even a broken bike helmet.

Nothing was giving me any inspiration. I returned to the road, one small kid rode her bike down the street. That's it! Of course! Why didn't I think of that sooner? I ran back to the bike rack and stole one of the kids' bikes, and I pedaled further into the neighborhood as fast as I could go.

I reached the town and I knew he would have felt tired and thirsty. Around me I noticed a few homeless people scattered here and there. I bet he would have found one isolated and drained him. Then he would have scavenged anything useful like I do with my kills. I ran my hand through my hair. What if I took a wrong turn? What if he didn't think like me?

Where would he go? He has some money, maybe, has a blood supply, and weak transportation. Where would I go? I stared at the sky and tried to think of ideas.

I looked around for a hotel or a motel. One was in my sight. The place had a broken light and a non illuminated sign that said "Been open and serving since 1972" I walked in and found a very old clerk playing solitaire with a bent up, greasy set of cards.

"Can I get a room here?"

He didn't even look up, he just said in a plainly bored tone, "I need your driver's license and we do not take anything except cash." I pulled out my wallet and looked at my license; it said Tracy, as usual. Wait, he didn't have a license, all of his stuff is in the slayer's possession.

I put my wallet away. "I, uh, don't have one." He looked at me with no interest, "No license, no room."

"Where do you think I should stay then?" He sighed, "I guess people call you homeless, so why don't you go stay with the bums? Or how about the beach? If those aren't good enough for your pretty little head to grasp why don't you go stay in HELL! I don't care where you go, just GET OUT!" He stood up and pointed to the door. "OUT NOW!"

I hurried out, giving him a mental five stars for wonderful, hospitable service. Then I stopped and popped my head back inside, and said sweetly "See you in Hell!" And before he could react I was already back on my bike pedaling away.

What an idiot, I wonder if Storid had to deal with him.

Where is Storid going now? The sun is looming in the distance and I still don't know where to go. I looked around again. Homeless people, garbage cans, cars, and more buildings.

Maybe I could break into a car, no, security is huge; the police and half the city would hear the alarms. Maybe I could break into a building, no, way too many problems with that, I would know.

I need to find Storid, maybe I could hide in the dumpster for a while until the slayers stopped searching for me. Several homeless people sat huddled with each other. I ignored them and opened the dumpster, an awful stench emanated from the dumpster and I immediately dropped the lid, "Yuck!" They sniggered behind me.

I ventured around the streets a little more and counted at least seven tents, not only that but everybody kept begging for money. Most of the bums sat and talked, not even noticing me. Their dialogue consisted of using an array of politically incorrect slang and keeping their intelligence level to that of a monkey. These are a strange kind of people, blunt and simple.

I've lived with these people before, and I was one of them at one point of time. Occasionally I would run into a smart one, and they would purposefully be homeless because they said they were rebelling and affronting conservative society, or have some other way of cleverly saying they were lazy and didn't pay the rent.

I sighed as I passed one picking his nose, everybody, and I mean the majority, will be like this one day. The news constantly talks about the stupidity of the masses, school test scores falling worse below standards each year.

Why would Chelsea want to live long enough to see the day humanity is too stupid to function? I wondered about what will happen to me, no real company, nobody intelligent enough to understand me.

Maybe it will be better, maybe some smart people will stay as consistencies. I could find them.

I smiled to myself, people of this time and the time before me were smart, those I hunt won't grow stupider, only reflect the intelligence born from their time period. They will be as salient as a ray from a flashlight.

A guy from the alley I just left whistled at me, and I broke my train of thought "Why don't you bring that tight little ass over ta meh?" I didn't answer him or any of the others, I continued on my way back to Storid's coven home where I parked the car.

Maybe...no, arrgh! Where is he? He couldn't have left Australia and he couldn't stay anywhere except the streets. Every other coven has been wiped out so he has absolutely no safe havens. Because he is so old, and from what I've read, prideful, he couldn't live with the homeless and their stupidity. I would rather have silence than their company.

He couldn't be in the sewers, even I couldn't be in the sewers. I nearly pulled my hair out as I paced around my bedroom. Where is he?

29
Options

About a week later I was packing to go home. As every slayer before me, I hit a dead end. I thought I knew what he was. I thought he was like me, I checked every place I knew I would have gone when hiding in plain sight, maybe he's hidden somewhere out in the middle of nowhere waiting for all the slayers to grow old and die off. Maybe there is something I missed, a note or some important location. Nevermind, I can't dwell on this forever.

I zipped my bags and carried them to the car. I haven't told anybody I'm going home yet in shame and I don't think I can ever look at Bill in the face again.

Rain poured down on the windshield as Chelsea and I sat in silence while she drove me to the airport. I looked out the window at the beautiful city. The buildings made the cityscape all the more admirable next to the ocean. It was cold, but not as dreary as England.

My flight had been delayed for about two hours, so I wandered around. I bought knick knacks, though I didn't know what to do with them after I got home, and after that I drifted into the airport bakery for a cookie.

It tasted stale and bland, though everything always tastes bland compared to blood. On my way back to the waiting area I stared into the confusing carpet and tried to read into the art, while contemplating why anybody would want to make a living designing airport floors. I wheeled my bags around and tried to think about something, anything, that didn't involve Storid or the slayers. I looked at the ceiling, the cream walls, and then moved on to the poster-sized ads hung onto the wall. One for Hawaiian Airlines, another for hotel points or something, and the last was a family smiling next to a river, it caught my eye. In big letters next to the family was the sales pitch:

Close to the city!
Beautiful views!
Privacy!
Great getaway,

Lane Cove River Tourist Caravan Park
Park it in Sydney.
Book it today!

I analyzed every corner of it, a getaway, and right here in the city. Behind me I heard the intercom lady call my flight. I ignored it for the moment and kept staring at the picture. "Storid's paradise." I mumbled to myself. Camping lots, he could spend years there, silence, close to the city. Bill's journals came into mind, Storid didn't flee, he stayed for five years in the same place, not even a mile away from his greatest threats.

Chelsea was surprised when I called her back, she didn't mind driving back to pick me up and thought I was strange when I told her Storid had gone camping.

But I'm almost sure of it, yes! How could I have not seen it before? I now know how he stayed hidden all these years!

June 5th 2021

"No! No! No!" I recounted the sites on the web page; I have to search so many campgrounds in and near Sydney. Back in the kitchen the coffee beeped and I rose to go get it.

The coffee maker asked what I wanted, I replied, "The location of Michael Storid" It just said error and asked me the same question again. "Cream, two sugars." It beeped again and I picked up the self recycling cup and drank it quickly. I wish I could give a reality check to the scientist who decided to make cups that ate themselves away in ten minutes when put in sunlight or water. Even in room temperature those things biodegrade holes in themselves so fast.

I sighed and threw the cup out. I miss the styrofoam cups that littered dumps since the beginning of time. If only Storid stood out like a foam cup in a garbage heap.

Wait, why am I comparing styrofoam cups to Storid? I shook my head and tried to clear the unnecessary thoughts out. In the other room I noticed Chelsea watching TV, I flopped on the couch and joined her; the news anchor was talking about a new policy on giving everybody jobs.

Australia's government wasn't the only one worrying about jobs, I'd heard the stories everywhere, the trash and pollution rates are skyrocketing. People are rioting because the trash is taking too much space and is greatly affecting the ecosystem.

Arizona never paid much attention to the garbage issue because we have miles and miles of barren desert we can dump our trash into. But I guess everywhere else it is a serious issue. The riots, actually more like angry demonstrations, have been going on for months, people tried everything all over the world to get rid of or recycle the trash. Right now the U.S. is trying to create a system to bring everybody on welfare into the trash sorting business, instead of just distributing money. People on welfare would be required to work a couple hours a week making the world a little bit less trashy. The mass population seemed to like it, especially because so many people have been on welfare for so long. Though it seems the ideas are just ideas at this point, and it will be a while until the system could be active. I guess Australia is hopping on the trash welfare system too.

Another proposed idea is that the trash already buried is hopeless and we should create trash cans that scan trash and divide it up into recyclable, non-recyclable, and other.

I think it's one of the stupidest ideas yet, replacing every trashcan with this super trashcan that right now costs more than the average house to make.

But I might be a little prejudice, because what I throw in the garbage might be classified as other.

Chelsea got up to go make a sandwich, I clicked off the TV and the holographic news lady disappeared. Alright, back to work.

If he's living in plain sight he would definitely want to be in one of two camp sites, one in the middle of the city and one further south. I decided to go with the one further south.

At around sunset I went in and started checking the lots. I had a slight idea of what he would be in, a tent, no car, no cooking materials, and relatively clean around him.

Van, Van, Van, too many grills, RV, where is he? Lot after lot of searching for him and I find two that fit what he carries around, a tent and a bike. One of the lots ended up with a very old couple having sex, (which I'm scarred for life now) while the other was a father and son on a camping trip. The father was too old to be Storid. Storid, from the sketches I've seen has him looking like guy with wavy black hair and high cheek bones going through his mid to late twenties.

The night went on and it got colder with heavy, chilling rain. I ran through a whole tent section and three quarters of them had cars, or other things to give them away as human. I started checking the suspicious ones, two women in one lot, three men in another, two men and a woman in the next, none fit. Maybe he's gay or a cross dresser, and has company with him, maybe my standards are too narrow.

What if he is with an entire group of unsuspecting normal people? It could be plausible, though extremely unlikely. If he is as old as I know he is, he wouldn't want to listen to a bunch of college kids goofing around. I went back to the start of the lots and searched again. Hour after hour of asking questions or making up a story of needing an egg or other foods at four in the morning led to nothing. My clothes were soaked to the skin and I removed all of my make-up because it kept running down my face.

Where is he? I thought I was on the right track! I stopped and leaned against a tree. I shivered harshly, my pants were splashed with mud, and a rock was wedged in my left shoe.

I angrily ripped it off my foot and chucked it at the tree. It ricocheted off and disappeared down in the muddy brush. I am such an idiot! Everybody in the chatrooms were right, I'm a stupid, inexperienced kid. Why should I bother trying to earn back their respect? They'll all just die in the end.

The rain hadn't cleared up when I got home. It didn't clear the next day, just darkness and wetness. Chelsea was at work and I was alone in the house with my pathetic self-esteem ruining the air.

I should just become a hermit like him, live out in the country and wait for anybody who would judge me to die off. My wet socks and muddy shoes tumbled in the washer/dryer machine that doesn't actually use water to wash the clothes; it was the third time I ran it through to clean them.

I'm such a stupid slayer, why would Storid camp? He probably has some mansion out in the middle of nowhere, living off an identity he stole. Or he stored money buried somewhere and flew to Vegas and has been living happily ever since.

Where am I?

I ruffled my hair and scratched my irritated scalp. My hair has been growing out again, I'll need to hack some more off before it touches my shoulders.

I left the laundry room and grabbed a pair of scissors from the kitchen drawer. In front of the bathroom medicine cabinet mirrors I carefully evened out my hair and shortened it about two inches.

The sections dropped piece by piece into a little golden pile in the sink. I could see every strand, a natural mishmash of dark golden strands to translucent yellow tinted locks. Intertwined were red hairs and dark brown hairs, but they didn't stand out until I really examined them.

Dejected, I lean forward into the mirror, rain pattered somewhere above me, and the old lights in the bathroom buzzed lightly.

"I'll never grow up." I said to the refection. "I will always be me." My reflection didn't answer, when I finished she held a blank stare.

My soft cheeks and freckles seemed to always be there, the lack of definition and grown up features granted my face a deficiency in appeal.

"I will never look like Melanie." I said. "Or be as beautiful as Angel." My refection blinked back a blank stare when I informed her of what she and I already knew.

Why did Dad do this to me? Why did he turn me? My thoughts of plenty filed back to the edge of my commonly ignored conscience. And then another question revived to the tip of my small tongue.

"What is the reason I'm chasing Storid? Is it smite?" I asked her. No reply. My life means nothing, there is nothing to avenge and nobody to look out for. I'm already dead to the world.

I combed hair with my fingers, I'm going to find and kill Storid, I need to finish what I started, with or without a plan.

I scooped up my hair in the sink and tossed it into the trash.

I never saw the sun rise, nor set, the clouds made certain of that. Chelsea might have come home, I didn't bother to check any clocks; I just got my clothes on, along with the half soaked shoes, and I walked out the door. I didn't stop walking until I reached the first campground and started the search again.

Weeks flew by; I broke into cabins, RVs, and searched every area I could. I reread Chelsea's books over and over, taking meticulous notes and trying to fit together his personality as much as possible. Sydney passed the dead of winter before I knew it. He wasn't in the latest camp I searched.

My motivation deteriorated every single day, some days I couldn't will myself out of bed, because all I could think about were the public humiliations I would endure for invading personal belongings in campsites.

I had walked in on way to many groups of people and been chased out. The mystical forests faded to lackluster, I was beginning to loathe the great outdoors beside the city.

Chelsea had gotten used to me, I helped her translate and transcribe some of her journals. She seemed to believe I was going to stay at the library with her permanently.

It looked like I was too.

October lead to my search spanning a bit farther from the city, every few days I checked rows of a new camp I located. I wasn't religious about coming back daily, especially with the longer drives. Several in this one were all-girl camping trips so I was able to go through them quickly, but I still haven't gotten rid of the cross dresser idea.

No luck, by midnight on the fourth night I had about a fifth of the RV section done and I'm not even close to the cabin or tent sections. By four in the morning the fires had gone out. I had reached the end of the RV section with not even a hint of Storid. By sunrise I took a break.

I didn't call Chelsea to pick me up; I was just going to stay the day. Nobody noticed me; other people walked around too, or rode their bikes. I wandered amongst the living, observing them. Such happy faces, well, except for that couple fighting over the TV to my right. Lots of people were on phones or laptops or something in between.

The past few months I've spent all my time looking for Storid's face in the crowd, I forgot about everything else. The city, my old life. The season even changed, without my notice.

The day passed quickly, night fell and I continued my search. I will get Storid one day.

October became November, and November came to the near end. On one of the spring November nights, before I left to go searching again, Chelsea caught me by the arm.

"Where do think you are going?" She said expectantly. I turned, "Out to the campsites."

She put her hands on her hips, "Just because we aren't in America doesn't mean we aren't supposed to celebrate Thanksgiving."

I stiffened in surprise, "It is Thanksgiving?" She nodded, "We should honor our home country by eating the premade turkey dinners in the freezer that I bought."

I shrugged, and we had a quiet dinner on the couch watching TV. Chelsea and I never really talked, she was definitely not Angel or Melanie, and she mostly did her own thing while I did mine.

Neither of us had been called back to the states, and the world seemed to revolve just fine without us.

My perpetually fruitless existence seemed content here, I was neither happy nor sad. At first I was angry for not finding Storid, but I realize he is just a ghost, one in several billion people on earth.

Spring grew into summer as November turned to early December. I wandered through the tent lots, my mind geared more towards trying to remember Spanish words, Chelsea and I have been trying to translate a few documents written in scratchy Spanish writing, and maybe I can pick up the language while I'm translating.

The night was as it always is in Sydney, in the low seventies; my eyes mechanically searched this perpetual paradise. I wore a sweatshirt incase it rained. The next tent I reached had a bunch of college kids dancing and hopping to music while steaks steamed on a grill.

They smelled good, and I drifted over to them. A few of the girls were dressed in short, skanky outfits. I imagine Angel would have had one of their costumes on at a party, wherever she is. One of the girls smiled at me, and came over to me while she adjusted her candy cane stripped push up bra, "Hello little girl, what can I do for you today?" I smiled politely, "Do you guys have any marshmallows? My sister forgot to bring them and we have all of these-"

"Pfft! We totally got some!" She interjected. And she shoved her red cup at me saying "Hold this." She opened the large tent in the middle of the camp ground, and appeared with a bagful of thick marshmallows.

She giggled and traded me the red cup for the bag. I smiled and she gently shoved me to go away. "Bye now!"

I turned and moved on, the entire time she had been there I scanned the area for Storid's face, nobody looked like him and he wasn't in any of the tents. All of them were unoccupied.

Throughout the night I continued my searching across the tent lots with the same excuses.

The third had an old man sleeping; it was definitely not Storid. The fourth had a bike and a tent. The tent was the newest I've seen, well, besides the one with built in security camera, which I thought was completely ridiculous.

The tent had polyester doors instead of a zipper opening and I almost moved on to the next one. But I had gotten sick of eating the entire bag of marshmallows, and there was a trashcan beside the tent.

I looked up at the door, I really hope this isn't going to be another wrinkly old couple having sex or another kid dissecting and stringing the intestines of a small animal. "Hello? Anybody in here?" I walked straight inside.

A young man was sitting on a fold-out chair with his feet propped up on a fold-out stool by a table with another empty chair across from him. He was drinking out of a coffee cup and reading the paper. "Hello young lady, how my I help you?" he gave me a warm smile. I smiled back "Hi, my friends and I are cooking some stuff and we ran out of eggs. Do you have one you could spare?"

He shook his head, "Sorry." I tilted my head slightly and put on a confused look, "Wait, do I know you?"

He stared at me, "Do you?" I sighed, "Are you Michael Storid?" I waited for the confused look to appear on his face. Instead he smiled, "Yes, who did you say you were again?"

I was stunned, adrenaline froze me in place. His face dropped the smile as he noticed my body grow ridged. Instantly I extended my Flashsword blade.

He stared at it with fascination, "My, my, what a shiny weapon you have!" I advanced towards him raising my sword. With slick, quick movements he managed to dodge me and I ended up cutting his chair. I quickly turned swinging the sword around. He jumped back into a corner and I rushed him again.

This time he grabbed my sword, and landed a punch in my side. His hit sent me flying back and knocked the wind out of me. He looked more interested in my Flashsword than me.

How did he do that? He just ripped it out of my hands as if I was a child!

As I got up to charge him again he still showed almost no interest in me and was completely absorbed in examining my Flashsword. I launched in the air to attack his left side. He was just too fast and fluent; I don't even know how he countered that time but I ended up on the ground again, pinned by his foot.

His strength was shocking; I couldn't move my upper torso. He looked down at me, "Are you done yet?" In a desperate attempt to get free I threw my feet around and hit his shins. He stumbled a little but I was free. I didn't hesitate, I just jumped and attacked. He had regained his balance as I was striking him and blocked me. He laughed, "They don't make them like you anymore! This is the most fun I've had in a while."

I ended up once again on the ground, pinned with almost no effort on his part. "I'm tired of playing this I-want-to-kill-you game. I could have killed you more times than you could count now, so why don't we sit down and let us talk like civilized people." He let a little pressure off and I put my hand down to steady myself, then slowly pushed up, humiliated.

He crossed his arms and shook his head, staring at the broken fold-out chair. "Those are extremely expensive. I'm going to have to order another one now."

He waved his hand to the fold-out stool, "Please, sit down." I was frozen. His voice grew slightly stern, regarding me as a child. "Sit down. Now." I quickly dropped down onto the footstool.

Storid's attention changed as he backed into the untouched chair, "What is this?"

He implied my Flashsword. A ping of shame shot through me seeing it in his hand. "My friend handcrafted it; I-I can take it almost anywhere." My voice was so weak, shrinking into a pettily little squeak. He collapsed it and put it on the table. "It's a neat toy, and a brilliant idea. I'm more of a gun person myself though; they get the job done in less of a primitive maneuver." He laughed a little at his comment. I gulped, still in shock.

"What is your name?"

I fixed my hair from how it got thrown and replied with a neutral look on my face, "My name is Moogie." He smiled brighter, "I heard of you, you are that little American."

He seemed to be teasing me now, his tone a biting sarcasm, "Such a sad story you have, and I knew Jonathan before he was kidnapped and experimented on." He looked at me again, "Now I seem to remember you were the slayer to kill Marian. He was very angry; she was his ex-lover and close friend."

"What?" I asked confused. He smirked, "I think you called her the esophagus ripper. It was her favorite way of preparing her food, but you made that title infamously hers."

He held up a finger, "And you are the one living in Marcus's condo in Phoenix." I shook my head, "I moved out." he knew where I had lived?

"Where is your little friend? Angel was it?"

I smiled politely, "She didn't want to come."

He nodded in understanding, relaxing a little as he said, "Yes, the hopeless quest of finding and killing a superior being like myself ends fruitless and in death."

I sat uncomfortably, ridged and fearful. "What else do I remember about you-oh! And Oklahoma, well, let's say everybody knows on both sides just what happened over there." My entire face broke from neutrality and filled with shame and embarrassment. He read my slip up.

I broke eye contact for the first time with him and looked down.

Then I looked back at him, his mocking smile had disappeared and he grew serious. "You know they will never accept you, no matter what you do."

My hand gathered into a fist, and he carefully watched me, now concerned. All taunting and pride evaporated from the atmosphere. His voice grew slower. "You are just lost, child, you woke up on the wrong side. It happens." He tilted his head, his grave face showing genuine empathy.

"Everyday you fight your existence. The pig's blood, the slaying, the constant work to make yourself fit in and look older. The slayers mock you for it, and they could never understand."

His eyes hardened, black and cold, "They have everything it seems, don't they? And we are forced to watch them throw away and take for granted what we will never have." I feared Storid greatly at that moment, but I admitted to myself I knew his envy. My thoughts drifted to the playroom.

"None of them have given you the respect you worked for. You are just a creature to them."

I bit my lip, listening. "I can see you are alone, I know nobody would honestly care if you returned tonight, or ever."

I fought the urge to cry at his words, my head spun, but I stayed silent for fear of losing it.

"I know Angel left you, they all left you."

"I have friends." I said weakly, my voice sounding more like the lonely child I was than the strong woman I know I am.

"No you don't." He said sympathetically, and leaned towards me, "But as I said before, you are lost." He smiled comfortingly, letting a silence linger for several moments.

"You see, I understand, this world is difficult. You are surrounded with nothing but the restrained life of the humans you spend so much time with.

They can only think in the small box of a short life they are given, they constantly have to worry about their minuscule time spans. But you, you are completely and utterly free. You don't have to live like they do, you don't have to find somebody to love in a short time bracket like they do, you don't have to choose which life pursuits you do, you can have it all for as long as you want."

I soaked in his words as they melted the trauma of my world.

"Child, there are so many gifts our forever can give you. The small, inevitable stereotypes of man you have known all your life are not the only people out there, with time you can enjoy honest companions, you can stop and truly enlighten yourself to things normal humans are forced to pass up. Our life has so much more to offer that you haven't begun to know. And your environment is trapping you into a one-dimensional state."

He was so close to me, I could feel his warm breath on the tip of my nose, "I know you suffer so much. You don't have to suffer, Moogie." His voice purred my name like no other. "You could stay here, become normal, you would easily fit in."

Then his voice changed, darkening, "I will compulse to all of our kind that you have transcended." His voice was near a whisper, "Eternity would never be lonely as you are now, and it would feel so right."

I closed my mouth and looked away, the world seemed to disappear, the universe could be in this little brown tent. Tears streamed down my face, I couldn't comprehend why. Or maybe I was crying because I was confused.

I didn't think. My thoughts and feelings were in a mess. I pulled back and wiped away my tears with my sleeve. Out of nowhere Storid silently offered me a handkerchief. I hesitated, but then took it as more tears fell.

He leaned back, watching me. And then stood up, turning to the small kitchen behind him. The kettle on the stove was boiling, "Do you want some tea?" He asked as I tried to collect myself. I nodded and he reached for the teacups hanging on the hook next to him.

On the table, I saw the Flashsword. Without thinking I lunged for it and flicked it out. Before he could turn I jumped and thrusted down with all my might, slicing him in half.

His blood splattered everywhere and on my sweatshirt. Gooey, dark red liquid spread and soaked into the tent's fabric.

The blood crept to my shoe, threatening to stain it. I stepped back a little, my adrenaline pulsed like fire.

My mind was still in a daze, I neither felt regret nor pride for what I had done. Body parts twitched and I stared down at him in disbelief for long moments. My fingers calmly carried the Flashsword, something inside of me felt limp, dead, and I just couldn't understand it.

What have I done?

Mechanically, I took a picture of his face and an overview shot of his body for proof on my phone. I sent it along with a text to every slayer on my caller contacts list.

I got Storid.

-Moogie

30
The Omission

I received video phone calls from slayers everywhere to see if the news was true, they all wanted to see the body live. I made sure to take copious amounts of video footage. Chelsea helped me dispose of the body, and I gave her a copy of all of the Storid files.

"This is the best Christmas ever!" She squealed. And she added the Storid evidence to a shelf in her library.

A day later Chelsea and I received invitations to a party in the Milton Mansion, sent by Bill to celebrate Storid's final death.

For the first time I smiled about seeing Bill. And although the party would make me happy for the next century, something felt wrong.

I opened up my phone's interface and dialed Angel's number. The line picked up and blaring music startled me. "Hello?" Angel's voice half shouted.

"Angel?" I said in a slightly loud tone. "Moogie? Wait one second-" I heard the sound of a door shutting and the music died into background buzzing. "Uh hi." She said, her voice apprehensive.

I opened my mouth to answer; nothing seemed to come to mind.

"Hi." I said quietly, I suddenly came to notice the light bulb above me buzzing. It didn't buzz rhythmically, so my sense of counting and time was impeded. "It is good to hear your voice again Angel." I said without thought.

"Um, yeah, your voice is a little odd." I listened confused at Angel's words, "Sorry." Was all I could say.

"Is the weather nice where you are?" I asked, Angel answered quickly, "Yeah, sure, I mean, for winter it is okay. I'd rather it be warm."

I chuckled, "You are in the wrong hemisphere for that, below the equator everything is flip flopped winter is summer and so forth."

"Where are you?" she asked skeptically, "South America?"

"No, Australia, uh, I have been hunting."

"Any luck?" she asked. "He was one of those really famous ones, and I finally got him tonight." I blurted. "Huh?" Her reply was slightly confused. "I was retracing some old coven busts and I tried to find this guy named Storid."

Angel's voice was pleasant. "Hey, that's really nice. I'm glad."

We quieted again. "Yeah, and the slayers were really happy about it too, they are throwing a party to celebrate me and the kill."

"They would do that for you?" I nodded, forgetting we weren't on video call, and switched to a verbal agreement. "It wouldn't be a party if you were not there."

"You want me to come to your party?" She said, her tone surprised. I held my breath "Yeah, it's at that Milton mansion in Oklahoma tomorrow night."

Angel was silent for a pause, "They really are happy about your kill, aren't they?" "Over the moon," I replied, my voice saturating in the air.

"Then I'll be there, see you tomorrow."

Australia was to my back on the plane ride back into America. Nothing could dampen my mood.

A car was there waiting for me when I reached Oklahoma, Chelsea eagerly rode with me, tightening her pony tail and fidgeting with her dress.

The door servants who resented me months ago gladly opened the door for me now. I wheeled in my luggage and they carried that up to a room for me, while the butler led Chelsea and me to the party room.

It was a ballroom, a glistening crystal chandelier lighted at the center of the room, everybody stared as we entered. Most of them smiled, and my cheeks grew red.

Then I made my way into the table of conversation, I found myself for the first time really having a conversation with these people. An early one was with George, "Moogie, congratulations." He said awkwardly, but not overtly cynical. "Uh, how did you do it?"

Chelsea left my side partway through the third explanation; she was bored of the story being told over and over. But groups of slayers listened eagerly. I found a corner of the room to make myself available to the people as I listened to some conversations at the far corner of the room ask about where I was.

Everybody, even if they had already heard it, was captivated by my story. I embellished a little, and left out the part where I was pinned on the floor a couple times, and I left out the last part of the conversation I had. But other than that my story was a true legend.

They laughed every time I told them I got him during his monologue, a few slapped me on the shoulder every once in a while, congratulating me.

Carrie and Candice approved, Mr. C wasn't there. I didn't see anybody else from Arizona either, but a bunch of people I knew from the chatrooms hovered. The couple from Switzerland, a Russian, about six people from India, I saw Dollys and Miltons together. It was a strange mishmash, one I thought I'd never see outside hunts.

Angel hadn't arrived yet, and every so often I'd glanced at the hallway watching for her. Angel would come sweeping in, wearing one of her corsets or miniskirts, and everybody would know she was there; she wouldn't even do self conscious tricks like making eye contact with everyone she sees, or talk a little too loud.

We were called to dinner sometime into the party, and on our way over an older Chinese slayer paced next to me. "Hello, I'm Bo; we've talked in the chatrooms?" I smiled and shook his hand, "Yes, BoJing, it's nice to finally meet face to face."

He nodded, "Now, you had a brief conversation with Mr. Storid. Am I correct?" I nodded at Bo's broken English words.

"Did he speak about myths or slayers?"

I ran over the conversation, so distinct in my head. "Um, he dropped a few names, I guess. He said the old condo I lived in was owned by his friend named Marcus. Oh! You know the esophagus ripper I had talked about a few years ago?" He nodded, "I remember Storid said she was an ex lover of Jonathan, and he was super pissed when he heard I killed her. Her real name was Marian."

Bo stopped, "That was after he was killed in Vegas, isn't it?" I stopped too. My memory is a little slow on dates. "Wait, yeah, I said it wrong. Sorry." I said to him, my voice shrugging off the comment. Inside and through, my thoughts remained at a mental halt. Maybe Storid said Jonathan would have been pissed. No, that doesn't sound right. Oh no.

I straightened up, keeping a neutral look. No, Vegas was later, right? No because Angel would have gone with me to see the bodies if she had been a slayer then.

Shoot, is my logic messed up? No. I turned to Bo, "He didn't say much after that."

My mind went back to the timeline in my head, and I didn't even notice Bo when he disappeared. I know what Storid said, clearer than anything else I knew exactly what he said. But, still.

Something kindling in my stomach flirted with embarrassment, a blush rose to my cheeks. The gag in my throat washed with confused stress.

Their skulls are on my dresser, I saw them dead, with my own eyes. With my own thoughts I accepted their deaths.

Storid's words gripped me, because they were so fresh and memorable.

At the dinner table, which every seat had been filled, and an extension was added to accommodate the amount of people, I took one of the last seats, between Candice and George.

As the servants passed out the first course, Bill, at the head of the table, stood up to make a toast.

"Attention everybody, a few words should be spoken to commemorate this event that we are celebrating as it goes down in history as one of the greatest achievements in the twenty first century." A few raised their glasses and grumbled in agreement to that before Bill continued. "Now I would like to thank a few people for their major contributions, first, Bo, for investing all of those years into chasing Storid through every corner of Asia, flushing him out like the vermin he was." We applauded to him, and I smiled proudly that Bill is recognizing some of the other slayers.

"Next I would like to thank those who were in the coven hunt of twenty fourteen, because they helped destroy Storid's truly disgusting occupation of Sydney and drove him to the streets." Several applauded and three of the younger ones whooped for being recognized.

"And last, but especially not least, I would like to thank our very young and talented Chelsea. For putting the puzzle pieces together and caring for all of the documentation that exposed and eventually killed the Weasel once and for all."

Chelsea froze, midway through retightening her ponytail. They all applauded the loudest for her, and I watched her from the other end of the table blush an almost maroon color as she smiled.

I looked back at Bill, shocked as he raised his cup to her, drank it, and sat down. Then they all started eating, gleeful and proud. My mouth dropped open, I didn't know how to feel. Is that it?

After all those months? After everything?

I stared at my food, fighting the tears that were about to fall. They were so selfish, this party wasn't for me; this was a party to congratulate themselves. My breathing grew irregular, blood rushed to my face; I looked at Bill one more time. He met my eyes for a brief moment and then returned to his food, smiling with the rest of them.

There I returned, an unnatural slight to knock me over. I tried to pick the silverware up and eat, but my fingers resisted wrapping around the smooth, polished handle.

The spoon finally could be gripped, and I realized my hand shook violently, I let go to hear the clattering on the floor. "Sorry." I mumbled. And nobody cared. I pulled out my handkerchief to wipe the dirt off, none of the servants offered to take the spoon or replace it.

The handkerchief was starch white and in the corner there was an embroidered M.S. That same one to predict this.

I folded it back up and stared at it, Storid's handkerchief, Storid, he was right. He was just so right. The disdain, the terrible taste in my mouth, I drew my eyes to each of their faces. The contentment in them as they had won in their minds.

I placed the cloth back in my pocket, my peers not even unsettled in a slight regret. I stared blankly at my undisturbed meal. Then I pushed out my chair and started to the door.

The exit made no difference to the conversation level. Going unnoticed for so long made my illusion of being seen so bright, but it made me forget what it was like to be unseen.

Suitcase in hand, I found myself outside to the gates, leaving the grounds without a glance back. And the moment the gates clanked shut behind me I realized I had nowhere to go.

Tears did not spill, I did not scream or act violent, only the consciousness of the world to become another memory. This inked in my mind as I realized I once again found myself in a position I couldn't reverse. This wasn't a time of division or distraught, it was my path.

I drug my suitcase up to the wall beside the closed gate and leaned up against it. The cold irritated me, making me shed goose bumps, but I could shrug it off.

An hour passed, then another half. A little economy sized car pulled up to the gates and stopped. "Moogie?" the driver called. My eyes slid to Angel's face. She looked fatigued from her flight, hunched; she was dressed in some worn out jeans and a loose blouse.

I picked up my luggage and tossed it into the backseat. She silently watched me as I passed the front of the car and got in beside her.

Angel brushed back her scarlet hair to look at me better. I didn't look at her; I stared with a dead expression at the gates. "Angel?" I said. "Yes?" she asked gently.

I paused, looking to the mansion one time. I mused so softly, "I just want to go home."

She put the car in reverse, turned it around, and we soon entered the highway. I turned to look at her; the last rays of the setting sun brightened the car, reflecting dimly off of the strands of her hair. Then I looked forward as we chased down the light.

Honey, we are just getting started.

MorganRouth.com

Made in the USA
Charleston, SC
26 June 2013